# MY GRANDFATHER'S FALSE TEETH

By
## ROBERTA AARONS

**IndePenPress**

First published in Great Britain by Indepenpress.

All paper used in the printing of this book has been made from wood grown in managed, sustainable forests.

ISBN13: 978-1-907172-95-3

Printed and bound in the UK
Indepenpress is an imprint of Indepenpress Publishing Limited
25 Eastern Place
Brighton
BN2 1GJ

A catalogue record of this book is available from
the British Library

Cover design by Jacqueline Abromeit

*For Nia*

# Acknowledgements

I would like to thank Roland Curram, Nancy Fisher, Simon Inglis, Derek McAllister, Louella Miles, Anna Millhouse, Judith Trepp, Leila Wallis, Crispin Wood and Anne Wooster for their support and encouragement.

I have used many resources for my research but I would particularly like to express my gratitude to the staff at the London Metropolitan Archives for their enthusiasm and expertise and to Jerry White for his excellent book *London in the Twentieth Century*.

Thanks are due to the team at Indepenpress for their hard work and belief in this book.

I am especially grateful to Joan and the late Paul Abbey for their infinite patience with my relentless questioning.

This book has been written in memory of Dimcha and Sam. It is not their story but could have been.

# About the Author

Roberta Aarons trained as a newspaper journalist and has worked as a writer and producer in television news and entertainment, documentary films, commercials, short feature films and corporate video in London and New York. She has lectured and taught proposal writing, presentation skills and video production.

She lives in London and now concentrates on writing full time. My Grandfather's False Teeth is her first novel.

# Contents

# 1900s

# 1902 Jacob

"You must come, quickly you must come," gasped the little boy from the doorway of the attic.

Jacob looked up sharply from the wooden bench and straightened the pattern he had been cutting, deftly arranging the edges beneath his thumb.

"Well, little fellow," he asked gently, "what brings you here in such a hurry?"

"Rosie, Rosie, they took her to the big hospital. The doctor said the baby is coming." The boy's normally pale face was red with excitement. "They sent me to get you…"

Jacob glanced anxiously at the calendar stuck prominently in the middle of yellowing patterns, snippets of fabric, scribbled measurements, bills and orders pinned on the disorganized wall. A date was marked in bright blue chalk. It was still a month away.

At twenty-four, Jacob's eyes were already wrinkled from years of tailoring in poorly lit rooms. He was tall, solidly built, his shoulders slightly bowed but his wide, carefully clipped black moustache gave him a certain dignity. His hands, with their long slender fingers sometimes shook like those of an old man but never when measuring a customer or fingering his beloved cloth. He marked out shapes with the flat, white chalk in absolutely accurate lines without the help of a rule. His movements were sure and swift, as he added a little touch here, a tiny tug there.

"Are you sure? Is that all he said? The baby is coming, is it true?"

"He said to tell you, you must go to the hospital. Quickly, you must go."

Jacob did not wait to hear any more. He had to go to Rosie. She was alone and in a strange place. Dragging on his jacket, he clambered over rolls of cloth, stumbled between tailor's dummies, some half-covered with cut fragments of material and some bare as if waiting to be dressed. He ran out of the attic, clattered down the five flights of stairs, two at a time, banging his arm against wobbly banisters and peeling walls as he fled. He hit at doors as he passed, wildly yelling at them, "My son, my son is coming today!"

Mrs Weinstein, who was tying up packages of buttons on the third floor, heard him and said to her husband, who was separating them into coloured piles, "We should say a prayer for his Rosie. She is not a strong girl and a month early too."

The neighbours respected Jacob for his hard work, his skill and his devotion to his wife. Now, with his first baby on the way, they believed he would make a good father. His business was building quickly and word was spreading of his perfectly-fitted suits. Recently he had even attracted gentiles, who usually did not like coming into the Jewish quarter, finding it alien and full of strange smells, but would travel far for such well-fitting suits. It was known that he was politically active and had been seen talking to small gatherings of men in the street. Some even rumoured that he had a printing press hidden beneath the bales of cloth in his attic. But he wasn't considered a trouble-maker and they chose to ignore these activities.

When Jacob married Rosie, he had been living alone with his mother in a village not far from the city for several years. His father had been massacred in one of the frequent pogroms. His mother never talked about it. "Cossacks" was the only word she ever uttered about her lost husband. Shortly afterwards, his only brother Bernard had emigrated to America. So the baby they were expecting, little Samuel, as they had called him from the beginning of her pregnancy, held all their dreams and hopes for the future. He and Rosie were determined to rebuild the family that had almost been destroyed.

His sons, for he could only imagine sons, would have opportunities. They would not be tailors. No, they would be doctors or lawyers, men of importance and influence, maybe even business men. That is why Jacob worked so relentlessly, in a shop during the day and for private customers at night. His commitment to a political group was to protect the community from further atrocities and to provide a safe future for their children. He knew in his heart, although it was a secret he kept, that this was more important for a Jew than lighting candles to a God he wasn't sure existed.

Jacob rushed into the hectic street. It was market day and the street was crowded with stalls and alive with boisterous traders' cries. As he ran, Jacob thought about how it would have been had he not insisted that they'd left their village for the better opportunities in Lodz. Rosie had not really wanted to come but dutifully followed, not quite understanding why he was sure, as he always had been sure, that his talents were way beyond the simple rural community where they had both grown up; though she knew that in the city he would be able to play a larger part in the changes he believed were coming. She had known from childhood that they would marry and while his dreams of grandeur meant nothing to her, his happiness meant everything. Jacob needed the city so Rosie followed, doing her best to make a home out of their tiny tenement attic, and to disregard the almost physical pain of separation from her family. Shyly and slowly she had started to make new friends despite her desperate homesickness, which she tried, unsuccessfully, to hide from him.

Now he cursed himself for his ambition; but for that, well-wishing, praying womenfolk, both family and friends, would now surround Rosie. She was beautiful, warm and gentle and everyone loved her so. Back home she was often followed by children, and old women used to wave and greet her as she passed, acknowledging her special aura.

By now the whole village would have gathered, they would be breathing with her, crying with her, holding her. The men would be outside singing, drinking and waiting for news. When the midwife sent the women outside the room to join the men, they would all fall silent and await the moment of birth with anticipation. Then when little Samuel arrived, they would all celebrate and double the drinking and singing and throw on their prayer shawls and add some praying for good measure. There would be kissing, dancing and hugging, running and jumping and more dancing.

"Jacob and Rosie have a boy, a great grandson to the Rabbi Samuel," someone would shout. Then they would pray and remember the late Rabbi Samuel. But now there was no one to laugh with him, sing with him, congratulate him and bless the new life, and no one to hold Rosie's hand except him. He felt so alone as he rushed towards the hospital, pushing his way ruthlessly through the startled crowd.

"Jacob, the tailor," he panted at the nurse standing by the hospital door.

"Is there another name, besides Jacob, the tailor?"

"Bromavitch, Jacob and Rosie Bromavitch."

The nurse looked up at a chart on the wall, then took his arm and led him past several numbered doors until they reached one marked 23c. Rosie was lying motionless on a high iron bed, covered with white sheets. Her dark brown hair, usually glossy and thick, was dull and straggly. Her eyes were closed in her drained face. Deep circles ringed her eyes. Her hands lay limp beside her swollen body but she was breathing peacefully. Jacob could hardly believe that a few hours ago this now still figure had sent him merrily off to the shop, teasing him as she plonked his hat upon his head.

"Off with you, my big business man, and don't be late tonight."

Then there was a quick change of mood. Sometimes the way her moods altered so quickly confused him and he did not know whether to laugh or not. She moved close to him so that he could smell her sweet perfume and feel her normally slender body, now awkward and large, pushing against him.

"One month to go, plenty of love is all he needs," she whispered, "so don't work too hard."

Jacob had known they would spend their lives together from such an early age that he could remember no time without her. Now he felt so far away from her. She did not even know that he was there. He watched anxiously as the nurse felt her pulse.

"The doctor is coming to see you." Then she left him alone with his silent wife.

The doctor came in. He was a round, short man with a shiny bald head and gentle eyes that concentrated on Jacob's face.

"Congratulations. You have a gorgeous baby girl, small but healthy."

"Thank God, thank God." Jacob shook the doctor's hand vigorously. "A girl, a girl," he repeated, as if he had never heard that word before.

A father to a girl, he thought. This would be different, but still the community would celebrate. Why had they been so certain, why had they never discussed the possibility? He did not even have a girl's name in mind. He wished desperately that he could talk to Rosie. She would know what to call a girl.

'Mr Bloomgarten, you must be very strong," said the doctor, his eyes serious.

"Bromavitch," said Jacob automatically, then: "Strong?"

The doctor put his arm around Jacob's shoulders. "Your baby girl is fine, but your wife is poorly. She will need lots of care and I am afraid there will be no more babies."

"No sons?" whispered Jacob.

"No more babies. I am sorry but you have a healthy girl and your wife will recover in time."

One child, he thought, one child only. He sensed the certainty of his dreams vanishing. This child would now carry the weight of the future, all his hopes, all his ambitions. This girl child, he vowed silently, must be protected at any cost. He and Rosie must be prepared to make any sacrifice for their only child.

"Anything," he whispered aloud to the God he now knew he did not believe in.

# 1903 Bella

Bella leant far out of the train window and welcomed the soot that flew up her nostrils. She breathed in the black particles, enjoying the sweet burning smell, which was a relief from the sour, stale air of the compartment. Looking ahead towards the engine, she watched the grey steam billowing out over the fields beyond the tracks, laying a thin veil of dirt over the crisp green leaves and luscious cornfields. She tapped her fingers on the glass in rhythm with the sound of the train.

"Da de da, da de da," she said aloud, again and again. It was a comforting noise and blocked out the sound of Rosie and Jacob's argument. They had been quarrelling for months because Jacob was sending her, baby Sara and Bella to America without him. Although he had promised to follow very soon, Rosie was wretched at the thought of leaving him behind.

Bella had been living with them since Jacob had sent for her after the difficult birth of Rosie's first and, sadly, to be only child. This had so exhausted her older sister that she showed no interest in looking after the baby. Bella had no family left in the village where they had all grown up and she had been staying with one of her late mother's friends. Feeling unwelcome, she had been glad to join her sister and brother-in-law in Lodz where, thanks to Jacob's thriving business, there were two rooms, not one.

Bella knew theirs was a happy marriage and hadn't questioned Rosie's decision to leave their small village to follow him to the city, leaving her behind to look after their mother. But Lodz had not been an easy place for Rosie. Jacob worked long hours and was also deeply committed to something called the Bund, which Bella didn't fully understand, but knew vaguely to be a political organisation dedicated to protecting the rights of Jewish workers. She was aware his activities were quite secret and took up a lot of his time. She knew also that this was another cause for disagreement.

Bella slept on a mattress in Jacob's working area, which she cleared out of the way each morning. As she lay down each night, she heard the slight crunch of pins beneath her. She would take baby Sara out in her arms every day and show her the bustling town while Rosie rested and Jacob worked. They trusted her with all the shopping. She had made sure that she knew all the market traders by name and could haggle for herring or bread or, on very good days, chicken. The traders enjoyed challenging this small, sharp, pretty girl who had an eye for a bargain. Her voice was strong for her tiny frame and the traders liked teasing her. They gave her the nickname 'Baby Bella', but they respected her and never cheated her. Far from it, she often left the market with extra vegetables or fish or flour. The traders said it was for her weak sister Rosie, but it was really because feisty young Bella had enchanted them so.

She was sad to be leaving this community but was also eager to experience another place and different people. The attacks on Jews were frequent in Lodz and had become part of their daily life and she resented that, because of them, they were restricted to the Jewish area of town.

Ignoring Rosie's pleading and the baby's whining, Bella leant against the carriage wall and once again read the letter from Nathan, Jacob's brother in Brooklyn.

*'This is the place for you and your family. There is always business for a good tailor in Brooklyn. It is not true the streets are paved with gold but at least not dirt and hate. Please work on your English and I will send you money for tickets as soon as I can.'*

The train jerked to a halt with a great crashing of metal and screeching of wheels. Carefully Bella folded the treasured letter into the large pocket in her skirt, where she had also tucked the two steamship tickets Jacob had given her to look after. 'New York' was stamped in large letters right across the front and a separate section was marked in small print 'via London'. Jacob had explained that they had to change to another boat in London and had given Rosie a small pouch of money to use during the journey. Just fingering the tickets thrilled Bella.

Leaning back against the window, she looked around the carriage. She observed her sister with concern, comparing her to the jolly, happy girl she had grown up with and shared a room with until her marriage. Rosie still looked frail from the birth but now she looked miserable and defeated as well. White-faced, she was holding Sara with one arm and clinging on to Jacob with the other. The train was crowded and their row was attracting attention from the other passengers.

"I can't leave, not yet," Jacob protested in a loud whisper.

"Then let us all stay," Rosie pleaded.

"It's too dangerous and there is no future for us. I want you and Sara safe in America. Bella will be with you, Nathan will look after you and I'll come soon. I promise you, Rosie, I promise you."

Bella was so thrilled to be going to America that she couldn't understand Rosie's resistance, but then she didn't love Jacob. Well she did, but like a brother. Bella knew Jacob would not leave his mother, who was too old and ill to move now. It would probably not be long before he could join them.

"It's not your mother, it's your Bund," Rosie was sobbing.

"The Bund is for all of us, for our future."

"How can it be more important to you than us staying together?"

"I won't give it up."

"So when your mother dies, you will still stay?" Rosie's voice was stifled with tears.

"We have been through this. The Bund will come with us. In

11

America we will need it even more. But I want you to go now. It is not safe to stay."

Bella had heard these quarrels so often that she barely listened now. She couldn't imagine how anyone, given this opportunity to go to America, would rather stay behind in Lodz, even for a husband.

"I can't manage alone," Rosie wailed.

Bella moved over and gently picked Sara out of Rosie's arms. The baby's body was rigid and Bella held her tight against her breast, stroking her head and murmuring until she felt her calm down.

"Bella will be with you and I will join you soon." Jacob pulled Rosie close to him and tucked her head onto his chest. He took some dark bread out of his worn leather sack and held it towards her lips. She jammed them shut and turned her face into his body, her back hunched in defeat.

"America, America," Bella cooed into Sara's ear. The baby giggled, burped, then fell asleep.

"Hold her." The memory of the last words Rosie had shouted stayed with Bella throughout the voyage, as did the image of Rosie running away from her and Sara. They had been standing close together on the crowded dockside at the foot of the gangplank that led up to the vast ship. Sara was tucked between them and they stood facing a photographer who was having a profitable day capturing last minute images. Rosie had wrapped the new shawl Jacob had made especially for their journey around all three of them as a protection against the sea breeze.

Surrounding them on the quayside was a mob of people clamouring to board. There were the very old, the very young and all ages in between. Some men wore smart suits and the women stylish dresses, coats and leather shoes but a lot were in simple country clothes and some were ragged and barefoot. Many were dragging bags along the ground or carried small cases and some clutched

12

improvised sacs. But the whole spectrum of society in all its variety shared an impatient need to escape.

The sea air was contaminated with the smell of dirty bodies and unwashed clothes; it had been a long journey for all. The noise was overwhelming. There was excited laughter, old people moaning with fatigue, babies crying and the shouts of young people. There was also the sound of horses' neighing and their hooves and wooden wagon wheels clanking along stone. The voices of officials barking instructions occasionally cut through the commotion.

The crowd pushed and shoved their way towards the walkway joining the boat to the quayside but as it was still cordoned off, they congregated in an agitated mass pushing forward.

Only Rosie was reluctant to move. Her shoulders were slumped and her face was wet with the tears that had finally fallen and streamed down her face after saying her last goodbye to Jacob. She had watched him stride away from them until he vanished into the crowd. But her eyes didn't leave the path he had taken, as if she was marking it in her mind.

"Smile, smile," Bella said "come on Rosie, we're going on an adventure. Please smile Rosie. It'll be such fun."

As if in a trance Rosie smiled for the photographer. Bella was irritated with her sister for the first time ever. She wished she would start embracing the experience and stop wallowing in the tragedy. Never having loved a man or, if she were truthful, anyone except Rosie, she could not understand why a temporary separation from Jacob represented such heartbreak. Bella was desperate to get on board but smiled joyfully for the camera. As the photographer's flash blinded her, she felt Rosie wrench herself away.

"Hold her," Bella heard as the baby was thrust into her arms. When her eyes adjusted, she glimpsed Rosie disappearing into the crowd following the route Jacob had taken. Eager to board, she assumed that Rosie had rushed back to Jacob for yet another farewell, even though it was unlikely she would find him now in the dense mob. Bella clung onto Sara and stared anxiously over the hordes of people.

"Hey lady, you, lady with the baby, get on board or you'll miss the ship." It took her a moment to realise that someone was shouting at her.

As the mass of people heading for the boat squeezed past her, Bella tried to stand still as they bumped into her, jostling her, unsettling her. Frantically, she tried to see over their heads. Even if Rosie had found Jacob, one more goodbye couldn't take too long, she thought. They had been saying tearful goodbyes endlessly, in her view, for weeks and certainly throughout the long train journey through Poland and northern Germany to the Hamburg port. Bella wondered if she should just get on board. Rosie would follow her and find them.

"Get that baby on board," she heard someone yell again "if you want a decent place."

Gradually the people milling around her pushed against her, sweeping her up the walkway and onto the vessel. As she stepped onto the deck she noticed below her still on the quayside, an old man bending down, picking up a clod of earth and putting it into his pocket. His eyes streamed as he too was pushed on board.

Through the crush on deck, Bella fought her way to the railings and clinging on, gazed down to the now nearly empty dock. She expected to see Rosie, still believing she would be rushing back to join them. The crew were preparing the boat to sail. Hugging the baby with one hand and fingering the tickets with the other, Bella wondered for a sickening, unreal moment what would happen if Rosie missed the departure.

Sailors were pulling and pushing at ropes, roughly shoving passengers out of their way as they strode around the decks. The sound of chains clanking on wood drowned the cries of the passengers as they surged towards the railings for a final wave. The noise was terrifying and Bella grasped Sara tightly to her body.

"Rosie!" she screamed into the air, gripping the guard rail as she felt it move away from the land. The baby cried out in distress as the great ship's horn let out a long, slow moan.

"Hold her."

The words echoed round and round Bella's head as she scoured the heaving vessel in search of her sister. At first she just assumed that Rosie had been late boarding and must be trying to find them. The ship was so crowded it was possible they had just not found each other. Bewildered and anxious, Bella clambered from deck to deck, from brow to stern, shouting her sister's name and asking anyone who would listen if they had seen her. Not many paid attention, busy as they were trying to find their way around and settle. Wherever she looked, no matter what else she heard, Rosie's voice never left her imagination.

Then, when she finally had to accept that Rosie was not on board, Lilly comforted her. They had bumped into each other as Bella rushed around in panic. The two girls, close in age and both alone on the boat crammed with families, had instantly formed a bond. Lilly had even shared her few coins with Bella until they ran out because, although Bella had taken charge of both tickets, Rosie had not given her the money pouch. To Lilly, she explained her total lack of money as a stupid blunder. "In the chaos, I left it behind," she said to a trusting Lilly.

Lilly was from Konin, a small town about one hundred kilometres to the west of Lodz. She was travelling to join her brother Oscar who was staying with an uncle and aunt in London's East End. She had remained in Poland with her parents while he worked to save enough money to send for them all to join him. But their parents had been slaughtered in a particularly vicious anti-Semitic attack, so now he was just waiting for her. It was a common story.

Lilly's hair was white, purer than snow. It had turned so overnight, the day she witnessed her parents' murder. Her round, sixteen-year-old face with its pale skin and jolly eyes was set in an ethereal frame. During the crossing, battered by sea air and neglected because of the primitive washing facilities, her hair became grimy and yellow but in the future it would become a blank canvas and could be any colour she desired. Now, despite the tragedy behind her and the anxiety of travelling alone, she was excited to be on her way to a new life.

Lilly enjoyed helping to care for the baby, and together they created a small but stable unit for Sara. Lilly was Bella's first friend outside her own family. With Lilly she begged for food and rags to make into nappies from other passengers, who took pity on the two young girls.

"They are only children themselves and with a small baby," Bella overheard one woman say as she regretfully told them she could give them no more food. Desperately, Bella traded the section of the tickets that would take them on to New York for far less than their value, but she needed food, soap and the occasional bucket of warmed water for the baby.

"You can stay with my family in England," said Lilly, "my aunt and uncle will love having the baby." She said this with confidence although she had never met her aunt and uncle.

"In London, we can get jobs for a while until we have saved enough money to buy tickets and then we can all go to Brooklyn together," said Bella, with equally false confidence. "It won't take long."

Throughout the day they stayed outside on the top deck, escaping from the smell and noise of the cramped quarters below. Despite the primitive conditions in steerage, the seasickness, hunger and cold, the atmosphere was joyous and full of anticipation. Everyone was leaving behind violent Cossacks, anti-Semitism and poverty. Some, like Bella, were leaving behind loved ones. In the turmoil of the desperate exodus, no one asked who they had left or even where they had come from, only where they were going. Shared dreams of a safe and prosperous future had created a mood of expectation that would sustain the hopeful passengers for the seven arduous days at sea.

In the night the girls huddled together deep within the bowels of the ship, cosy beneath the shawl that Rosie had thrown around Bella's shoulders at the dockside. It protected all three of them from cold but not the sounds or smells of fellow passengers. Bella and Lilly whispered their hopes and dreams to each other, ignoring the snorting, snivelling and farting. Sara seemed content and only cried when she was hungry. The closeness and attention of other people and the movement of the boat soothed her.

Despite their new-shared intimacy, Bella did not admit her doubts to Lilly, nor did she describe the anguish she felt. She told her only that Sara was her sister's child and that they were supposed to have made the journey together. Lilly, just like the other passengers, so many of whom had tragic stories behind them, accepted that Sara was Bella's responsibility now and, in the spirit of the times, asked no further questions.

But Bella now started to question whether Rosie had really missed the departure on purpose. The words "Hold her, hold her," persisted in her mind and waves of nausea occasionally overwhelmed her. Was it an impulsive decision, or had Rosie never meant to board the ship? Had the tears she had shed and the agony she had shown been an act, concealing her determination to remain? While Bella had been panicking, waiting for her sister to join them on board, maybe Rosie had already decided not to. She was certain that Jacob hadn't planned this and wondered how he had reacted when he discovered his wife's duplicity. Was it possible that gentle Rosie had betrayed her husband and her sister, and abandoned her own child?

Bella was tormented with questions and wanted to shout and yell her anger but Sara needed food, warmth and love so she concentrated on caring for her and making grand plans with Lilly. Despite her distress, she tried to quell her suspicions and persuade herself that Rosie had just made a tragic mistake. She tried hard not to think of the heavy responsibility she had bequeathed her. This was the adventure she had dreamed of but, despite the smile she forced onto her face, she could not help but be haunted by those final words: "Hold her."

Bella and Lilly had been standing in line for four hours waiting to be processed and allowed into England. Bella clasped Sara very tightly with one hand and with the other held onto the battered suitcase containing her few precious possessions. The joy of arrival was tainted by the unfriendly welcome in the barren, cold shelter that had been built especially for this purpose. This was not the reception they had imagined during the crossing. Lilly stood close, occasionally putting her finger into the baby's mouth as she had during the voyage when food was short.

Men and women were separated for their medical examinations. Officials checked eyes, chests and teeth. Bella saw with alarm that, despite protests, young women were being forced to strip off their tops with minimal privacy for the brief, probably ineffectual medical examination. It was not just her modesty that made her dread this; even a superficial examination would confirm that she had not recently given birth and questions she didn't want to answer would be asked about the identity of the baby.

She watched with horror as the official turned Lilly around, roughly pulling up her tattered shirt and listening to her back through a stethoscope. Lilly was crying deep, deep sobs and slumped almost to the ground as he let her go. She struggled to cover herself and glanced towards Bella as if to wait for her but was pushed out of the hall, still grabbing at her clothes.

Bella had never undressed in front of anyone except her mother and Rosie, and was shaking as her turn came to be confronted by the burly official. She wanted to look straight at him but also to keep eye contact with Lilly, whom she could just see outside through a broken window. Her sobs had stopped and she just looked tired and afraid.

"Name?" the official's voice was rasping.

"Bella Bromavitch." Bella knew it was deception to borrow Rosie's married name but she had no papers – hardly anyone had any papers – so she could choose to call herself anything she wanted. One day Sara would understand. The official seemed irritated at yet another unpronounceable, impossible-to-spell name. He glanced over her head at the queue still stretching behind her.

"Repeat," he barked as his hairy hand lowered a large, flat stamp onto a pad of forms. Bella was glad she had worked so hard to gain a few words of English during the journey. Despite seasickness, overcrowding, fear and hunger, she had studied the treasured book of English words she and Rosie had bought together to prepare themselves.

"Baby's name?" he asked.

"Sara," she said. *Hold her*, she thought.

Bella watched his pen slide across the columns and fill her answers in columns in a large ledger. His spidery handwriting reported her situation precisely as she described it.

"Father?" he asked.

"Dead," she said, surprised at how easy it was to lie.

"Job?" he kept his eyes on the paperwork in front of him.

"Seamstress," she answered, glad she had practised that word. A fellow passenger had suggested that without a man or apparent means to support herself and her child, she might be asked how she planned to live. Without an answer, she had been warned, she could be vulnerable to the awful exploitation that awaited young women. Bella knew that, if challenged, she could sew well enough to be believed. The official seemed satisfied and leant over, indicating for her to remove her top and turn around. Bella grasped her ragged shawl closely around her and held Sara across her chest.

"Please?" she pleaded, trying out another English word. His eyes stared steadily into hers, then at Sara sleeping in her arms, then again at the line of people still waiting to be processed. He dismissed her with a bored sigh. She stumbled gratefully out of the hall, ignoring the lines of con men trying to take the immigrants' last remaining pennies for leading them to 'a room, a cheap, clean room' or a 'job, you need a job, I can find you a job', and lurched into Lilly's waiting arms.

# 1904 Bella

Bella ignored the teasing of the other machinists as she disappeared beneath her workbench for the third time that day to retrieve a fragment of blue serge. Scraps of material, ribbon, discarded buttons and some complete spools of thread filled the large patchwork pocket she had hand-sewn to her overall. It had been a good day and the pouch was already bulging with useful items unwanted by anyone else and, had she not collected them, destined for burning as rubbish. Earlier she had scooped up a length of pale yellow muslin someone had dropped and she imagined the pretty dress she would make for Sara.

"Are you gonna make me a new dress too or is it only for the young and beautiful?" Like most of the other women working in the clothing factory, Hilda wore the same dress every day but it was never dirty. Bella knew that Hilda was only half joking and wished she had time to make her something. She looked at her large frame, calloused hands and drained, exhausted eyes.

"I will one day, Hilda. I promise I will." Bella and Lilly each owned several changes of clothes because Bella made dresses so quickly. They did not need to stand in their underwear in front of the fire each night whilst their one and only dress dried out, as Hilda and the other women did.

"She has a plan." Lilly laughed and so did several of the others, but Lilly knew that Bella did indeed have a plan. During the eighteen months since they had become inseparable, Lilly had learnt that Bella was always planning for the future. Now she watched her friend who was still concentrating on sewing the garment running through her machine, while the other workers started to pack up as the clock on the factory wall moved towards seven to mark the end of their twelve-hour shift. One hand was pressed down on the collar of a jacket, the other turned the wheel. Her feet were on the pedal but her eyes were scanning a book of English grammar that lay propped up behind the machine.

"I before e, except after c," Bella repeated again and again.

"Come on, it's time to finish. Aunt Milcah will need us and we mustn't be late," said Lilly.

Bella finished the jacket and handed it to the waiting manager. She closed her book and joined Lilly, who was waiting at the door. Bella was usually first in and last out. The factory manager did not mind her strange habits of collecting scraps of material and studying English while she worked as she turned out more pieces than anyone else and they were always accurate and never had to be remade.

It was still light and warm as Bella and Lilly arrived at the large Whitechapel house that was home to several families. They pulled aside the tarpaulin that passed for a front door and ran over the uneven wooden floor into a large room. Lilly scooped a crying Sara out of the arms of her brother Oscar.

"Haven't you fed her? Bella, look, she's hungry." Lilly pushed Sara at a reluctant Bella and the three of them walked towards the kitchen. Milcah was viciously chopping raw fish with the sharp, flat blade of a round-handled knife. A large saucepan of soup was steaming on the stove. The onion smell blended with different aromas created by other families in the same building.

"Stir it," Milcah ordered Bella, nodding in the direction of the soup. "Cut the bread," she ordered Lilly, pointing to a seeded loaf on the table. Sol, Lilly's Uncle, sat in a chair in the corner hammering a nail into the sole of a leather boot. Around his feet lay piles of shoes, nails, various tools and strips of leather.

"Ah, now you can take the baby and let me have my assistant back," Sol said gruffly. "Oscar has been acting as a baby's nursemaid all day, not a cobbler."

"Look, what do you think of these?" Oscar took a piece of crumpled paper out of his pocket. On it was a smudged charcoal sketch of a pair of shoes, which he showed to Bella.

"He thinks he is a shoe designer but first he has to learn how to make them and the only way to do that is by mending them." Sol pulled Oscar away from Bella as he spoke and pushed him towards a pair of shoes. Oscar winked at Bella and sat down on the floor. He picked up a wooden foot last and wrapped some leather around it.

"I know, Uncle, but if I…"

"Look what you are doing," Sol grabbed the unfinished shoe out of Oscar's hand. He pointed out a tiny hole in the leather. "Start again, but not now. First we have to mend Mrs Nussbaum's shoes and give them a new heel."

Bella held Sara out of the way of the stove as she stirred the soup.

"What have you brought home today?" asked Milcah, pointing the blade, now covered with small bits of raw fish, towards Bella. "More rubbish?"

"I'll make you a dress, Auntie Milcah, when I find a few more big pieces."

"Humph," was Milcah's answer. "Oscar wants to make shoes, Bella wants to make dresses, how do we get food?"

"Well, at least Sara is the best dressed child in the street," smiled Lilly.

"And you will be the best dressed woman, when I can find the time to finish," said Bella.

"Miriam – you know, the pawnbroker's wife – came by today. She asked to see the dress you are making for Lilly. The whole street seems to know about that dress." Milcah was irritated.

"It's beautiful but I have nowhere to wear it." Lilly sounded worried.

"You'll wear it every day," Bella reasoned.

"To the factory?"

"Why not? Can you hold her for a moment?" Bella asked Oscar, ignoring Sol's disapproving glance. Oscar cuddled Sara, who giggled as she always did in his arms.

Bella walked through the house, savouring the smells of the cooking, hearing singing, shouting, praying, laughter and all the lively sounds of a house full of people. She took a deep breath before entering the outside privy, where she was assaulted by the appalling smell of human waste.

She took a few coins out of her pocket and counted them aloud. Fishing a pencil out of her apron, she wrote a few numbers on the privy wall beside the scrawled messages and children's pictures already there. Next to the numbers she added some dates. She checked them then left, closing the door behind her.

After they had all eaten, Oscar dragged a tin bath in front of the fire and watched as Bella and Lilly washed Sara in water they had warmed in the communal kettle.

"Look what I found," he said, pulling some pieces of charcoal out of his trousers. "Someone dropped it on the street. Shall we do some drawing tonight?"

Oscar handed a few pieces of charcoal to Bella, who carefully wrapped them in a small fragment of soft fabric. "I can't, I promised Lilly that I would finish her dress."

Milcah, who was standing close enough to hear, grabbed Bella by the shoulders.

"What about your baby? You are working twelve hours a day in a factory. You are learning English. You are making dresses for everyone and now you want to learn to draw as well. What of this is for your baby?" Her voice was sharp.

"My baby is happy," protested Bella.

"Your baby is passed from person to person all day while you work and it's not right that we should be caring for her, especially Oscar. He is supposed to be learning a trade."

"I like looking after her while I work. She's happy and it doesn't interfere with learning to mend shoes." Oscar was adamant.

"It will do, she will be walking soon. Sara would be better off in a home. There are good homes for Jewish babies," said Milcah.

"Stop this," said Lilly. "Sara is not going into a home."

"What do you think, Sol?" asked Milcah.

Sol simply shrugged and hammered nails into a shoe.

"She is not an orphan," said Oscar.

"It's not just for orphans. She could stay there just until Bella gets herself established. Once she has her own place, she can take her back."

"You can't throw her out. We just don't do things like that." Lilly was trembling with distress.

"She is growing and starting to crawl, soon there just won't be enough food." Milcah placed the fish balls onto a plate and into the small oven.

Bella hugged Sara closer to her body. "I give you money for both of us. You do well out of it. If you don't want her, I won't stay either."

"At least look. Go see it. Lilly, you go with her."

Sara was dried and dressed and Bella took her up to the room the three of them shared. Bella placed the protesting child in a large drawer full of blankets and towels. Ignoring her cries, she emptied her pocket of all the scraps of material she had picked up that day. She sorted them by colour, folded them and put them into a sack at the bottom of the bed she slept in with Lilly. Then she counted the buttons and wound the thread and ribbons into neat circles. She pulled out a half-finished garment, a needle, thimble and thread, and in the low light of the summer evening, she began to sew.

She sang gently, "I before e, except after c." Gradually Sara quietened and slept.

Quietly watching her, Lilly asked, "Don't you think you ought to write to Rosie and Jacob? They don't even know where their daughter is. They must think you are in New York with Jacob's brother."

Bella shrugged and remained silent. Then later, lying in bed with Lilly, she said, "Maybe your aunt is right. Maybe it is time for me to find somewhere else to live. Milcah and Sol are getting irritated that we leave the baby with them all day, particularly as Oscar is supposed to be learning to become a cobbler and the baby is a distraction. Perhaps Sara could stay in that children's home just for a short while, while I look for somewhere. I wonder if I ought to at least look at it. Will you come with me?"

Bella and Lilly arrived at the gates of the large Victorian gothic building. Even for two girls who had travelled across land and ocean, the trip to south London still felt like a big journey. As they stood on the doorstep, Bella tried to cover up an abscess that had formed on Sara's neck. It was oozing yellow pus onto her fresh new dress. Bella had sat up all night finishing it, wanting Sara to look her best. She put her finger into the baby's mouth and rang the doorbell. Sara continued whimpering as she sucked. The door was opened by two boys and a girl. They looked about ten and twelve.

"I am Leah and that's Ruben and that's Seth. What's the baby called?"

"Sara."

"I am to show you around. Ruben, open the door." Leah was clearly in charge.

Bella and Lilly entered a long dark hallway. The floor and walls were tiled, the ceiling painted a dark brown. The air was bitterly cold.

"Are there any…?" Bella stopped, embarrassed.

"…grownups?" Lilly finished.

"Oh yes, but they are busy, it's lunchtime. They'll see you later. Can I hold the baby?" Leah reached forward as if to take Sara.

Bella clutched Sara closer, her hand still covering the child's neck. Ruben and Seth had marched ahead and were standing by a door with a glass window above it.

"She needs to get used to you first." Bella tightened her arms around Sara.

"Oh that's alright," chirped Leah. "I'm used to babies."

Bella looked through the glass into the long room behind the door. Lines of children sat on benches at long tables, eating in silence.

"Aren't you allowed to talk at meals?"

"Oh no," answered Leah "it's bad for you."

Bella and Lilly glanced at each other.

"Why is it bad for you?" Lilly noticed that the pus from Sara's wound was starting to seep through the handkerchief Bella had covered it with.

"Because you could choke and die," Ruben announced triumphantly.

Leah clipped his ear. "Go," she commanded, "I can manage this."

Ruben and Seth ran into the dining room, delighted to be released from their duties.

"Can we see where the babies are?" Bella looked towards a wide flight of stairs. She could hear babies crying above.

"Upstairs. They are all clean and happy," said Leah as she led them up the stairs.

The baby's dormitory was heated by gas fires at both ends and, although still chilly, was many degrees warmer than the corridor. There were twenty iron cots immaculately lined up against the walls. Each cot had a number hanging from its head. A few babies were crying but most were gurgling to themselves. There were several girls of about Leah's age or a bit older attending to them and a nurse in uniform walking around the cots. She gave instructions to the girls but did not touch the babies.

"Why do the cots have numbers?" Lilly asked.

"Because we don't usually know their names when they come to us," the nurse explained. "Some of them are foundlings, some have just become separated from their families or their families

27

just don't have enough money to feed them, so they bring them here. We wait and if nobody claims them or names them, we give them names. Do you want to put her down in a cot while you look around? I see you have a very good guide," she said, smiling at Leah.

"No, thank you. I'll take her with me."

"We'll take good care of her." The nurse held out her arms towards Sara.

For a moment Bella wondered: What would happen if I just handed her to the nurse and left? Sara would be fine with all the other orphans and I would be free of the unwelcome responsibility. She shuddered and for an instant she imagined Rosie's face, her eyes streaming. She clutched Sara tightly to her body.

"No." Bella's voice was determined. "Thank you," she added.

"I am going to train to be a nurse," said Leah as she led Bella and Lilly down the aisle. "We all train for something. We have to be able to earn money as none of us have parents."

One of the girls approached Bella and tickled Sara on the cheek. Sara screamed.

"Oh dear," said Bella, "she is not used to you."

Lilly took Bella's arm and led her outside the dormitory.

"Those babies seem very happy," she said once they were back in the corridor. "Milcah might be right, she might be better off here for now."

"She's not an orphan and she has a name." Bella mopped at Sara's abscess.

"Maybe you won't be able to manage after you move into your own place. You'll be on your own. You ought to think about it."

Suddenly there was the noise of children running and shouting. Bella and Lilly leant over the banisters and saw streams of children rushing out of the dining room.

"Lunch is over," announced Leah. "The Manager will be ready to meet you soon."

"What about you? What about your lunch?"

"Oh, they'll save mine till I have finished my job, that's looking after you. We have three meals a day and we do all the cooking ourselves."

"Can you cook?" Bella sounded surprised.

"Yes, of course but I am better at nursing. Some of the girls do cleaning but I hate that. We have to do an hour's work every day but unless they are short because someone is sick, you can choose what to do."

"Do you have any family at all?" Bella asked Leah.

"No, of course not, none of us have families. If we did we wouldn't be here," Leah giggled, as if Bella were deranged.

On the long journey back across London, Lilly comforted a stressed Sara by singing and whispering to her. Bella remained silent until they were nearly home, then she spoke resolutely. "I couldn't, Lilly, I just can't do it. She has a family – me. She is staying with me."

"I hate you!" Bella screeched at Sara, watching her attempt to stand up and then, defeated, crawl up and down in frustration. She was in the drawer that Lilly's family had lent to serve as a cot for the child and Bella slept on a mattress on the floor. Sara was still sick and the abscess had not healed properly. She cried a lot and only slept restlessly. The little dish of mashed carrots and potatoes, the food the chemist had recommended and which was a meal for both of them, lay uneaten on the floor. Sara gave up her struggle and lay back, howling deep, miserable sobs.

Bella looked around the tiny room she rented from the pawnbroker. In gratitude for dresses she had made for his wife and two daughters and those he expected her to make in future, he charged her very little money. Thanks to the low rent she just managed on her wages, although sometimes, particularly when there were extra expenses like medicine for the baby, she thought angrily about the money in the pouch Rosie had kept with her.

She had made the room cosy, using her dress-making skills to cover the bed and create curtains and cushions. Oscar had built her a table and dragged in a broken chair he had found in the street. He repaired it, Bella covered it.

"What a team," he had commented when it was finished.

He and Lilly popped by frequently to see if she needed any help, sometimes bringing food, sometimes just to say hello. Bella was always pleased to see them. She particularly missed Lilly who had recently changed jobs and was now working in a hat factory. Lilly had never liked sewing machines and was much happier blocking hats onto model heads. It was nearby but they no longer saw each other every day.

"Why didn't I give you to the orphanage?" Bella always spoke aloud to Sara, who listened intently as if she understood every word. Bella often wondered whether her decision was the right one but she had not been capable of handing the screaming baby into the care of strangers. Even now, although she had been told that there were places especially for mothers and babies without families and she could go to one of those, she did not want to give up her hard-won independence, or admit she was struggling to cope. She resented the responsibility but was comforted by the support she was given by the other women she worked with. She took Sara to the factory every day, carrying her in a large bag she had made that hung round her back. The baby crawled around the floor or lay on piles of material, with all the women taking turns to play with her, rock her to sleep or feed her. They brought special treats for her and Sara seemed happy there. Bella paid them all back for their kindness with new clothes and the manager had commented that his workforce had never looked so well-dressed. She would not allow herself to think of Rosie for whenever she did, a violent anger overwhelmed her and she did not trust herself to be gentle with Sara.

Then late one evening, when Sara was already asleep, Oscar arrived with a letter for her. The envelope was large, dotted with stamps and looked official. Oscar looked at Bella, expecting her to comment on the unusual receipt of a letter. When she didn't, he made small talk. He stayed for what seemed like a long time, excitedly chatting about the shoes he was now making, not just repairing. He commented on the baby's growth and confided his concern about his uncle's ill health. All the time he glanced at the letter, obviously hoping that Bella would open it in his presence. She stubbornly ignored this until he gave up, kissed her lightly on the cheek, tickled Sara under the chin then finally left her alone.

Turning her back on a fractious Sara, who was fussing because Oscar had left, Bella looked at the various labels on the package. One was dated October 1903, postmarked Lodz and addressed to Bella, care of Nathan Bromavitch in Brooklyn. It had been sent on to the headquarters of a shipping company in New York and returned to their offices in London, who had passed it on to the Jews' Temporary Shelter in London's East End. They had then forwarded it to the Jewish Agency, the organisation in England that kept records of the arrival of all Jewish immigrants. It had arrived there in an envelope addressed to Bella Bromavitch. From there it had been hand-delivered to Oscar. It had been travelling for eighteen months.

She removed the outer labels showing all this information, and opened the packet. Inside was a small envelope. She recognised Rosie's handwriting, neat and even. Holding the envelope as steadily as she could, slowly she opened it. A photograph fell out and fluttered to the floor. Nervously, she picked it up. Slightly blurred and pale, it was the photograph of the three of them at the dockside. It seemed like centuries ago. *'Rosie, Bella and Sara, from your loving mother and sister. 1903'* was written on the back in Rosie's handwriting. Then Bella pulled out the accompanying letter and reluctantly began to read.

*Dearest, dearest sister,*

*I know it might be pointless writing and this letter may never reach you. I only know you did not get to America because Nathan wrote to*

31

*Jacob asking why we hadn't arrived in New York. He went to the docks to meet us and had found us a room. He was very worried when the shipping line said we had left the boat in London. I am saying we, because the records show two tickets and at that time, Nathan didn't know that I had not travelled with you. We wrote to him to try to find you but he didn't write back. I think he took a lot of trouble to prepare for us and must be cross.*

*Even so, I will never regret my decision to stay with Jacob, just that I could not tell either of you because I didn't know what to do and Jacob was so determined and you were so excited. The truth is I didn't plan it and I wasn't sure until I saw that big boat. Then I knew I couldn't get on it without him. I couldn't bear to leave him and I could not manage without him. I didn't have time to think, but if I had, I would have been sure that Nathan would have looked after you both in Brooklyn until we joined you – together.*

*Lots of families are being separated in these difficult times but this is different. I don't know where you are and that is agony. It is as if I am being punished because I don't know what has happened to my daughter. Sometimes when I see a baby in the street, I feel as if all the bones in my body have become liquid. By now, naturally, I would be having another, but that will never happen, so I feel twice bereaved.*

*Jacob has changed. He acts as if he is disappointed in me. He has been cross with me since it happened and hardly talks to me. He just eats his meal, talks to his mother, who now lives with us, and then leaves. He never ever mentions Sara and that makes it harder for me. I don't understand because he is the one person I should be able to talk to about missing her. But he is so involved with his work for the Bund, do you remember that trade union that is supposed to make all our lives better? But I can't help thinking that he must be feeling it somewhere. I don't think we are as we used to be. I mean as man and wife. Is this a terrible thing to say? Something happened to us with the choice I made. I think that is unfair as he always said we should make any sacrifice for the good of our child and it was my sacrifice as well.*

Sometimes I still question why he had to wait here anyway. Why didn't we all leave together? Then this wouldn't have happened. But then, when we take Jacob's mother to the cemetery to visit his father's grave, I realize he had to stay to look after her. She could never leave because she still needs to talk to her husband, even though he died in 1892 – so long ago. Jacob said in the diphtheria epidemic of that year people died quickly and, surprisingly, not necessarily the weak ones. His father was strong and fit and yet he died and Jacob's life was never the same again. When we take Regina to visit his grave, she leans against the stone and talks down into it, as if he can hear her. Do you remember how large that cemetery is? Apparently it is the largest burial ground for Jews in all of Europe, can you imagine?

I am rambling on, because I haven't heard from you and therefore have nothing to answer. You know where to write to us, so I think you have chosen not to. Can you imagine how I would feel if I suddenly got a letter from you telling me that you are well and Sara thrives and is happy? I could die then, if that happened. I really could.

I am sending you a copy of the photograph that we had taken on the dockside. Jacob paid a lot of money to the photographer for a copy of it. It is my only record of my daughter and I couldn't bear to part with the original. I do hope you receive it and treasure it as I do, but perhaps in a different way because you have Sara and will be watching her grow and change. But maybe you will show it to her when she is old enough and tell her that is her mother. I don't look very happy, do I? I wasn't that day, of course. It was as if I was tearing my life into two pieces. I do hope you will remember the happy times we shared as sisters and cherish my child until we are together again.

From your beloved sister,

Rosie (and her darling husband Jacob and loving mother-in-law Regina)

Bella stared at the photograph as if she was looking at strangers. Then she read the letter again and smelt it, as if it held some answer. She folded it and placed it inside a pocket of her old suitcase.

She shoved the suitcase under her bed then gazed at Sara for a long time.

"You'll never be my daughter," she finally said to the sleeping child, then started to prepare for bed.

# 1908 Bella

As always the market was busy on Sunday with people jostling for bargains. Bella was standing in front of a stall beneath a large hand-painted sign, which announced:

*'Oscar's Shoes – a perfect fit for all the family.*
*Bella's Dresses – made only for you.'*

It was obvious that the name had been changed from 'Sol's' to 'Oscar's' and Bella's name had been added only recently.

The stall, where Oscar both repaired and made shoes, was in a much prized corner location and attracted customers from four different directions. Uncle Sol, who had died a year earlier, had worked hard and long to maintain its advantageous position. Now one half was piled high with shoes and boots, tools, large pieces of leather, pots of glue and old glass containers full of nails. Separated by a box, the other end held Bella's dressmaking paraphernalia, rolls of fabric, pins, scissors, a jar of crayons, a drawing pad and an order book. The area looked like a jumbled mess but Bella knew exactly where each item was, reaching into the clutter confidently as she needed it.

Now she concentrated on wrapping a swathe of material around a young woman over the top of her dress. She pinned it carefully around the waist and spoke through a mouthful of pins as she glanced briefly at the line of potential customers waiting for her attention. Her diminutive frame would have been swamped by the crowd had she not been surrounded by a small group of on-lookers. They had created a space around her to watch her work, just as if she was one of the street entertainers. Her hands moved swiftly and surely as she began to create an elegant outfit from the cloth. The bystanders watched in fascination as a shape emerged.

"Look, there's a queue of customers waiting for you." Oscar spoke as he vigorously polished a pair of newly repaired boots and nodded in the direction of a line of women patiently waiting for Bella's attention.

"They'll have to wait." She knelt down on the ground, holding a measuring machine against the long serge skirt. She puffed an even chalk mark around the hem as her customer peered down at her skirt.

"Stay still please, Mrs Huntley. Wait till I've finished pinning, then you can look in that mirror." Bella pointed to a cracked mirror leaning up against the back of the stall.

"You're getting wet knees," Oscar warned.

"I always get wet knees when I am measuring." She stood up and slowly turned Gemma Huntley around as she unravelled the pinned skirt, holding it above the wet ground. "It'll be finished in a week."

"Thanks," answered Mrs Huntley. "Can I send my sister Vera to you? She has a new beau and wants something to impress him."

Bella hesitated, glancing again at the people waiting for her. "I have too many orders at the moment. Can she wait?"

"Well, we picked up some material in Paris. Look, here is a sample." Mrs Huntley waved a wisp of pale blue silk in front of Bella's face.

Bella rubbed it gently in between her thumb and finger, then stroked it across her cheek, savouring its smoothness.

"Yes, lovely, it will make a wonderful dress as long as she is not in a hurry. I can't take any more on for now. I'll see you next week for one more fitting."

"You shouldn't have done that," Oscar remarked as he glued a sole onto a calfskin boot, half-watching Gemma Huntley disappear through the crowd.

"What?"

Oscar looked up at the sign above the stall. "Sol always said you mustn't turn customers away, no matter how busy you are."

"Yes and he killed himself working round the clock, even on the Sabbath. I can't take on what I can't do myself and properly. Customers come to me for personal attention and my hand-sewn clothes. Those women, the rich ones from the West End, boast about how much they order from a market stall in Petticoat Lane. I heard that Mrs Huntley laughing about it: 'A little Jewish seamstress on Petticoat Lane, not exactly haute couture,' she said, but she and her friends are happy to wear my clothes to posh places so I mustn't compromise on the quality they come for."

"Of course that is why they are coming. The same reason they used to come to Sol for their shoes – quality."

"I know, but if I made her sister a dress with that lovely fabric, it would have quality but smell of fish."

"The blue silk?"

"Yes, the blue silk. There is no point in working with such elegant fabric while I am still in the market."

"What do you mean, still in the market? We have only had the stall for a year."

"You want to stop mending shoes and only design and make them, don't you Oscar? That's your dream."

"Yes."

"Well, I want my own shop. Indoors, out of the rain and the cold, where my dresses won't smell of fish, or meat or worse. That's my dream."

Oscar pointed to a young man manoeuvring his way towards them. "Look, Isaac's here. He has come to see you. He will be a Rabbi soon. You can't have a shop if you are a Rabbi's wife."

"I am not going to marry Isaac."

"He will be disappointed, and you wouldn't have to work if you married a Rabbi. This could be a secure future for you."

"That's why I can't marry Isaac. He is going to be a Rabbi and I want a shop."

"Have you told him?"

"Not yet."

"But he wants to marry you."

"I can't, Oscar. Don't talk about it anymore. I am packing up. It's been a good day."

"A Rabbi's wife? Isn't that something good to be?"

"Not for me. I don't want to do charity work and follow someone around."

"Not *someone* – a Rabbi. You would make a perfect wife for a Rabbi."

"I would make a very bad Rabbi's wife. I am just getting established and I want a shop where I sell my own designs." Bella was folding her half-finished garments and placing them into large bags.

"What about Sara?" Oscar was putting shoes into large boxes, each pair tied together and labelled.

"What about Sara?" Bella's eyes narrowed.

"Sara would become a Rabbi's child." Oscar started dismantling the stall, unscrewing poles, lifting the base and pulling at the tarpaulin.

"No. Anyway, I don't want to live in that world. I can do better." She avoided looking at him as they continued to pack up for the day in silence.

# 1909 Rosie

In 1909 Bella received a letter. It was postmarked Lodz and addressed to the Jews' Temporary Shelter, London. She fingered it gently, smelt it, then read it quickly. Then she carefully placed it back in its envelope and put it with Rosie's first letter.

*Dearest, dearest sister,*

*I know this letter may never reach you but people tell me that the Jews' Temporary Shelter in London is very good at finding separated families, so you never know. I have sent you several letters over the past few years, but there has only been silence from you. I don't know if you received them so maybe this is a futile exercise but it makes me feel better. I wish I could talk to you.*

*There is bad news. Jacob was arrested. I am trying to think if there could be anything worse and of course there could. He could have been sent to Siberia – or maybe he could have been executed. He was picked up by the police carrying a pile of illegal political paperwork, the stuff I've tried hard to ignore. I don't know how serious is the crime he has committed. He can be very stubborn and he was furious that the Russians made it illegal to speak Polish. They don't want to keep the Polish language alive and he feels very strongly about that. He is very proud of being Polish and doesn't want to be called Russian. I doubt he kept quiet about that when they picked him up.*

*Mrs Mendel's son, Jonah, was in that prison for the same reason. He was let out after three months, but apparently some men were shot. He said the political prisoners are kept separately from the criminals, so at least that is something. But he said they are squashed in six or eight*

39

to a cell and the food is rotten, so they all get ill all the time. Sometimes the Russians just get fed up, clear a cell and shoot them all in the woods – just for fun. So I am very frightened. Jonah also said that if you volunteer for the Russian army you can get out. Some Jews have, he says. I do hope Jacob does that, although I can't imagine it. Can you imagine Jacob – a Cossack!

It's very hard trying to explain things to his mother when I don't really understand myself. She is now sewing buttons all day long and late into the night and I am out cleaning. Without Jacob there is hardly any money. Well, there is hardly enough with Jacob as it is anyway.

One piece of good news is that Jonah may be coming to London. I say 'maybe', because he has had some problems with his visa, because he was in prison, I think. But if he does, he'll ask around and I'll hope he'll find out where you are. He has promised if he does, he will write to me about Sara. Oh, I do hope so. But I have been warned that London is not like Lodz, although most Jewish people live close together. He is a very determined young man and I am sure he'll find you, if you are there. He plans to go to America afterward, just as we did. I hear there is a place in America that Jews go to called Ellis Island. Maybe you went there but it is so far away, I hope not.

Dear Bella, I cannot imagine your life now but for the first time, I am truly glad you are not here, nor is my darling Sara. Will you ever forgive me? I wonder that all the time.

Love, love, love

From your sister Rosie (and Regina, no Jacob this time).

# 1910s

# 1910 Bella

"Mind that lamp," Bella shouted at Sara, who was absentmindedly running her finger around the edge of an oil lamp. She held her slender body upright despite the large bulge that made her pregnancy look further along than it was. Watched anxiously by Oscar, she was bending down to unpack skirts from a large wicker basket, then straightening up again to hang them carefully one by one on rails. The shop was full of helpers, mainly market traders, painting, scraping, brushing and draping sheaths of cloth across poles. Lilly sat in a corner on a wooden crate putting finishing touches to a jacket.

"'Bella Designs'," she said for the umpteenth time. "I wish you would call it 'Bella Designs.' 'Bella's' could be anything, a sweetshop, another pawnbroker, anything – maybe a brothel."

"In Petticoat Lane, a brothel? Everyone's too tired," laughed Bella.

"Or poor," added Moses the butcher, with a wink.

Oscar took a break from organising the friends who had come to help them open their first shop. He tentatively approached Bella and gently put an arm around her thin shoulders, carefully pulling some strands of hair off her wet brow and pinning them back into her bun. She straightened her back with a low moan.

"Ooh, this baby better be a helpful one when it is born. Look at that child."

She pointed to Sara who was grumpily swirling strips of black material around a framed funeral photograph of Edward VII.

"Please sit down, bubbuleh, we have plenty of time," pleaded Oscar. "You are too large now, let me do this."

"No, Oscar, everything else, but not the clothes. There is plenty else for you to do. Only I touch the clothes." Bella lent down into the basket again.

"We have lots of help." Oscar pointed to the full shop. The other traders had watched Bella and Oscar's hard work and determination with admiration. Her flair and attention to detail coupled with his financial expertise had earned them this shop and they all wanted to help now, so they could celebrate later. They had shared so much in the market; the fight for fair rents; licence problems; the dreadful fire followed by the police investigation, which put them all under suspicion of arson; the constant vigilance for customers who stole and, always, the cold and wet.

Bella looked around at the people she had spent so much time with in the past two years. Some had just wandered in off the street after packing their stalls up for the night to see if they could help. Children popped in to see what the activity was about but they didn't last long as spectators. They were given jobs the moment they entered the doorway: a brush for the floor, a rag for the window or just some nails to hold. They either worked or were sent on their way. There was much noise, laughter and lots of gossip, always gossip.

From inside Bella could see Herman, who had the fruit and vegetable stall, painting her name on the shop front. 's'alleB' it said to her, confirming the realisation of her ambition. Across the road, she could see a shop front saying 'Kosher Butcher and Poulterer', in front of that a stall that seemed to sell second-hand everything: cutlery, pots, pans, brushes. Between them was Ritowsky's bagel stand, which always did brisk business. She could see children on the street hanging bunting onto the rails of the market stalls. Street parties were a tradition when a stallholder moved up to owning a shop; they were like family celebrations. It didn't happen very often but when it did, it was a reminder that advancement was possible. It promised hope, and that a better future was achievable for any of them. Pawnbrokers tended to make that journey first, making money from the poverty of new immigrants who frequently needed to pawn the few treasured possessions they had brought with them in order to buy food or pay rent.

Now Bella and Oscar were moving into a shop vacated by a pawnbroker who had taken that next step and moved into larger premises further west. It was a small shop on the corner of Petticoat Lane and Cobb Street, a short walk from Cable Street where she, Oscar and Sara shared one room. The drawer where Sara had spent her early months had been prepared for the new baby, but Bella was hoping that one of her regular customers would give her a proper cradle in return for a coat.

Oscar and Bella were stretching themselves financially to cover the cost of the lease and the necessary purchase of a sewing machine. But Bella knew her customers were loyal and she was a risk taker. She knew that without taking chances she would gain nothing. Oscar was the opposite but he loved and believed in her totally.

"Sit down," he said, leading her gently to the one chair, the only piece of proper furniture in the shop.

"I hate this brown, it's for pawnbrokers."

"The brown will go, I promise."

Bella propped her feet up on a wooden box. The heavy smell of oil paint obliterated the musky odour of the previous owner but made Bella feel slightly faint. She saw the chaos but it was good chaos. The shop was nearly ready and her garments, made during so many exhausting late candlelit nights, were safe. She saw Moses, the pots and pans man, hammering at the window frame. Harry, who supplied her buttons, was screwing a handle onto the rickety door. Mrs Ritkowsky (always Mrs Ritkowsky as no one knew her first name) had contributed bags of fresh bagels and was scrubbing the counter, trying to remove the stains of years of coins and dirty paper money. Her resentful son Danny was holding a bowl of soap suds in front of her. She skirted carefully round the heavy flat iron and giant tailor's scissors.

Oscar was scraping at the torn wallpaper hanging on the wall behind the counter. Bella smiled to herself. Oscar was good at money and they made a good couple, but scraping walls was a real labour of love for him. He was thin and pale, the strain of the last few years since their marriage showed on his face. As well as working long hours in a shoe factory and supplying bespoke shoes to his private customers, he still ran the Sunday market stall and spent occasional nights working as a caretaker for extra money. Bella hoped that this shop and the arrival of their first baby meant the beginning of a new life for them all.

In a box close to her feet was the Singer sewing machine, gleaming black with gold lettering. It was second or third hand and had been much used but was still accurate and sharp. Bella looked forward to unpacking it later. That would be the high point of the day. She closed her eyes and for a moment imagined the shop, pink and warm and full of customers. In her fantasy they were being measured, choosing fabric and ordering. There was a queue at the cash till and women looking in through a window displaying glorious Bella originals.

A loud crash dragged her quickly from her daydream.

"Look," she screamed, pointing at Sara. "She has dropped the King!" A portrait of the recently deceased Edward VII lay at Sara's feet in a mess of splintered wood and black funeral ribbons. "That child is so clumsy."

"It's only the frame, the portrait will be fine. I'll make another frame immediately." Oscar held a handkerchief out to the sniffling Sara, who stood staring at the shattered frame.

"Get her out of my sight," Bella dragged herself out of her chair.

"She is only eight, leave her, she is trying to help."

"She is never trying to help." Bella's tone was irritable.

Lilly left the jacket she was sewing and, taking Sara by the hand, led her into the street out of range of Bella's bad temper.

*

The street party had been a success, only a wedding could have created more excitement. A few of their closest friends had stayed behind to join them in the now pristine shop for a cup of tea and the festive unveiling of the sewing machine. Lilly had gone home, Sara sat cross-legged on the floor playing with a packet of buttons and Oscar was attacking the box with the giant tailor's scissors. Bella sat in a chair and laid her head against the back, fighting off fatigue. Oscar had suggested waiting till tomorrow but she had worked too hard for this moment.

She was the first to see the stranger peering through the window but many passers-by had stopped to look in during the day, so she didn't pay much attention. She didn't recognise him but noticed his long black coat worn open over black trousers and his flat black peaked cap. Beneath, over a white long-sleeved shirt, he wore a tight waistcoat. His greying, bushy beard and tiny round spectacles reminded her of Jacob. She hadn't thought about him or Rosie for a long time but now she glanced over at Sara who was creating patterns out of the buttons.

"Leave them alone," she said.

"Leave her alone," said Oscar.

The stranger wandered into the shop, his eyes fixed on Sara.

"I am looking for Bella."

Oscar jumped up towards him. "What do you want with her?"

"I am Jonah Mendel, I have come from Lodz. I am looking for Bella. Is this the child?" He pointed directly at Sara.

Bella felt a twinge in her belly and stroked the life growing inside her.

"Calm down, calm down," she spoke to the bump.

Oscar was standing directly in front of the man, as if protecting his women.

"I have news for Bella, and a letter."

"Letter?"

Bella tried to stand but found her legs were too weak. She took deep breaths. Oscar rushed to support her. The stranger walked towards Sara, who looked up but without any interest.

"This is our daughter Sara," said Oscar resolutely.

"Ah, I promised Rosie I would find her and I said I would write. Is she well?" The man calling himself Jonah leant down and placed a hand on Sara's chin, lifting her face up to see it clearly. He gazed at her with intense curiosity then, seeing the threatening look on Oscar's face, he let her go. He stood in front of Bella who continued to stroke her stomach. The twinges were worsening.

"It was not hard to find you. There are many Bellas here but only one, if you know what I mean. I said there would be a child of seven, or is it eight?"

"Eight," answered Oscar.

Bella, her breathing laboured and disjointed, asked, "What is it you want?"

"Rosie asked me to find you. She wants to know about her..." His voice trailed off and he looked at Sara again. "She asked me to find you," he repeated uncomfortably.

Oscar stared at the visitor, then decisively walked towards Sara, pulled her to her feet, sat her on his lap and held her close. She rested her head against his shoulder, eyeing the stranger with suspicion.

"How are they?" gasped Bella.

"Jacob is still in prison. I am sorry, maybe you didn't know. It is political, he didn't do anything criminal," said the stranger, directing his words to Sara, who, ignoring the visitor, had left the haven of Oscar's lap and returned to playing with the buttons.

"And Rosie?" asked Bella. Oscar had turned his attention to Bella and was patting her brow with a piece of torn fabric, still holding Jonah in his protective gaze. She was perspiring and he was worried about her breathing.

"Rosie can only see him once a month. Sometimes she is allowed to leave food for him. This child, Rosie keeps asking about the child..." He stopped as if realising that if he asked the question he had been sent to ask, something fragile might break, but he was not sure what. "Things are difficult." He looked at Bella with alarm as she panted and gasped, clutching her stomach and then finally crying out.

Years later, Etta liked to boast to her twin brothers that she was born on the floor of Mama's first shop. She wasn't. Oscar had carried her back to their home where hours later she gave birth to a girl. Bella and the baby were both fine. In the street they said that the excitement of the shop opening had been too much for someone that pregnant and she and the baby had survived only because she was so young and fit. When it was over, Bella wondered whether this early birth had left a mess of blood and awful things, which she imagined sullying her shop.

Oscar told her that Jonah Mendel had gone and he pointed to a letter in Rosie's handwriting lying beside her new-born in the drawer. She cried for the first time while reading it, blaming her weakness on her frail condition after childbirth.

The shop was immaculate when she went back to work a few days later with tiny Etta carried in a shawl tied around her shoulders. Everything had been cleaned, the clothes hanging neatly on rails or displayed on the mannequins, the windows were sparkling and the walls were the pale peach that she had so wanted.

'BELLA'S' was open for business.

# 1910 Rosie

The letter that had made Bella cry was dated April 1910 and had a label handwritten in large letters: 'DELIVER BY HAND'.

*Dearest Bella,*

*This is going to be very short as Jonah, you remember Mrs Mendle's son, came round and said he suddenly got his visa. He is definitely going to pass through London on his way to America. After being in that horrid prison, he is nervous and worried about everything. He thinks that at any moment the chance could be taken away from him so he is leaving right away.*

*I am so pleased he is on his way, for him but not for me. It will be one less person I know here. He was special because he could give me news of Jacob from prison. Now I have no one to tell me what is really happening. There is no sign of him being let out and it's awful because he did nothing wrong. Jonah says Jacob is very cross. Can you imagine Jacob being cross? I am allowed to visit him once a month, but the truth is I hate those visits. He never seems pleased to see me.*

*Things aren't any better for me and Regina. Maybe a bit worse, as Regina is getting so tired and her eyesight is troubling her, which is worrying because we need her to keep on sewing buttons.*

*Oh dear, I sound very depressing and don't mean to. Thinking of you and my little princess hopefully enjoying the good life wherever you are makes me happy. I have asked Jonah to kiss her for me, although I don't think he will. I hope that he is able to find you and remembers to write to me that he has. He is leaving now and I must finish this and give it to him – but I kissed the envelope first!*

*Love, love, love from your sister Rosie (and Regina, no Jacob again)*

# 1915 Bella

Disturbed by their father's cough the twins, Bernard and Simon, started crying loudly in unison, their usual way. They were curled up together in a single cot, which lived in the kitchen during the day. Now their fists and legs were thrashing around as they fought for the attention of their parents. Bella ignored the familiar routine.

"Look, Oscar, I told you, skirts are getting shorter. Shoes are going to be seen more now. Look." Bella was reading the Daily Mail and tried to show Oscar an article but he was concentrating on trying to calm the babies. He finally gave up and picked them up, hanging one over each arm.

Bella watched Oscar expertly juggling the twins and then read aloud: *'Now that the full skirt hangs a fair six inches from the ground, we shall see the ankle all the time. Silk stockings or patent leather boots are recommended.'*

"Shh, shh. Well then, I'd be better off making silk stockings."

"No, the skirts will go up further. Shoes are becoming so important. They'll be part of the outfit."

"Hmm, still silk stockings. Anyway how could they go any further? You can already see the calves."

The First World War changed many lives and also many businesses. Factories that had produced all manner of goods were commissioned to manufacture munitions and many people lost their livelihoods as certain products were considered a waste of resources. It was the opposite for Bella, who saw in the horror only a temporary hindrance to her expansion and an opportunity to sharpen her skills as an employer and as a designer. Her attitude was that

51

the more active women became, the more her skills were needed. The shop had spread to the premises next door but plans for a second shop in another location had been postponed, or "interrupted", as Bella described it.

Oscar, always cautious, warned that cutbacks might be necessary and urged Bella to concentrate on her few select customers who were riding out the war at the edge of fashion, as if there was no fighting in Europe. He even suggested giving up the site next door until it was all over and then maybe returning to her plans.

Bella protested that women were always interested in clothes but Oscar reasoned that labour was short and advised that she should go back to the days when she took on nothing that she couldn't do by herself. But Bella Unique, now both the name of her shop and her private fashion 'house', had become too successful to do that and a carefully selected group of home workers now supported her, although every design was uniquely 'Bella'.

"This war is changing things for women. It will show in the clothes. Women will be wearing trousers soon, you'll see, Oscar. Start thinking of shoes to go with women's trousers, really. Oh, Bernard, why are you such a whiny baby?" Oscar had thrust him into her arms as he placed Simon back in the cot and rocked him. "Maybe we should separate them. They keep waking each other up."

"No, they'll just scream if they are apart, this phase will pass. They'll probably end up hating each other."

"Never," said Bella, gratefully handing Bernard back to Oscar.

Having settled Simon in the cot, he held the miserable Bernard over his shoulder, patting him gently on the back.

"By the way, where's Sara?" asked Bella. "I need to work and I want her to give Etta her tea. I've got an idea for the wedding dress…" Bella picked up her sketch pad and started drawing a high-waisted bridal gown with a wide sash and a mid-calf skirt.

"I thought we had talked about this – you treating Sara like a servant. It's not right, she is only thirteen, a child."

"Yes, well at thirteen I was running the home for the whole family. I don't see why she can't do the same." Bella's pencil was busy outlining several variations of a neckline. Without looking up she shouted, "Sara!"

Nervously Sara popped her head around the door. She was thin and pale but, as Bella always noticed, she had Rosie's large, kind blue eyes.

"Where's Etta?" Bella was brusque as always with Sara.

"I am here," Etta answered quietly from behind Sara, expecting trouble.

"Can you give her something to eat and the potatoes need to be peeled for tonight."

Sara looked grumpy but disappeared to do her chores, closely followed by Etta.

"I think you are too hard on her." Oscar said quietly. Bernard had finally calmed down and snuggled close to him.

"Life won't be kind to her unless she learns how to work," said Bella.

"She does nothing but work. It is not fair just because she is the eldest."

Sometimes, Bella was overwhelmed by the desire to explain that her feelings towards Sara were so coloured by resentment that they verged on the violent, particularly when Sara called her 'Mama'. Bella wanted to shout, "I am not your Mama. She left you and I have looked after you, fed you, protected you, nurtured you, gone without food for you. Now I want something back from you." But she knew Oscar was right, she was unfair to the girl and her guilt made her even more unreasonable. After Jonah Mendel's visit she had told him the true story but she had never explained her feelings of betrayal and knew he would be devastated to find out that she had hidden such a trauma from him. From the beginning of their marriage he had just accepted that Sara was Bella's responsibility and therefore his own. Just once, before he proposed to her, he had asked, "Are you free to marry me? If so, I would like to ask you to."

"Yes, I am," she had answered in a way that invited no questions.

"Sara will be mine," he said, "like any other children we will have together."

Then she asked if she and Sara could still be called Bromavitch, which meant that their future family could be called Bromavitch. So many names had been changed or adopted during the mass immigration that it was not an unusual request, although Bella could not have explained why this mattered so much to her. Oscar agreed as he had no attachment to his own surname. It came with no happy memories. At a time when Jewish families were dispersed and disrupted, conventional family structures were frequently destroyed and when survival was the need, there was no more normal, just alive, fed and safe – or not.

For Oscar, his commitment to raise the girl as his own was sacrosanct and Bella felt that she could not tarnish this promise. But as her own children grew older her need to speak to Rosie increased. She wanted to say, "Look what I have achieved, see my shops, my clothes, look at my home, meet my husband, and hug my children." Even more, she still wanted to ask, "Why did you abandon us? Why didn't you tell me you planned to leave me with your baby?"

She was disappointed that the answer was not in the letters. She did occasionally pick them up and look at the envelopes as if her eyes could x-ray through the content but, having read them, she did not open them a second time, just placed them firmly back in the biscuit tin and put them above a kitchen shelf where nobody would look.

She knew it was entirely up to her to resume contact with Rosie. Communication was difficult, especially now Europe was at war but, thanks to the Red Cross, she knew that letters were getting through to Poland and in London the Jewish Agency would always find her. There was a saying in the community in the East End that no Jew could ever get lost.

All she had to do was reply. She ached to do that but knew that the life she had created with such hard work and determination would change and she would risk the destruction of the fine balance between her successful business and marriage. Involving Rosie in her new life would alter everything.

"Put him down, he is asleep now," she said to Oscar, who was still gently rocking Bernard. "We have to go to see the Goldblums. The whole family is working on this wedding wardrobe, you know for Mrs rich Amelia Bryant. Who would have thought a bride would want a golfing outfit, a tennis outfit, a cycling costume as well as day and evening wear? I was lucky to get a new apron when we married. The next thing she'll want is a fashionable swimming costume."

Oscar's laugh started a new wave of coughing. When he stopped he chuckled, "Don't forget the bridal dress amongst that huge order."

"Don't worry. The bridal dress is cream silk covered with Chantilly lace, with a high neckline, a detachable train and it is calf length – so think of the shoes. I know it is one of my best creations. Maybe we can copy it for Lilly when she and Saul marry."

"Keep the skirt long. I can't do frivolous shoes any more, they'll have to be simple. There are no buckles or buttons about and very little spare ribbon but I could put some laces in. There are some left over from the military footwear I am making. That's how women's fashions are decided these days: no buttons because there is no metal, and laces because I have some left over from soldiers' shoes."

"And flat, Oscar. Women want flat now, they don't want to struggle to walk."

"Saul's gone," Lilly announced to Bella while emptying a package of fatty meat onto the kitchen table. "I queued for two hours for this. I don't know if it is kosher."

"Does it matter?" asked Bella. "Does God want us to starve trying to find kosher meat?"

Bella and Lilly were alone in the kitchen. "Oscar! Sara!" Bella shouted at the closed door. "Someone please chop the onions. Whenever I do onions my dresses smell of them for days."

"So you don't mind if my shoes smell of onions?" Oscar had come in response to her shouts. "What's happened?" he asked, kissing his sister as she held her hands, which were covered with blood, up and away from his clothes.

"Lilly, can you?" Bella handed a sharp knife and three small onions to Lilly, who washed her hands underneath the ice-cold tap before taking them. "What do you mean, Saul's gone?"

"He has joined the army." Lilly pulled the knife through a steel sharpener twice.

"Fighting for England now? I suppose that means we belong," said Bella as she placed the pieces of meat into a large enamel saucepan. "Did you find any carrots in the market, Oscar? Does that mean you don't know where he is?"

"In Reading, it is a place outside London. It's in the country, I think. They had to walk all the way there carrying huge bags. He won't be there for long, he is fully trained now and going to France," Lilly said with pride. Her eyes started to run as she sliced at the onions fiercely.

Bella looked at Oscar watching her and was glad that he would not volunteer, as both the family and the business depended on him. Even if there was conscription, he would not be accepted because of his frail health.

"Carrots?" she repeated.

"No, hardly any vegetables, just those onions and I was lucky to find those. It's not just businesses like ours that are affected by war, there just isn't much food."

"Oh well, it'll be over soon," said Bella philosophically, as she put her arms around Lilly's shoulders.

Shaking with deep, deep sobs, her eyes streaming with tears, Lilly gasped. "It's just the onions making me cry but he looked so handsome in his uniform."

# 1915 Rosie

Bella received the following letter in 1915, dated September 1914 and postmarked Lodz.

*Dearest, dearest Bella,*

*Maybe you have chosen not to write to me but now with this terrible war on, I allow myself to pretend that you have but the letters just can't get through. A few years ago, I sent a letter by hand for you with Mrs Mendle's son. I waited and waited after he left. I was sure he would find you but we didn't hear anything from him. His mother just told me that he went to London and is now in America.*

*My darling child is nearly thirteen now, almost grown up. How does she look? I still imagine her as a baby. My mind has frozen you both in my memory.*

*I am sure you didn't find the pavements paved with gold but I hope your life is easier than it would be here. Here Sara would be working. Maybe in England she is going to school. I hear in England that girls are sometimes at school alongside boys. I would so love that for my Sara but I know you will have given her the best that you can. Maybe you are no longer alone. I hope you have found a husband. Maybe you have a child or even children. I can't bear not knowing. I think of you always at the end of the journey I left you to do on your own. But maybe you are no longer there. Maybe you did get to America and are in that place called Ellis Island where I hear that Jews go.*

*Jacob spent four years in prison. Now he is home at last but he is a changed man, angry deep down. He doesn't talk about it much but I know they kept him with criminals although they said they wouldn't. I supported us, me and Regina, doing cleaning jobs but Regina helped by taking in sewing. I wonder if you do any sewing, you used to be so good at it. I do not hear from you and the silence is unbearable. It is an ache that doesn't get better, not knowing what happened to you.*

*Your loving sister,*
*Rosie (and Regina and Jacob)*

# 1916 Bella

Bella had been trying to persuade Lilly to become a milliner so that together they could provide the 'total look' once the war was over.

"From top to bottom, Lilly's hats, Bella's dresses, Oscar's shoes, when this war is finished," Bella repeated frequently.

"I can't make hats, but I can cut hair," Lilly always protested.

"A head is a head, a hat or hair, does it matter?" was Bella's consistent reply.

A year after Saul had volunteered and left for France, Lilly was working as a domestic servant as well as cutting hair privately in people's homes. She wanted to save money for when he came home. Then she planned to open her own hairdressing salon. She hoped eventually to rent the ground floor of the house next door to Bella and Oscar's new home in Dalston. They had managed to maintain the shop in Petticoat Lane but had also opened a small boutique below their flat in the leafy residential street.

Bella's vision for the future of the shop next door, selling Lilly's hats and Oscar's shoes, either matching or enhancing her designs, was different from his. His was of clients leaving Bella's boutique after a fitting and popping next door to have their hair cut and styled. He also hoped that if Lilly established a hairdressing business in the neighbouring premises, Bella might give up her plans to expand further and not work so hard. Then, after the war, Lilly and Saul would have their own family and it would be cosy with them all living so close to each other.

But Bella was adamant. "I don't want bits of hair all over my clothes and the place smelling like shampoo," she said. "Hats and shoes, that's what we should sell next door."

However, that plan was delayed anyway as the war had created such a shortage of labour. When Bella and Oscar visited their most reliable home workers, the Goldblums, a family of thirteen, all of whom except the three very young children normally sewed for her, they were dismayed to find that it had become a small workforce of four.

There was grandmother Goldblum; nearly blind grandfather Goldblum; able but lazy fifteen-year-old Eli and the youngest girl, Eloise. The father and two older sons had joined the army. One sister had become a 'clippie' on the buses, filling in for the men who had gone to fight. There was an older sister who would not help as all her time was devoted to an organisation that was committed to gaining votes for women as soon as the war ended. Their mother, Lillian, Bella's best seamstress, was now delivering post.

"But why, when I pay her better?" asked Bella, sitting on the edge of a high backed chair in the large room that was a living room, bedroom, children's nursery and workshop for the whole family. "Why would she do that? She has a proper skill, I taught her. She has a future as a dressmaker."

Eloise, the thirteen-year-old, was Bella's personal protégé as she considered her to be naturally gifted. But she was constantly ill and was now suffering from weeping boils on the back of her legs, from thigh to ankle. They were so painful that she could barely stand. Sitting was even more uncomfortable so she spent her time lying down. Now she was lying on her stomach, holding tightly onto the metal railings at the top of the bed, while Bella placed strips of bread soaked in boiling water directly onto them. As each strip touched her skin, Eloise screamed out. Oscar watched Bella give Eloise the attention and nurture she would have begrudged Sara; but then she needed Eloise to get back to sewing as soon as possible.

As Eloise cried, grandma Goldblum stroked her tangled, wet hair with one hand and with the other pointed to a poster stuck crookedly on the wall.

"Look," she said and then read out in her crackly voice, "'Women of the country say GO!'"

"What does that mean?" asked Bella, preparing another boiling strip to lower onto the back of Eloise's knees.

"It means we have to do the men's jobs while they go off to defend the country," said grandma Goldblum with delight, "it's our duty."

"While they go off and get killed, you mean." Then Bella muttered under her breath to Oscar, "How can Lillian really like delivering post? Look at this weather, it's wet and it's cold."

Nothing got by grandma Goldblum and she replied, "She hates it, especially when she knows they are letters of dread."

"Letters of dread?" Oscar questioned, expertly folding finished garments on the kitchen table, which doubled as a work bench.

"The letters telling you someone has been killed. She says she knows which ones they are by instinct, but that's nonsense."

"I thought they were telegrams. Finished, child, all done, your boils will heal now, you'll see," said Bella, pulling a sobbing Eloise stiffly to her feet.

"No," said grandma Goldblum triumphantly, as if she were unveiling a great national secret, "the telegrams are only for officers."

Oscar was now filling a large box on the floor with the folded garments. Bella always admired his ability to pack clothes with hardly any creases noticeable when they were unpacked again. From his position on the floor, he talked up to the women. "Then if it's nonsense, how does she know which ones they are?"

"Because," cackled grandma Goldblum with delight, "they are in a funny brown envelope and have OHM on the front. She says it is good she knows because it gives her a chance to put an expression of sympathy on her face. She had two to deliver in one day to Mrs Geese. It was her husband and her son, the same day, the same day," she repeated, mesmerised by this information.

Bella and Oscar weren't too surprised, although they only read the fashion pages in English newspapers. Sara had told them that at school there were prayers nearly every day for someone's father or older brother who been killed. One day she reported passing a large funeral procession with lots of people in black, a coach holding a coffin pulled by horses with plumes. The leading horse had boots stuck in the stirrups the wrong way round.

"Toes facing backwards," she explained.

"Must be someone important," Oscar had commented.

If Bella was alarmed at the loss of her workers, she didn't show it. She only indicated her concern that they might not return at all. She had intended the Goldblum family to be the basis of her first factory, particularly as Oscar described their home working conditions as a sweatshop.

"It is certainly not a sweatshop. I know that, having worked in one. They are properly paid, the whole family is eating and I teach them skills. Young Eloise is so good at sewing that I have taught her to cut. She wouldn't get that opportunity in a sweatshop."

Nevertheless, Bella recognised hard work and expertise and wanted to reward them with more comfortable conditions. Despite her optimism, however, the war's impact meant that with a reduced order book, she was forced to return to doing nearly everything herself to uphold her immaculate standards of workmanship.

# 1916 Rosie

*Dearest Bella,*

*Here Jacob is so busy we hardly speak. The Bund takes so much of his time. I wish he wouldn't do political things because that is why he went to prison. If I say anything, he says I don't understand and it is not political anyway, just about getting treated properly and paid fairly for work done. He also says that it is not just for Jews and it is not just in Poland. Well, it's not Poland anymore, by the way, we are now part of Germany. I can't really tell the difference. We don't speak German, as always Polish, Yiddish and sometimes Hebrew. It certainly doesn't make any difference to Jacob. I worry because between his business and the time taken up with the Bund, which is meetings, many meetings, he has no time to relax. He tells me we will relax later, as if later is a special time with a date on it.*

*What he does is not popular. Many Jews now are Zionists and want a Jewish state in Palestine. They don't seem to care much what is happening here. I know they try to persuade him that we should be planning to go to Palestine and to make that our home. God gave it to us, but it was taken away so we must take it back. Sometimes I am tempted. I think the climate must be better there. It's so damp and cold here, especially in winter but what is the point of swapping one struggle for another? Anyway, Jacob says we must stay here because this is our home and our job is to make it better here. That's what the Bund is all about.*

*We have the printing press in the bedroom. Jacob says that although if people were seriously searching they would look in the bedroom, casual visitors and customers who come by for fittings shouldn't see it in the living room. He is right of course but the ink smells and I wake up* coughing. When he works at night, which is more and more often, I hear it churning away when I want to sleep. We share a kitchen and bathroom of course but there aren't too many families in the house so you don't have to wait too long. Anyway I like bumping into the children even if it is on the way to the toilets.

Don't misunderstand me. His business goes well. People come to him for suits from all over Poland, well I suppose I have to say Germany now, although it doesn't feel right just to change the name of the country your family have lived in all their lives.

Did I tell you that I left the factory? I was offered the job of cleaning for the owner and his wife. I go every day and look after his house and children. I keep it very clean. Jacob wasn't happy. He didn't like the idea of me doing domestic work for someone else, particularly Jews, and thinks that factory work is more honourable. But he soon changed his mind when he realised that I would be home earlier and his dinner would be ready that much quicker. I have to be careful what I cook though, between the shortages and not doing anything that would create a smell that could cling to the clothes he is making. That's the only good thing about bread and potatoes, they don't smell.

Oh, I so long to hear from you. It is so hard not knowing where you are or how my child is.

Your loving sister

Rosie (and Jacob and Regina)

# 1917 Bella

"I should be making her wedding dress," said Bella, furiously running black material beneath the needle of the sewing machine. "I am making it the same shape as one. Why shouldn't widows be elegant?"

As she was making the mourning dress for Lilly, she was working out how many more widows would need a black dress. She had the idea while cutting out the list of Jewish soldiers killed at the Somme from the Jewish Chronicle. The list covered many pages and included Lilly's fiancé, Saul Adler. Lilly was not exactly a widow as she and Saul had not married but that was just because they had not wanted a wartime wedding. They had planned to have a big, traditional wedding when the war was over. That was Lilly's dream. So they waited, but it was a decision she regretted for the rest of her life.

"Poor Lilly, I don't know how she'll manage now. I can't think of anything worse than losing a fiancée or husband at the Front. Look at these numbers. Thousands and thousands of men killed, that is thousands and thousands of women who will want to wear black dresses, and their children too."

"You shouldn't exploit my sister's tragedy." Oscar had protested vehemently enough to bring on a new attack of coughing.

"I am not exploiting anything." Bella was exasperated with Oscar. She thought he was too decent, caring for the world's woes over the family's needs. "We will be helping, Oscar." Then she added, "What about armbands? Maybe not, best stick to what I know." Although privately she thought black armbands would be simple and perhaps profitable because of that. "Anyway we need to do something, we have no other orders. Women aren't buying clothes, even the very rich from the country don't want to come into London for fittings now."

"It doesn't feel right to turn such a catastrophe into good business."

Bella wasn't listening but as always, when an idea took hold of her, she was sketching eagerly.

"Oscar, you must make many more black shoes, in fact only black shoes. We'll advertise, look," she pointed to a page of advertisements in the newspaper, which promoted everything from corsets to drinking chocolate to a day's outing at Selfridges.

"You can't advertise, you couldn't make them fast enough, we haven't enough help." Oscar was being calm and reasonable, his usual approach when Bella became excited about a fantastic idea that he was sure was not practical.

"Why, why can't I? I can do it all…"

"Myself," he finished for her. "Think about it, Bella. Someone is bereaved. They receive the news, come to you and ask for a dress. You discuss styles, choose a fabric, take measurements and then start making the dress. You can't do it quickly enough by yourself. Anyway, there is no fabric to be had."

"Yes, yes there is!" Bella shouted in her enthusiasm, "We can start tomorrow, look."

She opened a large trunk and showed Oscar rolls of blackout material.

"Blackout material, everyone has some spare. We go and collect all that extra blackout material. People don't need it anymore and they'll be glad to get a few pennies back for it. Then we soak it in the bathtub to get rid of the starchiness and we will have enough black fabric to make a shop full of mourning dresses. Women only have to choose what is already here. They won't have to make decisions at such a difficult time. There will be something for everyone, they will be made ready. Come on, Oscar. Can't you see it? They will be made already for widows to buy, children too. Maybe for children we'll do black and white checks, small checks for the little ones and larger checks for older children, Sara's age."

Oscar watched Bella as she hauled out rolls of the material and started measuring.

"Do you really think that children who have lost their fathers and brothers in this great conflict will care about the size of their checks?" he asked.

"Yes, I do," said Bella conclusively, "and their mothers will want them to as well. It will take their minds off their loss. See how much good we'll be doing at this terrible time. If you are worried about exploitation, just think of that. We will be contributing to the war effort with what we do best. It's brilliant."

"What will the advertisement say?"

"'Let us help you at this sad time.' I don't know – something like that."

Bella picked up her sketch-pad again and outlined a square. She placed the words within in it and quickly drew several dresses around the words. She then filled in the dress shapes with lines of black.

By the end of 1917 there were still queues for meat, bread and butter and a very long one for black dresses outside Bella's now famous shop in Dalston. Later, when the pain had lessened, those wives, mothers and sisters returned for more colourful outfits. These she had also made already or, as the fashion press called it by then, 'ready made'. It was an idea that accounted for Bella's first factory and financed the foundation of a separate couture house called BELLA UNIQUE.

# 1918 Rosie

*Dearest Sister,*

*Writing these letters is like talking to myself although I imagine I am talking to you. I have no one else to talk to. I hope for an answer but don't expect it anymore.*

*Jacob says the big war is nearly over but I am still confused about who is fighting who – or was. He tries to explain it to me but it doesn't make any sense. Now he says that the Poles and the Russians are going to fight each other but I am not sure why. He said we have to support the Russians but that doesn't make any sense to me because they blamed the Jews for their revolution last year, or so people were saying in the fish market yesterday. Anyway if the Cossacks hate us so, why should we support them? I don't understand and he just gets irritable if I ask.*

*Yesterday he delivered a suit to a gentleman in town and it had ink on it because of the printing press we have in our home. The man got very cross and refused to pay. Eventually things like that get around and people stop coming. He has fewer customers now than he used to anyway. I think non-Jews are not so comfortable about coming into the Jewish quarter now, even for a good tailor. It's more dangerous than it used to be.*

*This is such bad news because it means the Bund is more important to Jacob than his proper work, his tailoring, and that is what feeds us. Goodness knows politics won't.*

*But there seem to be as many arguments between Jews as between Jews and goyim. Jacob doesn't like me to use that word anymore. I can't remember why but his mother and I just use it when he is not around, which is a lot of the time. The arguments are because the Zionists believe* we have to support the Jewish state, as that is the only way we will be free of those who hate us. Then there are the Hassids who, Jacob says, don't care for anyone but themselves. He has started to hate them with their long hair, fur hats and unkempt beards. He says they smell. I am sure he is right. I can't remember anything in the Talmud that says don't wash. I can't understand why the women wear wigs. I know they have reasons but it seems so old-fashioned. Do you know they have eight synagogues, well not really synagogues but places to pray.

It is difficult here and it's very cold. Regina is feeling it more than usual. I suppose she is just getting older. I do wish Jacob would spend more time with her, but as always he is so busy. He goes into the centre of town every day and sometimes I go to meet him. Not as often as I would like because it is not fair to leave Regina alone for too long, so I don't stay long.

Dear sister, I so wish we were all still together. Sometimes I just pretend that we are young girls together and playing and laughing as we used to. Then I remember my wedding and how happy we were and so full of hope. Then the baby and being so sick and then all the old horrible memories come back. It is fifteen years now and I wonder if you think of me as often as I think of you and Sara. Of course I imagine you as you were.

Lately, I have started wondering if we will ever meet again. Up to now I have always believed we will. God knows. Jacob says there is no God. I don't know whether to hope he is right, so he doesn't get punished, or wrong because what would this life be without a God?

Your loving sister, Rosie (and Regina and Jacob)

# 1918 Bella

Bella and Oscar were sitting arm in arm on the top floor of an omnibus travelling along the road that ringed the outer edges of Hyde Park. Oscar had suffered a fit of coughing on the way up the stairs, which had left him breathless and perspiring.

"I hear it's like a palace on every floor. Look at the advertisement," said Bella, ignoring her husband's obvious distress and pulling a newspaper cutting out of her pocket. "It says 'Spend the day at Selfridges'."

"Why spend the day at Selfridges?" panted Oscar.

"I want to see what women are buying in these big department stores and I think you ought to see what is happening in shoes. Maybe that's where my clothes should go now, maybe your shoes as well. We can't open another shop until we have recovered from this dreadful war so we need to sell the clothes another way."

"We should cut back," advised Oscar, repeating again what Bella refused to hear.

"That's what everyone is thinking. I won't. I might tread water but I won't cut back. Any time now women are going to want to celebrate peace with new clothes and they will want different types of clothes. Work dresses, sports clothes, outfits for a more active life."

"You mean like Amelia Bryant? Nobody will have any money for such pursuits after the war."

"It won't take long, you'll see. Fashion will change and our business must change with it." Bella spoke with confidence. "Anyway the flat is getting too small for all of us and we have to think of moving somewhere bigger."

"We've only been in the flat for two years," exclaimed Oscar.

"And it's already too crowded. The boys are not going to get any smaller. When they grow more, I want a garden for them to run in and separate rooms for work, the girls, you and me."

"That's four bedrooms."

"Why not? I don't like Dalston anyway."

"What's wrong with Dalston? It's green, with lovely streets, and it's what you wanted. We can still spread to the shop next door when the time is right. We have good neighbours. What's wrong with it?"

"We moved to Dalston, found people who had moved here before us and then other people from the community started to follow us. It's as if the whole of Petticoat Lane is now living in Dalston."

"What's wrong with that, Bella? The whole community is moving to better parts of London."

"I want to move to West, or maybe to North London. I don't want my children to only know a Jewish world."

"What's wrong with a Jewish world?"

"It will never be safe. You'll see. The English will turn on us just as the Cossacks did."

"Of course they won't," replied Oscar, dabbing at his wet brow with a clean white handkerchief.

"I want my boys to be English, to be a lawyer and a doctor. That's what we need, a lawyer and a doctor. I don't want them to be tailors or traders. I want them to have responsible positions in society."

"Isn't that up to them?"

"No, it's up to us. We have to leave Dalston and work, work, work, work. We need money to educate our boys."

"And the girls?"

Bella hesitated. "Good marriages," she said thoughtfully.

"We were so lucky not to have opened that factory before the war," said Oscar. "Without the factory, we can still depend on our dressmakers, however few of them, to continue working for you loyally, without the interference of these new fangled Trade Unions."

"Oh, sometimes when my fingers are raw and my eyes tired, I wish I could just throw it all at a factory and say 'here, make ten of these.'"

"But, if we had gone ahead with the factory, we would probably have had to make ammunition, not frocks. And we would be battling with new labour laws about hours and pay. At least this way we haven't had to close or make uniforms and we can pick up where we left off."

"Maybe, Oscar, maybe, but think of Harry Myers. His whole factory just made uniforms. Those dreary khaki uniforms, but he made a fortune. He can do anything he wants now."

"Would you have wanted to just make uniforms – even for a fortune?" Oscar watched the traffic from the bus window. It was a crowded mix of horse-drawn carriages and motorised vehicles. "The worst of both worlds," he commented, "the smell of engines and the smell of horses and all of them in each other's way."

Bella shrugged and looked out of the window as the bus rounded the corner into Oxford Street.

"Look," she said, pointing out the sheep grazing in Hyde Park, "wouldn't you like to wake up to that every morning?"

"Sheep?" Oscar spluttered the word in astonishment.

"Not the sheep, the park. We could live near Hyde Park and we would be around the corner from Selfridges and near the West End but it would be like being in the country. It would be better for your chest."

The bus clanged to a halt at the top of Oxford Street and Bella lifted her long skirt to descend the stairs and avoid the muddy puddles between the road and the pavement.

Oscar helped her carefully off the bus. The stop was a short walk away from Selfridges' front door.

# 1919 Rosie

*Dearest sister,*

*It helps me to imagine I am talking to you. I know these letters probably go nowhere, but it helps. I wonder sometimes if someone else does receive them and read them. What on earth must they think of me?*

*There was an election here but I didn't vote. Jacob is really cross with me. There were gangs harassing Jews, and especially Jewish women, at the polling stations. I couldn't face it. I couldn't understand what to vote anyway and Jacob didn't tell me anything, just where to put my mark. I think that is not right because now women are allowed to vote, I think I should make up my own mind and make my own decisions. What is the point of women voting but just doing what their husbands tell them to do? They might as well give men two votes, married ones anyway.*

*Everything else is the same. Jacob has been more careful since ruining Mr Roysten's suit with the printing ink, so more customers are coming in. It is another cold winter and again more people are leaving for England, America and Palestine – the usual places. We haven't heard from Nathan in America for a while now. I think he got fed up with asking us to come and got bored with Jacob's reasons, excuses actually. Jacob didn't write very often and maybe Nathan just gave up. I am feeling a bit depressed, just tired I suppose, but wanted to say hello. I am sorry this is so short. I wonder where you are. Oh, I do long to hear from you.*

*Your always loving sister, Rosie (and Regina and Jacob)*

# 1920s

# 1920 Bella

The twins were in their favourite place beneath their mother's large drawing board. Simon was creating patterns out of shreds of fabric, which he stuck to the floor with fallen pins. Bernard had one finger up his nose and the other was stroking the strap across Bella's cream linen shoe. He stuck his finger into the buckle.

"Mama, my finger is stuck."

"Sara, take these boys to play somewhere else," Bella's voice was sharp. She spoke through a long cigarette holder, which was balanced expertly between her teeth. One hand was pressed down on large-scale graph paper, the other busy drawing. She sketched quickly with long flowing movements punctuated with brisk, feathery sharp flicks. She occasionally reached up to reposition a fragment of textile that hung loosely around the shoulders of a mannequin standing close to her drawing table, trying out different contours. She lifted the fragile material, placing it gently up and around, then down again. She let it go, drew some more then held it up again, finally pinning the shape to the mannequin's frame, satisfied with the silhouette.

"Sara, come and take these babies. And where is Oscar?"

"He went to pick up Etta from school." Sara spoke quietly, her eyes lowered. She was tall and thin with round shoulders. Her blue eyes, Rosie's eyes, were faded like those of an old woman and avoided direct contact with Bella's. They were set in a pallid face. Her translucent skin looked as if she had never seen sunlight. She was wearing a worn apron covered with flowers, which might once have been brightly coloured.

Where is Rosie in you? thought Bella, as she so often did.

Oscar was still convalescing from the influenza that had killed so many millions across Europe in 1918, but miraculously no-one else in the family had caught it. His dose was mild and the doctor said it was not the fatal strain of the virus, but he hadn't fully recovered. His breathing continued to be laboured and he reacted so violently to the dust that floated up from the tailor's chalk that he had to stay clear if Bella was marking material. Tiny fragments of fabric, which clung to the air when Bella was cutting anything, caused violent coughing fits that weakened him terribly. He helped wherever he could in the home. He loved reading to the children and was still a valuable advisor to Bella but he no longer made shoes.

"He shouldn't have gone out in this cold. Why didn't you go?"

"I was cooking supper." Sara's voice was flat.

"Mama, my finger," wailed Bernard.

Bella shook her foot, releasing Bernard's finger from the buckle and causing him to yelp.

"I have a collection to finish, I have a baby kicking my stomach as if it's a football, twins who are driving me crazy and I'd like you all to let me get on with my work. Oh dear, listen to that, he has got worse."

Oscar's cough was dry and breathless as he entered the room and nearly drowned out the happy squeals of Etta.

"Mama, look what we did today," she shouted in Yiddish, bursting into the room holding a paper model of a Crusader on horseback.

"No Yiddish! We do not speak Yiddish in this house."

Etta looked chastened. "But Sara does in the market."

"That's right," said Bella, "in the market, that's where it belongs. We are English, we speak English. Oscar, I need your help. Are you sick or just coughing again?"

"Daddy is always sick because he won't wear his hat," said Etta brightly. "I kept telling him to put it on, just as you do."

Oscar playfully cuffed her on the head and that triggered another coughing fit. Bella sprang up, her petite frame rigid with frustration.

"Out," she shouted, "everyone out. I have to work, NOW! Do you want to spend the rest of your lives in these squashed rooms? Tell me, do you? Let me work. Oscar, go and get some soup or something to calm your chest. Etta, go, just go and… I don't know, help or do your school work. Oh why did Lilly have to leave?"

They had both tried to persuade Lilly not to go to America but as soon as the war was over and she was free to travel, she had torn up her only picture of Saul, spread henna over her hair (a procedure which was distinctly unsuccessful and left her head an assortment of stripes ranging from yellow to orange to bright red), and set off by boat to New York.

"I have no reason to stay," she had said.

"Us, your brother and your best friend, we need you. Doesn't that mean anything?" Bella had argued hopelessly, but in the end she had provided a new wardrobe for Lilly to take with her, partly out of generosity and partly with some vague idea that it might be good to have her clothes seen by New York society, a world she imagined Lilly would inhabit.

"If Lilly were here, she would have got these boys out of here and let me work in peace." She kicked at the boys who were now cowering together.

"Dearest, calm down," Oscar begged Bella, who was working herself into a familiar rage. Gently he reached beneath the table and hauled the twins out and away from Bella's feet.

"I will not calm down!" Bella's face was red with irritation. "This is it, Oscar. This is the opportunity you and I have been working for. But I have to be able to work. What's the matter with Sara, why isn't she helping with the children?"

"She does, you know she does." Oscar's voice was placating. "But she is still young herself."

"Eighteen?" Bella was shouting again "By the time…"

"I know, I know, by the time you were eighteen you had... I know, darling, I know what you had done. But times are different now."

"Times aren't different, *she* is different. Sara has no energy, no fight and no ambition."

"Maybe that's so and it's just as well because you have enough for all of us." Oscar coughed again and, pulling a boy with each hand, left the room. Bella stared indignantly at the door closing behind them, then she picked up her pencil and turned her attention back to the gown she was creating.

# 1922 Rosie

*Dearest Sister,*

*I always seem to write to you when things are bad, but I suppose that is why I do. Things are very difficult again and Jacob is agitated all the time. He says things are about to change because the new Jewish state in Palestine is going to happen very soon. I don't understand why that means things will change here and I don't understand why he is so cross.*

*Sometimes I feel that I would like to go there, because if we live in our own state, no-one will be able to harm us ever again or chuck us out. Then I think of you and Sara and know that I want to find you more than anything. But he still believes our lives are here and our job is to make Poland safe and secure for Jews and all the other people who have been treated badly.*

*I wish he would meet with the government instead of fighting them. They certainly know of him as he is important now and apparently in charge of things at the Bund. But he is so hot-headed and when I suggested this, he said that I just don't understand what is at stake. I think he is feeling deserted and that is why he is so cross, not that he would explain it to me anyway.*

*David, do you remember little David the grocer's son? He is thirty now and has two sons of his own, so not little any more but grown up and going to Palestine. He says it's pointless to stay, as it is over in Poland for Jews. He believes he might as well fight where there is a future for his boys. Myra, his wife, is sorry to leave her friends but ready to go now both her parents are dead.*

*I think that is something to do with Jacob being so sad. David was always around from when he was a little boy. Then later he helped in the tailoring and then they were practically partners in the Bund. Also Isaac, who is a neighbour and we thought a friend, has let Jacob down really badly by joining the Communists, the bit called KPP. I don't know what it means and I don't dare ask but Jacob says twenty per cent of the KPP are Jews and many of them are leaders. I don't know if he means Jewish leaders or Communist leaders, anyway he is livid. He says they think joining will protect them from anti-Semitism and it won't. It seems so unfair. We've survived the pogroms and his prison sentence, why should we still have to survive anti-Semitism?*

*It's funny really. He talks to me the way I talk, or write anyway, to you. Except he knows I hear but assumes I don't understand and I just write, assuming you don't hear.*

*Dear Bella, I hope you can hear me.*

*Your loving sister, Rosie*

# 1925 Bella

Etta, sitting awkwardly on a pouf opposite, watched Auntie Lilly sip tea through a cube of white sugar, which she clenched between her front teeth. It was exactly in the centre of her mouth and framed by her bright red lips. Lilly sat deep within a large winged armchair, her arms resting lightly on lace antimacassars. Her long swept-up hair, now an elegant deep auburn, was still neat despite the removal of her hat, which was now positioned carefully on her knees beside her gloves. Both were balanced on her decoratively arranged skirt.

"Where are the twins anyway?" Lilly sounded peeved.

Etta placed her hands behind her back and crossed her fingers on both hands.

"They are at Hebrew school. Only six months to their barmitzvahs."

"Don't you want to come to America, Etta? Can't you persuade your mother? Why is she looking for another house here? You have two flats side by side and she has a big workroom. Dalston is lovely, why move again, unless to America? I do wish you would all come."

"I can't persuade my mother to do anything, you know that, particularly now. She is determined to move to Hampstead Garden Suburb when Daddy is better and the boys have had their barmitzvahs."

"Are all your plans arranged around the barmitzvahs?"

"No, usually the fashion seasons and her order book."

"I hope she likes what I am wearing. I bought it in New York just for this visit."

The door crashed open and the twins rushed in. Without noticing Lilly, they hurtled across the lounge towards the piano, plonked themselves on the stool and started to bash chopsticks onto the keys.

"Sshhhh! What about Daddy?" admonished Etta.

"It was amazing, there was a chariot race." Simon gave this information in an exaggerated stage whisper.

"It was so fast," Bernard added, emulating his twin brother's stage whisper and bouncing his rear end on the stool.

"You should have seen the organ. It came right up out of the floor! Mighty Wurlitzer, it was called." Simon, suddenly noticing Lilly's presence, stopped his babbling and thumping at the piano.

"Say hello to Auntie Lillie," said Etta with a warning gesture.

"Hello, boys." Lilly stood up, her hat and gloves sliding to the floor. "Did you enjoy your Torah study?"

The door opened and Bella came in, dwarfed by several outfits draped over her arms. She was followed by Sara who, although tall, was even more weighed down by clothes. Three-year-old Sam tailed behind, carrying some hangers almost as long as he was tall and looking important.

"Lilly, I'm sorry I have kept you waiting. Sara, put the clothes in my workroom and make us some tea," she said sharply and handed over her whole load to Sara.

"We've had tea," said Etta.

Bella embraced Lilly and after kisses, there were mutterings and pulling and tweaking, each taking note of changes in the other.

Etta manoeuvred the boys towards the table and indicated that they should bring out their books and study. The boys placed their school books on the table, sat down and brought out pencils and rubbers. Etta sat between them with a wriggling Sam on her knee and watched as the old friends' ritual was played out.

"Sorry, Lilly, they are allowed into the lounge for homework and piano practice. When you have finished your work, go to the kitchen and listen to the radio," Bella addressed the boys, who groaned in unison.

"Why?" asked Lilly.

"So that they speak the King's English and don't sound like market traders," whispered Bella into Lilly's ear, brusquely adding to the twins, "and sit up straight!" The boys groaned again but both pulled themselves upright.

"Have you seen your father today?" Bella asked Etta, then addressing Lilly added, "He was asleep when I left this morning."

"He is the same," said Etta.

"I'll pop in soon," said Bella. "So… tell me all about America, Lilly. I can't believe you are here, how did you get here?"

"By boat, though not that kind of boat." Lilly and Bella exchanged knowing glances. "A large liner and in luxury, everything we dreamt of once. Bella, you really should come over. They love the clothes you send me and always ask where I buy them. You would be very successful in New York and there is a lot of money to be made. Just come for a visit, look at the shops we have."

"We? You really are an American!" laughed Bella.

"I am now and it's good. My husband makes money and we are safe. It's easy. We see a piece of land, buy it and build a house. We live in it for a while, then buy another piece of land and do it all over again." Lilly's eyes were roaming around the crowded living room as she spoke.

Lilly has gained elegance, thought Bella with approval; and an American drawl, she mused, with less approval. "Why do you need so much money? You have no children?" she asked aloud.

Etta noticed Lilly draw in her breath and purse her lips.

"Children aren't the only reason to make money." Lilly glared at Bella.

"I didn't mean…"

"That's alright, it wasn't to be and we have a full life without children but I would love to have yours closer. The opportunities for you in New York would be huge. Businesses are growing. There

85

is a lot of money around and women spend a lot on fashion; New York is getting to be as important as Paris. You would love it, Bella, you really would."

"Maybe someday, but now I have four children, three shops, a business and a sick husband. But more importantly, I am established here in London and I don't want to start again. Bernard, concentrate." Bella had noticed Bernard whispering into Simon's ear and passing a tiny piece of paper to him. She strode towards the boys and grabbed the paper. "What's this? It's a cinema ticket. When did you go to the cinema? Look, today. Today!" Bella screamed. The boys cowered. Lilly covered her mouth with her hands. Etta stood watching apprehensively.

"You were supposed to be at cheder. That's where I sent you. You should have been studying, anyway you are too young to go to the cinema alone. How could they let you in? Did you lie? How could…?" Bella was so angry that she was struggling to finish her sentences.

Etta watched Simon, knowing that he would find a way to negotiate himself out of trouble and curious about what he would invent as an excuse this time. Bernard stood silently behind him, slightly hidden from Bella's onslaught. As always, Bernard would benefit from Simon's ability to reason with his mother. Lilly followed the argument with fascination.

"It was for history." Simon's eyes were narrowed and he looked boldly at Bella as he waited for her next attack.

"What do you mean, history?" she asked surprised.

"Ben Hur. We saw a film called Ben Hur. It was for history."

"It's a film, not a lesson. You were supposed to be at a lesson."

"It's a history lesson. It's about a Jewish slave. He beat the Romans. He led a revolt. It's history. It's Jewish history."

"Did the Rabbi send you?"

"No, but…"

"You won't be able to do this kind of escapade when you go to your new school," Bella addressed Simon, who looked embarrassed.

"Do you know, Lilly, that Simon has won a scholarship to a grammar school? They would have taken Bernard as well if he had bothered to do any work for his exam."

"I didn't want to go anyway." Bernard was petulant.

"Why not?" asked Lilly.

"It's too far, what's the point?"

"You didn't try and now we won't be together," shouted Simon.

Bella, Lilly and Etta silently watched one of the rare angry exchanges between the twins. Despite Bernard's obstinate attitude, the family was wary of his feelings. Their separation was going to be a huge adjustment for them, and the news that Simon had passed and Bernard had failed had been a shock to all, except Simon. He had been helping Bernard with his school work for several years now, but told no one.

"He is asking for you." Sara had entered the room without anybody noticing and interrupted just in time to save the boys from a serious rebuke and maybe even a punishment of some sort. "I told him Lilly had arrived."

"It's time to see your brother, Lilly, but be prepared, he has changed a lot. He has not been out of bed for weeks now. I'll deal with you later," she added, looking ominously towards the twins.

The children watched as the two old, close friends walked towards the sick room.

They found the note from Sara the day after Oscar's funeral, which was the day after his death. This was the day Sara decided to walk out of her home and leave the only family she had ever known.

Sam had been howling for Sara and Etta could not console him. She picked him up and tried to place him on her knee but he made his body rigid. He arched his back and slid onto the kitchen floor like a plank of wood.

"Play with your brothers," said Etta as she heard another knock on the door. She had been opening the door all day long as neighbours, friends and even some of Bella's customers arrived with dishes of cooked food and cakes. Bernard and Simon were hitting each other with prayer books and ignoring the visitors' arrival. They were enjoying a moment when nobody was paying attention to them, telling them off or giving them instructions. Sam loved playing with his older brothers but it usually didn't last long before they bullied him and now they couldn't be bothered with a crying child.

Through the bedlam, Etta tried to listen to the row that was coming from the living room. Sara and Bella were supposedly preparing it for the mourners, who would arrive later for the second day of prayers.

"You are not my mother!" Sara shouted.

"Stop it, stop it," returned Bella.

"You should have told me."

"Everyone will hear." Bella was covering the mirror that hung on a wall in the centre of the living room. "Are you going to help me?"

"No!" screamed Sara. "Why should I help you?"

Etta had never heard Sara raise her voice before and it frightened her. She thought it was unfair that anyone should die, because of the pain and grief it caused. She knew that Sam could sense her anxiety and that is why he would not quieten. He scrambled across the carpet and flung open the door of the living room, rushing to Sara, who ignored him. He screamed again.

"Well at least look after your brother" Bella shouted.

"He is not my brother."

"Shhh, your father has just died and you are upset." Bella tried to touch Sara but she pulled away. "Don't you think I might be upset too? Or have you forgotten that I have lost my husband?"

"He's not my father," sobbed Sara, "and you are not my mother. He told me, he told me. You should have told me."

"What should I have told you? That I am not your natural mother? What would that have done? I have been a mother to you, always." Etta could tell that Bella was angry but trying to control herself and she could hear Sam crying.

"He said there were letters. He said my mother had written you letters. That means she is alive. Is that true?"

"Be quiet. Look at Sam. See how you have upset him." Sam let out a howl at the mention of his name.

"I want to see the letters. I want to know who she is." Sara was shouting.

"Your father was delirious," said Bella as she left the room. She brushed past Etta, who was standing so close to the door she was almost touching it, and Etta saw that her face was distraught, her shoulders uncharacteristically bent and her eyes moist. "See to Sam," Bella ordered, her voice tight. Ignoring the visitors who were waiting in the lounge for the Rabbi's arrival, she charged upstairs and the bedroom door was heard slamming. Those who saw put it down to distress at the loss of her husband and muttered sympathetically.

When Etta went into the living room to comfort Sara, she saw her pulling plates and cups out of a cupboard and viciously crashing them onto the table. Etta stayed in the corner, hoping that she would not be noticed. Sam was still crawling around the floor trying to get Sara's attention. Sara stopped her hysterics, looked at him and started gulping hopeless, loud sobs. She rushed across the room towards the door, ignoring Sam. He put his hand out to grab her as she passed and bashed it on the leg of a chair.

In her effort to comfort a howling Sam, Etta did not notice that Sara had run to the front door and was only vaguely aware of the front door slamming. This was followed by the familiar rattle as it juddered on the shaky frame that Oscar had always meant to repair. The vibration was felt throughout the house.

Although there was a house full of people all day long for most of the following five days, not one of the neighbours or friends asked where she was. Because Sara had always adopted – or been given – the role of servant, everyone just assumed she was in the kitchen.

Only Bella, Lilly and Etta knew that Sara had walked out, but they all thought she would just walk back in when she had calmed down and resigned herself to whatever information Oscar had given her on his deathbed. Bella dealt with her distress and her grief by keeping busy, busy, busy. In that sense, Sara's absence contributed to her ability to cope with her loss. With the help of Lilly and Etta, she now had to do all the jobs that Sara would normally have done.

"Brave," the mourners muttered as she sat stony-faced on her low seat and received their traditional condolences, shedding no tears.

"I wish you long life," they repeated, bending low to kiss her dry face.

"Brave," they whispered as they watched her stay emotionless while prayers were being recited.

Etta, unsettled by the episode but nervous of Bella's state of mind, wanted to confront Lilly and ask about Sara's claims. If there was a story going back to their past, Lilly would surely know. But Lilly was devastated by Oscar's death and was simply going through the mourning rituals automatically weeping constantly. It would have been cruel and pointless to upset her even more.

Etta knew she had to challenge her mother but realised that with another five days of prayers to get through and visitors to cater for without Sara's help, this was not the time. But still she hoped for an opportunity and it happened when they passed on their way to the newly installed flushing toilet.

"What was she talking about, Mama? What letters?" Etta asked urgently.

"Your father was delirious," whispered Bella, repeating the phrase that would become her mantra for dealing with this question in the future.

"We must find her," Etta insisted.

90

"And how would you do that?" hissed Bella.

"She can't just disappear. She must have gone to someone. Someone will know where she is."

"What a time to pick to just leave her family, just when her father dies and we need her most. Why should we look for her?"

"She's all alone out there in this beastly fog. She doesn't go out alone much."

"She'll come back," pronounced Bella, "she was just upset. She wouldn't leave us like that."

But Sara didn't ever come back. Etta remembered some things about the second day of prayers for Oscar, Bella shouting at Sara and Sara, surprisingly, shouting back. She remembered a flurry of searching and dramatic tears from Lilly and cold detachment from Bella. She remembered rushing into the street to look for Sara, walking up and down, unable to see clearly through the smog that enveloped the town. She shivered in the grey, damp air and placed a hand over her mouth to protect herself from the fine particles that restricted her breathing. She tried to call out but, gasping, returned to the warm house and the mourners who were ignorant of the drama.

She remembered finding the note Sara had left on her bed. *I hate you*, was all it said. It was there for all to see as she had scribbled it on a piece of paper and not put it inside an envelope. She remembered Bella's hands, normally so steady, shaking as she read it. Then she tore it into tiny pieces and Lilly tried to stick it together again. Etta remembered Bella and Lilly arguing but Bella was cross with everyone that day. In time the memories became blurred but what she was sure of was that she never again saw Bella look close to tears as she had been after the row with Sara over the letters.

Etta was the only one who continued to look for Sara and she didn't tell her mother. She went on asking neighbours, friends, local shop-keepers, convinced that someone knew where Sara had gone, maybe was even hiding her. She thought that Sara, so domestically able, might have found a job in someone's home, perhaps caring for children. She left messages at the synagogue, although the family were not active members and only went at High Holidays and for family rituals.

The twins remembered Sara for a while and occasionally asked for her but they forgot her quickly. In their minds it was all confused with Oscar's death. Sam did not remember her at all. Gradually everyone stopped thinking about her as the twenties gave way to the thirties and other priorities took over. Sara's name was just not mentioned.

Later, years and years later, Bella's granddaughter Sophie found out that Sara had gone to Soho. It just happened. She hailed the first cab she saw in the street and, since she had no address to give him, the driver asked if she wanted to go to Soho. She said that was fine although she had never heard of it; she was just glad to have a destination. Anyway that is where he was going, so he took her.

# 1926 Rosie

*Dear, dear sister,*

*I know my letters may never reach you and I may never have a reply but somehow I think, in your heart of hearts, you know that I am communicating with you. Anyway writing makes me feel better, stronger even. I imagine you sitting beside me and listening and we are talking together just as we used to so, so long ago.*

*It is Sara's 24th birthday. I am so tempted to write to her but I have never done that before and I have no idea what she knows of me, Jacob or her past. I keep thinking that if I keep writing letters, one day she might understand what I did and that I have never forgotten her. I know it is for the best that she has your family, whoever and whatever it is now, as her own. Maybe you have formerly adopted her? I hear sometimes that is allowed, even for Jews.*

*Here Jacob is busy with his meetings. They take so much energy and time but I wonder what is being achieved by all those meetings. Nothing really seems to change and when the present is so difficult here it is hard to remember that what he is working for is the future. I long for the old days when he would read the Talmud and not political literature. He wants me to join a women's political group but I say that I am busy looking after his mother. She is seventy-five now and getting frail but honestly, I could really. She is perfectly safe on her own and has many visitors. For your ears only (and God's) I don't really want to. Strange, isn't it, that I have no one of my own to look after but am attending to Jacob's mother.*

*Money is a bit tight. When we went to the fish market yesterday, Jacob bought cigarettes from a boy in the street. I felt really cross but* didn't dare say anything as he is so sensitive. But I wish he wouldn't. We can hardly afford the fish. It is so silly really. I speak three languages, Polish, Yiddish and Hebrew. Surely I could teach. But Jacob says no and we should always talk Polish because we are Poles and we must save Hebrew for prayers because we are not Zionists, and Yiddish isn't a language anymore. Can you imagine? I have to talk Yiddish to his mother and if I didn't talk Yiddish in the market, we wouldn't get any food. I just wonder what you speak now – and Sara. I suppose she doesn't speak Hebrew or Yiddish and certainly not Polish.

How far away you suddenly seem.

From your loving sister Rosie (and Jacob and Regina)

# 1926 Etta

Bella was kneeling in front of Etta, carefully lifting navy blue material from the floor and pinning a hem precisely six inches below the knee.

"What strike?" Bella's voice was strong and rasping, an effect that Etta believed had been carefully contrived, then nurtured with the intake of much tobacco smoke in order to compensate for her short stature.

Etta had been taller than her mother from the age of twelve and now, at fifteen, was not only taller, but bigger and fuller. As a child she had observed that the clothes Bella wore were the opposite of the flowing feminine garments she made for her clients. They were tailored and sharp and Etta guessed that they were chosen to give her a business-like, slightly masculine image.

Etta peered over Bella's head with its short-cropped black hair, beyond her own reflection in the long mirror and into the living room. Despite the size of their new flat in Crouch End, it resembled all their previous living rooms. Every surface was piled with cut lengths of material and half-finished garments, the dining table held school books, the piano lid was open and sheet music was spread on the stool. There were pins on the floor, as there had always been.

Etta was sure that she admired, but didn't love, her mother. She knew that Bella cherished her boys in a way she could not treasure her daughter. Sara's name was never mentioned but Etta wondered whether she might have left as much to escape Bella's expectation that girls were there for her domestic support, the support she herself had never given anyone, as because of any revelation of Oscar's.

"Slave labour," is the way Etta remembered Sara describing it. She thought about her sister often and when she did, she felt guilty at not having done more to find her and helpless as she didn't know what else to do. She wondered if Bella felt the same. Etta was given the job of clearing out Sara's clothes when preparing for the move from Dalston to Crouch End. She packed them carefully and threw nothing out. Etta noticed Bella didn't comment when she saw a case labelled 'Sara's things' join the family's belongings being transported.

Sara would, Etta knew, have relished the opportunities that she herself was being given. Sara would have welcomed the shorthand and typing course that she so detested, as it would have given her a chance to get a job outside the Bella enclave and away from her control and the kitchen. However, Etta wanted to study 'properly' and resented being forced to do it. Although the boys were two years younger, she borrowed their school books and read late into the night under her blankets in the bedroom she shared with Sam, who never woke.

Bella pushed the twins to study and, as soon as their barmitzvah was over, she had started to talk about matriculation. "The only route to success is education," was a frequent refrain.

"But you didn't go to school," the twins would always answer.

Etta loved her brothers. Simon, with his easy charm and liquid black eyes set in olive skin, was relishing the challenges of his new school with its broad, very English education. Uncomplainingly, he walked the miles every morning from Crouch End to Bethnal Green, his head held high, his back straight, proud in his uniform. In the evening, after a few riotous hours mucking about with his brother, he settled down to twice as much homework as Bernard. He was mixing with people from different backgrounds and Bella was proud that he mingled well. She was less pleased when he announced that he had been cast as one of the three Kings in the school's nativity play. With Etta helping with her written English, which did not match her verbal fluency, she wrote a furious letter to the Headmaster. A rebellious Simon then asked for a Christmas tree, claiming all the other boys had them. It was a request that Bella dismissed without discussion. None of the family realized that Simon never told his new friends that he was Jewish and his family did not have Christmas trees.

Bernard entered his teens suffering from constant sniffles, which had given him a permanent nasal drawl and an itchy skin, which flaked from persistent scratching. He pretended that Simon's success did not bother him but Etta knew that he missed his twin and felt their separation keenly. He enjoyed disrupting Simon's homework.

"It's stupid stuff, who cares?" he once claimed when Simon showed him his Latin text books. Then, when Simon returned home one day wearing a soccer cap, complete with badge, he grabbed it and threw it in the rubbish bin in the street outside. Simon removed it, cleaned it and said nothing. Nor did anyone else.

Sam was the baby, spoilt and adored. He looked different from the other two, with his sandy hair and blue eyes. His temperament was different as well. Simon was competitive and ambitious, Bernard anxious and moody; but Sam was a placid, easy child, who laughed for no reason. He had slept through the night from an early age and always ate everything put in front of him. He was cuddled by everyone and was happy to be picked up by strangers. He watched his older brothers with fascination and followed them around, dragging his toys behind him.

Etta looked over at Nat Goldsmith, a widowed neighbour who had slipped into the family effortlessly soon after Oscar's death. She could barely remember a time when he had not been there, as a close family friend supporting the grieving widow. He would bring them fresh fish from his shop for supper until he and Bella married, then Bella decided she would rather have less fresh fish and a husband who didn't bring home the smell of it. So he sold his business and became her business manager.

Because Bella and Nat had married with only two local witnesses, none of the children had observed their union and there had been no celebration. Bella just came home one day and told them, without warning, that she and Nat were now husband and wife. Nat moved in that day and life went on. The neighbourhood knew they had married and were pleased that two people on their own had found new happiness but as it was so soon after Oscar's death, the couple wanted to keep it discreet. Bella still called herself Bella Bromavitch, but as she had with Oscar, she used Nat's surname when it was useful to do so. Without children of his own, Nat was particularly devoted to Sam, who didn't remember Oscar and so called him Papa, but the other children continued to call him Nat.

Nat's sales skills contributed hugely to the fast growth of Bella's business. Etta did not want to compare him to her father but Nat was more ambitious for Bella and the family. Maybe because by the time he became part of their lives, Bella was already successful, he managed her differently. He respected her creativity, sometimes treating her like a prized race horse and at other times a piece of fragile, valuable china. He also ensured the whole family respected her talent in the same way. Bella glowed in response.

Nat was responsible for the move to Crouch End. They were both eager to move away from Dalston, where Oscar and Nat's late wife had been known. But he had convinced Bella to delay relocating the family to Hampstead Garden Suburb, arguing that it would not be fair to disrupt Simon's schooling. While Bella concentrated on her designs, the quality of manufacture and personally nurturing her customers, Nat managed the shops and staff. He also read the newspapers and was concerned that there were troubled times ahead. Having adopted this family, he was committed to protecting it. Bella accepted Crouch End as an intermediate move, but held onto her dream.

Nat also insisted that their home was geographically separate from her boutiques. There were now four and although Bella continued to sketch, cut and pin in the kitchen, the bedroom or wherever she was, and read fashion magazines in bed, for the first time she valued having a haven where customers could not call. Even the demands her children made on her were controlled by Nat, and business was not discussed. He tried to forbid any conversations about expansion, collections, styles or money at home and for a while, Bella tried to comply.

He humoured her out of her tantrums and calmed her when she was unreasonable, as she was now. The war had not destroyed her business; in fact, Etta knew that Bella was ready to expand again. The success of the ready-to-wear black clothes for World War One widows had turned her small boutique fashion house into a growing, thriving business. She was determined that a general strike would not hinder her progress either although she hadn't yet worked out how she might benefit from it.

"Strike? We do not strike," she bellowed.

"You might have to, if it's a general strike."

"I don't, I won't. Don't forget there is nothing on any outfit that I can't do myself, down to the buttonholes. In fact my buttonholes are still better than anyone else's and customers used to come…"

"…all the way to the East End for my perfect buttonholes," finished the twins in a chant.

"Owch, be careful!" Bella had stuck a pin ferociously into the collar of the blouse Etta was modelling, sliding it straight through the material and scratching her daughter's neck.

"No, I'll look like a man," protested Etta, pulling at the tie Bella had thrown loosely around her white blouse.

"No you won't, men don't have boozies," giggled Simon.

"No, they don't," sniggered Bernard in agreement.

Etta threw them a look of total disdain. "It's mannish."

"No, it's for a working woman. It won't crease at the typewriter." Bella grabbed some of the fabric and scrunched it tightly. They all watched as it sprang back into pristine shape the moment she let go. "Rayon," she announced triumphantly.

"The typewriter, the typewriter, that's all I know, the typewriter," said Etta, wriggling her neck to a more comfortable position.

"You are lucky that you will have that type-writing. I never—"

"I know, I know you had to learn on the job, arrived with no skills, no money and I am privileged. But not as privileged as the boys, who are getting a proper education but don't seem to appreciate it. Do they?" Etta snarled at the last remark from her twin brothers.

"Stand still," growled Bella. "I have to finish this because next I have to make a ball gown without any staff."

"Calm down please," said Nat in his moderate tone. "If there is a general strike, no one is going to expect new clothes. No one will work."

"Mr Morrison next door says he is going to his job on roller skates. He doesn't approve of striking and nor do I. We are lucky enough to be working and should remember that. Time for bed, young man," Bella addressed Sam.

"No, can't I stay up a bit?" Sam objected.

"Just for a little bit but only if you go on reading quietly. Mama is busy and the boys have their homework and Etta—"

"Is being pinned," interrupted a petulant Etta.

"If there is a strike, will the schools be closed?" asked Bernard in his nasal voice.

"Of course," answered Nat, "the teachers won't work."

"Oh good, let's strike too," shouted Simon with delight.

"Mrs Amelia Bryant is even richer than she was when I made her bridal trousseau during the war. Now her father-in-law is dead, she's a Lady, a proper Lady, and she has come to me, Bella Bromavitch, for a ball gown. It is not the time to strike."

"If there is a strike there will be no need for ball gowns," said Nat, pulling Sam towards the door. "Bed!"

"And she wants me to design something for skiing." Bella wasn't listening to anyone.

"Skiing? There is a strike around the corner and she is going skiing?" Nat was incredulous. "What do people wear for skiing anyway?"

"I don't know. I'll think of something. I can't decide whether it should be white to match the snow or bright, so that if she falls, they can find her." Bella sounded thoughtful.

"Who would want to stand on a couple of planks of wood and slide down a mountain in the snow with only bamboo poles to help them?" asked Etta.

"Warm, I suppose." Bella wasn't listening to Nat or Etta. "Lady Amelia Bryant needs a new wardrobe and has come to me and all you can think about is the strike."

"We don't know yet." Nat's voice of reason, which so reminded her of Oscar, sometimes irritated Bella and yet she knew he was usually right and was secretly grateful for it.

# 1930s

# 1930 Rosie

*Dearest sister,*

*How is London in the winter? Do you remember how cold it is in Poland? (Well, it's Russia now). This is a cold, cold winter, the lake is frozen and I haven't seen that for years. There is very little work here for anyone. There just aren't any jobs so no one has any money. Jacob has had to give up his business and would like to get a job. He doesn't care if it is in a factory. He used to, but now he says he wouldn't mind, as we have to eat and that comes first.*

*He went to see Mr Solomon who still has his glove factory. I suppose people still can afford gloves and need them in the cold even though they can't afford good suits. He used to live next to us and he and Jacob were always friends. He moved away into a nice house in the centre of town about five years ago and we used to go to visit him sometimes. Jacob knows that the factory works on the Sabbath, it was one of the first Jewish owned factories to do so. Jacob says he wouldn't mind that now because God, if there is one, would forgive him doing what is necessary to feed his family.*

*Mr Solomon says that the only Jews who work on a Sabbath are Communists. He thinks Jacob might organise the workers and get them to join the union. Actually I think Jacob would like to organise the workers as they get so little money and work such long hours and it is so filthy. Someone got fired for bringing food in even though they are not allowed to have breaks to eat for at least twelve hours. But Jacob just wants to work now and wouldn't bother to organise anything. But Mr Solomon (we used to call him Samuel but now he is Mr Solomon) would not hire him. It's unbelievable for Jews to treat other Jews like this.*

*So I am cleaning again for gentiles at a house on the other side of town. I go by tram for some of the way and walk the rest to save the fare. But Jacob says I should take the tram back as I am so tired by then. My dreams of being a teacher seem so far away.*

*I wonder what it would be like if we ever met again. I am beginning to think we may not. Hoping that we will is what I live for.*

*Your loving sister, Rosie (and Jacob and Regina)*

# 1930 Etta

*'To whom it may concern:*

*Miss Etta Bromavitch has been my secretary for nearly two years. She was at all times most efficient, reliable and tactful in her dealings with staff and with the many people with whom her post brought her into contact. She is exceptionally quick in performing all her duties, she has very high speeds in shorthand and typewriting and her English and grammar are excellent.*

*I highly recommend her for any position in which initiative is required and a degree of responsibility called for. Please do not hesitate to write to me if you require any further clarification of my comments.*

*G.R. Scott*
*Managing Director*
*G.R Scott and Co Ltd*
*Mechanical and Electrical Engineers'*

Etta showed her reference proudly to Bella, who read it in silence. Then, waving the letter around, she said, "So what is the point? All that skill and all those expensive classes and you chose to work for mechanical engineers. Who on earth are mechanical engineers? Do they make something you can eat? Do they make something you can wear?

"Anyway now you have given it up you are finally free to work with me. I could do with a fast typist. I educate my own daughter and she gives the benefit of all that education to others – mechanical engineers!"

Etta was determined to ignore the tirade she had expected from her mother. "No. I've got another job. I am going to work for a newspaper, as secretary to the editor. It is a good job, more money and maybe I can start to write some news reports or articles." Etta was defiant.

"Where is this newspaper?"

"It's in Stratford, in the East End. It's easy to get to from here by bus and tram."

"The East End? You know how hard I worked to bring us out of the East End? And now you go back there."

Etta recognised the signs of imminent rage.

"Mama, I don't understand this obsession about the East End and getting away from it. I just have a job on a newspaper, that's all. I am not moving back there to live. Anyway, the East End is ours, it's still a Jewish community and where we belong."

"There are people I knew in Petticoat Lane who are still in Petticoat Lane. Is that what you want? Anyway, it won't stay Jewish for long, it will soon belong to someone else and the Jews will feel like strangers there." Bella's voice was raised.

"I like Petticoat Lane and I won't feel like a stranger there since that is where I was born. I just want a chance to be a journalist. I am going to be a journalist and that's that."

"Etta, I need you, I need you in the business." Bella changed her tone to conciliatory. "It's a family business. I would like a member of the family in it."

"Why me? Why not the boys? There are three boys and two..." Etta just stopped herself from mentioning Sara, the name that was never said. Her memories of Sara were still vivid and she always felt uncomfortable, particularly at times of family celebration, knowing that out there somewhere was a sister, a sister her mother would never mention.

"Can't you see, doesn't anyone understand? My business has supported you all and now you are all grown up, well except Sam, we still eat because of Bella Unique. You should all contribute to it, even you."

"Mama, you have a collection coming up. It's always like this, a new shop, a collection, it's like getting your period." They both heard a small giggle from Sam. "There you are," said Etta, seizing an opportunity. "Sam's our hope for the future."

"Ah, so it's me to save the day, is it?" asked Sam, unable to resist joining the argument now his name had been mentioned. "You'll have a bit of a wait, Mama. Anyway I am going to be a doctor."

"Well, we need one. Goodness knows what Simon plans to do with all his fine education and Bernard…" Bella shrugged. "My children have choice because I pushed them but sometimes I wonder if there was any point. What is the point of a family business if there is no family in it?" She turned again to Etta. "I have a collection coming up, and I need you to help. This is not the time to be working on newspapers in the East End."

"It'll be fine, it always is in the end. You don't need my help. You have never really needed any of us. You have always managed to do it all yourself, yes, down to the last button hole. It's just an excuse to stop me taking a job on a newspaper but you can't stop me. Nobody stopped you running your own business, which is what you wanted. Nobody expected you to do something you didn't choose."

"Nobody stopped me because there was nobody around to stop me. Alright, if you want to be a journalist, you could be a fashion journalist. That should keep you happy and could be useful to me too. I can get you a job on Vogue. I have friends there and they will give you a job. There, satisfied?"

"No, I don't want a job on Vogue. I am not interested in fashion." Etta wished she could reach into the air and pull the words back.

Sam, who had been sitting silently in a corner during this exchange, holding his head very low over his school books, now glanced up. He had one chewed pencil behind his ear and another sticking out of his mouth. Both hands covered his ears but Etta could tell he had heard every word. She waited for Bella to react but, before she could, Sam slid over to her and held her in a large and comforting hug.

Bella Unique had continued to grow and Etta knew that Bella would actually benefit from a good secretary now but she just didn't want it to be her. Bella and Nat had ruthlessly reinvested profits into the business and, other than her ambitions to move into ever more middle class neighbourhoods, the family continued to live frugally, as if they were still poor. Bella was not mean, just cautious. She trusted Nat to run the business and Lilly to supervise the boutiques. Lilly had proved herself to be a versatile and enthusiastic member of staff. She could be looking after three customers, taking an order, fitting or showing and, at the same time, still notice the new person entering the door.

Lilly had returned to England at the end of 1929 after her husband's property empire had crashed and he had thrown himself out of a window from the last of his homes to be repossessed. He had lost his fortune suddenly, not an unusual story in 1929. It was a black year for entrepreneurs. But the spirit that had carried Lilly from Konin to London and then to New York, the spirit that had attracted Bella and maintained their friendship for so many years, saved her again.

Lilly sailed back across the Atlantic to the Port of London, not in steerage as with Bella, and not in luxury as she had with her husband. This time she had travelled in the kitchens, washing dishes for her passage. When she arrived on Bella's doorstep, Bella welcomed her, recognising that once again they needed each other. It was the perfect opportunity for her to have the trusted, reliable, mature help she needed to continue to grow.

As Lilly unfolded the story of the end of her life in America, Bella rubbed Ponds cold cream gently into her friend's hands and continued to do so, until those hands recovered from the weeks of washing greasy dishes in cold water and were ready to attend wealthy, fussy customers in elegant, expensive frocks.

# 1933 Rosie

*Dearest sister,*

*It is getting harder and harder here. I can't understand why Jacob is so committed to staying, especially when he was so keen to send his only daughter away. I know thirty years have passed but I still burn with the pain of it. Even now I think of you as you were. It seems like yesterday although I know my daughter is now grown up and you may have grey hair. I certainly do. I am not fat though, none of us are, how could we be on this diet?*

*We lost touch with Nathan in America as well. I don't know what has happened to him but I am sure he is still in America. I have never written to him, as I write to you and I know Jacob didn't, but lately I have been thinking that I might try to find him. Maybe he could persuade Jacob that it is time to go. I don't feel comfortable in the street anymore, it is as if something is threatening us all the time. It doesn't feel like our home this place, so many are leaving. I feel more and more lonely as if something possible has passed us by.*

*Jacob is so moody at the moment, I get quite frightened. Yesterday he shouted at me that I should have left when I could have left. He has never said anything like that before. But he still didn't mention Sara, he never has, not ever. I would love to talk about her and what I did, how it happened and what it has done to our lives but I can't really and I don't want to make him any more bad-tempered than he is.*

*He seems very distressed that some Communist Jews have gone to Russia and more are planning to go. He thinks a person gone to Russia is a person dead. He doesn't complain so much when people go off to America, but still says they should stay in Poland. He thinks that people*

111

*running away will destroy the community and doesn't accept that the community is disappearing anyway and that's why people are going away.*

*He wants me to speak only Polish now, except for prayers. He won't go to synagogue anymore anyway and we only do prayers on Friday night for his mother to light the candles by. But I have to talk Yiddish in the market or no one will understand me. I can't believe that once the Torah was his only daily newspaper and now he devours all the newspapers.*

*I don't understand why he works so hard for other workers and their rights when his own wife is so exhausted cleaning for other people and looking after his mother as well. The Bund isn't helping me – that's a fact.*

*Your loving sister Rosie (and Jacob and Regina)*

# 1935 Bella

Nat was stirring a large saucepan of porridge and occasionally peering into the large brown earthenware teapot beside him. Simon was striding around the kitchen, eyes closed, air conducting with one hand and stroking his new moustache with the other. Etta was tucked up in a corner scribbling notes into a large notebook labelled 'Silver Jubilee'.

"Watch out," she hissed as Simon bumped into her, knocking her pencil to the floor.

Bernard sat at the kitchen table fiddling with the disassembled parts of a camera. Beside him was a pile of business cards announcing 'Bernard Bromavitch – Photography. Weddings – Barmitzvahs – Engagements.'

"Clear all that stuff off the table please, Bernard," said Nat. "Is anyone going to put out some cups and bowls? Come on, let's have some help around here please."

"Not stuff," said Bernard grumpily. "It's a genuine Wetzler, made by Ernest Leitz himself."

"Who is that?" asked Etta without raising her head from her notebook. "Where did you get it from?" Bernard shrugged.

Despite the major move from a flat to a house in Crouch End, the centre of family life was still the kitchen. Simon, who was studying business, spread his books over the table, as did Sam his school books. The chaos created by Bernard's various ventures added to the disarray. Etta had created a cosy hideaway in her own bedroom, which Bella called 'Etta's luxury'. Now that she contributed some of her wages to the family budget, she felt she had the right to privacy and she spent most of her free time writing.

The other living area, the formal lounge, was supposedly for adult relaxation or guests. The furniture was always protected with white dust covers, unless there were visitors. Only Sam was allowed to go in for his piano practise and Bella and Nat used it as an escape from the boys.

Nat, though self-taught, was now a fully qualified accountant who was able to total three columns of figures at the same time by running his fingers down them. He continued his transformation of Bella Unique as its business advisor, accountant and marketeer. Chasing customers for payment was his speciality and now even Bella's regulars knew that, except in extreme circumstances, there was no credit and all purchases were to be paid for when received. This strategy partly accounted for the company's steady growth.

He had been less successful at keeping the business away from the home. When not actually designing, Bella scoured fashion magazines for any trends she might have missed and any references to herself. When not poring over large ledgers of figures, Nat read the business pages of the newspapers, checking for any financial or political movement that could affect them.

Nat nearly always made breakfast for the family, accepting that Bella was not at her best in the morning. Now, as Nat gave a final swirl to the porridge, Bella came into the kitchen carrying a copy of Woman's Own in one hand, a coat, bag and gloves in the other. She wore a crisp navy blue two-piece suit with calf-length skirt and a white blouse. A flamboyant silk bow, navy with white spots, softened the impression. Even in middle age she needed little help from make-up. Her skin remained unlined, her eyes clear. Her hair was without a touch of grey. Not one inch of fat had been added to her still straight frame.

"Etta, please," protested Nat, signalling for her help.

"Sorry," said Etta, getting to her feet. "Come on you two, breakfast. Morning, Mama."

"Bernard, move that stuff please. More to the point, young man, where did you get that expensive looking camera?" Bella asked tersely. "Anyway, take it out of the kitchen or it'll get covered in porridge. Where's Sam?"

"Listen," said Etta, her eyes softening.

For a moment they all quietened and heard the thump, thump, thump of a ball being hit against an outside wall.

"Tennis, of course," announced Bella. "Someone call him for breakfast. Bernard, no, maybe not you, you need to pack up all that junk…"

"It's not junk, it's a valuable camera," whined Bernard, piling camera parts hurriedly into a box and awkwardly carrying them out of the room.

"We are eating, at least anyone in here is eating, anyone not is…"

"…not," laughed Sam as he rushed into the room, flinging his tennis racquet into a corner. Tennis balls tumbled out of his hands and ran around the floor. "I can't make up my mind whether to play at Wimbledon or be a doctor," he shouted with excitement.

"Watch out!" shouted Nat.

Bella looked at the disorder in her kitchen in despair.

"I have to go. I've got an appointment to see a vacant shop. It's on the Finchley Road just at the bottom of Frognal, very convenient for the well off people moving to live up near Hampstead Heath. I need to establish myself there. I'll see you later."

"You haven't eaten," Nat said, stating the obvious.

Bella shrugged her shoulders, took a sip of tea from a cup that was already cold, then picked up her handbag, pulled on her white leather gloves and without looking backwards, left the kitchen. They all heard the front door slam.

"Where did you get it, by the way?" asked Nat as Bernard returned without the camera.

"Where's Mama?" asked Bernard.

"Where did you get the camera?" Nat repeated.

Bernard looked at Simon for support, "I didn't steal it."

"Well?"

They all looked at Bernard expectantly, except Sam, who filled a bowl with porridge and started eating.

"From Mr Katz."

"The pawnbroker?" Etta sounded worried.

"Of course, the pawnbroker."

"Just don't tell Mama," warned Simon, "she'll go mad."

"Why? I paid for it."

"You know how she feels about buying from pawn shops," Etta added.

"I don't see why. They have to make money and if it has been there for more than a year, it's for sale. Why shouldn't I buy it?" Bernard still sometimes sounded like the petulant little boy he had been.

"You know what your mother thinks. That people only pawn goods when they have had a really difficult time. Or they might be new arrivals or refugees and we, who have been lucky, shouldn't benefit from others' hardship."

"Not exactly luck," whined Bernard. "Anyway, somebody would have bought it."

"But it shouldn't be us." Etta was filling the bowls with porridge.

"Let's change the subject. Who is going to the street party?" asked Simon.

"All of us, I think," said Nat. "How often do we have a Silver Jubilee to celebrate?"

# 1935 Etta

Etta lost her virginity to the Sports Editor the night of the celebrations for George V's Silver Jubilee. Looking back, she could only remember his name was Paul something. She had become separated from the family and, wandering amongst the joyous crowds, was stimulated by the freedom of being on her own and the jubilance around her. The spontaneity was infectious. She talked to and laughed with strangers, although the massive display of patriotism on May 6th 1935 on the streets of London ensured there were no real strangers that day. Waving a flag that had been thrust in her hand, she joined in the singing and banter. She realised that this was an opportunity to write a story from the point of view of the people in the streets. She knew the reporters who had been assigned to the story would concentrate on the pageant, the spectacle and the historical significance. But she didn't want to write about royalty or the famous, but about real people and their reactions to the event. She planned to describe the streets decorated with patriotic red, white and blue banners and bunting, the cheering, singing and flag-waving. She wanted to capture the mood of optimism and joy.

Etta rushed back to the newspaper office in West Ham late that night to file her report. She still wasn't actually a reporter, only secretary to the editor. Nevertheless, from her first day in the job, she had submitted articles, news reports and reviews. Occasionally they were published, although she was never given a by-line. She pursued every opportunity to display her writing skills, as she realised this was the best way for her to get the chance she wanted to become a journalist eventually.

She and Paul found themselves alone in the editorial office late that night. He had been interviewing sportsmen about the Silver Jubilee. They had both drunk too much champagne and the exhilaration of the occasion was overwhelming.

It happened on his desk. Her back was crushed up against his typewriter, her buttocks scratched by paper clips and scissors. Glue stuck to her as Paul fumbled his way past her cami-knickers and tugged at her stockings. She quite enjoyed it – not the sex, that had hurt a bit and left her feeling sticky and smelly – but the danger. For the rest of her life, the chemical smell of newsprint reminded her of their undignified encounter. As a journalist, that smell surrounded her frequently, and the memory always returned, sometimes only for an instant. She felt slightly comforted by the fact that he was Jewish, but not that he was married or that they had both been drunk.

She did not 'fall' pregnant, which was her biggest concern, she just 'lost' her virginity As a wordsmith she was fascinated by these negative descriptions, which matched her own attitude to the event. It was a long time before she had sex again. It was never central to her marriage, which took place four years later, and that was a relief to Etta.

Alan had arrived at the house one evening, to pick up some Bella Unique dresses to deliver to Debenham and Freebody. He started chatting to her while waiting for them to be packed.

'He'll do,' thought Etta. She probably chose him because he was uncomplicated, grateful and available. She respected his integrity and kindness and knew he would pose no threat to her career ambitions. He also appeared just when her unmarried status was starting to become an issue with Bella and the neighbours.

"Just in time," Bella had commented when Etta had announced her engagement, possibly referring to Etta's age but possibly to the fact that Simon was showing a healthy interest in a series of eligible girls he had met at the very sociable Anglo-Palestinian Club. The twins spent a considerable amount of their free time there and Bella was sure it was only a matter of time before at least one of her sons would want to settle down. Having an unmarried older daughter did not fit in with Bella's drive towards convention and respectability. She wanted Etta 'married off' before the twins.

It was not a passionate coupling, more a warm friendship. Had Alan pounced on her during their wedding night in the Grosvenor House bridal suite (a wedding present from Bella and Nat), she would have complied in the same way that she had agreed to the marriage. But he didn't. He approached her gently with a copy of Marie Stopes' *Married Love* in his hands and suggested they read it together "before". As there was not an "after" that night, The Grosvenor House's finest double bed went to waste.

Alan moved into her room, and as well as giving practical help in the house and the garden, he became an invaluable support in Bella's business. His contribution was complementary to Nat's business skills. He carried racks of dresses and fixed broken clothes rails. He saw things that needed doing before anyone else noticed them: the cupboard door that was about to fall off, the rail that was crooked. He took over the responsibility of the packing and unpacking, and all the delivering. Alan became an essential part of the business and the household.

Bella was relieved that Etta was finally married. She never questioned the state of the marriage. Had she done so, she would have found out that every night he and Etta slept back to back, as far apart as a double bed would allow. Other than the occasional thwack, delivered by Etta to interrupt his snoring, there was little physical contact.

As Etta entered her thirties, no one questioned that she had no children. It was just assumed she was too old to conceive when she married and the neighbours just thought that she was lucky to have married at that age anyway.

# 1935 Rosie

*Dearest Sister,*

*I do so want to sound happy for you in these letters but it's hard. Writing to you, I don't have to pretend to be brave. Everyone here has so little money. It's dreadful when we all worked so very hard all our lives. Yet people are still collecting for Zion, always collecting for Zion. Why are we so divided when we all want the same thing?*

*Jacob was attacked today and not by anti-Semites. Jew attacking Jew. It is because he wouldn't put something about Zionists in his newsletter. Oh yes, it's a proper newsletter now, distributed by hand but still printed in my bedroom! He still doesn't like the Zionists. He insists we have to solve the problems we are having where we live and not run away. This is our homeland he says but so many are leaving I sometimes think we are going to be the only Jews left in Poland.*

*There are queues at the passport office and sometimes people stand outside there for days. Many are going to Palestine and some are studying skills to take there, where they plan to build this new land. Mendle, do you remember the butcher? I suppose not, anyway he was a child and not a butcher then. He is learning to be a builder. He is a very old apprentice. I would have thought being a butcher was skilled enough but apparently they will need practical skills in Palestine so that they can build homes. Jacob says it is all desert and nothing is growing but people think it is better than Poland. How can you grow things in the desert? I wonder what they eat in the desert. I don't suppose I will ever find out.*

*From your loving sister, Rosie (and Jacob and Regina)*

# 1936 Bernard

Bernard stood in the damp, freezing cold of a December night, in the queue outside a newsreel theatre near Victoria station. He blew warm breath into his hands. It was ten o'clock and the line curled round the corner and into the next street. A small group of buskers were torturing Irish ballads, one of them fiddling the refrains. They stood strategically at the corner where everyone needed to pass by. A hat, holding a few coins, lay on the ground in front of them. They occasionally glanced at it hopefully. Bernard wanted to pay them to be quiet but knew that, if he gave anything, it would encourage an even more enthusiastic performance. He had already visited two cinemas that day armed with a notebook, pencil and a list of questions Simon wanted answered.

From the moment Simon and Bernard, aged twelve, had snuck out of their barmitzvah classes to visit the Perfect Picture House in Crouch End, Simon knew exactly what he wanted to do with his life. He was entranced by the flickering screen accompanied by the tinkling piano, but his interest was in the cinema itself.

"It's a palace," he had whispered to Bernard, as they ran down the stairs to find seats in the front row. Through the years they had seen Charlie Chaplin, Rudolph Valentino, the Marx brothers. They had watched cowboys shoot Indians and heroes rescue maidens. He had frequently gone with Bernard, sometimes Etta and occasionally he had taken an underaged Sam. Bella and Nat made sporadic visits, mainly to see what outfits the glamorous stars were wearing. Simon didn't mind how often he saw a film. He was fascinated by the audience, when they laughed, when they shouted at the screen, even when they walked out in the middle. Whilst everyone else stared at the screen, Simon looked around the building. He observed the way the seats were numbered, how the box office worked, the layout of the corridors, what worked and what could be improved. His eyes roamed to the ceiling and around the walls. He visited the lavatories so that he could see how often they were cleaned. He chatted to the ticket sellers and the usherettes. Eventually, he cajoled his way into the projection booth and watched mesmerised as the large reels of film were changed from one projector to another. Quickly he learnt how to do that and gained the respect of Ronnie, the Perfect's resident projectionist, by managing a slick change over while Ronnie took a break to smoke a cigarette.

While studying for a business degree at London's University College, he took a job at the newly opened Apollo Victoria. He spent his evenings polishing the winding brass banisters, until an opportunity arose for him to demonstrate that he understood quite a lot about the projectionist's work, thanks to Ronnie from the Perfect. He was offered the important position of rewind boy. After he graduated, he was given a promotion from rewind boy to number three projectionist. Happiest in front of the house, where it was noticed that he spent most of his spare time, he was offered the job of assistant to the assistant to the assistant manager when it became vacant. From there he plotted his career and started calling himself Simon Broom.

"Make yourself useful," Simon had said to Bernard. "I am working most days and every night and I need to know what other cinemas are doing."

"Why, why does it matter what they are doing?"

"Then I can do it better, when I have my own cinemas."

"Cinemas? More than one? How many do you plan to have?" Bernard laughed.

"More than anyone else," replied Simon, deadly serious.

"How much will you pay me?"

Bernard was without work again and grateful to have a purpose. He was conspicuously not being persuaded to join Bella Unique by his mother. His vocational path had wound around many different callings. His career as a photographer had been brief and humiliating. He had dropped his Wetzler camera with the Ernest Leitz lens, of which he had been so proud but which had caused so much stress in the family, at the first wedding he had been hired to photograph. He not only lost the irreplaceable camera, together with all the memories of that special day, but any hope of building a reputation as the chosen recorder of momentous events in the close-knit community of Crouch End.

There had been a flurry of energy over his fleeting involvement as a dealer in cigarette cards and then an embarrassingly short and unsuccessful stint in the administrative office of the Anglo-Palestinian Club. The club still formed the basis of the twins' social life. The position had been manipulated by Simon, who hoped Bernard might work his way up to being Club Secretary. He expected to cover his brother's errors so that only they would know he was not up to the job. Bernard was given free access to the bank account as part of his training. It was too tempting. Simon hadn't contemplated that, confronted with so much available money, Bernard might 'borrow' some to replace his beloved camera. He had meant to pay it all back very quickly, assuming that no one would notice a temporary reduction in the bank balance. Then a smart accountant had seen the gap and had a private word with Simon. Bernard was out. Everyone agreed that Bernard was not a criminal, he had indeed seen it as a loan and no charges were pressed.

Bernard regretted that he had borrowed the money but worse than that, Simon had lost confidence in him. Now he desperately wanted to regain his trust. Maybe, he thought several times during the day, if Simon did really become a successful cinema owner, he might give him a permanent job. Perhaps Simon would always need someone to visit other cinemas, to see what the competition was doing. So, although he didn't relish another visit to a cinema so late at night after his long day of viewing and travelling across London, he knew this was his opportunity to prove he could be valuable.

Bernard had been so captivated by The Thirty-Nine Steps, which he had seen in Tooting, that he had struggled to remember that it was the cinema and the environment that Simon wanted to know about, not the film. He had fallen asleep in Shepherds Bush during Modern Times, only woken occasionally by the surprise of Charlie Chaplin's innovative sound effects. On both occasions he had made copious notes.

Simon had insisted that he visited newsreel cinemas as well as conventional picture palaces. Now Bernard took out his notebook and wrote that the audiences at the other two cinemas had been mainly families but this queue for a newsreel was mostly men, not surprising late at night. He noticed a tall black man wandering up the line, stopping in front of people and asking, politely, for money. Bernard was fascinated by his wide shoulders and the thick neck showing above his coat collar. The coat itself was several sizes too small, his trousers were short and there was a gap between his socks and the bottom of his frayed trousers. As he approached, Bernard noticed that the toes had been cut out of his shoes and remembered that Bella had done that to their shoes when they were little. He wanted to pull away when the man stopped directly in front of him but felt that it might be offensive to someone in such a poor state. So he stood still, concentrating on the sound from the buskers and stared directly into the man's eyes, trying not to blink.

The man moved closer, until he was just touching him, and Bernard could smell his body. He was surprised that he smelt clean and even faintly perfumed.

"Anything you want, sir?" he whispered and Bernard felt hot breath in his ear and the full length of the man's body touching him. He stayed still. For a moment, Bernard enjoyed the close contact with another human being. It was rare in his life. His only physical contact was duty kisses with his family. He felt the man push a little closer.

"I need money for my ticket," he rasped.

Bernard jerked away, pulling himself backwards, releasing the contact and breaking off the mood. He shook his head violently and then, deliberately, removed some coins from his pocket and threw them into the buskers' hat. He was glad that the queue was starting to move forward.

In the flickering light of an animated cartoon, Bernard balanced his notebook on his knee and looked at Simon's questions.

*'Is it clean?' 'Not really,'* he wrote.

As he entered he had noticed that the air was thick with smoke and a musty smell, like sour onions, filled the atmosphere. There was old newspaper on the floor and something sticky on his seat.

*'Were the staff helpful?' 'Not really.'*

"Sit or stand?" the attendant had asked brusquely as he reached the top of the queue. He held his hand out for money and seemed to be indicating some people towards the far wall of the auditorium when Bernard answered, "Sit", ignoring the attendant's hand as he had already paid one shilling and sixpence for his seat.

*'Did you get in quickly?' 'Not really.'*

*'Are the seats comfortable?' 'Not really.'*

There were men lying down in the aisles and he needed to step over them, which slowed down his progress. He bumped into two who seemed to be tucked up together under a blanket, he assumed to sleep for the night. As he made his way unsteadily down the aisle stairs in the dim light, a young man leaning up against the wall stuck a foot out as he passed, as if to trip him. When Bernard looked at him, he gave an angelic and slightly apologetic smile.

*'Is there enough time between programmes?' 'No, no, no!'* he wrote as the newsreel of Edward VIII's abdication speech started to wind through again.

'*The year of three Kings*,' screamed the title in large white letters across the black screen and then moved on to a full repeat of the abdication speech.

"…found it impossible to carry the heavy duty of responsibility and to discharge my duties as King as I would wish without…."

Over a few short, sad scenes of the new George VI, his gentle smiling wife and two pretty daughters playing with corgis, the abdication speech was played again and again.

"He has one matchless blessing, enjoyed by so many of you and not bestowed upon me – a happy home with his wife and children…"

By the time Bernard had heard this several times, in between two cartoons, a short film about Wedgwood china and another about haymaking, he waited for those words. He enjoyed the emotion each time, relating to the abdicated King's pain. He felt he alone understood the poor man, who knew he had let down his family, his country and even his Empire.

"…the ministers of the crown, and in particular Mr Baldwin."

Bernard didn't know whether he was exhausted from his long day or by his empathy for the abdicated king but by 2 o'clock in the morning, he desperately wanted to sleep. He didn't want to join the poor souls who were camped out for the night in the aisles but understood the need to lie down. By 3 am he could recite the whole speech by heart. Simon had asked him, ordered him really, to stay for at least fours hours so that he could report on the type and size of audience, how it changed at different times and when the cinema was full and when empty.

"I now quit altogether public affairs and I lay down my burden. It may be some time before I return to…"

Bernard, dozing, was woken by a man sitting next to him touching his elbow. The man moved away when he withdrew his arm. Glancing around the auditorium, he noticed that several men were changing seats. He made a short note and got up to leave.

On the way out, he glimpsed two men seemingly glued to-gether leaning up against a wall. One faced the wall, the other was leaning against him. Disturbed, Bernard rushed into the street. The black man who had confronted him four hours earlier was still there and as Bernard passed, he shoved a card into his hand.

"Thanks," whispered Bernard, not knowing what he was thanking him for, and shoved the card unread into his pocket.

The next morning, late and after a long sleep, he looked at it and saw that it said:

TURKISH BATHS
DISCREET AND PRIVATE

There was an address in the Edgware Road.

# 1937 Rosie

*Dear Sister,*

*I think it has been ages since I wrote to you. Sometimes I get dispirited as nothing seems to change and if I look back it just seems that everything is a bit more difficult.*

*I so want to come to England to find you. Although I never hear from you, my letters are never returned, so I think you are still there. It doesn't make any sense that we are stuck here. Magda, she's the other cleaner at the big house where I work, thinks we should come to England but just to pick you and Sara up, together with any family you might have, and just go to America. We haven't heard anything from Jacob's brother for years now and, quite honestly, I can't remember what he looks like. But anyway Jacob will never leave and now he says it is because his mother is too old to travel and the journey would kill her. Of course he is right. He says also that they don't need any more tailors in America.*

*Anyway he says we are weakened by so many leaving here and we must stay here. I think he means all the Jews, but he might just mean Bund members. Honestly I don't want to question him when he is so angry at everything. We nearly quarrelled when I told him I wanted to get a passport just in case. He asked, in case of what and I didn't really have an answer but I just want to be able to leave if – I don't know, just – if. You must think I am very stupid. Jacob is quarrelling with everyone now, even his mother. But she is so old, she just cried and he stopped. She said the meat he had brought home wasn't kosher, although I don't know why she said that, as he bought it from Mendle. Certainly it wasn't very nice meat but, despite learning to be a builder, Mendle is still working as a butcher and it will be kosher, even if not tasty.*

*Jacob hasn't much time for being observant anymore and has no more time for the orthodox Jews than he does for the Zionists. He says orthodox Jews just keep their heads in books and don't see what is going on around them. He says man exploiting man NOW is more important than what happened four thousand years ago. He thinks they don't support the workers who are so exploited and that without the workers, who provide a valuable and very cheap labour force, we would have been thrown out of Poland a long time ago. He thinks that the workers should stick together and if we all refused to work long hours, we wouldn't have to.*

*I know though that it is dangerous what Jacob thinks and I wish he would keep it to himself. I feel so tired that I can't even think for myself anymore and feel like a machine in a factory doing the same thing again and again every day.*

*Blessings and may God grant you safety (I still believe in God).*

*Your loving sister, Rosie (and Regina and Jacob, the stranger)*

# 1938 Bella

Whatever was happening to the Jews in Europe did not impinge to any degree on the successful, socially mobile, middle-class Jews in England. There were rumours of anti-Semitism but these were old and familiar stories. Whenever Bella thought of Rosie and Jacob, which was only when she received a letter, it was only of their betrayal and never with sympathy. Sara, who represented their betrayal, was never mentioned or enquired after.

By the time the twins were twenty-five, Bella owned a chain of boutiques in London and several in new towns around the country. Bella Unique was established as a famous couture house and the Bella Unique ready-made collection featured in the most prestigious department stores. The vision and the designs were all exclusively hers, but the business was managed by Nat and the clients were nurtured by Lilly. Bella's reputation remained, as it had been in the days of her market stall, quality in design, fabric and workmanship. Her styles were always just within the guidelines of each year's fashions but she considered any outfit that could not be worn comfortably for at least five years to be a failure. Her customers relied on her judgement, her reliability and her speed. Her team of home dressmakers and piece-workers had been carefully selected and trained. They knew without doubt that if they did not match her exacting standards, Bella would give them no more work. A small factory in Manchester provided the ready-made collection.

Bella continued to hope that one of her children would join her and, eventually, take over. Too much had been invested in the enterprise for her not to consider its prospects. Now over fifty, she needed to think of what Nat insisted on calling 'the succession'. It was a description that made her distinctly uncomfortable, but encouraged her to think seriously about the future – Bella Unique without Bella. The generation of Bella, Nat and Lilly were entrepreneurial because they'd had no choice. But the next generation were expected to become lawyers, doctors, dentists and accountants, except neither of her older sons were planning to follow any of those careers.

Bernard had grown into a stocky young man. He had broad shoulders, the beginning of a belly and his unfortunate teenage attack of psoriasis had left him with a scarred face. He spent time improving his appearance, placing pomade on his wiry, auburn hair and all manner of unguents on his face, in the hope of clearing his skin. He was excitable and enthusiastic about everything, particularly his 'projects'. It was a useful device for covering up his limitations. Bella loved but didn't trust him.

Bella and Nat were so worried about Bernard being unemployed again that they failed to notice that Simon had decided on his future and was never going to use the skills he had learnt at university to expand Bella Unique. With his quick mind, business degree and natural charm, he would have been a great asset. He was tall, languidly attractive with blue-green eyes shaded by long lashes. Yet his permanently smiling eyes belied his savage ambition. He had not outgrown his obsessive interest in the cinema and his success so far indicated that this might never happen.

Sam was good at tennis, good at the piano and good at his studies. At seventeen he resembled a puppy Great Dane, with arms too long, hands and feet too large. He showed signs that he would be painfully handsome when older. Bella's clients would adore him but he showed no interest in business, design or any other skill that could be identified as being useful to a chain of fashion boutiques. He was set on his course to become a doctor and Bella knew that it could never be right to persuade anyone to abandon medicine.

By the time the family had finally moved to Hampstead Garden Suburb, into a white, circular fronted house just in time for Passover in 1938, she had nearly given up hope that any of her children would join the business.

Hampstead Garden Suburb had not been built as a Jewish suburb, but as a green, healthy environment on the outskirts of London for the new middle class. However, the Jewish community continued to cling together, creating ghettos, albeit now frequently rich ghettos, wherever they settled. The synagogue had been built in 1933, the architecture was controversially modern and on Friday evenings and all day Saturday, the nearby streets were full of men in skull caps wandering towards it. Shops in the High Street closed for the Sabbath and gradually the non-Jews left the area.

The houses, all attached to each other, formed a curved private close. They had long thin gardens with low walls, a cause for great excitement. The family now had four bedrooms, one for Bella and Nat, one for the twins, one for Etta and Alan, one for Sam. Sometimes when Lilly visited she would stay in Sam's room and he would sleep with the twins. All three enjoyed those nights and could be heard talking and joking late into the night. Lilly's home was a rented a flat in Maida Vale, in one of the newly built blocks of flats. She could afford it with the salary that Bella paid her as her top 'vendeuse', the one assigned to her richest and most demanding clients. Lilly's time in New York married to a millionaire, albeit briefly, helped her to relate to the very rich and speak their language without intimidation.

As well as the lounge, with the furniture protected under dust covers and mainly used for visitors, there was also a dining room for very special occasions, like Passover. It had a pale green carpet with a raised Chinese design that blended with the pale mauve walls. The windows looked out onto a private close lined with young cherry trees but as the curtains mainly remained closed, these were rarely seen from inside the house. The modern mahogany table, with matching chairs, had a central section that could be added when the whole family came to eat.

There had been a massive rush to move in and be settled in time for the Passover meal and service. Everyone helped with the packing, the moving, the unpacking. Not one set of dishes but two were swept up in the hurry to be ready for the traditional celebration.

Bella employed two young sisters from the Ukraine to prepare the house and meal. They were refugees from an observant Jewish family and needed little instruction in the frenzied preparations. The cleaning, scrubbing, putting away plates, taking out plates and cooking of special dishes, as well as a final scouring of the home for any errant breadcrumbs, were second nature to them and allowed Bella and Lilly to work up until the last moment, finishing outfits for her loyal and dependent customers.

The chicken soup, chopped liver, latkes, and matzo pudding were made from recipes straight from the girls' mother's table, as were the Passover delicacies. They had arrived with little English but a desire to secure their future, so that they could bring their parents out of a Europe they no longer felt was safe. They had brought little with them and were grateful for the clothes Bella gave them. They enthusiastically studied a book she had given them called *How to behave in England*. It dealt with table manners, queuing, when to say please (all the time) and when to say 'thank you' (also all the time).

It was customary for the mother of the house to be near exhaustion by the time the candles were lit for the service. Bella remembered her mother telling her of the relief she felt when she heard that first question, "Why is this night different from all other nights?" It meant that most of the hard work was done and the rest was not too different from serving any other large family meal, until the end of the period when all the plates and cutlery had to be changed again.

The Bromavitch-Goldsmith family, as it was known in their new neighbourhood, was observant but not particularly Orthodox.

They continued to follow the rituals but more out of habit than belief. However, it would be inconceivable for Passover not to be a big family feast, complete with ceremonial food, prayers, candles and songs. But as the younger generation became busier, their lives became more assimilated. Even though they lived in the middle-class ghetto of Hampstead Garden Suburb, their work put them in contact with non-Jews and the customs were being observed only out of respect for parents.

There had been a last-minute rush in Bella's boutiques before they closed for ten days but she arrived home in time to check every detail and try every dish, all of which she found perfect. Nat struggled with the accounts in the privacy of their bedroom till the last possible moment and Etta arrived from her office just in time. Simon had arrived early and threw himself into a flurry of helping, making sure that Bella noticed his contribution. Bernard, who had spent the day at home doing something unidentifiable, stayed in his room until called for. Sam just got in the way in the kitchen, sticking his fingers into a mixture of fruit, nuts and honey, salt water and then, much to the Ukranian girls' amusement, the traditional bitter herbs.

The table for that Passover was laid for a large family, which now included Alan, Lilly, and Simon's latest girlfriend, Judith. The Ukranian girls, who were organised enough to cook, serve and sit at the table, were also included. After the formal service had finished and the meal eaten, Nat allowed a special toast to Bella, whose skill and hard work had allowed them to spend "this year in Hampstead Garden suburb", a play on the traditional Passover words of "next year in Jerusalem".

The table had been cleared and the family were relaxed at the end of the long meal and service, leaning on the white lace tablecloth that now sported a few red wine stains and many crumbs. Simon had an announcement to make. He had been working full-time at the Apollo Victoria for three years and believed he could do every job in the cinema better than the people he had shadowed. He had been promoted to assistant manager but was now ready for his own picture palace.

Bella and Nat rarely argued. Theirs was a benign relationship based on his careful respect for her talent and her wise understanding that she performed better with his total support. But when Simon asked to borrow money to rent a run-down theatre in the East End to develop into what he saw as the first of a chain of cinemas, they disagreed violently.

"How can you discuss money at Pesach?" Bella was furious.

"Come on, Bella, why not?" Nat's voice was conciliatory.

"When else can I talk to you when you are not busy? I am asking for a business loan, not a gift. I am going to do this, Mama."

Etta and Sam sat silently, watching for the duel that would surely follow. Bernard nursed half a glass of wine, which he had not allowed the maids to clear.

"What do you mean you are going to do this? Where will you get the money? I didn't pay for your education so that you could take more money from me."

"I am not taking money. I am asking for a business loan."

"Shall we go into the lounge?" Etta's voice was tense with worry. She didn't want there to be a family row in front of Alan, who became agitated when there was conflict, or in front of Judith on her first visit for a family occasion.

"Lounge?" queried Bella. "Will this sound better in the lounge?"

Etta signalled to Alan to leave the table with her.

"Sit!" screeched Bella. "This is a family matter."

"Why is this a family matter?" Sam asked innocently.

Bella's eyes softened as they always did when addressing Sam.

"If I give Simon money, what if he loses it? What if you need it? You are only seventeen. You want to go to medical school. That will cost money. What if Simon loses the money put aside for your medical studies? What will you feel then?" Bella's voice rose at every word.

"He might be successful and make money. He has worked hard and deserves a chance." Nat's voice was still calm.

"Hmmm. From a run-down dump in the middle of nowhere he is going to make money?" Bella wished she could retract those words the moment she heard herself say them. She knew exactly what any one of her children could say to her.

Bernard did. "That dump is right in the middle of the district where you had your first dump, Mama."

"I made clothes. People need clothes. Do they need picture palaces?"

"Yes they do." Simon's confidence was growing. He was hearing the arguments he had expected and prepared for. "People always need entertainment. The cinema is here for good. Nothing can replace it. Look at these figures." He reached into a large leather bag he had stashed under the table and brought out some documents. He spread press clippings and sheets of numbers on the table.

"Why are you in such a hurry?" Bella's voice sounded as if she was trying to get her voice back under control.

"I have to hurry. There are chains of cinemas spreading throughout the country. If mine is not one of them, it will be too late. Look – ABC. Look – super cinemas. This is it, this is the future. The way people will get their entertainment for generations. Nothing can change that, nothing can compete with that."

"Simon, is this the right moment? Really, it's Pesach." Nat's protest was unconvincing as he stood up to look at Simon's research.

"Can we leave you to it?" Etta had moved towards Alan and was beckoning him to leave the room with her.

"No. You stay and listen. This is a family decision." Bella was starting to show interest in the press cuttings Simon had spread out.

Etta shrugged and winked at Alan. There was only one decision-maker in the family and they all knew it.

# 1938 Rosie

*Dearest Sister,*

*Jacob's mother died this week. She was 87. The whole neighbour-hood came to her funeral and my home seemed so small when crowded with people for the Shiva. My back is so bad from looking after her that I found it hard to sit on the low chairs the Rabbi had lent us. By the end of the week, I was in great pain. Although Jacob says he doesn't think there is a God and he doesn't want any more prayers in the house, there is something comforting about the old rituals. People came into the room and knew what to do, who to greet and what to say.*

*I wish I could feel sad. That is what I am supposed to feel, I know, but for you alone, I have to say that I am fifty-eight and my life is just beginning. I feel bad, saying it is actually better here, now. We will have two rooms again. We haven't had two rooms since his mother came to live with us. One is for living, eating and working and one is our bedroom. No more printing press in the bedroom.*

*I despair about the future. I thought now Jacob would consider leaving but he said no, nothing is changed. He is not blind, he must see what is happening here for Jews but he still thinks that we must stay and work for a better future here in Poland, our homeland. The surprise is that he said we don't have to keep kosher anymore. Can you imag-ine? A Jewish home without prayers, candles, kosher? He even thought we might start celebrating the Polish holidays. I don't even know what they are.*

*But it is different on the streets, because so many people have gone now. Some have just crossed the border to go to Germany, where there are jobs. Whole families are just crossing the border. I don't understand that either as some say the Germans are coming here. But people will go anywhere there is work, particularly Jews. The government will only grant passports now to Jews who are going to Palestine. I don't know why. Mendle went to Germany, without a passport. He, his wife and all the five children and his brother's family just crept out one night. He told me that now he is a bricklayer and not a butcher, he will get work in Germany. I suppose we will never see them again. Now I have to go to the market to buy meat. Although, Jacob doesn't think I need to find kosher meat, I don't know how to choose any other meat, so we will still eat kosher!*

*I still need to talk to you even though I know I will never have a reply. It calms me down. But then again, every day, and it is every day, I still wake up and think of you.*

*From your loving sister, Rosie (and Jacob, how empty it feels not to say, from Regina.)*

# 1939 Bella

"Flat feet! I have got flat feet so, apparently, I can't fight the enemy," Simon was spluttering with frustration.

It was a gentle June evening, the cloudless sky was deep blue. The family had gathered to celebrate Nat's birthday in the rose-filled garden. Neighbours had popped by earlier for a light supper but now the family, plus Lilly, were on their own. Bella relaxed in a canvas deck chair on the daisy-covered lawn, a sketch pad on her knees.

"And you. Bernard, why aren't you allowed to defend your country?"

"Medical reasons." Bernard looked shifty as he answered. He and Sam were hitting at golf balls with small putting sticks.

"Well, I can't say I am not glad my sons won't be going to war. If this is really going to be a bad war, there will be plenty to do on the home front."

"Well, I am signing up," Sam announced, glancing through the chestnut hair that flopped in front of his face.

"Don't be ridiculous," snapped Bella, "you have medical school and will be much more value as a doctor. Anyway, you are too young."

"Not too young, you can enlist at seventeen." Sam hit a ball into one of the rose bushes. "Sorry, Nat."

"But you don't have to, because you are going to medical school," offered Lilly, shouting across the garden, where she had been cutting herself the bunch of roses Nat always invited her to take home.

"I'm redundant," announced Nat as he joined them, carrying a tray of homemade lemonade, which he planted on the grass. "That teas-maid is amazing. Thank you all. What a great gift. A device that heats water, makes tea, has an alarm and a light. I can get an extra quarter of an hour in bed in the morning. Most welcome." Nat's hair was now nearly all grey and his back slightly stooped. His fingers showed the first signs of arthritis but his eyes were still bright, his skin warm and golden from as much gardening as he could find time for.

"So," he said, "we are to have no soldiers in the family. Thank God for that."

"Sailors, pilots? I would like to be a sailor. They are going to need doctors on ships when they pull all those wounded men out of the sea." Sam was bored with his golf game and had joined Nat, who had started wandering around the garden with a tape measure.

"Oh, Sam, you have to finish your qualifications to be of any use."

"We are all going to have to be of use."

"How are we all going to be of use?" asked Etta, as she and Alan entered the garden by a private path running beside the house. "Sorry to be so late, everyone. It is very busy at the moment. Wars do that to newspapers. Gorgeous roses, Nat, and a very happy birthday. What on earth are you doing?"

Bella sat up straight, hearing the tone in Etta's voice, and put down her sketch pad. Nat was placing the end of a tape measure over one of the fence poles, then slowly walking across the lawn, letting out the tape as he walked. As he did so, it kept dropping out of his hand.

"Sam, grab the other end of this please. Air raid shelter, I am measuring for an air raid shelter. There is room."

"In the garden?" Bella gasped.

"Where else would you like to go when the bombs fall?" asked Etta, sitting down next to her mother. She flicked through the copy of *The Spring Wartime Gardening Guide* that Nat had left on the ground beside his deckchair. "I bet that if this war really happens, Nat will transform all those roses into marrows and potatoes. How sad, but I bet we'll be grateful that he is a keen gardener."

"Ah well, let's hope it never happens." Bella picked up her sketch pad again. "You'll be glad to know that your twin brothers have both been rejected for the fighting. It's the first time Simon's flat feet have been useful. And Bernard, why did you say you were turned down?"

"I didn't," Bernard answered sharply.

Etta and Simon exchanged glances. Then Etta leaned over her mother and peered at her sketch pad. "Let's see what we are going to be wearing in the war."

"War changes everything," mused Bella, as her pencil deftly cut the corners off the bottom of a jacket then trimmed some length off the hem of a skirt and, with a flourish, reduced the width of the collar.

"That's smart," said Etta.

"Hmm, rationing, it's no longer about fashion but less material. I wonder if I can really keep my customers cooking smart through rationing and shortages? They expect it, but I am running out of buttons and it is only one year in. A customer brought over an old pair of silk curtains yesterday. She wanted me to make a dress for her to wear to her daughter's wedding. She said they were of no use any more as the windows were covered with blackout and anyway they let in the light."

"Can you?" asked Lilly.

"Can I what?"

"Make a dress out of curtains."

"Why not? But the daughter is driving ambulances and the son-in-law-to-be is a pilot. She has no idea if they can get leave at the same time and is very distraught. So maybe the curtain dress will cheer her up."

"Oh, how depressing," muttered Bernard, in an exaggerated show of disdain.

"Bernard!" Simon and Etta shouted, both disapproving and almost in unison.

"I'll be making uniforms soon," said Bella.

"Well, that would be better than making shells." Nat tried patting Bella on top of her head but she ducked to avoid his hand messing up her neat hair.

"Shells?" Sam was curious, as he was about everything.

"Yes, in the last war, clothing factories were recommissioned to make shells. The staff worked in shifts around the clock. All part of the war effort." Nat shrugged. "Who knows what will happen this time."

"Maybe it won't happen," Alan said to no one in particular.

"Bernard, why were you turned down?" Bella tried again, ignoring Alan's comment. Bernard pretended to be absorbed by a ladybird crawling up a stalk of grass.

"Lady bird, lady bird…"

Bella shook her head in frustration and turned to Simon.

"Your cinema won't last. It will have to close when—"

"No, it won't and I have an announcement to make. Is everybody listening?" Simon mimed carrying a loud hailer and raised his voice.

"Well, I expect the neighbours are." Nat had rejoined the group and was calculating the measurements for the air raid shelter.

"People need entertainment, the cinemas will remain full. They'll go for safety or distraction or to be with other people. The business will boom, you watch."

"But last time all the cinemas were closed the moment war was declared." Sam liked to think that he had his finger on the pulse.

"Only for a few days while the government decided what to do. So the announcement is…" Simon mimed a drum role "…we are buying two more derelict cinemas, but that will be it, three till the war is over."

"Oh, I thought you might have an announcement about Judith. Where is she, by the way? Nice girl," Bella added pointedly.

"She is with her family. I like them more than they like me. Her father is none too pleased with his beloved daughter having a boyfriend in the entertainment industry or the son of tailors."

"Outrageous. Who would have thought that we would not be considered good enough for the Ritowskys? Her grandmother sold bagels in Petticoat Lane and all her father Danny did was buy a hovel when everyone else was still renting hovels. Then he turned it into a property empire and now he owns several blocks of flats. That doesn't make them any better and no one knows where he got the money in the first place. You are well out of it, Simon."

"Mama, he is not out of it." Etta supported her brother as always. "Just waiting to become a cinema-owning millionaire. Isn't that right, Simon?"

"It is. We are fed up with meeting privately and she is fed up with lying to her father. It's hard to understand. I am an educated Jewish boy with prospects but I am not a dentist or a lawyer or a doctor, so I am not good enough."

"What have they got that we haven't got?" Sam sounded indignant.

"Radiators with a gas boiler. Their house is always warm all over, not in little pockets like ours. Her father thinks that makes him better than us." Simon shrugged.

"Well, we have a telephone," countered Sam.

"So have they."

"Well…" everyone could see that Sam was struggling for ideas "…we have an electric sewing machine."

"But only an electric fire with bars," Simon added. "They have an electric dishwasher, oh, and a car."

"Car? Maybe Judith would wait for me," laughed Sam. Simon jumped up and chased him round the garden, whacking at him with a rolled up newspaper.

"Do they think that car is going to be any use to them? There will be petrol rationing, they won't be able to drive their car as

143

there won't be any petrol," said Lilly, concentrating on slitting the ends of the rose stalks.

"Or food," added Nat. "It's not even the rationing, it's the shortages."

"Maybe we should be storing food, tins of food, baked beans, pilchards, corned beef, evaporated milk and stuff. What do you think, Nat, or is it unpatriotic?"

"I don't think it is very patriotic to starve." Bernard held a handful of golf balls collected from various parts of the garden.

"Maybe you could do that, Bernard, start collecting tinned food to keep. You don't seem to have anything else to do." Lilly found herself talking to Bernard's back, as he turned away from her.

"It's chilly, time to go inside, anyway the news is on in a few minutes. I don't suppose it has got any better," said Bella, leading her family towards the french windows.

"Ah, the military situation," snarled Bernard.

"Bernard, can you put away these deckchairs please, and those golf balls before you drop them again. And you still haven't told me why you were rejected. Etta, I want you to try on a siren suit I made. I think they will be very popular. They are practical, all one piece with a zip…"

# 1939 Rosie

*Dearest sister,*

*It is very strange, suddenly Jacob has decided that he wants to leave Poland. He didn't say where he wants to go but I know he has now had enough. I don't know what happened to make him change his mind and he won't tell me. He came back from the centre of town one day and he was very dirty and very agitated. I think I saw blood on his clothes, certainly lots of dust. I am waiting for him to tell me where we are going and when but I think it is too late now they won't give Jews passports anymore.*

*I bumped into Mendle in the street. It was a surprise as I didn't know he had come back. He said he did not get building work in Germany after all, as now Hitler is there, they are taking the jobs away from Jews. So he wanted to come back to Poland to get away from Hitler. His brother stayed but Mendle and his wife and children came back. 'To my homeland,' he said, 'where I will be safe.' They left everything behind he told me, and snuck back in the way they snuck out. They spent days outdoors in something called a transit camp. Must have been dreadful because it is quite cold already and he said the children got very hungry and two of them were quite sick. But at least they are now safely back in Lodz. He did it quickly because he thinks Hitler is going to close the border to keep the Jews out of Germany. Poor Mendle, he has nothing again but although there are few jobs here, we certainly need our butcher. Let's hope he can find some meat.*

*Jacob is so pleased to see him back. I saw him smile again, that wonderful smile which I have almost forgotten. But he started to put him under pressure immediately saying we must help Poland now. Poor*

*Mendle, who is only worried about how he can feed his children, didn't need to hear this really.*

*Jacob is now trying to raise money for the Army although I don't know who has money to give. Today he even said he would join the Army if that is what it takes to keep the Germans out. Lots of Jews are joining the Army. I wish they wouldn't fight but at least we know we are safe in Poland. But most people are saying that we should leave here too. Well, we can't go chasing around the world but Esther and Yokel, who were our neighbours, have actually gone to China! Can you imagine? Shanghai! Doesn't that sound far away? She didn't want to go really but would always follow him and she says that there are lots of Jews there.*

*Sounds like a muddle here, doesn't it? You must be so pleased that you are so far away from any war that might happen.*

*With love, from your dearest sister, Rosie (and Jacob)*

# 1940s

# 1941 Bernard

Crossing a darkened Trafalgar Square, Etta's hand covered her face to ward off the dust and smell of burning from the savage bombing the night before. The square was sinister in the eerie light created by the reflections of the searchlights that criss-crossed the sky overhead. She relived Bella's cries over and over again. She could not dismiss them. They had been like those of a wounded animal, deepthroated, raw and wild. The family had been sitting around the radio, concentrating on the latest news, when the doorbell rang. Etta read the formal letter from the Navy aloud. Bella sat motionless in her armchair, clutching at her stomach as if she needed to wrench something out of it. Her eyes stared sightlessly at a point on the wall.

One thousand four hundred people had been killed aboard the HMS Hood. Sam Bromavitch-Goldsmith was one of them. He was twenty years old. His medical ambitions had led him to serve with the Royal Army Medical Corps as an orderly. That was the closest Sam came to becoming a doctor. The battle cruiser had been hit by a shell on May 21$^{st}$ 1941, during the battle of Denmark Strait, somewhere between Iceland and Greenland. It was freezing cold and the confrontation had only lasted seventeen minutes.

Some remembered it as the most shocking news of World War Two. For Bella it was the worst news of her life. She placed a photograph of Sam on his piano and lit a candle in front of it. First thing in the morning, sometimes even before she dressed, she stood in front of it. She muttered in a low voice, not prayers, just random words, but never mentioned his name. She suffered a very private grief.

Now Etta, a turban covering her head, wearing a long, slim dark brown coat with large shoulder pads, heavy shoes with high wedge heels and a gas mask swinging defiantly from her shoulders, passed Nelson's column and the famous lions, their shapes now unrecognisable beneath their protection against bomb damage. Etta rehearsed her speech to Bernard, while automatically registering the positions of the public air raid shelters.

Before she entered Lyons Corner House at the end of the Strand, she watched him for a moment through a gap in the blackout material covering the window. How sad he looked sitting alone in a corner, a newspaper in one hand, a cigarette in the other. The table was laid with silver and porcelain. Thick slices of white bread with very yellow spread lay untouched in front of him. He heard her heels as she crossed the pale, green marble floor.

"Even in wartime, a Bromavitch manages to look smart," he announced, getting up to greet her with a kiss. "You are cold."

"My legs are freezing. Painted stocking seams just don't keep you warm."

"I like the coat."

"A utility Bella design," she laughed, kissing him, "and she still hasn't made a uniform. How I hate brown but we are all lucky to be dressed at all, despite rationing and shortages, in some vestige of smart clothes. Mama is as creative with clothing coupons as she is with fashion."

"Tea?"

"How do they do it? I can't believe there is sugar on the table."

"How is she?" Bernard poured the tea out of a silver pot.

"In some kind of deep pain, like a coma really. Just sitting and staring. I've never seen her still before."

"Has she said nothing?"

"I heard her repeating 'no grave, no grave, just the sea'. It was like some kind of chant."

"Do you think she would feel like this if it were any of us?" Bernard stubbed his cigarette out then drew the packet from his pocket. "Smoke?"

"That's a vile thing to say," said Etta, taking one.

"But a genuine question."

"He was her baby, her last child. I am sure all mothers would be the same." Etta picked up a lump of sugar and placed it close to her nose.

"Isn't it a shame that sugar doesn't smell? I bet there won't be any more until this wretched war is over. I'd like to remember the smell." Etta placed the sugar lump into her cup.

"And Nat?"

"He lost a son."

"Stepson."

"Sam didn't remember Oscar. Nat had him from a baby, so he lost a son." Etta's voice was flat. "Bernard, I don't think you should be going away now."

"Is that what you have been sent to say to me?"

"Nobody sent me."

"Not my brother?" Bernard stubbed out his newly lit cigarette.

"For goodness sake, stop wasting cigarettes!" Etta picked up the stub and pointed it at him for emphasis.

"I have to go now, while I still can. I have a friend to go with. It may not happen again."

"Tangiers? What on earth for? Why do you want to go there anyway?

"Adventure."

"We're in the middle of a war." Etta pointed around the restaurant. "Isn't this enough adventure for you? It certainly is for everyone else."

"Tangiers is not really touched by the war in Europe. I have heard of some property and…"

"Property? You have tried that before, wait for the end of the war and there will be plenty of opportunities in property here."

"There is nothing I can do here." Bernard's voice held traces of his childhood whine.

"There is plenty to be done here." Etta's pragmatic reply was the familiar response.

"What? You make spitfire parts, albeit in Slough. My brother entertains people in his cinemas, my stepfather fights fires every night, goodness knows what important work your secretive husband is doing. My mother still manages to dress people even though nobody knows how she gets hold of the materials. There is nothing for me to do. Home Guard, that's what's left. I hate grey, miserable, frightening London. I am fed up with wondering whether I will wake up alive every morning."

Etta sipped at her cold tea and grimaced. "Yuck, that can't be real tea. I miss real tea more than meat or fish or eggs. This is disgusting but honestly, we've got to hand it to Joe Lyons for trying to make it look like a normal time when we all wonder whether we will wake up alive. Is it a woman, Bernard? Is that why you are going?"

"No women, Etta."

"Oh. I'm sorry. It must be difficult with Simon spending most of his time with Judith now…"

"It's everything. I need to go. I have friends there."

"Bernard, everyone needs to go in wartime but people stay. We owe it to one another. What's wrong with the Home Guard? We need the Home Guard."

Bernard stuck his fingers into the full ashtray and pushed the ash into little piles and shrugged. "Boring," he said.

Etta reached one of her chapped hands across the table and placed it on top of his. "I am sorry, Bernard, but I still don't think you should go. It's not right or fair and won't make you happy. It is just running away."

Bernard stroked her hand. "Oooh, spitfire parts aren't good for your skin. Of course it is running away. Doesn't everyone want to run away right now? Why shouldn't I go, if I have a chance?"

"The family is in mourning, we should stay together."

"Bella and Nat can comfort each other."

"They seem to be avoiding each other. I think they are both just too sad. We need you here."

"Do you think I am not affected by losing my younger brother?"

"Are you telling me that this is more difficult for you?"

"No, but Simon has Judith. You have your friends." Bernard stirred his cold tea, picked up a new cigarette, then put it down again. "Do you miss working at the newspaper?"

"Yes, but I make notes, lots of notes. I'll write something about the war when it is over and who knows, maybe go back to newspapers."

"What will you write?"

"I don't know, maybe about being a woman in London during the Blitz."

"Did you walk through Leicester Square, by the way?" asked Bernard.

"No, why?"

"The queues outside the cinema. I bet Simon is going to be a very rich man after the war. They say people are staying to see films three or four times just to stay indoors."

"Good for Simon."

"Yes, good for Simon."

# 1943 Etta

"Oh, we've stopped again," shrieked Debbie.

Etta and her two new friends, Mary and Debbie, had been lucky to find three seats together in a carriage in an otherwise crowded train. It stumbled towards London along the dark tracks, frequently stopping. A spew of grey steam and the rhythmic chug of the engine were the only indications of its existence.

Suddenly it halted so quickly that Debbie's attempt to paint a bow on her lips was ruined as the crimson lipstick jerked across her chin. "Blow!"

Etta laughed as she observed her in the dim light sneaking through the blacked out blinds covering the carriage window. She held a notebook on her lap with one hand, a pencil in the other. "I don't know how you can put makeup on in such darkness."

"Got to try to look good for the returning soldier," Debbie tried again, feeling the shape of her lips with one finger then following the shape with lipstick.

"Is he – returning, I mean?" Etta's voice was gentle, as if she expected bad news.

"Who knows? And what about your old man?" Debbie asked, pointing at Etta's hand, which had swollen in the stuffy overheated train. "I've noticed you wear a ring. Funny, isn't it, we worked side by side in that factory for so long and I've never asked. But I suppose under the circumstances you don't dare. Is he, I mean…?"

"Don't worry. I haven't a clue what he is doing or where he is doing it. Something very confidential, I am not allowed to ask, so I don't."

"Golly. Is he a spy?" asked Mary.

"No, I don't think so, but maybe."

"My younger sister is a pilot," announced Mary proudly.

"That's brave," said Etta, her pencil scrawling across the rough pages of her notebook, ignoring the printed lines.

"I think so too," said Mary, "but she loves it, says it saved her from the boredom of cleaning the kitchen."

"No children?"

"No, they had only been married a few months when he was called up. So she volunteered. Apparently he went mad."

"Mad?"

"Not actually mad, but cross, livid. He wanted her to wait at home for him, but she was one of the earliest women to volunteer."

"Oh, we're off again," said Debbie, checking her face in a tiny mirror.

"Honestly, we could circle the globe in the time it is taking us to get from Slough to London."

"After this war, we'll all be like bats, able to do everything in the dark," Debbie was trying to fill in her lipstick again. "Look, you're writing in the dark."

"Oh, I can write anywhere." The train jerked again and Etta's pencil broke. "Damn, it's my last one. You don't have a pencil, do you?"

"No. How did you end up in the factory? You seem too educated," Mary asked.

"Well, it was a choice between the services or industry. No one is too educated to do war work."

"Me too, and I like it, it's fun even if the hours are long but I am looking forward to my own bed. That factory camp bed felt as hard as these seats." Mary tapped her hand against the resistant wooden seat.

"I hated staying over," said Debbie, "didn't you? Everyone snoring and other personal noises."

"Well, it just isn't worth the struggle to get home. We've been on this train for four hours now." Etta was trying to peel the wooden pencil tip back to reveal some lead.

"But don't you miss your family?" Mary's face was framed with wisps of straggly hair, which she pushed back from her forehead whenever she spoke. "Do you have any other family?"

"Lots," Etta laughed ruefully.

"Don't you like them?"

"Yes, I do really. But it has been good to get away from them."

"So how many brothers and sisters do you have?" Debbie was curious.

"I have twin brothers and my youngest brother, Sam, died at sea."

Mary put her arms round Etta. "I am so sorry. This wretched, cruel war. You have all brothers and no sisters and I have all sisters."

"I had a sister once—" Etta stopped, realising that for the first time she was going to talk about Sara.

"Once? Ooh, a mystery?" Debbie sounded excited but Mary nudged her and she looked contrite. "Sorry."

The train started off again slowly and Etta looked at her companions. They were so different but wore the same overalls underneath their coats. Mary's eyes were dull and fatigued. Etta guessed she was aged somewhere between forty and fifty but looked older because of a lifetime of tedious, backbreaking work. Debbie, not yet twenty, had layered her face with colour that was now badly smudged. Her unkempt hair was streaked yellow where she had attempted to become a blonde. Just below her hairline the peroxide had caused a vicious rash.

"It's alright. She ran away and my mother was so angry she just stopped talking about her and we were never allowed to mention her."

Mary held Etta again. "Wasn't she worried about her?"

"I don't know, I just don't know. It's as if she never existed."

Saying those words aloud to strangers emphasised how irrational Bella had been about Sara.

"She must be worried about her now, surely, bombs and stuff. Why didn't you try to find her?" Debbie was curious.

"I was fourteen when she left. My mother just closed the door on the whole subject."

"You could now, dear," said Mary.

"I wouldn't know where to begin. Maybe, when the war is over."

"Whatever she did, at a time like this, mothers need to know their children are alright. She lost a son and anyway, war changes everything." Mary's voice was comforting.

"It certainly does. We wouldn't have met before."

"No, but why?"

"Why?" Etta echoed, desperate to change the subject. "I am Jewish, you're Catholic."

"How do you know?"

"You wear a cross, I hear you pray. It's obvious. I've never met a Catholic before."

"I've never met a Jewish person before." Mary sounded embarrassed.

"That's what's been great about this, meeting women outside my family."

"I know and you're right, we wouldn't have met." Mary looked down at her hands, roughened by years of housework. "But what about the work? I mean, you're educated and you worked on a newspaper. I was in service. This is better for me, believe me, it feels like I am doing something worthwhile rather than just keeping rich people's homes clean. Oh sorry, maybe you are stinking rich."

"No, not stinking rich, anyway everyone in my family works." Etta laughed.

"Do you have someone cleaning your home?"

"Well, I suppose we did, before the war."

"It could be me, after the war."

"No, Mary, not after all this. You could get a better job now."

"What could I do? I am nearly fifty, too late to learn anything new. It's OK for Debbie."

"Look at what you are doing now," Etta protested.

"What? Helping the war?"

"Precision engineering."

"What's that?" Debbie asked.

"What we do. Precision. Precise. It means exact. You've been trained and you have a proper skill now, you could go on doing it afterwards."

For a moment Mary looked hopeful, and then sighed. "I don't think so. The men who are fighting have to come home to jobs. I am so hungry. Do you think we are nearly there?"

Etta pulled a corner of the blind away from the window then, seeing nothing, started to roll the blind up.

"Don't!" shouted Debbie.

"Alright, no I don't think we are nearly there. I could do with some air. It does smell in here, and look." Etta pointed at a dirt streak running down the carriage wall.

"So filthy. I hate the idea of going back to being someone's servant." Mary rubbed at the dirt with her handkerchief.

"Maybe people won't have servants after the war, well, except the very rich," said Etta.

"Yes, the very rich."

"What do you want to do after the war, Debbie?" Etta asked.

"I want to marry a GI and go to America and have lots of children and a swimming pool!" Debbie sounded very sure of her ambition.

"Oh, we've stopped again. Will we ever get there? So what's your diary about?" Mary asked.

"How the war has changed our lives."

"Has it though?" Mary stretched her back against the seat. "Oh, I am so stiff."

"Yes, it has. I mean, do you think you are good at your job?" asked Etta.

"Yes," Mary answered.

"There you are. Would you have thought that you could have done such a job before?"

"No, but…" Mary was doubtful.

"You see, maybe war did you a good turn. Just think of the fun we have at work, all the singing and silly jokes and laughter, even when we are staying overnight."

"Oh, I hate that," said Debbie.

"Oh, I think its fun, but it's not right to enjoy war," said Mary.

"Not enjoy exactly, but maybe some women have benefited." Etta was at her most reasonable.

"How?" Mary was curious.

"Women have worked out that they can do many jobs as well as men, sometimes even better."

"Still doesn't seem right," said Debbie.

"Maybe not, but isn't it right to try to find something good in this mess?"

Debbie pulled a packet of cigarettes out of her overall pocket, peeked inside and saw only one. "Share?" she asked.

"No, you have it." Etta, forgetting her pencil was broken, attempted to write something, then gave up in frustration.

Debbie lit her cigarette and inhaled deeply. "What jobs?" she asked through a carefully exhaled smoke ring.

"Women are working as labourers, on railways, as plumbers, electricians and of course in the forces."

"Puff?" Debbie held the cigarette out towards Etta, who shook her head.

Mary took the cigarette and dragged slowly onto it. "Is that what you are writing about?"

"Was, until my last pencil broke. I want to write about what has happened to women during the war."

"Don't you think it will all go back to normal afterwards?"

"No, normal will never be the same, not for women anyway."

Suddenly there was boisterous male laughter coming from the train corridor.

"Hey, I think we've got company!" Debbie rubbed viciously at her lipstick-stained chin with a grubby handkerchief. "GIs," she announced.

"You might be in luck," said Mary, nudging Debbie and returning the cigarette. "How can you tell?"

"Well if they were ours, they wouldn't be here, would they? Any nylons, bananas?" she shouted towards the door.

The carriage door was opened by two friendly-looking GIs and Etta noticed how healthy they looked compared to the English forces.

"Hi, girls," said one, plonking himself beside Debbie, who wriggled over to make space beside her.

'War is changing our lives in many different ways,' thought Etta as she watched Debbie give a welcoming smile to the handsome American. She wrote down *Women and Men* with the stub of her pencil.

# 1944 Bella

"Take your shoes off!" Three-year-old Joshua's attempt at a shout was muffled from inside his Mickey Mouse gas mask. His devotion to it was so extreme that no one could persuade him to remove it, so his skin beneath was scoured with a rash that was kept permanently covered with a bright purple antiseptic liquid. Etta obediently removed her boots as she stood on the oak parquet floor. She noticed Bella's look as she observed her grandson. She had only ever seen that look when her mother had been looking at Sam. Etta picked Joshua up and swung him in the air, making a mental note to add it to her notes in the section entitled 'Loss.'

The house was now full. Simon and Judith's wedding in 1941 had been unopposed by her parents after Judith announced that she was pregnant. Her family planned to move to the country but, as Judith refused to join them, they decided she would be safer married to Simon, even though he was well below their expectations, than being single and alone in a Blitz-torn London. As a married woman and a mother she would not be conscripted to war work. Simon was a protective husband and although his career as a cinema-owner did not please them, old values had to change when bombs were dropping.

One had dropped directly onto the little flat in Victoria Street where Simon and Judith had started their married life, which was round the corner from his basement office. Bella and Nat were perfectly happy for them both to move into the Hampstead house and they were given the second largest bedroom. Joshua occasionally slept with them, sometimes in the single room with Etta and occasionally, as a special treat when Uncle Bernard was staying over, on the sofa in the living room with him. This was an arrangement that worried Bella and Judith, as Bernard frequently left his Home Guard rifle propped up against the dining room table. But Joshua mainly chose to tuck up with his Granny and Grandpa Nat in their big double bed, cosy amongst the large soft bolsters and covered by a gold-quilted eiderdown.

Joshua's arrival had given Bella the distraction she needed to make at least a superficial recovery from the loss of Sam. Judith had joined the Women's Voluntary Shelter and while she was out doing what Bella had described as "serving soup, cabbage, bandaging and lots of hugging", Bella looked after him. Bella Unique still kept her busy, although her work was now more to do with 'make do and mend' than fashion, as she improvised, lengthened, cut off, shortened, turned bedspreads into skirts, added patches to knees and elbows. But she continued to design dresses for the future when rationing was over and her clients had money again. The picture of Sam had been moved to her bedroom.

Nat's air raid shelter – it was always thought of as Nat's air raid shelter – could just about accommodate everyone, albeit in cramped and uncomfortable conditions. But Bella said once during a particularly long night inside it, "At least we are all family and not with strangers."

"What are you doing?" asked Etta as she lowered a protesting Joshua to the floor. "Why are you cutting his shoes up?"

"Not up. I am cutting the toes out of his sandals. His feet are growing so quickly. No point in using up his clothing rations when he'll grow out of them in a matter of months. You are late. How are you, how's the factory?"

"Hours longer and longer. Just not enough of us now to keep up the output. It's exhausting but in a strange way, I like it."

"What on earth do you like about it?"

"The other women. It's the first time I have ever had a chance to talk to women out of my own circle."

"Not quite true. What about the newspaper?"

"It's different. I was a secretary and worked for men. Oh, I know I had the odd story published but the men all stuck together. At the factory, we are all in it together, we have a laugh and sometimes a cry. Most of the married women don't know where their husbands are. They just assume that they are alive."

"Come here, Joshua, let's try these on." Bella pulled a protesting Joshua onto her lap.

"They've got holes," he whined.

"Just room for your toes to breathe. Why do they assume they are alive? Joshua, stop that now." Joshua was poking at his exposed toes.

"Because they haven't been told they are dead."

"Oh." Bella went quiet and pushed Joshua off her knees. He peered at his sandals in dismay for a moment and then lost interest.

"Who's here, by the way? Is there by any chance any food?" asked Etta.

"First answer is everyone except the twins. Second answer is the tomatoes are almost ripe, and Lilly brought a tin of dried eggs." Bella pointed to a row of green tomatoes on the window ledge.

"Right, I'll make a powdered egg omelette, my speciality, with water not milk and green tomatoes. Is Lilly staying?"

"Yes, she's resting upstairs right now."

"In my bed," wailed Joshua.

"You are a young man with many beds. Come on, little fellow, you can help me make an omelette." Etta led Joshua into the kitchen and Bella followed.

"It doesn't seem so long ago that we were joking at the very idea that Nat's roses might be replaced by vegetables," said Bella sadly.

Etta placed her arm around her mother's slender shoulders. "You are so thin! It's not like you to look back, Mama. Oh, look who is here," she said as Joshua pushed his way between them and hugged Bella's knees.

"I know and look, we'll have cauliflower and potato soup soon. The veg are nearly ready for eating."

"Self-sufficient. Maybe we'll stay a lot more self-sufficient when this is all over."

"What on earth is all this?" Etta asked, pointing to the sewing machine on the kitchen table surrounded by bits of material and cotton reels.

"Nowhere left to work in this house. The Frognal shop is now full of people camping out. Four shops in four years lost."

"Not lost. You'll get them all back when—"

"I know, the war is all but over and we are lucky, we still have our home."

"And our lives." Etta realised she had made a painful mistake as soon as she opened her mouth. "What's this jacket?"

"Women still want to look smart."

"It's nice. I like that shape," said Etta, starting to pour the powdered egg into a bowl, measuring it carefully. "Don't distract me, I don't want to use too much."

"The shape," laughed Bella, "glad you like it. I actually ran out of material so decided to cut the corners off the jacket to make pockets. It really wasn't a design choice but suddenly I am in business again. People are bringing in their lengths of material for me to make them a jacket with a diagonally cut hem. It's become a Bella design."

"Where are they getting material from?" asked Etta, trying to select the least green of the tomatoes.

"Oh, anywhere they can. Look at this, Mrs Mills brought an old blanket she picked up after a bombing raid. I made a coat for her and I think there is enough left over to make a pair of trousers for Joshua. Come here, Joshua, let me measure you again. I know you will have grown since yesterday. By the way, Judith is pregnant again."

"Oh, is that good? It's hard to feel good about another mouth to feed."

"This time she'll have to breastfeed as there is no baby milk. Hopefully by the time he, she…"

"…or it…."

"…is weaned, the war will be over." Bella sat at the kitchen table and started working on the frayed piece of blanket material. "Have you heard from Alan?"

Etta whisked at the powder and water mixture with a fork. "No. I don't know where he is or what he is doing. Something very secret is what he told me before he left. He looked quite pleased with himself actually. Ah, I wonder who is at the front door. Joshua, go and see but please take your gasmask off first."

"Mama, we need to talk," Etta said suddenly as Joshua scuttled out of the room still wearing his gas mask.

"We are talking."

"No, I mean without Joshua. Some things we need to talk about."

"I won't talk about it. It doesn't help."

"I don't mean Sam. I really don't."

Bella's expression contorted for a moment, then resumed her normal tight control. "What then?"

Against the background noise of Joshua greeting his mother at the front door, Etta confronted Bella. "Sara."

"Out of the blue, or did your new friends just feel like interfering in private family business?"

"The more I talk to other women, the more I think we should try to find out if she is alright."

"What has this got to do with other women? Is this what war does? Suddenly family business belongs to other women?" asked Bella, putting a fork into the egg mixture and watching it run through the prongs. "This looks like egg soup."

"She is my sister and there is a war on."

"Why is this gun still here?" Judith's voice shouted from the hallway. "It's so dangerous."

"Oh, dear. Can't you get Bernard to be more careful? Judith is right, it is dangerous. Even if we are at war, we shouldn't have weapons hanging around." Bella ignored Etta and left the kitchen, slamming the door behind her. Etta sighed in frustration.

# 1945 Jenna

Bernard was one of the very few Londoners not to celebrate VE day in June 1945. It had been a good war for him. He had given in to pressure from both Simon and Etta to stay in London and, coerced into doing 'something useful', resentfully joined the Home Guard. However, like Etta, he had found himself relishing the companionship of people from different backgrounds, many of whom had also been rejected by the forces. As a young, articulate and apparently fit man, he was warmly welcomed and promoted quickly to Commander. He felt worthwhile for the first time in his life, even for once superior to Simon. For although during the war Simon's cinemas continued to be full, serving both as entertainment palaces and air raid shelters, Bernard felt that his Home Guard duties were tangible and directly contributed to the war effort. It gave him the confidence to court Jenna, his first and last girlfriend.

The dinner at the Mansion House, which was given as a thank you to Home Guard officers on the day the organisation was officially disbanded, would have been a bleak and depressing evening for Bernard, except that he took an impressed Jenna as his date. She was dressed in an elegant, navy blue Bella design, which Bella had hastily added inches to around the waist. The colour was chosen to narrow her shape.

"Black would be even better, but I don't want her to look as if she is going to a funeral when we are hoping for wedding bells," said Bella privately to Lilly.

Jenna was short and round, a figure that seemed charmingly appealing in her early twenties, but turned to unattractive fat as she aged. After Bernard had proposed and Bella, who had never gained an ounce in her life, was fitting her wedding dress, she tried to gently suggest that Jenna might be more comfortable in her wedding dress if she shed a few pounds.

"It would flow to the ground more easily," Bella lied.

Jenna responded with her jolly, loud laugh and a bit of cheeky mime, implying that Bernard was happy with her body and therefore so was she. Later, after Bernard had confessed his different sexual preferences to Simon, he claimed it was her body he couldn't stand.

"I couldn't bear to touch her, all that flab. She wobbled when she walked and when I touched her I kept thinking I would get lost in the folds."

Jenna's mother had died in childbirth and she had been raised by her widowed father. Always a demanding and difficult man, he became ill when she was entering her teens and wasted no time in turning his daughter into a house maid, nurse maid, parlour maid and every other kind of maid, long before she had grown up. He made a hobby out of criticising all her efforts at cooking and cleaning as well as her weight. She responded by continuing to give him devoted care out of a sense of misplaced guilt that she was responsible for her mother's death, and by eating more.

After his death she needed to find a job. Having spent her life in domestic service to her father, she had no skills to trade, no way of earning a living and no inheritance. She noticed an advertisement in the local paper for various different levels of staff at a company called B.E.E. and was thrilled to discover that it was a chain of cinemas. Her ready smile and enthusiasm captivated Simon's manager and she became an usherette at his new cinema just north of Oxford Street, happily making the long journey each day from Stoke Newington.

After being confined indoors for so many years, she enjoyed the freedom the bus ride allowed her and every day sat on the top deck gazing down at the shops. At the cinema she was enthralled by the stories unravelling on screen in front of her. When her audience was seated, she would lean against the back wall near the exit sign and imagine herself wearing one of the dresses she had seen in the shop windows. In her fantasies she became the slender, elegant heroine being chased, kissed, maybe even ravished by the handsome hero. Jenna was happy and she had never been happy before. With the little amount of extra money she earned for the large amount of extra hours she worked, she was proud to be able to keep renting the two rooms she had shared with her father.

She noticed Bernard's frequent visits, that his tickets were always marked 'complimentary', and also that he wore the badge of Commander in the Home Guard. He always entered by the door she managed and greeted her warmly when she led him down the steps to his seat. Sometimes she shone her torch a little higher than necessary to look at his face. He occasionally commented on the weather, remarked on the film or muttered a compliment about her appearance. Then one evening, as he made his way out, he asked if she would like to go for a walk when she had finished. Their courtship was quick. Two needy people had by some miracle found each other, just at the right moment.

Simon shared the cost of the big synagogue wedding with Nat and Bella, giving Judith a good reason to complain. Judith had given birth to their second child, Brynah, earlier in the year and regained her figure quickly. She was derogatory about Jenna's shape but it was probably because she couldn't see any reason for Simon to pay for a big wedding, particularly as her own had been a hurried wartime affair.

There was a large reception in a newly built hotel in Portman Square and the guests included many of Bella's clients and Simon's business contacts. There were six bridesmaids dressed in pink and pale green net dresses, designed by Bella, which matched the soft icing on the many-layered cake. The girls were all daughters of friends and contacts, as Jenna had no family. The Bromavitch-Goldsmith family were making a statement.

Whether Jenna ever loved Bernard or just loved being part of the family Bromavitch, no one knew or discussed. She certainly enjoyed the attention he gave her and the promise of an alternative future. She welcomed the opportunity to move out of her father's home and into the first of many marital homes, finally cutting the ties to her past. Despite her background, she was a cheerful young woman and Bernard liked her jolly demeanour, her energy and her wholehearted acceptance of all his wild plans. She treated each new scheme as an exciting adventure and gave her unconditional support when they failed.

For the first time Bernard's projects had the encouragement he craved. Jenna didn't complain about their frequent house moves, attacking all the packing and unpacking with good humour as they moved from rented flat to rented flat, the size and location of each an indication of the success, or otherwise, of the current business venture.

As if in rebellion against her background, she was a lazy housekeeper but Bernard did not appear to notice and the family were never invited to any of their homes. For a while the family, particularly Simon, thought that Bernard was finally settled. He had a good woman who would look after him and stay with him.

Their relaxation did not last long.

# 1946 Rosie

This letter was dated December 1939 and there was no postmark. It arrived in 1946. It was in a Red Cross envelope and bore several official stamps. It was unfinished and was Rosie's last letter.

*Oh dearest sister,*

*I have such bad news. Our magnificent synagogue has been destroyed. Why would they do that? It was just a place of worship and one of the few places left that poor Jews were able to be together. Everyone is very frightened.*

*We have no radio anymore, I don't know why, so my radio is Jacob. When he goes into town he brings the news but he certainly doesn't tell me everything. Yesterday he told me to pack two small suitcases and to put Regina's jewellery into both, splitting it in half as if we were going away separately. That scared me but as I didn't want him to find out that I had sold one of her rings a few months ago, I just did it and didn't ask why. Aren't men strange? I know he wouldn't have noticed what she had and that one piece had gone!*

*But at least he is here. My poor neighbour Miriam, who moved into the room left empty by Esther and Yokel, is by herself with small children. Apparently her husband went into town a few days ago and didn't come back. She is hysterical with worry. They weren't very happy together so she thinks he might have left her. But it's not like a Jewish husband to leave his children. I don't tell Jacob but I try to give her food for the children because I think she has even less than we have.*

*I didn't finish this letter yesterday and today Jacob came home with big news. We are going to have to leave our home. We have lived here* for our whole marriage but I am trying not to be depressed because apparently it is good news although Jacob looked very tense when he told me. Anyway, it's good because we are going to be moved east where there are jobs for everyone. We are going to meet in the town centre (thank goodness I nearly finished packing last night because it is happening very quickly) and take a train to the Baluty district, although apparently it has been renamed Litzmannstadt by the Germans. I don't really like it there and for some reason all the Jews are being put together. With the differences between us, I can't see that this is a good thing but I think we have no choice. However we have been told there will be work for everyone, so that at least is good.

We went to the cemetery to see Regina's grave. Jacob I think was saying some kind of goodbye. He held onto the stone and it reminded me of when we took Regina to see her husband's grave and she talked into the stone. He didn't do the same but I think in his mind he was. In the cemetery the rich and poor are together. Artists are with factory workers, the rich are with the poor. Those who wouldn't eat together, lie together forever.

I have to finish packing now but I'll take this with me to finish as soon as we are settled. I really don't know...

# 1947 Bella

"Judith's pregnant again. I wish it was Jenna." Bella's stocking-clad feet were resting on her drawing table. She balanced a cigarette holder in her mouth and ash fluttered onto the tracing paper, missing the ashtray that stood beside her, amongst other smoking paraphernalia. A cigarette box engraved with her initials was left open, displaying rows of slim cigarettes, each a different pastel shade. The harsh glow of a standard lamp lit the charcoal sketch of a model with tiny waist and a skirt that fanned out to a mid-calf-length hem. Her fingers had remained agile and the outline emerged quickly.

"A line," she announced to Lilly, who stood up to peer over the drawing then returned to lie on the pale green velvet chaise lounge.

In their sixtieth year, the two women could not have looked more different. Bella was still compact and slender, her short boyish haircut was unchanged from the thirties but was now showing a few streaks of grey. She wore less makeup than she had when young and this revealed how unlined her skin remained.

The years had been less kind to Lilly and her complexion confirmed her liking for alcohol. She had blossomed into a buxom woman, now benefiting from the new girdles and waist-length brassieres that controlled the folds but allowed movement as well. Her hair, which had passed through many shades, was now long and bright red. She piled it on top of her head, held up by masses of hairpins, which kept falling out. The children teased that they could always find Lilly by following a trail of fallen hairpins.

Bella was worried about Lilly's drinking and suspected that she sometimes popped back to her flat in Grove End Road from the Bella shop in Finchley for a few sips during the day. Lilly had an office in the headquarters of Bella Unique, which were above the shop. Bella had noticed alcohol on her breath and knew that she had started making mistakes with orders.

"Simon and Judith want a big family, why not, he can afford it. We need to repopulate the country. Shall we have a sherry?" Lilly noticed that Bella checked her watch at this suggestion.

"It's only four o'clock, too early for sherry. Let's wait for Etta, then have tea. Still, I am glad I will have lots of grandchildren."

"Replace the ones we've lost." Lilly realised as the words came out that she had been insensitive. It was an unspoken rule that Sam was never mentioned.

"She had such a difficult time with Brynah, I would have thought she'd take a break. Still, that will silence all those rumours about his film star mistresses and unhappy marriage."

"The price of fame."

"The price of being in the entertainment business, all those long hours and dinners with glamorous women, while Judith is at home getting fatter and drained from childbirth." Bella, who had never become drained by childbirth and had had her children as effortlessly as she designed her dresses, said this with less than total sympathy. "Still, it's Bernard I'm worried about."

"Hm, strange, isn't it? I thought that once he got married he'd settle down and sort out some sort of proper career for himself." Lilly picked up a crystal decanter full of sherry and pointed it towards Bella. "May I?" Lilly gave up waiting to be asked and poured herself a sherry.

"We have to get dressed soon. Don't have any more sherry, for heaven's sake. Simon said there'll be plenty of champagne there." Bella took the decanter away from her.

"Do you think he is going to have more cinemas than children?" Lilly giggled.

174

"Simon? I hope so and I expect Judith hopes so too. Oh, here's Etta, someone who has really left it too late to have a family." She added under her breath, "Shame, Etta would have made a wonderful mother."

"It's not too late." Lilly was still swilling back the remains of her glass. "At least she has a husband. There are hardly any men around now because of the war and anyone any good would have been taken by now."

"Maybe a thirty-six-year-old journalist, whose ambition is to go to war zones and report on women fighting, wouldn't make such a good mother after all." Etta had confided this dream to Bella once, when she was frustrated with her job. She had returned to her east end newspaper as soon as the war finished and was initially treated as a reporter and given important assignments. Then, as the men who had survived started to return, she was relegated back to being the editor's secretary and sometimes, if lucky, covering local events. It had happened throughout the work force and although women might have found it individually frustrating, the need to provide jobs for returning heroes was accepted.

Etta was busy all the time but assigned to the stories the newspaper's stars avoided: dog shows, council meetings, fete openings and occasional trips to court for minor cases. Even a local newspaper reported on much more exciting news than Etta was covering and she listened with interest to her colleagues as they discussed gang murders, corrupt officials and robberies.

Nonetheless, she was valued as a reliable and objective if uninspired 'hack' who could be depended upon to check her facts and cover a story in detail with the minimum of drama. When the paper was ready for printing, the editor often called upon her if he was short of a few lines of copy. Etta always had something non-confrontational in her desk drawer, immaculately typed out with three perfectly edited carbon copies. Etta seemed satisfied to write and get published usually for interviewing a local VIP or visiting celebrity. She was chosen for these tasks as she was unimpressed by fame but admiring of achievement, so the articles were free of overt enthusiasm.

As a female, she knew she was lucky to maintain the job and have so much trust invested in her, but mainly she appreciated that, unusually for a woman, she was not expected to write for the fashion and domestic pages. She had made her only mistake the one time she was sent to an haute couture show in Park Lane. There was no one available from the women's pages and it was assumed that, as the daughter of Bella of Bella Unique, she would be completely at home in the world of fashion. However, having paid so little attention to her mother's business, her report was a disaster and it was the last time she was sent out to such a story.

"Hello, you're late," Bella turned to greet her daughter.

"Sorry, I met Bernard. He wanted to have a cup of tea with me to explain why he couldn't come tonight. We met at Lyons Corner House in the Strand, our usual place, and guess who I saw there?"

"Who?" Bella was intrigued.

"Shouldn't you be getting dressed? I'll come upstairs with you and chat while you change. I'm going like this, I hope it's OK, not exactly a Bella design but I am going to report on this for the paper anyway, so it's a working wardrobe."

They made their way upstairs. Lilly went into the spare room she had inhabited for the past week and Bella and Etta went into the main bedroom.

"Where's Nat?" asked Etta.

"Oh, he can't come tonight, he has something else to go to," Bella answered evasively.

"Should you be there too?"

"My son is opening his fifth cinema. That is where I must be. I am so proud he has been so successful despite the war."

"The war was kind to some people. People wanted entertainment, cinemas grew. Look at you, clothes rationing, uniforms, bombed buildings and yet your business survived."

"Mine just survived, his thrived. I wish you would—"

"I think you are going to start on me. Is it the journalism or the lack of children you are in the mood to attack tonight? Leave me alone and by the way, Lilly is drinking too much. You should say something."

Bella sighed and pulled a mauve silk dress over her pale, skin-coloured petticoat and asked from inside the silk, "So, who did you see?"

"Oh yes, one of the waitresses, Eloise Simmons, used to be Goldblum. She used to sew for you. I think you trained her up as a seamstress before the war, then gave her a job in the factory."

"Oh, little Eloise, my goodness, that poor child had dreadful boils. I remember treating them for her once. I wonder if they left scars. Did she recognise you?"

"Oh, yes we talked. I asked her why she left you. She said she lost her husband. He was caught in the Bank station bomb. He was in the army and had been home on leave. She and her baby were living with her mother-in-law. She wanted to earn more money to get one of the new flats being built to replace what was bombed. It was money, nothing else. She said that there is lots of work now for girls, particularly waitresses and sales girls in the new shops. Those jobs pay better than factory work now, she said."

"I remember Eloise, she was very good, she had a skill. What a waste for her to be a waitress."

"I am thinking of doing an article about how the war has changed women's lives."

Bella sat at her dressing table, her makeup now immaculate, trying out different combinations of jewellery.

"When you are completely dressed, look in the mirror and take something off!" she announced, removing one strand of pearls. "Don't forget to include employers like myself, who can't compete with the wages and keep losing good girls to restaurants and shops. My working life has also been changed by the war. How do I look?"

# 1949 Simon

Simon clipped his carefully nurtured moustache into the exact shape he preferred. He raised his face so that his chin pointed directly at the mirror and he could see the hairs inside his nostrils. Gently, he cut away the longest, until he was satisfied with his appearance. From his dressing room cupboard, he chose a shirt from a large collection hanging neatly in rows ordered by colour, from pale to dark. Each one of his selection of ties was placed next to the appropriate shirt.

Stravinsky was playing on his radio. Simon enjoyed the coarseness of the sound, it jarred his imagination. He had tried to introduce the music to Bella, thinking that she should understand the mood of the post-war world.

"What is this noise?" she had said dismissively, preferring to hear romantic melodies on the phonograph he had given her for her last birthday.

Stravinsky was a good start to this difficult day. He had done his exercises particularly vigorously in the morning, preparing himself for two arguments. One was a minor but ongoing disagreement with Bella about Saturday daytime openings for children. In all his cinemas, Saturday tickets were cheap and set aside for children's films. Bella disapproved of making entertainment, which she considered frivolous and a second-rate pastime compared to work, so available. She had never forgotten the twins dodging their lessons to go to see films, and was convinced that it was possible to run a successful cinema empire without this additional service. Simon, irritated but familiar with her interference, knew that it was an opportunity to capture the audience of the future.

The other was a major row with Judith about another despatch of money to Bernard. He didn't want to argue with her as she was so close to giving birth. He couldn't understand her constant anxiety about money. He recognised that she was a born worrier, despite having been brought up with wealth. He did however recognise the pattern that, towards the end of each pregnancy, she became even more nervous. Etta explained that it was something to do with the mothering instinct and natural stressing over being able to shelter one's baby. He did not think Etta was the ideal advisor on such an issue but she was a ferocious researcher and had an enormous amount of information available to her in the newspaper's library, so usually her facts were correct.

Simon stroked a delicate touch of pomade onto his hair then took a nail file to his cuticles. He looked rich and indeed he was now nearly rich. His elite group of cinemas had started in converted theatres and dance halls but he had based their design on his early experiences as a cinema-goer. He wanted the opposite of the uncomfortable seats, murky screens, unnecessary queues and dirt of his youth. His creed was that the environment itself should be part of the film-going experience, and this should start the moment the audience walked through the entrance. And indeed, he was renowned for the comfort of his premises. A Broom's cinema was always beautiful, clean, well-organised. Each one had a different theme. One featured shells and sea colours on the walls and the proscenium. This was The Grotto Picture Palace. The Festival had plaster palm trees wrapped around the pillars surrounding the entrance. The Palace glittered like a mini Versailles. His latest, The Oriental, was an uneasy mix of Chinese and Turkish. Despite their different names, they were all recognised as Broom's and Simon Broom was admired by distributors, producers and audiences. He installed innovations the moment they were available. His London cinemas had wide screens and sound systems that were so real, he had watched audiences turn around to look for a horse and carriage that sounded as if it was coming towards them, or duck beneath a bullet that seemed to be whistling past their ears.

No food was allowed inside the auditorium, so the kiosks did brisk business in the intervals, which were slightly longer than the large chains offered. To anyone who grumbled at not being able to munch sweets in their seat, he replied, "You are here to watch a film, not eat a meal!" It was a saying he became famous for later.

He had learnt key lessons of diversification from Bella. Her couture business, ready-made shops and mail-order business were paralleled by his new-release cinemas, news cinemas and classic film cinemas. His chain spread beyond London and its suburbs to Manchester, Birmingham and Newcastle, and when new towns like Harlow and Hemel Hempstead appeared on the map, Simon Broom planned to build modern cinemas to attract a new audience. He did not compete with the large chains yet, although that was his ambition. He wouldn't until he was ready.

Still, Bella thought he was in too much of a hurry but Simon's expansion was steady, and he knew that with the growing popularity of cinema after the war, he needed to move quickly. She thought he took risks, but he pointed out that he had never taken the type of risks she had. But these complaints were nothing compared to the outrage she had expressed when he had changed his name legally to Broom just at the beginning of his remarkable climb to fame. His explanation that Bromavitch was too complicated did not impress her and she alone continued to call him Simon Bromavitch. What he hadn't said was that it was too Jewish, which worked in Hollywood but not in England.

Simon's office remained in the same building, just off Victoria Street, where he had first proudly placed his name plaque on the cellar door. 'Broom's Entertainment Empire' it had proclaimed to the few people, mainly cleaners, who passed his door on their way to the rubbish bins. No one else went to the cellar. From the beginning he had fantasized about a large, brass sign announcing B.E.E. right across the front door of the whole building.

The space had originally been lent to him by the husband of a client of his mother's, who was intrigued by his determination and enterprise. While Mrs Bentley had been choosing a selection of dresses for a cruise, Simon's visionary ideas had caught the attention of Mr Bentley, who promptly offered his derelict cellar to the young entrepreneur, assuming that either the dream would die, or he would actually survive working in the damp cellar with the rats for company. If that were the case, in future Mr Bentley could proudly boast that he gave Simon Broom his first 'break'. Now that cellar was pristine and clean, the rats had long since been sent on their way and Broom's Entertainment Empire stored its filing cabinets down there and operated from the top two floors.

Simon himself worked in the penthouse overlooking the rooftops of Westminster. His desk and all his office furniture were chrome and shiny glass. A cocktail cabinet had recently been installed; it was delicate inlaid rosewood and mahogany and its label had claimed it was eighteenth century French. He had bought it at a Sotheby's auction, to the consternation of Judith and total disapproval of Bella.

"Old furniture, why?" Bella had protested when invited to view her son's new acquisition. Coming from the wrong generation to appreciate an antique, she did not recognise that this piece was merely the beginning of Simon's collection, which would one day be sold for a huge sum of money. His offer to Mr Bentley to purchase the entire building had just been accepted and agreed on a very emotional handshake.

"Little Simon Broom," Mr Bentley had said, sucking on his unlit cigar, "it is like handing over my child, a treasured first-born, so I am glad it is you."

No, Judith certainly had no need to worry about money, but Simon had every reason to worry about Bernard.

*

"This is just like a film," Etta whispered nervously to Simon as they stood together outside the Greyhound pub in Hackney. It stood on a dark corner where two residential streets met. The pavements and gutters held the residue of the day's market. Etta and Simon had picked their way through rotten vegetables, egg-shells, paper rubbish and slimy things they didn't want to identify. The stench was of mould and decay.

Approaching the doorway, Etta had tripped over an abandoned shoe and gasped in relief as Simon grabbed her arm, saving her from slipping into the debris. The glow through the frosted glass windows provided the only light. Paint was peeling from the bottle-green doors. Simon held Etta's arm protectively and, leaning over her, peered through the window. The engraved word 'Greyhound' presented him with a clearer view and he could see that people were leaning on the bar and moving around inside. There was a low murmur of voices and the occasional raucous laugh. Somewhere in the background he could hear a voice singing to a piano that was bashing out a jazz tune.

Simon wished he was anywhere else, preferably back in the comfort of his own office, but he was concerned that as the son of Bella of Bella Unique and the brother of a highly regarded cinema entrepreneur with a growing reputation, Bernard's exploits, if illegal, could attract the interest of the newspapers.

Recently, when Bernard had been arrested wandering around the women's lingerie department of Swan and Edgar, it was mentioned in a small paragraph in the London newspapers. Simon knew that he, Simon Broom, was really established when Bernard was described as his twin and not Bella's son in the reports of the scandal. There was an explanation, written by B.E.E.'s public relations department, a police apology and Bernard was released with a caution, after providing the apparently acceptable reason that he had been choosing a present for his new bride. The family did not accept this excuse as readily as the police, but were publicly more than prepared to give him the benefit of the doubt.

Nevertheless, Simon had not felt at ease having Bernard followed by a private detective, so he and Etta had decided to follow him themselves. He justified his decision to Etta because his instincts and long experience warned him that Bernard was likely to be involved in some unsavoury activity. Simon could not, in all conscience, bear the idea of standing by and watching his brother get into trouble again.

Simon's bond with his twin had been stretched to the limit over the past ten years. From their first serious row, which had taken place the year he met Judith, just when he was trying to impress both her and her family, he knew that he had been manipulated by Bernard.

After the war and since losing the status he had gained from his position in the Home Guard, Bernard's business endeavours had gone from the pathetic to the dismal, to the catastrophic and the borderline illegal. Bankruptcy had been avoided on more than one occasion only because of Simon's frequent last-minute interventions and rescue packages. His property enterprises were disastrous; his strategy of cashing in on the post-war property boom looked promising on paper but his choice of locations and, worse, his selection of business partners was always dubious. What he built all but fell down, what he rented out remained unpaid for. Court cases were frequently threatened and fending them off had become a way of life.

The hope that marriage to Jenna would change him and encourage him to become more responsible had not been fulfilled. Simon and Etta had been disappointed that Jenna seemed unconcerned and continued to laugh her way through his exploits.

Finally, after several other near-misses with the law, Bernard had recently announced that he had a job. "A proper job," he said.

Both Simon and Etta noticed that for a while he had been wearing smart suits from Saville Row, silk shirts and ties almost as wide as his grin. He had brought strawberries out of season for Bella one evening, in a Fortnum and Mason box, and Jenna flaunted a pair of sapphire and diamond earrings. His accent, carefully nurtured at Bella's insistence to be upper-class English, now displayed a touch of the very Cockney she had worked so hard to avoid. All those hours of listening to radio announcers were, for the moment anyway, wasted. Lately, Bernard had claimed to be very busy working, though he did not say at what – all anyone knew was that he was too busy to visit the family, particularly in the evenings.

Simon and Etta had agreed that ensuring his safety and legality was in his own best interest and together they questioned Jenna. First she said he was "at business". Then, after further persuasion, she had told them that he often met his friends at a pub called the Greyhound in Hackney, and they had taken the tram east.

"What can you see, what's happening?"

"Nothing much. There are a few people at the bar. Some are standing round a piano. Nothing much really, it's just a pub."

"Shall we go in?" Etta's voice sounded excited rather than nervous. "I've never been inside a pub."

"For heavens sake, you are not here on duty as a journalist!"

"What next then?" whispered Etta.

"Wait, I suppose, till he comes out." Holding Etta tightly, Simon glanced away from the door and down each side street in turn. "Look, there is another window. Let's have a look, but be careful."

Slowly they made their way, Etta striding ahead, warming to the adventure, Simon gingerly guiding himself by touching the dank walls. The window they reached was covered with what looked like two leftover wartime black-out blinds. There was a gap where they did not meet exactly. Brushing his jacket, Simon stared in.

"Can you see what they are doing?" asked Etta, straining to see over his shoulder. Giving up, she leant against the side of the building and waited for his report.

"Hard to see," he said, squinting, "it's very smoky. There are some people sitting at a table in the corner. There is money on the table."

"Poker?"

"I don't know, maybe, but I can't see any cards."

"And Bernard, can you see him?"

"No."

"Are they drinking?"

Simon stood back from the window and stretched his back, putting his hands above his head and pulling. He leant his head slowly to each side.

"Owch, I don't think I am cut out to be a detective." He looked at his dusty clothes in disgust.

"Go on," Etta encouraged, "look again. Tell me everything you can see."

Simon peered in.

"I can't see any cards, but there are lots of beer glasses, two telephones, paper, pencils and lists. I can't quite see, but looks like numbers."

"Numbers, oh it's gambling. Simon, it's gambling. Why didn't we think of that? Do you remember that summer when he decided he wanted to be a bookmaker's runner? He has always been fascinated by gambling."

The sound of a car approaching interrupted their conversation.

"Oh my God, it's a police car!" Etta was suddenly terrified.

"Stand back, look here, let's hide in that doorway." Simon pulled Etta away from the window. They dashed across the street and huddled into a shady doorway on the opposite side of the road. It was covered in cobwebs and smelt of stale urine. Simon recognised the irony that he and Etta might be arrested. After all, Bernard was just having drinks with friends in a pub and there was nothing illegal about that, but he and Etta were loitering, which was at least sinister, if not actually wrong.

"Is snooping against the law?" he muttered to himself.

Etta glanced at her watch. "It is nearly ten o'clock. Past drinking time, oh my God, they are going to raid for illegal drinking."

Nervously they crouched down and saw two police officers bang on the door of the pub. It opened and Bernard came out accompanied by another man. They were laughing and obviously drunk. Bernard and his companion greeted the policemen jovially and the officers responded with familiarity, like old friends. Simon tried to hear what was being said but was too far away.

Bernard, who seemed to be joking with the officers, took a wad of notes out of his pocket and carefully counted them out. He handed a pile to one of the policemen, who laughed, counted the money and then, with a friendly wave, returned to their car and drove off. Etta, shaking with tension, held on tight to Simon's arm as they watched in astonishment. Bernard put his arm round the other man's shoulder and together they walked unsteadily towards a Cadillac, which was parked down one of the side streets. They laughed and hugged each other close before getting into the car.

"Let's go home," croaked Simon huskily, pretending he had not noticed that Etta, strong, tough Etta, was crying silently.

"Oh, poor Jenna, poor, poor Jenna," she sobbed.

Simon had parked his black Morris Minor in a field next to a lake. It was one of the first of the newly launched cars and he was extremely proud to own it. He had wanted a Jaguar but Judith was opposed to him spending so much money on what she considered to be an unnecessary purchase. With her anxiety about his support for Bernard, he had decided that acquisition could wait.

The grass, parched from a long, hot summer, was now sodden from a recent rain burst, which had hit them as they arrived. They waited in the car for a while, Bernard chain-smoking, as they talked.

It had taken Simon weeks of persuasion then finally a threat to withdraw financial support to convince Bernard that they needed a serious and private talk about his future.

"Who was that man?" asked Simon, rolling down the window to clear the smoke.

"A friend."

"A gambling friend?"

"A friend," Bernard repeated defensively.

"But what kind of friend?"

Bernard shrugged his shoulders and stared out of the window.

"And what about Jenna, what happens to Jenna?" asked Simon.

"Nothing happens to Jenna. I'll take care of her." Bernard's voice was husky, maybe from the cigarettes, maybe from emotion.

"How, you can hardly take care of yourself?"

"I'll find a way."

"What way, illegal gambling?" Simon was furious. "The rain has stopped, let's walk to the lake."

Bernard looked down at his patent leather shoes that were fashionable but not appropriate for an outdoor walk. Cautiously he stepped outside the car. They passed hedges displaying small green blackberries, which Simon hit at absent-mindedly as he passed and then rubbed his hands where the thorns had caught his skin. They reached the edge of the lake, which was surrounded by tall purple reeds, yellow wild flowers and bullrushes. A moorhen floated close to the bank where the dandelions were seeding.

Avoiding the nettles, they stood together quietly for a while, watching ducks swim past, showing no curiosity. A dragonfly hovered over the water, which was carpeted with patches of green weed. A gentle wind, augmented by the calls of different birds, rustled the leaves and loosened a few. Simon watched them fall gently onto the water's surface.

"Why did you marry her? Bernard, for God's sake, why did you marry her?" Simon's voice broke through the natural sounds of the countryside.

"It was expected of me." Bernard shrugged and took a few deep breaths. "Anyway, I like her."

"But don't love her?" Simon grabbed Bernard's shoulders and forced him to look him in the eyes. "How could you do this to all of us?"

"Ah," said Bernard, slowly releasing air from his lungs, "this is about the wedding, the costly wedding. Is that why you care so much? Nobody asked you to pay for it."

"That's unfair," said Simon, swiping at a bush displaying a few young hazelnuts.

Bernard lit a cigarette and threw the match onto the ground.

"For God's sake, be careful," scowled Simon, "you will start a fire."

"For God's sake," imitated Bernard, "it's wet, look." He splashed his feet into a puddle that indicated recent rain. "I got married because it was expected of me and I genuinely liked her. I still do."

"What did," Simon hastily corrected himself, "do you like about her, as it appears that you don't like women at all?" He kicked at the ground.

"Now who is being unfair?" whined Bernard, sounding remarkably like his fourteen-year-old-self. "Of course I like women, what are you talking about? I love women, just not that way. It just doesn't happen for me, don't ask me why, I don't know."

"But what happened with Jenna, I mean what happened? Don't go away, where are you going?" Simon's voice rose as he watched Bernard wander away from him, then return.

"I am not going anywhere, this conversation is well overdue," Bernard said, looking Simon directly in the eyes. "Do you mean in bed? On our wedding night? Nothing. We cuddled, that's all, and went to sleep."

"But didn't she…oh God." Simon's voice was tense and incredulous. "What am I doing?" he asked in despair to a pigeon flying by overhead.

Bernard scratched randomly at the bark of a tree, leaving tiny shavings at the base of its trunk. He churned the earth around with his feet, then shrugged and looked helplessly up towards the sky.

"Answer me, just answer me, what did you like about her?" asked Simon, as if that question held all the answers he needed.

He moved closer to his twin and placed an arm around his shoulders. Together they stared across the fields into the distance, neither one of them wanting to break the mood.

"Why are we doing this?" asked Bernard eventually, his head just reaching up over Simon's shoulder so that he could breathe. "I am very busy, you know."

"Ah, ha," said Simon, "you are very busy, I know."

"Well, why are we doing it here?" Bernard's voice once again assumed its youthful whine.

"Why not, do you want to have this conversation in front of the whole family? Is that what you would prefer?"

"No, of course not."

"So why did you marry her? It's obviously not what you wanted."

Bernard moved slightly away from Simon and breathed deeply, filling his lungs with the fresh, damp air. A heron swooped down towards a tiny island in the middle of the lake, landed and folded its wings. Bernard watched as the graceful bird settled and became still.

"We have to work out what to do." Simon was brusque.

"We?"

"If it is a divorce, it's a family matter."

"Why, it's my divorce? Anyway, I offered to divorce her but she doesn't want a divorce. Anyway, one of us would have to claim adultery. If it was me, it would look bad for her and if it was her... well, it would look even worse for her, so we'll stay married. I know I shouldn't have married her. I ruined her life."

"Oh, don't be so dramatic, Bernard. Her life is still better now than it was before you married her and Jenna is family now, we'll take care of her." Bernard watched the heron fly off, its wings momentarily blocking out the sun.

"I wish I could fly away, just fly," he said wistfully, waving an arm towards the sky.

"When did it start?"

"What do you mean – it? You sound like a doctor. It is not a disease."

"It is a disease. There must be some treatment. You have to stop. It is not right."

"I can't stop, anyway, why should I? Who am I hurting? I am happy for once. I'm with someone who understands me and I understand him." Bernard shrugged.

"Oh, don't Bernard, it's wrong, it's—"

"Perverted? Is that what you were going to say? That is what Bella would say. You sound like your mother."

"Our mother, except that she doesn't know and must never know."

"So she doesn't know and will never know, and Jenna doesn't, so who am I hurting?" Bernard kicked at a nettle bush.

"They'll find out. Someone will tell them, you know what it is like."

"No, I don't. I am so careful, boringly so. I don't pick up men in the street, or parks or urinals, any of the obvious places."

Simon placed his hands firmly on his brother's shoulders and stared down into his eyes. "Where then?"

"Private parties and sometimes clubs, but I don't do that anymore. I don't even go to Turkish baths anymore."

"What anymore? What anymore, did you pick up men in Turkish baths?"

"Well...once, it was only once, the ones on Marshall Street. You don't want the detail."

"I do want the detail, I have a cinema around there."

"I know, a newsreel cinema. I go there sometimes."

"What happened?"

"I met someone."

"Did you pay?" Simon's voice boomed into the quiet air and several birds left the safety of their perches from the trees above them.

"Pay? I don't pay," Bernard sounded outraged.

"Anything is possible with you lot," said Simon disdainfully. "It is a good thing you didn't get into the forces. Oh God, is that why?"

"Why what? Let's go back." Bernard started to walk away from the lake.

"No, we haven't finished. Is that why you were rejected by the forces?"

"Maybe, I had a medical. Heavens, Simon, you know. You had that medical too. You know what awful things they do – up your... oh you know." Bernard marched ahead, his head raised high. Simon could not see that there were tears in his eyes.

"Bernard," Simon shouted, "is that why you were rejected?"

Bernard stopped, turned his head and answered quietly, "Yes."

Simon caught up with him and stood in front of him. "Is that why you are going to Tangiers?" His voice was full of disgust.

"Yes."

"Not property?"

"Not property." Bernard broke away from his brother's gaze and restraining arm and walked forward again.

"Is it a queer's place, then?" Simon shouted at his back.

"People don't mind so much, that's all. I don't spend my time worrying about Bella or Jenna, or whether that gorgeous man following me or even touching my thigh in your cinema, yes, by the way, in one of your cinemas, is a plain-clothed policeman."

Simon's back crumbled in defeat and he sank to the ground, not feeling the wetness beneath him. "Are you going with him?"

"Yes."

"Then don't come back till it is over," said Simon, his voice ice cold.

It was over long before Bernard left but Simon never knew that. Bernard discovered the hard way that being the brother of a rich man had its drawbacks. When he told his 'friend' that Simon would not support their trip to Tangiers or invest in their property venture, he found he was on his own. He told Simon none of this; he just took his hurt with him.

# 1950s

# 1950 Etta

Etta and Alan were packing up their room in the Hampstead Garden Suburb house, having rented a small flat in a new block overlooking Regent's Park.

"Waste of money," had been Bella's reaction. She was not only infuriated because she wanted her daughter and the very useful Alan to continue living with her, but also because the block of flats was one of those owned by Judith's family. She didn't want any member of her family, whom they perceived to be inferior, paying them rent.

She had said, "Why can't you stay here? It is not as if you need room for children." Bella never missed an opportunity to remind Etta of her failure to produce grandchildren.

"Let's hope Madam Bella is not going to make a fuss again." Etta had invented this nickname for her mother when she was being particularly impossible and demanding.

Alan was struggling to pack bedclothes into a trunk. "You've got to understand that it is hard for her to see the last of you leave."

"Not the last. There's still Bernard, he hasn't really left home. He can't stay in Tangiers forever."

"A year now, do you think Jenna misses him?"

"I don't know. She seems very happy being nanny to Simon's children. It's the perfect arrangement. Simon helps her without anyone losing face and the children dote on her."

"What did his last letter say?" Alan asked, trying to close the lid of the trunk.

"Oh, well, you know Bernard, another project, another disaster, another excuse."

"I was a bit doubtful about his idea of buying property and developing it for tourists, he wasn't very successful with property here."

"There was a war on. There isn't in Tangiers and they say that it is becoming a popular tourist destination." Etta displayed the optimism she always pretended to have about Bernard. "It is warmer than the South of France and the war finished off Europe anyway. No one is going to want to go to Europe for their holidays. Let's hope for once he has got it right."

"I hear some very weird people go there…oh sorry, I didn't mean Bernard. Right, I think we are nearly done," said Alan.

"Well, he had to do something, he couldn't go on relying on Simon's help forever because Judith will stop Simon giving him money eventually, particularly if she goes on breeding."

"Yes, and Simon says money is tight now that his newsreel cinemas are being threatened by television, not that we should worry about Simon, he will always have some plan up his sleeve."

"Maybe making a complete break was the right thing for Bernard to do. It is hard for twins, especially when one is so… well, everything: clever, good-looking, successful with women, you name it and Simon is it. Bernard just got a bit left behind." Etta always managed to remain sympathetic to Bernard despite the aggravation he had caused the family.

She looked around the room as if she was never going to see it again. She had never liked the pale pink walls, shiny pink bedspread with the baby camel motif, the bedside lamps with pale cream pleated shades, but it had been Bella's choice for her daughter. Etta, though recognising that Bella's taste in soft furnishing did not match the expertise of her understanding of fashion, still appreciated the hard work that had gone into building this home.

"Anyway, there is no sign of him returning and that's just as well as he and Jenna would now be left living alone with Mama, and we all know that couldn't work." Etta was wiping dust off the now empty dressing table.

"I don't know, that might have been his chance to have Bella's undivided attention. Simon was always so brilliant, Sam was the perfect baby and then there was you, the only girl…" Alan finally shut the lid on the trunk. "What next?"

"Curtains. Not the only, don't forget Sara." Etta had told Alan the story of Sara before they married. It was a secret he wished he didn't know as, working so closely with Bella, he frequently wanted to ask questions. But he didn't.

"I don't, although because she is never mentioned, it is easy to forget you had an older sister."

"I know, I learnt to forget about it a long time ago. Then something reminds me and I wonder what happened to her. The older I get, the less I can understand Bella just letting her go and never trying to find her, particularly during the war."

"It is as if everyone believes that the superstructure that is Bella Unique—"

"Madam Bella."

"Alright…Madam Bella would collapse if she was ever confronted with it."

"You know, during the war I used to have this fantasy that Sara would show up at the front door, needing us and all would be forgiven and forgotten, whatever it is that we are forgiving and forgetting."

"Do you think Bella worried about her during the war?"

"I don't know. In a funny way she was happy during the war with all of us at home, Nat devoted to her and Bella Unique surviving against all odds. I don't understand why he decided not to carry on working with her after the war. I think that was unfair."

"Here, hold the ladder," said Alan as he climbed up to take down some curtains. "Why unfair? I think he did it to save their marriage. Working and living together, not easy with someone as strong-willed as your mother. Anyway, he still runs the mail order business."

Etta looked around her bedroom, now packed up and looking forlorn. "Nearly forty and finally a home of my own."

"You specialise in doing the major events in your life at nearly something, like marrying me at nearly thirty."

"I wonder what I will do at nearly fifty and then at nearly sixty."

"Right, we are ready, I think. Come on, before you change your mind, or Madam Bella changes it for you."

The move was supported by the proceeds of Etta's syndicated column in a national newspaper. She credited Alan with the idea of turning the meticulously ordered notes she had taken so obsessively during the war, into a series of articles. He had watched her boredom increase and recognised that she had found it hard to settle back into a routine after the war.

"Night court is occasionally interesting but I only get to cover that when someone is sick and I can't stand another council meeting or school sports day. I have to find something else to do. If I don't, I will go on just going to work, coming home, arguing with Bella, then going to work again. And living here is getting tedious because there are so many subjects that are forbidden."

She dared not show any interest in Bella Unique for fear of being coerced into getting involved. Etta knew that mentioning Sam was understandably too painful for Bella, but she remained frustrated that she could not ask about Sara and find out Bella's reasons for completely cutting her out of her consciousness. Since the war, their loss of Sam and her experience of other people's tragedies, Etta's memories of Sara's constant presence during her childhood had become more vivid and her curiosity about her whereabouts more intense. But it was fruitless; Bella could not be persuaded to even acknowledge her existence. Etta needed a new challenge, a new place and new people.

"Like your mother," Alan had commented about her once, "only her challenge was constant and about survival so she didn't have the luxury of feeling bored. What about that idea you had about women's lives in wartime? Why don't you do something with that?"

The inspiration for the first article originated from the overwhelming need Etta still felt to communicate with Sam. She didn't believe in reincarnation, she was far too down-to-earth for that, but she did take comfort from talking to him as if he were with her. She needed to say, 'Listen, Sam, we were with you, you were not alone, the suffering also happened on the home front. We were all part of the same tragedy.'

Struggling to find a way to express this, she turned her notes into narrative.

She wrote at home, with a picture of Sam in front of her large yellow writing pad. Her pencil raced across the pages, her own grief affecting the mood of the piece so intensely that she captured the tragedy of millions. She wrote of women coping with the loss of husbands and sons and the horror of the unknown when 'missing in action' was the only information given.

The article was entitled 'Loss, Women at War', and printed below the title were the words 'by Etta Broom'. She thanked Simon for her new name.

"It is not about myself," she had told the editor of the East Express, when presenting the idea. Like many editors, he was looking for a way to attract and keep intelligent women who didn't just read fashion pages now but wanted their more active lives reflected in the main body of the newspaper. Researching readers' views was a new technique and editors had learnt from retailers that they needed to understand and adapt to women's changing attitudes and spending power if they were to maintain their circulation figures. Etta's timing was perfect.

Although the concept was based on her own experience, she concentrated on writing objectively and so hit a nerve in the collective female post-war psyche. Women who had lived through such times relished the opportunity to relive them and were grateful that the significance of their wartime roles had been recognised, although in a different way from those of the returning heroes.

The first article was controversial. In some readers' views, it suggested that women bore the brunt of war. That is not what Etta had meant at all, but the numbers of letters the paper received created the right environment for a second article appearing in the paper as 'Women in Wartime – Endurance' by Etta Broom.

She wrote about women dealing with shortages, blackout, rationing, losing homes and having babies while the bombs fell. She did not mention names but described Bella and Judith taking it in turns to look after Joshua, and Judith rushing through dangerous streets to do her shifts at the Women's Voluntary Shelter. She described women who had never done anything for themselves learning new skills, becoming experts at first-aid and learning not to cry at the sight of dead bodies and wounded children. She wrote about loneliness and fear.

Her mailbag was growing and many letters of thanks flooded in. The editor decided to print several of them on the letters page, so a dialogue began between Etta and the readers and she was given a weekly series in the East Express. It was called *Women in Wartime*, and was announced with a banner headline on the front page.

Her article, 'Work', contentiously suggested that many women had benefited from war. She compared the value of contributing to the common objective with the mundane existence of a housewife, maintaining that once they had experienced the exhilaration of independence and decision-making, women would find it impossible to return to any type of subservient role, either in the home or the work place. She remembered her conversations with Mary, her colleague in the factory, about her sister and was glad of the detailed notes she had taken. The article used the example of a pilot who had always wanted to fly but had never been encouraged or indeed allowed by her husband. She had described her flying career in the RAF as five years of bliss. The heated response in the letters made it clear that this was an issue that attracted as much agreement as disagreement.

Etta was interviewed on radio and she spoke clearly and surely. An editor from one of the Sunday papers telephoned to ask if she had any more stories like that. Out came Etta's wartime notes and diaries and the series *Women in Wartime* was established nationally. The money from the syndication rights meant that she could became a freelance journalist and she and Alan could move to Regents Park.

"You can't give up your job," warned Bella, "it is a well paying job." Etta and Simon laughed that the job on the East Express that had so upset Bella when Etta first took it was now considered good enough to hold on to.

Etta realised that even Bella's attitude had changed since the war. Then she thought about other women and how their outlook had been altered. That gave her the idea for a new series of columns. By the time they were published, Etta was a celebrity.

*Women After the War – Adjustment* was the first of many syndicated columns, examining how women's circumstances were now different. She wrote about wives and fiancées whose men had returned from the war, but were badly injured or virtual strangers who needed constant care.

In her second article of the new series, called 'Returning', she exposed the resentment of women being made redundant from jobs they had performed more than adequately, in order to make way for the returning men. She used the example of a woman who had served in the War Office as a wireless operator and wanted to continue using these new skills in civilian life. She veered between anger and guilt when her husband returned as a hero and expected her to return to life as a caring housewife.

After two years Etta decided it was time to move on from the war theme. She recognised that the war would soon be history and her readers wanted to forget and rebuild.

Her new series, *Women at Work*, concentrated on the new employment opportunities for women and this opened up a broader range of issues. Her mailbox grew and grew and a campaigning element entered her writing. She started to support the move towards equal pay for women and believed that her voice and substantial readership would be valuable in that campaign.

After Etta was given a weekly radio programme, as well as her regular column in one of the Sunday papers, Bella finally recognised her achievement and started to be proud of her. When clients were being fitted, instead of her usual refrain, "My son Simon owns six cinemas", she would sometimes say, "My daughter is Etta Broom, you might have heard her on the radio or maybe you read the Sunday News."

# 1951 Bella

Bella dreaded the train journeys around the country, visiting her local outlets and small factories. When she had first started her nationwide expansion and began to extend her manufacturing base, as well as her shops, beyond London, she had found these trips exciting and rewarding. They confirmed her status as a businesswoman and designer and she was always welcomed with warmth and admiration. She was responsible for creating many jobs so there was gratitude as well. But it was now becoming more of a chore and, although she wouldn't admit it, at the age of sixty-four, physically exhausting.

She particularly disliked the trips north and joked that any place north of the Finchley Road gave her a nosebleed. She felt the grey drabness and, as a typical Londoner, couldn't tell the difference between Doncaster and Derby. But the north was a lucrative market. Running costs were low, labour was available and the prices competitive. So she still felt the need to go even though now she had perfectly adequate managers and a staff of loyal and well-trained executives. She knew that an appearance by Bella herself was motivating and she had been determined, despite its substantial growth, to maintain the culture of the personality-based company.

She was uncomfortable staying in hotels that were intended for delegates to conventions. She felt old and invisible if she visited the lounge before retiring, as she watched smart young male executives hanging around the bar waiting for smart young female executives. She watched with irritation and an unwelcome touch of jealousy as they coupled up, then disappeared together.

She had taken Lilly with her once but was aware that out of their own environment, they just looked like a couple of old bingo ladies. She had once travelled with Irene, one of her senior managers, hoping that this would both encourage Irene's development and give her geographically spread staff another contact at the London hub of the company. The trip had ended in disaster when Irene had her first attack of morning sickness at Doncaster station and Bella had ended up taking care of her.

"Dudley, Derby and Doncaster – nose bleeds and morning sickness," she reported to Lilly. Now she preferred to do it on her own.

Simon, who travelled everywhere by chauffeur-driven limousine, tried to persuade her to go by car. She could well afford it now but her background, the struggle, the habit of being frugal wouldn't allow her to relax into the luxury she actually deserved.

After one of these arduous journeys, arriving back in London late at night, she decided to visit the warehouse of her extremely successful mail order company, Bella by Post, to pick up some designs that she could work on at home.

From the doorway, she was surprised to see a woman's shoe on the floor, then a camisole and then a man's shoe. The door to the packing department was slightly ajar and she heard female giggles and a man's voice. Her surprise turned to shock, then rage as she realised the man's voice was Nat's. She quietly followed the trail of clothes into the packing department, holding the large files she had intended to carry home.

The first Nat knew of her arrival was feeling the weight of a huge ledger crashing down onto his back. He looked up in horror and saw the bundle of raw energy that was Bella dropping the remainder of the files as she retreated backwards towards the door, her face shrivelled in fury.

"Stop it, get off her!" Bella screamed, throwing another file, which missed its target and landed on the floor in front of the distraught couple, who were a tangle of naked limbs crushed together atop piles of folded brown cardboard packing boxes, their bodies half-hidden by rails of clothes. Their attempt to disengage was both inelegant and embarrassing.

The frequency of Nat's absences from family occasions had been noticed by everyone for a number of years, and Bella herself had nursed her suspicions. The possibility of him having another, or even several other relationships, was just something no one ever discussed. Nat, a fit and energetic sixty-year-old and Bella, a work-obsessed sixty-four year-old, had not, after twenty-five years of marriage, settled into comfortable and united middle age.

Etta and Alan knew that her mother and stepfather had not shared a bedroom for a while but from their perspective, it was not surprising, older people often slept apart, and they themselves did not have a physically passionate relationship. They had also heard and seen at first hand the fights and arguments, mainly instigated by Bella and concerning Nat's handling of some business transaction or other. Nat for some years had been the Managing Director of the mail order business, with Bella maintaining control as Chairwoman.

"A bloody interfering Chairwoman," Nat had raged in one of their battles.

They rarely attended social events as a couple unless they were business related and, with the excuse of the various companies needing their attention, seemed only to be together for meetings and at essential family occasions. Nat even found urgent business to do during the Friday night family gatherings that Bella tried to maintain.

Now, her worst fears confirmed, she charged out of the building, yelling obscenities Nat had certainly never heard her say before and was surprised she even knew.

"Strumpet, whore, pimp, bastard!" she yelled. On the street she hailed a taxi and was driven directly to Simon's house.

When Judith opened the door, she was alarmed at Bella's frazzled appearance and gently led her into the living room, calling Simon urgently.

"I need a solicitor, now," Bella demanded as her son poured a large glass of Scotch from a cut-glass decanter. One large mouthful and a number of deep breaths later, she told an appalled Simon and Judith about her encounter.

"My assistant, that snot-nosed girl. I hired her. What on earth is he doing? Stupid old man. He'll be sorry. He'll lose everything," she announced. Judith and Simon watched in amazement as she ranted away. Joshua, Brynah and Rachel hung over the banisters in excitement, until two-year-old Sophie was woken up by the noise and started to cry.

The family expected her to fall apart, but from the moment she burst in and found him, Bella once more took control of her life. She cleared his belongings out of their home in record speed and had them couriered to a hotel address he had given. She engineered his suspension from Bella by Post pending the resolution of a court case. She was inflexible throughout and showed no emotion.

"Just like sacking a husband," growled Simon, whose legal department advised her.

The divorce came to court a year later. Bella sued Nat for adultery – a claim she won – and mismanagement of the accounts of Bella by Post – a case she lost.

From then on, Bella took Simon's advice and hired chauffeurs. They were always young, attractive and articulate and she always sat in the front passenger seat. They frequently joined her at the bar during her hotel stays and she welcomed their companionship.

# 1951 Bernard

Bernard's liberation started the day he abandoned his European clothes and swapped his suit and tie for a kaftan. He had not intended to 'go native'. It was just more comfortable in the heat and he was able to wander through the streets of Tangiers without being accosted by locals trying to sell to him, touch him, crowd him. Little boys, who had previously shoved themselves against him, promising that their 'uncles' had special delights for him, ignored him. He nodded in greeting to stall holders, then picked up packages of herbs, materials, beads, vegetables, just to look, and replaced them without buying. The kaftan was the uniform that signalled he was local. Long hair, pierced ears and a chain of crystals round his neck followed.

Roaming the labyrinth of alleyways and meandering through the souks, he relished being invisible. The spicy smells and vibrant colours, the very foreignness excited him. The sounds of different languages – French, English, Portuguese, Dutch – resonated around him. He loved the gleaming white buildings, the surprising street corners. He spent his days roaming and his nights drinking in all-night bars. Occasionally he strolled along the beach, escaping the putrid heat of the town and invigorated by the sea air. All his senses were alert.

He was still living on the money Simon had given him before his departure, which was the moment he realised Simon really wanted him to go away. The sale of his London clothes and some of the books and objects he had brought with him fed him for a few weeks, but despite the cheap rent he paid, his money would run out soon and he knew that he would have to find a way of earning some funds.

He had found a room to rent in a boarding house near the centre of town. He shared it with cockroaches, spiders and various insects he couldn't identify. He had bought his own linen and a fan but, other than those essentials, he lived with what it provided: creaky floors, wobbly bed, a central bare light bulb and a stained washbasin. He avoided the bathroom and kept himself clean with body washes in his own basin. The toilet down the hallway had not been cleaned for many years because nobody could be bothered or would take responsibility. Other than at night, he preferred to use the facilities in cafes and bars.

There were three other inhabitants of the small boarding house. Charles Baker was a writer, whose book in progress was called *The Centre of the Universe – Tangiers*.

"It is all here," he told Bernard one night, leaning heavily on a bar and waving his arms towards the throng of people queuing for drinks, "the centre of the universe where everyone, all nationalities, all sexualities converge. This is what I need to capture in words, the freedom, the birth of hope. If everyone moved here there would be no more wars."

Bernard loved Charles's enthusiasm, which bordered on the obsessive, but having witnessed several street fights, he was not convinced about Tangiers as an antidote to war. He was also not sure how this theory tackled the issue of overcrowding in a city that was already overcrowded. Charles, however, was oblivious to the anomalies in his argument and Bernard recognised that it was not in his best interest to enter into philosophical dialogue with him, particularly when they had both been drinking. Charles confided that he existed on inherited money and had been in residence for two years when Bernard arrived. He claimed he needed to be living in the poverty of the boarding house because he could not personally experience the reality of the centre of the universe if he upgraded his accommodation. Occasionally, Bernard saw him arrive late at night with young Arab boys, and on those nights he stuffed his ears with cotton wool.

Zeki was a middle-aged, overweight Turk. His shirt never quite covered his large belly, his trousers never quite closed, his armpits were always wet with sweat. He described himself as a businessman.

"My name means smart," he told Bernard when introducing himself, "and I am. You want land, drugs, girls, boys, stick with Zeki. I know where to get the best of all things and," he added ominously, "the best deals."

His habit of thwacking Bernard round the shoulders to emphasise a point was alarming to start with, and then became a welcome feature of their tenuous friendship. Zeki's most recent business deal had fallen apart, apparently, due to the treachery of his business partner. He claimed his sojourn in the boarding house was temporary until funds arrived from his successful enterprises back home. He had deals to discuss with Bernard, who was prepared to listen to anyone who had done business in Tangiers and certainly someone who had purchased land and property, even unsuccessfully. But the deals were only suggested and never described.

Bernard was given his first employment by the third resident. Paul was a painter from the Basque country, on the border of France and Spain. He drew charcoal portraits of tourists from a pitch in the central square and although he rarely achieved a likeness, he took cash in advance and no visitor dared to challenge his interpretation. Paul was over six foot tall and very thin. His grey hair framed a gaunt face and he had perfected the persona of the easily-offended, hysterical creative artist. So his 'victims', as Bernard liked to call them, felt it best to take the picture and run, however disappointing the end result. Bernard's job was to stand amongst the tourists handing out leaflets and entice them towards Paul and his easel. On a makeshift panel he displayed finished pictures of people who had long since gone away, so that no one could identify the sitter and whether the likeness was in any way close.

Bernard was supposed to receive ten per cent of the fee of anyone who agreed to pose. He had to remind Paul of this arrangement every time he brought in a new customer, and Paul would laugh at his own forgetfulness and reluctantly hand over the few coins owing. They would then go off together to one of the all-night bars and drink away their day's earnings.

Bernard's three new friends considered it their duty to initiate the newcomer into the joy of a society that lived by its own rules. All four men were escaping from some former life, nobody asked questions and everything was possible if not exactly legal. Bernard tried and disliked opium, marijuana and cocaine. They were all openly available and they all made him sick but he didn't tell anyone as the drugs were a passport to new friends. So when the communal joint, paper or pipe was passed, he pretended to inhale or sniff, smiled benignly and watched other people succumb.

He quickly learnt the art of trying anything on offer. He saw girls, boys, animals in positions he had not imagined possible. Occasionally, he brought a young boy home – sometimes procured by Zeki, sometimes in response to an approach in the streets – for a fumbled sexual encounter. The sex was like scratching an itch. His excitement came more from the release from guilt, the feeling that he was part of a thrilling culture and the lack of responsibility than the bodily contact. Bernard was content for the first time. He belonged in a society of misfits and planned to stay in Tangiers for ever.

His letters home to Jenna told none of this but reported, truthfully, the glorious scenery and, not so truthfully, his property deals. He promised her that money would come soon and that he would send for her when he had built her the perfect home. He sent postcards, photographs, once a small packet of saffron and even a whole nutmeg. He gave her the number of the telephone that sat on a wooden table inside the front door of the boarding house. It was for emergencies, his letter said. For a while he wrote regularly and then, gradually, intermittently.

Then Simon telephoned and it was like receiving communication from another world that meant nothing to him anymore. On the crackly line, he demanded that Bernard return for the fortieth birthday party Bella had planned for her twins.

He persuaded him with a substantial sum of money.

Alan's car swept under the archway of Victoria station. The Southern Railway sign was prominently engraved onto the high lintel. The car was a pale green Hillman, a colour Bella described as 'sick green'.

"How can you tell which is the front and which is the back?" she had asked when they picked her up.

Alan, Bella and Etta had come to collect Bernard. Jenna had stayed at home to prepare a welcoming meal. Simon claimed that he had a meeting and declared it was not necessary for them all to go. He was furious that it had taken Bernard eight weeks from his telephone call to cable his return date and details.

Bella had dressed carefully to welcome her son home. She wore a navy blue suit with a tight-waisted jacket. Her bright magenta blouse was tied with a bow beneath her chin. The ribbon, which ran round her pill-box hat, matched her blouse and the umbrella was striped with both the navy blue and magenta. Bella was excited but the rest of the family were anxious.

The rain was falling flat against the window screen and the wipers were not up to the task of clearing the view. The early evening sky was leaden, without a patch of relief. The light from cars and street lamps was diffused by the water.

"London is grey, grey, grey! Wet, wet, wet!" exclaimed Etta, peering out of the window. On her lap was a pack of photographs of scenic views of Tangiers they had received from Bernard. "Look at these pictures, how colourful it is. Can you blame him for wanting to stay?"

"It's time for him to come home now. I can't give a fortieth for my twins, if one of them is absent." Etta and Simon had argued that, between Simon's cinema openings and his son Joshua's bar-mitzvah approaching, there was no need for more celebration but she was adamant. "He is a married man. He can't leave his wife alone any longer."

Simon did not admit that he was glad that Bernard had stayed away so long or how little he had wanted to make the call to summon him back. His four-month visit to Tangiers, ostensibly to look for property to develop, had lasted over two years and had shown no sign of coming to an end. His letters sounded happy although everyone except Jenna distrusted the reports of his business ventures. She needed to fantasise about his abilities and exaggerate his achievements.

Bernard's return trip through Europe, which had started with a cargo crossing from Tangiers to Gibraltar and continued by rail and bus to Paris, had been depressing. He was struggling towards a destination he did not want to reach. The weather grew gradually colder as he moved north and he wanted to turn around and run back to Tangiers. His friends had been disappointed that he was leaving so soon. They protested and pleaded. They promised obscurity, great riches, more fun and idleness, anything they could think of. The group considered it a failure on their part if any one of them dropped out of the circle. In Tangiers, everyone was used to people coming and going, but his close friends knew that Bernard's family ties were strong and doubted his promise to return quickly.

As the train pulled into the station, he thought of the farewell party that had been thrown for him on his last night. More than a hundred people arrived to celebrate, although most were not sure what they were celebrating and Bernard did not recognise many of them. Zeki had invited all his 'contacts' and there was alcohol and drugs in potent mixtures.

"You must not forget all this," said Zeki as he led a conga through the streets. Then, whispering into Bernard's ear, he asked, "How do you want to say goodbye to Tangiers? A little Arab boy, a sexy little Arab boy?"

Bernard's hangover had taken days to pass and accompanied him on the first leg of his journey home. The emotion of the hugs and tears also stayed with him. He concentrated on remembering that warmth as he stepped out of the Golden Arrow third class compartment and on to the platform. Underneath his arm he held a large roll of multi-coloured silk that he had dragged all the way as a present for Bella. It had left Tangiers carefully covered in brown paper but arrived in London unwrapped and exposed, covered in dust and grime from his journey.

His three relatives stood upright and expectant by the barrier. Through the crowds he saw them before they saw him. He noticed that his mother was shorter than he remembered, Etta looked thinner and Alan looked fatter. He was surprised that Jenna had not come but not surprised that Simon had stayed away. Then Etta noticed him and pointed him out to Bella. He saw shock in all their eyes at his dishevelled appearance. He knew that Bella would have expected him to be clean and smart for this reunion but that was impossible. As he had come home in response to her summons, he resented the coldness of her greeting.

"Sorry," he apologised, "no washing facilities." And all at once, the familiar lack of confidence gripped him.

# 1953 Etta

"How could you do this to her?" screamed Etta, watching the needle spin round and round on the record, skipping the grooves in the middle.

"Who?" shouted Simon. "Do it to who?" He was shaking Bernard's inert body violently from the shoulders but Bernard's head only flopped backwards at every shake. Vomit covered the bed and the floor where old cups of half-drunk coffee, cigarette ends and pills, many pills, all different sizes, shapes and colours, were scattered. A whisky bottle lay empty on the carpet, a small trickle of the spirit still dripping from its rim.

Simon stared at his brother and the mess around him in horror. "What the hell has he taken? Do it to who? For God's sake, call an ambulance."

"Bella, Jenna, I don't know who, us maybe," Etta answered angrily, her voice shrill with panic. Etta staggered around the room trying to avoid pools of sick, looking for a telephone. Finding it, nearly obscured beneath a pile of unwashed clothes, she picked it up and, hearing no signal, bashed frantically at the receiver.

"Dead, cut off of course, oh God."

"Go, go find a telephone box," Simon was still shaking Bernard with one hand and with the other, trying to prise open one of his brother's eyes. "Go Etta, go."

"But he has been sick, they are not supposed to die if they are sick," she offered in a whisper from the doorway. She looked with disbelief at the scene in front of her.

"Ambulance, go!"

Etta ran down the two flights of stairs, battled with the front door lock, then escaped gratefully into the street, breathing the traffic fumes with relief. While crossing the road and running towards the telephone box on the other side, she rehearsed an explanation to Bella.

"Died in an accident – tragic!" "Victim of a murder – tragic!" "Bravely and secretly suffering a terminal illness – tragic!" They would try to protect her from the truth, but she knew it would be impossible.

Inside the telephone booth she fumbled with some coins. She retched at the smell of stale urine and old tobacco smoke and probably in shock at the scene she had just left and must return to. Her shoes stuck to the floor and she wondered, with a shudder, what might have caused the stickiness. On the sides of the booth there were cards offering massage services and personal grooming and a note, scrawled in purple, said, "I fucked Johnny right here." Somewhere in between this concoction of messages, was a sign, saying 'Police, Fire, Ambulance – dial 999 – free call'.

"Ambulance," she finally managed to say into the mouthpiece.

Bernard's funeral took place while the rest of the country watched a twenty-five year old Queen Elizabeth II commit herself to duty for the rest of her life. The new television set, bought especially for the occasion, sat unwatched in a corner of the lounge.

For weeks after the funeral, Simon and Etta spoke daily on the telephone. Etta had decided to delay her planned visit to Israel and Simon, whose marriage to Judith had been on the brink of collapse for several years, decided to abandon his mistress and try to cement things, at least for a while. They both felt that the enormity of Bernard's actions was such that their mother needed protection, for a while, from change. Bella, who had looked forlorn for so long after the loss of Sam, now just appeared bewildered. There were moments when they questioned whether their decision to keep Bernard's sexuality a secret from her was the right one.

"Maybe she would have understood his guilt and confusion and it would have made more sense," Etta had said in a telephone call to her brother shortly after the funeral.

"No, no one who fought for survival the way she did could ever understand this. I can't understand it, why should she?"

Etta knew that Simon was angry with his brother for not warning them of his creeping despair.

"You can't be posthumously angry with him," reasoned Etta.

"Apparently I can. From the moment I gained that scholarship, I have been made to feel guilty about my success and Bernard's lack of it."

"That was nearly thirty years ago, for heavens sake. Anyway, who made you feel guilty? I remember everyone was so proud of you."

"My twin. We were supposed to stick together. Everything changed from then. I was propelled into a different world and I never looked back."

"You can't blame yourself for being brighter. Come on, Simon, this isn't your fault. He got lost, we didn't see how badly."

"Yes, we did, we just assumed he'd be OK because, somehow, we are always OK." Simon's normally strong, steady voice was quiet and came from somewhere at the back of his throat. "I sent him away and I have to explain this to my children," he added in despair.

"What do you tell them about Sam?" asked Etta.

"They didn't know Sam, they weren't born. Anyway, I tell them that I had a brother once, who died a war hero. All children want heroes in their own family. They boast about him in school when they do the Second World War in history."

"They'll forget about it, really they will." Etta's voice was as comforting as she could make it. "It's Mama we have to think about. I saw her last night, her lips are tight, pursed, her eyes dry and she is not talking about it."

"She didn't cry at the funeral. I think she was ashamed. A son's suicide is not something to be proud of," added Simon. "I am going to see her tonight, she wants to talk about what we can do for Jenna. She thinks I should give her a better job than looking after the children."

"Will you?"

"She's my brother's widow and I have to do something but she has no skills that I can use, except helping with my children."

"Surely you can find something for her?" Etta was appalled at what she perceived as her brother's ruthlessness. "It's a big enough company."

"She's a good nanny, maybe she could live in. I'll talk to Judith."

"That's outrageous. You can't make her a family servant and put her around children when she will never have any of her own." Etta was frequently astounded at her brother's lack of sensitivity.

"She's around our children anyway, she seems to enjoy it. She is a very good nanny and now she has to give up her home, she would have a place to stay if she lived in." Simon spoke as if he had just solved a very difficult problem.

"I can't believe you are so callous. Let me know what Mama has to say tonight."

Etta slammed the telephone down.


Those who questioned Bella's determination to take care of Jenna did not understand Bella. She needed a personal cause to displace the abhorrence she felt at her son's choice to end his own life. To her it was incomprehensible. She also considered Jenna family and, as such, naturally assumed that the family should take responsibility for her.

She discussed her idea with Lilly after watching her comfort a weeping Jenna at the small funeral. Where Simon saw lack of skills, Bella saw charm and warmth. Where Simon saw an awkward liability, Bella saw enthusiasm. Jenna became Lilly's assistant and Bella acquired another devoted and personally committed member of staff. Simon and Judith had to find a new nanny.

# 1955 Etta

'More money for the hangman!' screamed the headlines, rousing the crowds waiting outside the austere Victorian Gothic building that housed the most infamous of women: Holloway Prison. Ruth Ellis, the murderess or the abused, depending on your point of view, had the support of thousands of signatures on a petition pleading for a stay of execution during her three weeks and two days as a condemned prisoner – but to no avail. On the eve of her execution, more thousands waited through the night and on into the morning. As the appointed time approached, many more came. There were men and women of all ages, some women had brought babies in prams and many were sobbing and wailing. Some were on their knees praying but most were angry. They threw stones and pushed forward, breaking through the police barriers to bang on the prison gates.

In her life as a journalist, Etta had spent little time in crowds, in fact she had not been near such a mob of people since George V's Silver Jubilee. She was not skilled at approaching an event with her elbows sticking out protectively, as she noticed other reporters doing, but this moment was the challenge she had been waiting for and all her senses were alert. There was a notebook pressed closely against her body and her pencil was poised as she mingled. She was not concerned by the police cordons or throngs of people. She was not even disconcerted by flying missiles. She had the manner of someone who had every right to be there in the middle of the action. She listened carefully and within the buzz of those protesting, she heard many, though less vociferous or sure of their ground, who approved the verdict and the punishment. As many people were shouting 'villain' as 'victim'. She wrote down their comments.

The crowd swayed forward, eager to see the death announcement pinned up on the gate by a lone policeman. Sobs and the murmur of praying filled the air, then nothing. After about half an hour, the crowd fell silent and shuffled off. Etta's instinct told her that this was the most important story she had ever covered.

It was all such a stroke of fate. She had been assigned to one of the most notorious legal incidents of the twentieth century because the news reporter who would normally have covered the event had flu. Had the editor known what a huge story this would become, he would certainly have sent one of the paper's male, though not necessarily more experienced reporters, simply because, in his view, a man would have had more authority. But his lack of judgement provided Etta with the opportunity that she had craved for so long.

From June 20th, she had sat in the Old Bailey's number one court, through the trial of prisoner 9656, recording not just the evidence, witness statements and pleas, but the comments and whispers she heard around her. She made notes in her astonishingly speedy shorthand and her notebook confirmed that the jury had taken fourteen minutes to condemn the accused. Etta noticed that Ruth Ellis (she refused to dehumanise her by calling her Ellis, as some of the papers did) showed calm acceptance, almost relief when the verdict was read and the punishment announced. Maybe, thought Etta, the relief is real as she has no more fight left and knows she cannot change the result. There even seemed to be a faint, knowing smile on her face.

Despite her reputation as a columnist, specialising in what the editor sarcastically called 'feminine issues', Etta was still not normally considered serious enough to report on major news items. Any career progress she had made was considered to be good fortune rather than gainfully acquired. However, she always searched for the chance to enhance the success she had achieved and use her popularity to improve women's lives. She struggled to quell her disappointment that, however well she wrote, however controversial her words, however reliable her submissions and large the female readership, she was not assigned to important events, even if they bore a direct relationship to her articles about women. The contributions of the male journalists would always be accepted ahead of hers, whether the work was better or not. She was aware that it was a common dilemma across many fields of work and she was determined to fight off bitterness and concentrate her energy on watching for the opportunity to prove her worth, whenever and however it appeared.

She was aware that Alan was also frustrated and faced a similar predicament for different reasons. His war work, the detail of which still remained a secret although Etta knew it involved code-breaking, had given him a sense of value. He knew that the skills he had learnt could be useful during this new period, which the press had dubbed 'the Cold War'. However, there were not many jobs for men who could not explain their wartime experience and he had crawled back into Bella's employment, discouraged and disappointed.

This they shared as a couple but little else, except a commitment to family. She and Alan still lived in the small flat in the block originally developed by Judith's grandfather in the 1920s. It overlooked Regents Park, so while he merely 'popped' to Bella's house or one of her shops, Etta struggled across London by bus to West Ham. But she enjoyed the opportunity to read as many newspapers as she could carry and arrived at the offices very well-informed about the competitive press. It was useful knowledge for a journalist. Bella, with the location pretentiousness acquired from her climb from east to north London, was comforted that Etta lived in Regent's Park and therefore was able to ignore that she actually worked in the East End.

Etta and Alan's life was quiet, occasionally punctuated by the glamorous events that were associated with Bella's business or

Simon's cinemas. Their flat was simply furnished and convenient for a busy working couple. The walls were decorated with maps and posters of Israel. They followed the struggles of the new state and they shared a dream to live there one day, but knew that day was far off. They were content in the summer, to sit on their small balcony overlooking the park and watch its wildlife. In the winter they enjoyed their new television and played dominoes, although Alan was always on call to Bella to deal with a crisis and Etta's hours were varied depending on how close her deadline.

They shared a bed but had developed a technique of not touching and never seeing each other in any intimate moments. The schedule they invented for use of their one bathroom was an exercise in discretion. For anyone looking closely, the whole arrangement might have seemed bizarre and the relationship questionable. But it worked for Etta, whose ferocious ambition was balanced by an accepting and sympathetic character. She was at peace, albeit in waiting.

Her life changed on July 13th 1955. The national press was universal in its condemnation of the use of the death penalty. So was Etta in principle, but she believed if Ruth Ellis did not hang, the opportunity to kill in revenge would be opened to all thwarted women. She knew her opinion would be criticised but she knew it would be noticed. The exhilaration gave her energy as she rushed to the office to write and file her report.

On the bus on the way home she wrote a passionate article in defence of the death penalty in this case and others similar. Her large notebook, precariously balanced on her knees, was covered in scrawled writing by the time she got off.

She walked in the front door, exhausted from a physically and emotionally tiring day and the rush to file her report to hit the morning's special edition, but elated by the experience. It was close to midnight. She kept a small typewriter at home for her freelance columns and late night assignments and couldn't wait to get to it. She opened the front door and saw that Alan was waiting for her with a sombre look on his face.

Alan's cancer was aggressive and speedy. The compassionate leave she was given by the newspaper only lasted for a few months. She knew that her critical editorial about Ruth Ellis had been widely syndicated and had attracted columns of letters, some supportive and some irate, but she paid little attention.

Alan died with as little fuss as he had lived, with dignity and no complaints. He seemed more concerned about the upheaval he was causing than what was happening to his body.

"I hate to be such a bother," he whispered to Etta as she tried to feed him during his last few days.

A few weeks after his small, simple funeral, Etta left for Israel, leaving controversy and grief behind her. She was armed with introductory letters from national newspaper editors and contacts given by Middle East experts. She made a will before she left.

# 1956 Sophie

All families have secrets but Sophie was convinced that hers had more than most. Like all stories in immigrant Jewish families that were exaggerated, confused by generations of telling and eventually lost as those who knew the truth grew old and died, the details were unclear and certainly not confided to children.

Perched on top of the little hill that had once been the roof of the family's air raid shelter, Sophie peered down towards the two women who had been central to her life as long as she could remember. She pretended to be engrossed in the daisy chain she was making but her eyes were running and her face was red from holding her breath in an attempt to hear what they were saying.

Granny Bella, who preferred not to be called Granny, and Lilly, who wanted to be called Auntie although she was not really related, were sitting side by side in striped canvas deck chairs. They chatted confidentially in the familiar tones of old friends. Lilly was enthusiastically drinking sherry from a whisky glass, Bella was sipping from a china tea cup with one hand and waving a blue air-mail letter with the other. Sophie thought it might not be good news as her grandmother's face was grim.

Once she had heard her grandmother and Lilly whispering about family in Poland. She was immensely interested in the possibility of more relatives but then Sophie, at the age of eight, was curious about everything, although she wasn't sure where Poland was.

She had tried to excite her older sisters about this prospect but Brynah and Rachel were only eighteen months apart and they seemed to exist in their own universe. Her brother Joshua, at fifteen, just responded with a grunt. In fact, he grunted about everything. Her father described each day by the number of grunts. It could be "a one-grunt day", "a two-grunt day", or very occasionally, and to be celebrated, "a three-grunt day". Joshua would, her father assured her, get over this stage when he grew up. Sophie just wished he would hurry with his growing up.

She hoped that one day, maybe today, her grandmother would mention this mystery family again. It was an exciting notion that went into the 'family secrets' file in Sophie's orderly brain. This was much more promising than the vaguely interesting rumours that Aunt Etta, the famous war reporter, had gone to Israel to escape her grief after her husband died. Sophie remembered Uncle Alan and he had seemed perfectly reasonable but not particularly jolly or warm. These were the two qualities she valued above all others, so he didn't really seem to be the type of person it was necessary to grieve for.

On the scale of one to ten, Sophie's scoring system for the stories she considered herself to be investigating, Aunt Etta's reasons for going to Israel notched up a lowly three. Sophie was especially fond of Aunt Etta, who always seemed to show real interest in what Sophie was doing, asking questions about her school work, her friends and the diary she had persuaded her to keep. Aunt Etta was fun and full of tales of adventure on her infrequent visits home. She brought exotic presents for her nieces and nephew, so although Sophie missed her when she was away, she thought it was actually more useful that she was abroad a lot and didn't really care why.

More fascinating was Uncle Bernard, who had apparently taken his own life. She could never imagine how anyone could 'take their own life'. *Take it where?* she wondered. There were no photographs of him in the house and nobody would talk about it, not even Joshua, who Sophie was sure must remember it. Bernard's story achieved a five, sometimes, on really boring days, a seven, as it presented a situation she couldn't contemplate and something new to learn. Once she understood where Uncle Bernard had taken his life to, she planned to grade it down to three.

Then there was Uncle Sam, a name rarely mentioned. He was the blue-eyed, bushy-eyebrowed young man in naval uniform, warmly glowing out from the silver frame that sat on the sideboard in the living room. Sophie had been told that he was a war hero and had died defending his country. She told her school friends about him proudly because, in 1956, what your relatives had done in the war was important to your status in the school hierarchy. But as there was no mystery to pursue, that story wasn't rated.

So with two dead uncles and one missing aunt, Sophie felt she had been seriously cheated and hoped she really did have other aunts, uncles and maybe cousins, even if they were in Poland. The possibility of a whole new family rated a resounding ten. But Sophie would have to wait until she was grown up to find out about it, by which time she had long since abandoned her childhood scoring system.

Soon she would be called into the house for dinner and the opportunity to gather any useful information would be over for the day. With the family all together, Sophie knew that the conversation would be lively and loud but the subjects would be chosen carefully. There would be a check around the table about jobs, school reports and who was marrying whom and when. Then the conversation would move onto boring things like the rising price of food.

When Bella called her to come into dinner, she ran down the slope towards the house, hoping that her parents would not have another argument tonight.

# 1956 Etta

*Dear Mama and everyone,*

*I have no idea when this will reach you. It is taking infinitely longer by airmail now, as the post offices are so short of staff. Then it all gets delayed going through the censors. I tried to send it by hand with a photographer who has been out here for Picture Post, but I missed him as he had to return to England unexpectedly.*

*I got your message telling me to come home and I can imagine what you are reading in the English newspapers. As far as I am concerned, I see no reason to change my plans because the Israeli army decided to march into the Sinai peninsular.*

*You tell me it is not my war. It is my war, your war and every Jew's war. And we are and will always be Jewish, however much we are all trying to be English. Simon's children will always be Jewish, despite their very English education, and even if Joshua wants to go to football practice on a Friday night. But that is not why I am here. I am a journalist, that's why. In the eyes of the newspapers, I am the expert on women in wartime and women are at war here. I am finally in the right place at the right time. There aren't any other women in the pack of war reporters, so I get treated rather well. You mustn't worry. The press are very well protected by the Israelis, who want them to stay alive to report their victories.*

*Anyway, it seems the worst is now over. The campaign was incredibly quick, decisive and well ordered. Where Russia and the USA come in, I am not quite sure. The political jigsaw puzzle is so complicated that I won't try to unravel it for you, even if I could. Seen from the Israeli point of view, particularly the young, it has been interesting and exciting. Of course none of them believe death is for them, even if they are surrounded by it.*

*I am nowhere near the front line and spend my time trying to get interviews with female soldiers. A surprising number of them are officers but they don't want to talk. So I pursue politicians or hang around the Dan bar, the press information office and the censor's office. I waste lots of time at the airport trying to get reports onto planes going out to anywhere in Europe. The streets are still empty of cars, the black-out is over, there are no more air raid sirens and life has, on the whole, returned to normal.*

*So please stop worrying. This is what I do. I know I sound like a broken record but then so do you. I can't go back to where I was, who I was and where I was living, without Alan. I know I came out to fulfil a dream that we both had and didn't expect to meet conflict when I came. But I would lose all credibility if I missed the final scene. Anyway, I am so involved, I miss Alan less and less and sometimes, I even forget he is no longer there.*

*Good luck with your new collection, Daddy's new cinema (I've lost count now!) and Sophie's piano exam.*

*Big kisses to everyone and lots of love to all,*

*Etta.*

# 1959 Sophie

Their last family holiday was remembered not for the final break-up of Simon and Judith's marriage or the introduction of the word divorce into the family, but for the moment Sophie flung herself out of a tree. Or at least that is how it was described later.

The farmhouse Simon and Judith had rented on the Mull of Kintyre was bleak, desolate, deserted. It was supposed to be the perfect family holiday, with no one around to talk to except each other and sheep. Joshua, at 17, was bored and stayed in his room most of the time. The girls made their own entertainment, telling stories and chasing each other around the grounds. Sophie liked to play tag as she always won.

"Only because we let you," chanted Brynah in her familiar nasal tone, which unnerved her father as it reminded him of Bernard.

"Because you are the youngest," added Rachel arrogantly.

Now, resting after a race, Sophie was sitting on a log scribbling her name in the mud with a stick, over and over again. Brynah and Rachel sat beside her, playing cat's cradle with a piece of old twine they had found in an abandoned chicken coop.

"I'm bored," complained Sophie, "what shall we do next?"

The girls saw Joshua approaching, kicking twigs and stones as he walked.

"I am bored." Sophie looked at him, hoping to find a sympathetic audience.

"They're fighting again," offered Joshua.

"I wish they wouldn't." Brynah looked distressed.

"They hate each other," said Rachel.

"They can't, can they? They're married," Sophie appealed to Joshua.

He patted Sophie on the head. "Don't be stupid, of course they can." He wandered away, grabbing long sticks and throwing them at trees. In late August the colours were just starting to change, green was becoming tinged with gold, horse chestnuts were forming but still small. The air smelt of wet earth from the previous night's rain. Joshua disappeared into a wooded area and Sophie watched him until she lost sight of him.

"I wish Joshua would play with us," she whispered, not meaning to be overheard.

But Brynah heard her and answered, "He can't, he's a boy."

"Then let's do a boy's game." Sophie sounded as if she had just discovered the mystery of the universe. "Then he will."

"It will have to be something very difficult," said Brynah nervously.

"But something we can't get caught at," Rachel was taking charge.

Sophie poked her fingers into the middle of the cat's cradle, destroying its pattern. "Stop that boring cat's cradle and let's concentrate," she said, jumping off the steps and leading the way towards the trees where Joshua had gone.

"Don't go in there, Mummy said we mustn't go in the woods," Brynah protested.

"She'll never know," shouted Sophie over her shoulder, daring the others to follow. "Too busy fighting with Daddy anyway."

Sophie rushed into the woods, weaving between the trees, knowing her sisters were stumbling along behind. She heard them giggling nervously and their feet crackling over pine needles and twigs. Deeper she went into the forest, then stopped in front of a huge, gnarled oak tree. She stared up through the branches, studying the intricate shapes of the dark green leaves against the sky, which, in the slight breeze, was changing patterns like a kaleidoscope. Hanging from a high branch, which stuck out at a right angle from the massive trunk, was an old rope. It was twisted and frayed, brown and green with mould. Another shorter rope, which had been cut or damaged by weather and time, hung about two feet away from it.

"Look," cried Sophie as her sisters reached her, both breathing heavily, "there must have been a swing once and someone has tried to mend it. There's a ladder." She dragged a rusty but quite solid metal ladder from behind the trunk and placed it directly beneath the large metal hook deeply embedded into the branch over which the rope was lashed.

"Let's climb it." Sophie was too excited to consider the practicalities of this new adventure.

"Doesn't look safe." Brynah was as always the first to suggest caution.

"Don't be silly, Sophie." Rachel was alarmed. "It might break."

Sophie reached out and curled her fingers around the coarsely-woven strands. They were worn smooth by many hot greasy hands but here and there stray ends of fibre, like prickly animal hair, stuck out from the tightly spiralled twist. She tugged at one of the strands and it came away in her hand. She stared at it lying in her palm, no stronger than a corn stalk.

"Let's climb up to that fork…look, the ladder reaches…" Sophie indicated where the massive branch joined the parent tree "…then swing down on the rope."

"I won't," Rachel was very definite.

"Cowardy custard." Sophie was rubbing the bits of string between her forefinger and thumb, watching it separate into even tinier strands.

"We can't, if the rope breaks it's too high to jump," said Brynah, looking at the scattered yellow strands on the ground. "This is stupid, let's go back. Come on, Sophie. Anyway it must be tea-time and they'll be mad at us."

Sophie, ignoring the attempt at older sister authority in Brynah's voice, jumped up and down on the rope, testing it out.

"Look, it's fine. I am going up." Her bravado didn't betray the slightly nervous twitching of her stomach. She banged the ladder hard against the tree, rooting it firmly into the earth then, glancing back at her aghast sisters, slowly started to climb. Sophie felt the solid rungs comfortingly on the ball of her foot. Her legs felt heavier and heavier the higher she reached.

"Don't look down," she said to herself, quietly but aloud. She looked straight at the bark six inches from her face, counting notches in an attempt to concentrate. The pungent smell of sap was in her nostrils. She watched little black and grey insects running between the cracks and studied them closely. She felt as if she was invading their world and wondered how she appeared to them.

"Don't look down," she repeated aloud. Nearing the top of the ladder, she saw directly in front of her some wet, yellowy-white bird dropping that had slithered in a slimy line down the trunk. Nausea taking over, she blindly groped her way up and off the ladder, pulling herself onto the branch.

"You're there," she heard Brynah cry, relief in her voice.

Sophie perched in the crook of the branch and leant against the trunk then, breathing deeply, opened her eyes. It felt as if she had climbed a hundred miles straight upwards and now she couldn't remember why she had needed to do it. The urge to pee was strong; she carefully swung one leg over the branch and, sitting astride it, pressed down. When the need had passed, she breathed in deeply and looked down. She kicked the ladder away and heard the sound of it crashing to the ground mingle with the shocked cries of her sisters.

"Sophie, you've broken it!" screamed Brynah. "You have broken the ladder." Rachel was crying quietly.

Sophie felt comfortably alone now, no one could reach her, the ladder was broken, the tree was high, the rope dangerous. The fear in her stomach was replaced with calm and a little spark of excitement. She was going to do this, although she didn't know how to or why she needed to: maybe to scare her sisters, maybe to stop Mummy and Daddy fighting. They couldn't go on fighting if she hurt herself on the way down. She ignored her sisters' pleas to be careful and, holding on tightly, lowered herself slowly towards the rope. Her fingers were an inch away but she couldn't reach it.

"Let's get that ladder out of the way," she heard Brynah say and knew they meant in case she fell on it. Sophie heard it being dragged along the ground. The ground looked further away with the ladder gone. She wiggled her bottom further back into the comfort of the tree.

"I think I'll just stay here forever. I'll never come down and no one can reach me," she shouted to the ground. But as she did, she was looking at the rope and wondering how to grasp it. She was hungry and it was getting chilly and she knew that either she would have to climb down or Brynah and Rachel would fetch their father and she didn't want to deal with his anger – and anger it would be.

"We are going to get Daddy, he'll bring another ladder," shouted Rachel.

"We can't go and leave her up there alone, we must stay with her." Sophie heard the argumentative tone in Brynah's voice but was very glad one of them had made that point. She enjoyed pretending to be alone but knowing that her sisters were waiting below was comforting. She leant further out over the branch, feeling its roughness scratch the soft skin of her inner arm and thigh. This time she managed to touch the rope with the tip of her finger and push it slightly, so that it swung a little outwards and then back. When she pushed it a second time, it swung back far enough for her to catch. She snatched at it and pulled it towards her. At the top, it was clean, smooth and tightly twisted as if it had never been touched. Brynah and Rachel were shouting suggestions from the ground.

"Swing your legs over and hold it further down," yelled Rachel.

"Hold it very tight and push yourself away from the tree," suggested Brynah. Sophie sat still hugging the stiff part of the rope to her body. It smelt of wet fibre and mould. Tucking it over the crook of the tree, she clung onto the trunk and gradually edged herself into a crouching position, still leaning backwards. The nausea returned and bile came into her mouth. She let her breath out slowly until there was nothing left in her lungs, hoping to quell her fright by breathing slowly; but she could only manage short, disjointed pants. She grabbed the rope with both hands and waited. There was only one way down.

Suddenly, clinging as hard as she could, she flung her body blindly forward, away from the safety of the branch. One foot hit the branch as she fell and she groped wildly for a firm hold with the other, but her legs jerked out against nothing. She swung out and around and then her hands loosened and she slid down, twisting like a rag doll. The rope cut into her palms like fire. Down she fell, winding and swinging, helpless. She saw crazy upside-down trees and an upside-down house. Her two sisters, standing on their heads, rushed past her in a confusion of streaking colours.

After what seemed like a million years, she hit the ground, stones and earth dragging along her skin. The rope, not yet finished with her, relentlessly swung her around, out and then in again. She yelled at the searing pain as she crashed up against the trunk like a tiny piece of driftwood tossed up by a stormy sea onto a rocky shore.

Through what felt like warm black velvet all around her, Sophie saw her father, his taut face very close to hers. Her hands were stiff in white bandages.

He gazed at her anxiously. "You foolish, foolish girl," he said gently.

She opened her eyes slowly and, looking beyond Simon, saw Rachel and Brynah standing close together near the door. They looked very frightened. Behind them was Joshua. She heard her mother's sobs and looked around for her. Judith was standing up against a wall, her body shaking, tears spilling. In her hand she held a string dishcloth, which she kept scrubbing up and down the wall, trying to remove spattered brown, glutinous globules of gravy, bits of carrot and peas. On the floor near her feet a bright orange casserole dish lay upside down, surrounded by the remains of the family meal.

"Mummy threw the saucepan at Daddy," Sophie heard Rachel shout, full of importance at her superior knowledge of this event.

"Shut up," said Joshua.

"It was stew," said Brynah.

Simon reached down to Sophie, lifted her into his arms and carried her to an empty bedroom.

"My brave, wild child," he cooed gently as he covered her with blankets. "You are very lucky, the doctor said you could have broken…well, everything, your legs, your back." He gasped a moment as the idea took hold.

"Is the doctor here?"

"Well, he is a vet really. He just happened to be close by. We'll see how you feel tomorrow and maybe take you into town for a check-up. But the vet knows you haven't broken anything."

Sophie was strangely comforted by the thought of being cared for by a vet. "Did Mummy really throw the supper at you?" she asked.

"It's my fault, I upset her," Simon said, stroking her hair.

"But what will you all eat?" Sophie didn't stay awake long enough for the answer.

# 1960s

# 1964 Bella

"Wheeeee…I am swimming," gasped Bella nervously, sucking in more water than air. Her face contorted as she struggled to keep her feet on the ground. She flailed her arms about as she fought the gentle ripples as if they were killer tsunamis. One strap of her bright, floral costume slipped off her shoulder, revealing a sagging breast and prominent brown nipple. Her spectacles slipped off and sank slowly down to the bottom of the pool.

Bella and Etta were in the deepest part of the shallow end but well out of the way of the children splashing about near the edge. Etta, who had been holding Bella's head with one hand and her slippery shoulder with the other, was reliving their annoying row over breakfast in the hotel's quiet but busy dining room. She had suggested the holiday in Bournemouth because Simon had asked her to take Bella away from London during the week his divorce from Judith came through. Etta hoped it would be an opportunity to spend some time with her mother, perhaps get to know her again and give Bella a chance to understand her better. But the week had been marked by arguments, recriminations and Bella's constant nagging.

"I understood that you went to Israel but not why you stay there."

"My work is there. Why can't you be proud of me? Look how proud you are of Simon and your grandchildren."

"Proud of what?" Bella sounded vicious.

"My achievements. In case you hadn't noticed, I am a well known and successful journalist."

"What is that to be proud of? I got you a job on Vogue and you turned it down."

"That was thirty years ago. Come on. I didn't want fashion, I wanted news."

"News isn't right for women." Bella crunched at her toast and marmalade.

"You didn't do things that were right for women yourself. You started and owned your own shop before women even had the vote. I became a news correspondent when women were stuck on the fashion pages. Can't you see the parallels?"

As soon as the words left her lips Etta realised she had been unnecessarily provocative and felt ashamed. She took a deep breath and waited for Bella's inevitable response.

"What do you mean, 'stuck'? Fashion is about making statements about women, women making statements about—" Her voice was loud enough to break through the hushed breakfast murmurings, the gentle clink of cereal and egg spoons, and attract the attention of the other diners.

"I didn't mean stuck," Etta quickly interrupted. "I just wish you could recognise that I've worked really hard and am highly regarded by everyone, it seems, except my own mother. You are a career woman, why can't you respect that I am too?"

"It's different," said Bella, her voice now suitably lowered. She put down her coffee cup and gave up on her breakfast.

Etta also stopped eating and shook her head in frustration. "Why is it so different?"

"Because I did it for my family, my children, my home."

"I have no children."

"I had noticed." Bella sounded vindictively pleased with this statement. "That's the point. You do it for yourself."

"It's not like that, I am just a different generation." Etta's tone was kinder. There would be no winning this argument, which was pointless anyway as Bella was just being cantankerous, so Etta tried to close the subject. "I know I didn't have to work to feed a family and I could choose what I wanted to do but there are other pressures."

"Feeding a family when there is no money is the only pressure I understand and you chose not to have children."

"That again. Well, it's too late now," Etta countered, trying to make a joke of it. They had four days left of their week together and somehow the tension had to be eased. She came back to England so rarely and was infuriated that her mother still had the power to aggravate her.

Bella stood up and roughly threw her napkin down onto the table.

"Well? Are you taking me to the pool?"

The water kept Bella's body buoyant but as she thrashed about, her head kept sinking. She tried to shout but floundered and kicked violently at Etta instead, taking in more water as she did, and coughing and spluttering. Etta, knowing Bella had never been swimming before, tried to hold her upright and drag her feet to the bottom but her thrashing around and the resistance of the water prevented it.

Etta knew that without her glasses, Bella could not see and would by now be terrified. Etta let go and dragged herself backwards so she was no longer trying to support her. Frozen, she watched, enthralled by Bella's helplessness. Her short, dyed black hair fanned around her bulging face like a halo. The top part of the body was all exposed. There was no dignity in this kicking, panting creature. *This is it,* Etta thought to herself, *she is going to drown. It will be over.* She moved further away then, standing still in water just up to the top of her thighs. It felt as if hours were passing and the choking, spitting, struggling body in front of her, half-naked and sightless, was a stranger's body. Etta felt nothing but cold curiosity about what life would be without Bella.

Suddenly, she was violently shoved aside by two large lifeguards. They grabbed Bella and dragged her high out of the water. Coughing and wheezing, she was carried over the surface of the water and unceremoniously laid by the edge of the pool, face down. Etta watched, mesmerized, as the lifeguards thumped hard on her back, as if in brutal punishment for some wrongdoing. A crowd gathered around the scene as Bella, after choking up some water, was turned over like a tiny bird ready to be carved up. She was pulled into a sitting position, propped upright by the lifeguards. A small trickle of sick oozed down her chin. Her eyes, blank in horror, looked around but seemed to see nothing.

"She'll be alright!" shouted one of the lifeguards at Etta. "Come on out, it's alright now. You'll get cold. Do you have her glasses?"

Etta plunged her hands, now both wrinkled from the water, downwards and scooped the glasses up from the bottom of the pool. She half-paddled, half-walked to the edge and pulled herself up the metal steps and onto the side. The small crowd encircling Bella, intrigued by the drama, made room for her to pass. Disgusted with herself, she approached her mother, her eyes streaming with tears and chlorine, and placed the glasses on her face. Bella gazed at Etta and suddenly gave a little giggle. Etta guiltily put her arms around her.

"It's alright," Bella said. "It wasn't your fault."

# 1967 Sophie

"Auntie Etta, no, no!"

The bathroom was heavy with a musty lavender aroma and the bath water swirled as Sophie tried to reach the pale green gel. The bottle seemed to move further and further away from her. She wanted bubbles, lots of bubbles and heat and steam, anything to wash away the grief – anything to wash away the truth.

"Aunt Etta," she cried into the water, surprised it wasn't running any more. Somehow she must have managed to turn off the taps. But where were the bubbles? Her legs felt weak and she collapsed onto the hard floor and lay down.

Later, much, much later, waking up stiff, she tried to remember every detail of her father's telephone call. His voice had sounded muffled and strained. But she didn't know whether it was due to the news he had told her or the effect of the drugs she had taken.

It had been a fun evening with lots of music, laughter and not much food. There had been dope and wine and the promise of sex. She and James had flopped onto the sofa, then the floor, giggling together. It was so neat. She would fall into bed with James, although she had only been dating him for a few weeks, and Charles and Jose would fall into bed. Then James had suggested acid. He knew well that she had never tried it, never wanted to. She loved the gentle release of cannabis and joints were regularly served at all their gatherings, but she didn't want anything harder than that. Surprisingly, her head had been clear enough to resist.

"You'll love it," he said, "just try half."

Charlie and Jose didn't help. "It's fun," persuaded Jose.

"Let's go all the way," added Charlie, one hand clutching onto Jose's exposed breast, the other just above her knee.

"Here," said James.

"No, I don't like to lose control."

"Control? Why do you always need to be in control? It is time to have some fun and maybe lose some control." Sophie was hurt by the criticism in his voice.

The small white pill had been cut in half and carefully positioned in front of her on a saucer that was grimy with cannabis dust and red wine stains. Charlie and Jose watched as she stared, then suddenly picked it up, placed it in her mouth and swallowed it. James slid his arms round her expectantly. She felt nothing, no effect at all.

"OK," she said, "I've tried acid, are you happy now?" Suddenly the evening seemed over. "Call me a cab."

"Wait," said James, startled.

"For what?"

Sophie looked at Charlie and Jose. They were ready to have sex and didn't seem to care whether anyone was watching or not. With much rustling and grabbing of half-abandoned garments, they staggered towards the open door of the bedroom. James looked expectantly at Sophie.

"No, James. No. I am going to leave now."

Sophie walked out of the basement flat and into the cool night of the square. She picked up a taxi on the street. Later she realised she must have given her address correctly, paid the driver, hopefully the right amount and with the appropriate tip. She must have staggered to her front door and managed to unlock it. She couldn't remember any of it, only that as she entered she was the glad to find the flat was empty.

The telephone had been ringing as she walked in to the hallway of the luxurious flat she shared with her mother, sisters and brother since her parents' divorce. She ignored it, dumped her clothes and headed for the bathroom. The telephone went quiet.

She ran the water into the bath. The telephone rang again. She remembered going to answer it. She struggled now, straining to remember the details of her father's call and hated herself for being so drunk, stoned, hungover. She had probably sounded unsympathetic and uncaring. But she did care. It was a terrible loss, an unbelievable loss.

Etta had been her mentor, her muse, her guide through her troubled teen years. Etta had tried to persuade her to go to university, pointing out that it had not been an option for her. She must have been disappointed when Sophie chose not to. It was Etta who listened to her dreams and ambitions, then convinced her to get a job, "any old job", if she wasn't going to study. Etta encouraged Sophie's achievements and, although she was probably unimpressed with her choices, never showed it.

Unlike the rest of the family, she did not question or criticise when Sophie volunteered to be a guinea pig for a research scientist. He was writing his thesis on plains of hearing. She was eighteen and very vulnerable. Every morning for six weeks she climbed into a black, velvet-lined box and perched on an uncomfortable wooden stool. She spent the day listening to a series of differently pitched sounds. When she heard one clearly, she had to press a red button. Some of the sounds were so eerie and high that she could not be sure whether she had heard them at all or whether the last sound was still reverberating in her brain. She could see nothing except the red button, at which she stared for three or four hours at a time. She was totally isolated and could only relate to the professor's voice. He assumed a God-like power over her. She was frightened of him, of getting it wrong, which might make him angry or, worse, scornful. She would strain her whole body in an attempt to be right. He was the puppeteer and Sophie was the puppet. When she climbed, shaking and covered with sweat, out of the box each evening, she fantasized a dramatic and tragic liaison. It was, of course, a teenage crush. Her parents and grandmother were horrified but Etta advised them to wait patiently for Sophie to grow out of it.

243

Later, her CV read:

'Research Assistant to Dr. Abbey Brown. In charge of project to discover relationship between sound and body movement. General organisation, analysis of findings, typing and editing report. Resigned to continue education.'

Although Etta's home was now Israel, she telephoned and wrote frequently and came home at least once a year. She was busy with her own career yet always found time for Sophie. It was obvious to everyone that they were especially close. Etta rarely showed interest in Brynah or Rachel, but they had each other. Sophie was like her, the daughter she'd never had, unconventional and bold but born at a time when her wilfulness was a benefit rather than a hindrance. Recently, they had been planning Sophie's visit to Israel and were in the middle of working out a way to persuade Judith and Simon that it would be a good idea. Etta could give Sophie work, so that she could decide whether she really wanted the life of a journalist, or whether she just wanted to emulate Etta.

Etta, with her courage, her originality, her strength. Gone now, all gone. What had her father said? A land-mine? A lorry? Why was Etta driving a lorry? The war, the remarkable six-day war, was over. Sophie knew that because above the map of the Middle East Bella had stuck up in the kitchen was a headline from a London paper. The front page banner headline said: 'ISRAEL SWEEPS TO VICTORY'. This was the first time that Bella had shown any interest in Israel. But the map had drawing pins where she knew Etta was: Jerusalem, Beersheba, Tel Aviv. Arrows in coloured crayon showed the progress of the Israeli forces towards its enemy's borders and down into the Sinai peninsular. Etta's reports were published in the London papers and the Jewish Chronicle, so they could keep track of her, even when they didn't hear from her.

Bella had only recently become a supporter of Israel. She and Lilly had joined a Zionist movement for women. They collected money fervently, gave clothes and went to functions. Bella claimed it was because she needed to meet and develop contacts with rich Jewish women and where Bella went, Lilly followed.

In one of her regular telephone calls, Etta had complained about going backwards.

"I am reporting women at war again," she said, but the articles described a more aggressive involvement of women in the Israeli army. They were soldiers as well as ambulance drivers, they dug ditches as well as making food, but it was not enough for Etta.

All these disjointed thoughts ran through Sophie's mind as she tried to remember what her father had said. She felt despair and disgust with herself. How could she call him and ask him to repeat such a message? Why was she still lying on her bathroom floor? Etta, the brave, was dead and Sophie, the stupid, was lying shaking and senseless on her bathroom floor next to a bath full of cold, pale green water. She concentrated and slowly her father's words returned.

Etta had been driving a lorry towards the West Bank to interview Arab women who were interned in refugee camps. She said she was looking for a different story, a new angle on the conflict. The truck ran over a stray land-mine.

"Auntie Etta, no, no please, not Auntie Etta."

Sophie felt the physical pain of loss for the first time. It was her first taste of bereavement. She wished she had not been indulging in alcohol and drugs. She wished she could clear her head and that when she did she would realise it was merely a bad dream. But in her daze, she knew it was true.

"Oh my God, Bella, Gran, oh my God," Sophie heard herself talking aloud. This would be too much for Bella at eighty. She pushed herself off the floor and leant over the basin, splashing water onto her ravaged face, under her arms and across her neck. A change into fresh clothes helped her focus and realise what she needed to do. She raced downstairs, jumped into the first taxi she saw and gave her grandmother's address.

# 1968 Bella

"Dear All, especially Bella," read Simon, as he removed his skull cap with one hand and carefully placed it beside his plate.

"I've got four grandchildren and not one of them calls me Granny," complained Bella, ringing the bell vigorously to signify that the next course should be brought in.

"Do you really want to be called Granny, Granny?" asked Joshua. He leant over and kissed her on the forehead. "Well, Granny?" Bella pinched his cheek.

"Owch!" yelped Joshua. "Are you ever going to stop doing that?" He rubbed the patch on his face that her fingers had attacked. His fiancée, Hester, pale in a cream and green blouse over a darker green skirt, looked down at her hands uncomfortably.

"Shall I go on?" asked Simon patiently.

The oval table was covered with a lace cloth and silver cutlery. Crystal wine glasses lay beside wooden table-mats decorated with Victorian London scenes. The Sabbath candles wavered slightly in the breeze from the open window. Bella sat at one end with Joshua and Hester on either side of her. Lilly, now blousy, heavily made-up and with hair that was back-combed, lacquered and had multi-colour stripes from a lifetime of colouring, was next. At the far end of the table, directly opposite Bella, was Simon, his new wife Stella beside him. Brynah and Rachel were placed on one side of their father, Sophie on the other. All three were wearing Bella Unique dresses, Brynah in blue, Rachel in pale purple and Sophie in plum.

Judith, who, despite her acrimonious divorce from Simon, was always invited to family occasions and always accepted, not wishing to miss the opportunity to humiliate her ex-husband, sat next to Sophie. She wore, as she always did, an expensive couture outfit and a great deal of jewellery to remind Simon how much money his 'dalliance' had cost him.

There were three empty chairs.

Bella, now a straight-backed eighty-one-year-old with expertly-coloured dark brown hair cut into a short bob, had command of the room despite her tiny physique. She had never put on an ounce of weight but now her slender frame was starting to look scrawny. She had added long sleeves to her own designs to hide the ageing arms she so hated, and chose from an exotic collection of scarves to cover her neck. She still wore little makeup, just a dab of face powder on skin that only showed a few fine lines around her mouth and eyes. Her beauty routine was to wash her face thoroughly with ordinary soap and water morning and night and apply a thin layer of Ponds cold cream. Her eyes, emphasised with mascara and pale shadow, were still clear.

Two young girls in their late teens, wearing black dresses and white aprons, carefully pushed in a trolley burdened with a large chicken, a variety of vegetables in silver salvers, a plate of roast potatoes, and gravy in a silver sauce boat. They rolled the trolley over the pale aquamarine carpet, lifting it over the edges of a large rug, past the family and the three empty chairs, which they glanced at uncomfortably.

The domestic staff made fun of Bella keeping chairs empty for her three lost children and it was always one of the first of her eccentricities to be reported to new girls. Joshua had warned Hester, whose first Friday night dinner with his family this was. and she had tried to avoid looking at the vacant places. Nobody knew how Bella coped with the loss of three of her children. It was as if she had a box where she put their memories, then locked it and never opened it.

"No, you carve or it will get cold," ordered Bella. She took the blue, flimsy aerogramme covered in Sophie's familiar scrawl and held it out towards Brynah. Then, looking roguishly towards Simon, she changed her mind and handed it across the table to Judith.

"I'll read it," protested Brynah petulantly, holding her hand out to Bella, who looked dismissively at her and shook her head.

Simon picked up the carving knife and started to scrape it skilfully against the sharpener. He indicated to one of the girls to place the vegetables on the table and to the other to hold the first warm plate up in readiness for the precisely carved meat. Judith held the letter in her pale hands, which were punctuated with long pointed nails covered by startling bright red nail polish.

"I am now in Lake Charles – a somewhat uninspiring spot, somewhere between New Orleans and the Texan border," she read.

"Why, what for?" said Bella. She knew that Sophie had escaped to America to avoid the pain she felt over Etta's death. But she felt that grief was best supported in the heart of the family, although the family was now becoming complicated.

"I have done a tremendous amount of travelling over the past week since leaving Jacksonville," Judith read, ignoring Bella's interruption.

"Jacksonville, what's in Jacksonville?" queried Bella.

"Please, Mama," protested Simon, glancing apologetically to Stella, as he placed the first slender slice of chicken breast on a warm plate.

"A smelly industrial town," Judith continued.

"A smelly industrial town!" Bella squeaked.

"Come on, Granny, let's hear what our adventuress is doing." Joshua laid his arm gently on hers. Bella shrugged and held his hand. He stroked hers gently.

"No more interruptions," said Simon, sculpting more chicken onto plates, "or we'll be here for breakfast." Hester started to laugh, then controlled herself and pretended to cough into her white linen napkin.

"We crossed northern Florida to the State capital, Tallahassee, through little towns with names such as Live Oak and Two Egg. The countryside from Tallahassee to Mobile is not interesting, flat and…"

"Dark or white meat?" Simon asked Hester, watching Bella, who was about to protest again.

"No interruptions," said Bella.

"That doesn't count," Joshua reprimanded her.

"White please," said Hester apologetically.

"Actually, she's a vegetarian," said Joshua.

"Vegetarian?" Simon sounded astonished. "Why didn't you say so? Would you like an omelette?"

"Meat is such a privilege," commented Bella in a stage whisper.

"No, no, honestly, that's fine. Please don't worry, I sometimes eat chicken." Hester pulled nervously at the many coloured beads hanging round her neck.

Simon had finished demolishing the chicken and the pristine carcase, absolutely clear of meat, was carried out. He sat down next to Stella. Judith looked uncertainly at her full plate and the letter she was still holding.

"Shall I finish this later?" she asked Simon.

"Yes, let's eat now," said Bella. "I don't think we need to read any more about Sophie's exploits in industrial towns. Will somebody please tell me what she is doing there?"

"It's a man." growled Joshua with his mouth full, making a comic threatening face.

"Is it?" piped up Rachel. "Has Sophie got a boyfriend?"

"No, she would have told us," Brynah offered.

Joshua caught his grandmother's eye then quickly looked away. They both knew Sophie would not confide in her sisters. Hester kicked him under the table and he slowly raised his foot and stroked hers. She smiled to herself and attacked her chicken.

"So, Hester," said Bella as she carefully picked at her food, "what does your father do?"

# 1968 Bella

Bella was disappointed with her grandchildren. Weddings, bar-mitzvahs and funerals, and the occasional Friday night gatherings were the extent of their Jewishness. They considered themselves assimilated, though still aware of their heritage.

Then Brynah surprised everyone by marrying an Orthodox Jew.

Lionel Glazer was a decent man, quiet and steady. Even a phi-losophy degree from Oxford had not diminished his religious beliefs and he encouraged the family to reinstate the tradition-al rituals. He took over the responsibility of ensuring that correct procedures were maintained during the Jewish festivals and ev-ery Friday night. Brynah seemed to relish the behaviour expect-ed of her, claiming she found comfort in the isolated community they inhabited. She gave all the clothes Bella had made for her to Rachel and replaced them with modest, high-necked, long-sleeved outfits. Bella said nothing, but she secretly confided to an equally surprised Judith that it was a shame Brynah's hair, her best feature, was now to be covered under a wig.

Lionel had what were known as 'expectations'. His father had made a remarkable success out of the manufacture of jigsaw puz-zles and Lionel, at twenty-eight, was learning about the business he was due to inherit one day. He patiently spent time in all de-partments, working harder and longer hours than the staff, but leaving in time for the Sabbath on Friday afternoons and breaking all contact until Sunday morning.

Their engagement had been a surprise. Brynah had always been so locked into her closeness to her sister that her social life was limited and neither of them was expected to marry early. Yet she and Lionel had found each other and it was generally acknowledged that he would make a good husband and father.

Brynah was no beauty but Bella created a wedding gown that enhanced her bland looks, emphasized her better features and somehow illuminated the sweet and gentle character that she normally hid beneath a wariness of strangers.

"Perfect for her," Bella had commented to Lilly, "all she has to do is make the home efficient and warm and keep food on the table."

"And observe correctly," Lilly added.

The congregation remarked that Brynah looked radiantly happy as she walked down the aisle of St. John's Wood Synagogue to the encircling sounds of its magnificent choir. "Smug," was Sophie's whispered observation later to Joshua during the five-course dinner at the Holiday Inn in Swiss Cottage.

"Don't be bitchy," he whispered back.

The couple moved into a small house bought for them by the Glazer family and announced Brynah's pregnancy two months later.

Rachel treated Brynah's early marriage and impending motherhood as a betrayal of their relationship and, without the companion with whom she had shared everything, seemed to shrink into a well of lethargy. The family 'elected' her to live with Bella, supposedly for a short time while she recovered from her depression. Judith had remarried and the presence of her three grown-up children was a hindrance to her new life. Joshua would move out soon when he and Hester married. Sophie was unsettled and although her bond with Bella was close, she was considered too young and unreliable.

So Rachel moved in to keep Bella company. Although she resented it, the move gave her an excuse to avoid decisions about her own life. She took herself out to what she called 'business' every day as if she were running a mighty empire but was in fact selling at the counter of a jeweller's shop in Hatton Garden. It was a job she took very seriously. She had no social life, despite Bella's badgering her to go out to meet people or find a more rewarding job. At night, after supper and washing up, she curled up in an armchair with the Daily Mirror and at weekends washed and re-washed curtains. The family tacitly accepted that Rachel's life had been sacrificed to the companionship of Bella.

Sophie had returned to England for Brynah's wedding but was considering returning to New York. She knew she couldn't stay with her mother for long and impose upon her new marriage, and would need to find a flat of her own. She remembered Etta saying "Take any old job" and, if she stayed in England, she would have to. Despite her expensive education, she had no qualifications, no skills and nothing other than a determination to succeed – but at what was still a mystery. The ruin of her plans to join Etta left her without direction. Bella was concerned about Sophie and determined to give her more attention, which made it hard for Sophie to leave London again.

Joshua was a worry as well. Despite his grand education, his business degree and his obvious talent for drawing, he still worked for Simon. This was a choice that Bella could not understand. In B.E.E. Joshua would be junior for many years. Being the son of the all-powerful Simon Broom actually hindered his progress. To her it seemed obvious that of the two businesses, hers could offer the most to an enterprising young man. She knew that, as she had passed her eightieth birthday, it was essential that she found some-one to take over and Joshua was the obvious choice. He had all the necessary skills, drive and ambition. More importantly to Bella, he was family. However large the organisation grew, it was still, in her mind, her own personal achievement. She would not be comfort-able replacing herself with any one of the applicants she had been interviewing lately. Joshua could proceed with his career faster if he stopped working for his father, where he had admittedly gained very useful management experience, and joined Bella Unique.

In reality, Bella had now started to feel isolated in her own company and remembered Oscar and even Nat, now both gone, with sadness. No one would have guessed this from her daily workload or the power that she so easily wielded. But as she sat alone in her Belgravia office, she just wished there was someone in the next office sharing her decisions, supporting her judgement or even arguing with it. She couldn't accept this from anyone outside her family.

She decided to add some pressure to Joshua.

# 1968 Joshua

Simon was having his portrait painted in the dining room. Lady Penelope, his third wife and always called Lady Penelope, objected violently to the loss of the dining room. Simon, however, had presented her with two choices.

"Either I go to his studio directly after I finish my normal fourteen-hour-day, or I come home and get painted here. With the first one, I never see you; with the second, the dining room smells of oil paint for a very short period of time. Your choice."

Lady Penelope, aware that his previous two marriages had probably failed through neglect, opted for the pungent oil paint smell, even though it also meant that evening meetings took place in the dining room so they were invaded by a constant line of business colleagues. The dining room furniture was piled up against one wall and the easel placed at the serving end. The family ate in the kitchen. As a concession to the sensitivities of the artist, the pictures and ornate mirrors hanging on the walls had been covered with white sheets.

"Looks as if we are about to have a funeral," commented Lady Penelope as she watched her dining room being converted into a studio.

"It will take six weeks," Simon had reassured her, omitting to add that that schedule depended on his availability and meant a commitment to at least one sitting a week for six weeks. With cancellations and unexpected urgent business trips, this had now been going on for three months.

When she had married Simon Broom, Lady Penelope was

determined to be flexible, tolerant and to look glamorous at all times. The last resolution was easier to keep than the first two.

Joshua had been booked into his father's diary for weeks. Bella had been particularly persuasive and Joshua thought that out of respect for her, he should consider the six-month trial she suggested. He needed to discuss the situation with his father and wished he could do so immediately, as father and son, rather than having to book appointments through diary secretaries. But at least, he thought as he entered the dining room, I am in his home and not sitting across a desk with telephones ringing.

"I can't move." Simon tried to talk without moving his lips. "Just find a chair and put it where I can look at you without moving my head."

Joshua, who rarely saw his father in casual clothes or even without a tie, was surprised that Simon had chosen an uncharacteristically sporty look for this perpetual image of himself. As children, he and Sophie had teased their father that, even when taking them to the beach or on an outing in the country, he still wore a shirt, jacket and tie and laced-up shoes with socks. They had giggled at their favourite game, which was trying to remove his shoes and socks. Sophie, always imaginative, had invented the story that her father had no toes, which was why he kept his feet covered. Brynah and Rachel never joined in and called the game stupid. They thought that their father was always formally dressed because he was an important man.

Now Simon was wearing a pale grey cashmere sweater with a blue zigzag pattern across the chest, which was repeated in the pristine shirt collar that peeped above it. His grey slacks were exactly the same grey shade as the jumper.

Joshua placed himself next to Harry Zsigmund, RA, commonly called Ziggy – a painter well-known for his extremely expensive society portraits and now, certainly, as famous as his sitters. A refugee from Romania during the war, had arrived in London via Paris and his accent was a fractured combination of middle European,

French and English. He wore a traditional painter's smock covered in multi-coloured stains with brushes stuffed into the large front pocket. Underneath were blue baggy trousers and no shoes, a mark of respect for Penelope's gold carpet. A folding table holding tubes of paint, bottles of various oils and spirits and a selection of palette knives stood on a stained sheet.

"Further away," Ziggy demanded dramatically. "I cannot move freely." Emphasising the point, he picked up a brush, waved it in the air and attacked the canvas, hitting Joshua's shoulder as he did so. Joshua moved back, out of reach of his waving arms.

The portrait had been commissioned by Simon's company as a tribute to his thirty years in the entertainment business. It was due to hang in the corporate headquarters, with a print to be placed in every cinema lobby. Glancing at the unfinished canvas, Joshua recognised how distinguished Simon now looked. At fifty-five, his hair was a steely black with a touch of silver at each temple. His bushy eyebrows slanted wildly upwards at each side, emphasizing his wide blue eyes, his nose was straight and his mouth showed only a few crease lines at either side. He was tall and slim with a rod-straight back, a result of Bella's indoctrination throughout his childhood.

"Talk English, sit up straight" were his lifetime mantras. The first no longer resounded in his mind but the echo of the second, even though he was now a millionaire several times over, was still constantly with him.

Ziggy was working with a pallet knife, layering paint in thick blocks onto the large canvas. He had taken liberties with colour: Simon's pale blue tie was represented as a vibrant red, his pale grey outfit transformed into a dark blue. The portrayal was robust, capturing Simon's vitality and exaggerating his distinctive eyebrows. His hands, one now resting on his lap, the other poised in the air as if pointing to something, were, on canvas, sinuous and full of life. In order to achieve that pointed hand, Ziggy had propped Simon's right arm on a wooden rest, which was balanced on his knees. The prop did not appear in the picture.

At first glance the portrait, which was now more than half-finished, looked like an impressionistic series of swirls. Joshua noticed that beneath its wild strength lay a precise pencil drawing, now almost covered by paint. Every detail was exact and considered. Harry Zsigmund RA was a true craftsman. He was also irritated and not afraid of Simon.

"Well, what is so urgent?" Simon muttered in an attempt to stay still.

Ziggy threw up his hands, waving drops of oil and paint onto the dust-sheet covering the carpet. "'ow can I paint you if you keep zee visitors coming in?" he asked in despair.

"It's just my son," protested Simon, "he has come to talk to me. I don't need to talk to him, and I'll stay still."

Ziggy grunted in disapproval.

The meeting with his father had not gone the way Joshua had wanted. He had hoped to clarify his future prospects within B.E.E. and expected Simon to object when he reported the pressure Bella was putting on him to resign and join Bella Unique.

During a short break for Ziggy to visit the bathroom, the still immobilized Simon suggested that Bella would be impossible to work with and Joshua should stay on course as he was still training.

"Your future," he pronounced, "is with B.E.E. Do you really want to work in the fashion industry for an impossible woman who won't let the future touch her world?"

"She seems to be very successful in her world." Joshua was angry at his father's dismissive tone. "I would have a lot to learn from her."

Simon moved, knocking over the armrest as he did so. "You have learnt a lot from me."

"I never see you."

"You don't need to see me, that is just the way my business works."

"I have to talk to her. I think she needs me more than you do."

"Maybe, but it's your future. She's impossible, you know that."

"They say that about you." Joshua attempted to sound confidant.

"I tell you what, just ask her to install a facsimile machine in her office. Not just like that but explain, clearly, that she can use it to communicate more quickly and efficiently. Well, instantly actually. See what she says, and if you get what I predict – an outburst about modern machinery and how 'hand is best' – then I suggest you stay where you are, complete your training and continue to work your way up the business you may, or may not, one day inherit. If you leave and join Bella, I propose that you buy yourself a couple of homing pigeons to deliver your correspondence because nothing in her office works."

Joshua escaped just in time to miss the rest of Simon's lecture and Ziggy's tirade.

# 1969 Bella

Despite her eighty-two years and her tiny frame, Bella's hand on Joshua's arm felt firm and steady. Her back was still straight despite years of poring over patterns, sewing in low light and kneeling on floors while pinning up hems. Her head was always held high and if her hearing was perhaps slightly less sharp, her eyes were still bright and her voice strong and husky, as always, due to years of smoking, which seemed to have had no other ill-effect.

Bella had not allowed her hair to show so much as a single wisp of grey for years, but she had recently lost the battle of colour and overnight, it became completely grey. No one commented on its perfectly even, steely shade. Aided by her expert colourist, its brilliance emphasized the clarity of her skin. The short bob, which had been her style for so long, was now longer and softer.

Simon had finally succumbed to his mother's nagging, which had switched to him, and encouraged Joshua to spend six months working at Bella Unique, as a trial for both of them. He hoped that Joshua would either stay with Bella and make a total commitment or return to B.E.E. settled, having alleviated the pressure from her. The time was nearly up and Joshua had decisions to make. He also had conditions Bella would need to meet.

Persuading her to accompany him to Kensington had taken Joshua days of cajoling. It wasn't relevant, she was too busy, she knew what was happening in that market anyway – these were her usual excuses. Eventually, he negotiated a wander down classic, expensive Knightsbridge to visit Harrods and Harvey Nichols (her choice), with a trip to trendy Kensington High Street (his choice).

Bella loved window-shopping, which she rarely had time for, relying more on Women's Wear Daily than shop fronts, and she also loved to barter.

Now they were wandering down Kensington Church Street from Notting Hill Gate, where her car had left them. Joshua could feel her excitement as she peered into boutiques. While dressing so many other women in seasonally changing clothes, Bella had developed her own distinct and lasting style, which bowed to no fashion trend. She wore a black skirt just on the knees, black tights, and a black top. She added single coloured jackets – pale blue, or pink, or Joshua's particular favourite, tangerine – and one of the multi-coloured scarves from the vast collection she was so famous for.

Today she had chosen a lemon yellow jacket. She kept several of these in her office and had been known to change them during the day according, not so much to her appointments as to her mood. She wore, as always, plain black medium-heeled court shoes, gold and diamond earrings and a jet and gold lapel pin. Despite now owning a significant collection of jewellery, she rarely changed these. Bella could confidently appear at any event looking absolutely elegant, and this wardrobe simplified her life without wasting precious time on wardrobe decisions. She had been wearing spectacles for twenty years and had managed to turn even them into a fashion statement. Their shape remained unchanged as the lenses strengthened to adapt to her weakening eyesight, but she had many pairs in colours that matched her jacket collection.

Joshua planned to stop at several coffee shops so that he did not tire his grandmother, then to treat her to lunch at the roof gardens at Derry and Toms, where he had booked a table. But Bella didn't want to slow down and was moving Joshua forward with little cries of interest.

Joshua knew that Bella, who read the fashion pages avidly and had contact with manufacturers, importers of everything from cotton thread to fabric as well as other designers, was well aware of what she called 'the 1960s' scene'. He would be underestimating her to think otherwise, even though she had not actually visited any of the boutiques.

They arrived at Biba on Kensington Church Street, where she was intrigued by displays of makeup, accessories, shoes and the circular rails, heavy with outfits. She wandered around them, always just a step ahead of Joshua, and embarrassed him by feeling fabric between her fingers and attracting the interest of a sales girl.

"Can I help you?" The sales assistant, noting Bella's age, glared at her suspiciously.

"I have to feel, I can't see anything. Why is the music so loud and why is it so dark?"

"Is there anything that you are particularly interested in?"

Bella picked up a suit with a swirling skirt and flowing jacket, accompanied by a wrap-round scarf. Its colours were gentle beige with wide damson stripes, a theme that followed through all three pieces. She removed the scarf from its hanger, flung it around her neck over her fox pelt coat and headed for the glass exit door. On the way she glanced disapprovingly at the cosmetic counter.

"Gran," protested Joshua, "what are you doing?"

"How can I buy anything I can't see?" Bella was determined and he knew better than to contradict her when she was being determined.

The assistant followed her towards the door carrying the rest of the suit. A bemused Joshua followed. She removed the scarf from Bella's shoulders, placed it back onto the hanger over the jacket and held the entire outfit in the light, using both hands to demonstrate the way all three pieces fitted together. Bella lifted up the skirt and looked at the reverse side.

"No lining," she said dismissively, "how can it hang properly?"

Showing more patience than Joshua was currently feeling, the assistant gently swayed the skirt backwards and forwards. It slid off its hanger and onto the floor. All three stared at the garment on the ground.

"No lining," said Bella, as if that lack had caused the skirt's downward slide.

Joshua's arm strengthened beneath her elbow.

"Thank you, thank you, sorry," he called over his shoulder as he led Bella away.

It was a bright day and the exotic gardens at the top of Derry and Toms were showing spring promise. They chose a window table inside the palm court restaurant, so that Bella could see outside but not feel the chill air. Joshua was aware that although he, and indeed everyone else, treated Bella with the deference due her age, she always appeared to be stronger than anyone else. It was the younger members of the family who had colds, flu, allergies and tummy upsets, while Bella ploughed on, seemingly impervious to hard work, winter cold or passing bugs.

They ordered salads and cappuccino. Bella twiddled her spoon in the frothy coffee, but if Joe thought that he had managed to persuade her that she was part of the new fashion scene, he was wrong.

"Do you see what I mean, Gran? We need to go 'up-town'."

"Mine is a different kind of business. Anyway, what do you mean 'up-town'?"

"Well...here for instance," he pointed over the garden and into Kensington High Street, "or the King's Road, or maybe we should have a boutique in Harrods and sell to America."

"You mean like Mary Quant or Barbara Hulaniki?" Bella was disdainful.

"What's wrong with Mary Quant and Barbara Hulaniki?"

"They are a sign of the times, fit only for the Sixties and a new throw-away world."

"But Gran, you did something different once. Bella Unique is still capable of doing that again."

"I only followed fashion basics, no trends or fads, long skirts, short skirts, women working, women playing. My clothes are personal and made to last. They make my customers happy. It's quality, it's about feeling valued. They feel comfortable but also desirable in them."

"Desirable?" Joe respected Bella's loyal clientele but privately thought many, if not most of them, were well past the need to feel desirable.

Bella opened a black and gold box of slender cigarettes, each one wrapped in pastel coloured paper. She contemplated for a moment, then picked out a pale green one and placed it in a long black holder. She waved the holder around the air in emphasis and rattled the box of matches in her other hand.

"Paper knickers," she exclaimed. "They say she makes paper knickers."

"I bet paper knickers are selling very well," Joshua whispered under his breath. Bella did not hear or, if she did, chose to ignore the remark.

"The women who come to me have been dressed by me for a long time. They rely on me to concentrate on what is best for each individual. They are always smart." Bella lit a match and held it close to the end of the cigarette without touching it. She watched the flame flicker and die, then placed the dead match in the silver ashtray in front of her.

"Yes Gran, that's the point, they are not getting younger and I am sorry, nor are you. You have held a unique place in a cut-throat market but I am not sure that place exists anymore. Its haute couture or high street now."

"Cut-throat," commented Bella dreamily.

Joshua stretched his hand out and placed it over hers. "It is now and in order to survive, we have to change – that is if you want this business to continue, perhaps, for another half century. If you don't," his voice was gentle, "it will die with you, a small mark on the history of fashion. All your hard work and that's it. But only you can choose."

"Is there any way we can make the changes you are suggesting and keep what is unique about Bella Unique?" Bella asked thoughtfully. "How can we be sure that once we are touched by outside influences, the quality doesn't go, the customer service and my understanding of the needs of each customer is not lost?"

"You already have too many shops for that, Gran. I measured Mrs Grossman last week. She said she had been coming to you since Petticoat Lane. Is that possible?"

"Ah, Gemma, dear Gemma Huntley, yes, she has. You measured her?" She looked at her handsome young grandson. "She must have enjoyed that," she smiled, "but you don't know how to measure. Where was Bernadette?"

"At lunch, and I have been watching you measure all my life and she wouldn't have come back if we hadn't attended to her then and there. The point is that the dress will be made to a design and quality of your standard but you won't actually see it from the measurement to the fitting. That is the reality of what is happening." Joshua was still stroking the back of Bella's hand but his voice was taking on a sterner tone.

"But I'll be at the fitting."

"Not if it coincides with Countess Rene de la March, who is booked into Finchley Road at the same time. Is she really a Countess, by the way?"

"European Countess, she married someone who called himself a Count. When they arrived here before the war no one was interested in questioning her title. It gets her good tables in smart restaurants."

"Gran, we have to hold on to your younger customers in a different way, those who perhaps don't know you. There is a lot of competition for them," said Joshua, choosing his words carefully. "I am going to put a business plan together for you to look at, then you can think about it and take it to the bank."

"Business plan? Little Bella Bromavitch with a business plan," she mused and finally lit her cigarette.

"For goodness sake," Joshua's voice showed his irritation but he waved at the waiter to bring more coffee, which gave him a few seconds to calm down. "We need to develop other lines, scarves for instance. Scarves would be perfect. You are famous for your scarves, it would be a natural next step. You could design scarves that go with your outfits. Better still, I know someone we could bring in who specialises in textile design. He would work directly with you Gran, absolutely up to your standard of design."

"Joshua, women buy my vision of how they should look. That is the way it has always been."

"But you are a world-class designer, you can't design everything yourself." Joshua was nervously tapping his teaspoon against the edge of his cup.

Bella stretched her hand towards him and held his steady. "I am not a designer, I am a dressmaker. Women come to me for quality and because my clothes last. They always have. If we lose that, we lose everything."

"If they last too long, women won't need to come back, they will wear them forever."

The coffee arrived and Joshua put two large, uneven lumps of brown sugar into his. "Come on, Bella, can't you see? It's time to move forward."

"You called me Bella," she said, surprised.

"I didn't mean to. It's just that you are two people to me, my grandmother and the stubborn, talented, successful designer – yes, designer." He raised his voice and leant across the coffee cups, placing his hand gently over her mouth. "Don't argue, entrepreneur. I want to take Bella Unique into the future. What about scarves?" Joshua removed his hand from her face and was relieved to see she was smiling.

"No scarves, no makeup, no perfume and definitely no bathroom towels."

Later that year, while Neil Armstrong hopped on the moon, Joshua skedaddled to a Caribbean island to marry Hester. On his return,

265

he accepted Bella's offer to become Assistant Managing Director, on condition that he was allowed to develop his business plan – and call her Bella during working hours.

# 1970s

# 1970 Sophie

With financial help from her father for the large deposit, and a small income from temping to cover the rent, Sophie moved into a flat at the top of a converted house in Notting Hill Gate. It was a notorious area with a high crime rate and reputed to be the location of illegal landlords and brothels. She shared with Maggie Byrd, whom she had met while working in an architect's office, filing blueprints.

The flat had one bedroom, which they shared. There were decrepit kitchen units hanging off the wall of the living room, which the landlord described as a galley kitchen. Despite the landlord's denial, Sophie was sure she could both smell and hear gas escaping from the back of the ancient stove. The bathroom featured a giant enamelled Victorian bathtub with claw feet, leaking taps and a permanent water stain. They moved in winter and the only heat came from gas fires in the bedroom and living room. They slept with their clothes piled on top of their beds, so that whoever's turn it was to jump up first in the morning and light the gas fire could get dressed under the covers first. Occasionally Sophie noticed that Maggie tried to bargain her way out of her turn by offering to do another chore instead.

"I'll carry the shopping up," she would say, "if you'll get up first tomorrow."

"No, we'll share the shopping and it's your turn." Sophie would not be pressurised. The morning leap to light the fire was the worst part of the day.

Together, they rearranged the few pieces of furniture that

269

allowed the flat to be described as furnished, bought some cheap throws and cushions at Kensington market and made the living room into a cosy den. They painted the bathroom brilliant red and the underside of the bath deep purple.

Simon, who had not been at all happy about his daughter's chosen neighbourhood, came round to check that all was well with his youngest and most wilful child. He said nothing about the colour scheme but sent an engineer round the next day to sort out the gas stove. A new sofa was delivered from John Lewis a week later.

Judith protested that five floors was too much for her and sent the girls a lavish bunch of flowers from Constance Spry as a moving-in gift. They sat in a bucket by the front door for months until even Maggie complained that the whole flat smelt of rotting vegetation.

Maggie was tall and gawky, with thin angular arms and slender hands with talon-like manicured nails. Her startling green eyes were shaded with long lashes, which she curled with tongs every morning. Her tense body resembled a stick insect in flight from some unknown hazard. She was unpredictable, neurotic and as generous with miscellaneous information on the subject of herself, as she was revealing gossip about other people.

Neither of them liked their tedious jobs. They worked for a large practice and had their own small airless room in the basement of a building in Gower Street. The architects, all male, treated them as if they were invisible, just wordlessly handing them completed plans for filing. The work was repetitive and they relied on each other for entertainment during the monotonous days. Sophie learnt that Maggie had always wanted to be an actress; that her makeup always wore off by lunchtime; that her older brother had died as a child and her parents had always resented her for being the sibling who lived. Maggie also divulged that she had not slept with a man for six months and it was starting to be a biological problem.

Although their wages were small, they managed to budget for cigarettes and alcohol. After work, they visited a cocktail lounge where free canapés were served between 5 and 7pm. They filled up on half-price gin and tonics and stuffed themselves with mini sausage rolls and baby Welsh rarebits. As this eliminated the need to cook, it became a regular routine.

Sophie knew that she only had to call her father and she could be whisked away in a chauffeur-driven limousine and taken to any of London's finest restaurants for dinner, but she was determined to prove her independence and not call upon his help. Maggie was thrilled to hear about Sophie's family and asked her endless questions. She was not able to separate the idea of Simon's cinema-owning from her own dreams of becoming an actress, no matter how many times Sophie explained it. Maggie thought that she had chosen her flatmate wisely, hoping that a Bella Unique wardrobe at a wholesale price and invitations to Broom's film premieres might be part of the package.

Sometimes, but only sometimes, Sophie accepted Brynah's invitation to a Friday night dinner, which she knew would be a lavish, kosher five-course affair, all punctuated by prayers. Maggie, who had no such family invitations, found it hard to understand Sophie's disregard for such invitations. She would have been happy to say prayers if a good meal were being offered.

"I don't believe in God, I don't speak Hebrew and candles make me cough," said Sophie, ending the discussion.

"Orgasms," announced Maggie one day, "we deserve to have them."

They were spending a rare evening in the flat. Maggie had bought two bottles of cheap red wine and Sophie had volunteered to cook spaghetti Bolognese, the only dish she knew. Maggie had discovered feminism but only because there was no man around to entertain her. Sophie continued to stir the Bolognese sauce, waiting for Maggie's next revelation, which was about her latest interest, a women's theatre.

"Only women in the audience, no men allowed," she pronounced.

"But…" Sophie stirred vigorously, deciding not to say that she thought that was futile. If the message needed to be given to men, what was the point of banning them from the audience? But she let Maggie ramble on.

During Maggie's feminist phase, which was destined to be short-lived, she went to self-help groups to "bond with the sisters" and karate lessons to "improve her self-defence". Initially, Sophie accompanied her, until she was repelled by a consciousness-raising meeting, run by a group of disgruntled women who sat in a circle having intense discussions about how frequently they should examine their own vaginas. She agreed that the situation for women needed to change but found Maggie's involvement frivolous.

Sophie was genuinely interested in playing an active role in the women's movement, but had a difficult time reconciling that with her family's history. Bella had survived and thrived before the word feminism was invented. She had created her own opportunities and allowed no law or act of discrimination to obstruct her. Sophie was also inspired by Etta's articles about women's experiences, during and directly after the war. She kept these in a treasured scrapbook, reading and rereading them. She missed Etta, knowing that she was the one person with whom she could have discussed her disillusionment about the peripheral activities surrounding what the newspapers had dubbed 'Women's Lib', a title she hated.

Nevertheless she was excited by these new ideas, eager to contribute, and eventually joined a political group committed to militant action. She marched through the streets of London for abortion on demand and then, on November 20[th,] headed for the Albert Hall.

Bella and Rachel saw Sophie's arrest on television, only at the time they didn't know that it was Sophie. They had finished supper and were tuned in to watch the Miss World contest. The radio had already reported that there had been violent protests at the Albert Hall, led by 'unruly female anarchists'.

"That's not the way to gain independence," Bella had commented as a small group of women were shown forcing their way through the entrances, down the deep stairs and onto the stage.

"Stupid," Rachel concurred, as always agreeing with Bella.

Beefy security guards, who had been employed to fend off over-enthusiastic male admirers of the beauty queens, found themselves grappling with a bunch of wild young women. They were chanting, "We're not ugly, we're angry!"

The level tones of the newscaster reported flour bombs and fruit being thrown at the stage. The contestants, in bathing suits and high heels, were seen being shoved unceremoniously out of the way of the mayhem. The camera settled on a squashed banana at the feet of Bob Hope, the bemused master of ceremonies, before turning back onto the intruders. Bella and Rachel gasped as they saw a woman fall. She had been leading the rampage into the hall. Her arm was outstretched directly towards the camera, her eyes distorted with exhilaration. She tripped and slipped down the aisle, bumping down the stairs. Her long skirt was inelegantly dragged up to her shoulders, leaving her knickers in full view of the audience.

"Someone's been hurt!" screamed the newsreader over the riotous noise in the hall.

The television wobbled and went black. An announcer apologised for the lack of picture and vowed to return to the contest as soon as possible.

"Pretty girls don't have these problems," commented Bob Hope when asked for his opinion.

As soon as he had returned from bailing his daughter out, Simon telephoned Bella to tell her that Sophie was one of the women arrested at the Albert Hall. He felt it best she heard it from him, before it hit the headlines of the morning newspapers.

Bella telephoned Sophie immediately and was vehement in her disapproval of her granddaughter's militant activities and subsequent arrest. She was sympathetic with the view that Sophie and her group of active, able women friends had the right to have significant careers, equal pay for equal work and to get mortgages in their own names. However, she disapproved of the methods of realizing it and was sure that the only way to progress was education and hard, hard work. Sophie enjoyed discussing feminist issues with Bella, as she felt that Bella had a balanced view and a wisdom the strident women of her own generation had yet to attain.

"It is about choice, Sophie. Are you judging Brynah for choosing to stay at home to breed babies?"

"Of course not, how could I? It is what she wants."

Bella told Sophie of the pride she had felt when she was first allowed to vote in an election. As her naturalisation had not yet been approved, there was confusion surrounding that momentous event.

"But I stood and waited," she reported triumphantly, "and shamed them into letting me vote."

"You probably scared them, Gran. Who did you vote for?"

"I can't remember," admitted Bella, "it just seemed important to use my vote."

Sophie tried to persuade her grandmother to visit one of her women's group meetings but Bella was not keen. She had given Bella a copy of *The Female Eunuch* by Germaine Greer. Bella never read books but she left it conspicuously on her desk for visitors to see.

"Please reconsider, Gran, we could learn so much from you."

"I can't, I don't approve. Disrupting an entertainment event is just behaving like a hooligan and leaving men out of everything, what is the point of that?"

"How could you, of all people, not approve?"

"Me, of all people? Do you think that throwing flour and going on marches will change anything?

"Yes, we are listened to, we have a voice, we have made progress."

Bella lit a cigarette. "Tell me about this arrest. Do you have a criminal record now?"

"No, they released us all. Daddy didn't have to pay much bail. It was worth the risk, it achieved a lot."

"Like what?"

Sophie thought for a moment. Despite her closeness to Bella and the love and support she always knew she had, Bella still had the power to disconcert her. "Publicity," she said finally.

"Not good publicity," Bella responded quickly. "You looked un-disciplined and out of control, certainly not worthy of powerful positions – which is, I believe, what you are after."

"Now women can do many things they couldn't do before." Sophie knew Bella was scrutinising her and felt ill-prepared to face her grandmother's fierce logic.

"I am sure, but are you too busy making a noise to get on with it?"

Sophie knew she had lost her way in her own argument. Bella was not often confrontational with her, but when she was, Sophie was reminded of Joshua's complaints that he found her impossible to negotiate with and frequently gave up. It was known that Bella won many arguments with this method, which Joshua called 'the Bella Unique oblique technique'.

"Jockeys, women can be jockeys now." Sophie wished she could cancel her words as soon as they were uttered, mortified at how trivial she sounded.

"Jockeys, is that what you have campaigned for, the right to ride a horse?"

"No, that's not the point, it is the principle." Sophie tried to sound profound but, faced with Bella's defiance, even her voice sounded feeble.

"Explain the principle then. I am listening." Bella was the only person in the world who could make the strong-willed Sophie feel like a four-year-old.

"It is about having the right to everything we are capable of doing and being paid the same as men for the same job. Women are now flying with the Red Devils…"

"Who?" Bella was mystified.

"The Red Devils, the pilots – you know, the formation team." Sophie pointed at the sky out of the office window, as if she expected them to fly past on demand.

"Ah, so is your work done now? Pilots and jockeys. I am not making fun of you and I know that the Director of the Royal Observatory in Greenwich is a woman because I met her at a business lunch. Fascinating woman, but I can't connect that achievement with the activities of your group of hippies."

"Maybe it is connected, because they couldn't refuse her the job just because she is a woman. We, and the publicity you so scorn, have achieved that."

"Not scorn," Bella interrupted, "question."

"Can't you see? Do come and at least meet them. They are a serious group of women who, I know, would prefer not to have to pull off stunts to get noticed. Your opinion is important and will certainly spark a valuable debate."

"No, Sophie."

"Why not?"

Because I believe that what you are doing now will backfire."

"What do you mean, backfire?"

"Women will get men's jobs and the status they want but, by demanding it this way, they will not lose any of their domestic duties. They will just add another layer of responsibility. They will still be in charge of the home, so they will be doing two jobs, not one. Do you really think that men, even if they have to allow women on the Board, are going to suddenly start doing the laundry? That's why I don't want to meet your 'women's lib' ladies. I believe women are heading for catastrophe by demanding, rather than earning, equality."

When Sophie reported this conversation to her group, the women did not seem to think that a woman of Bella's generation could add anything valuable to the debate anyway.

*

Yet Bella did want to be part of the debate. She enjoyed challenging Sophie, who often popped in to have lunch with her or visit her at home in the evening after work. Sophie's relationship with her mother was cautious and distant. Her affections seemed to have missed a generation and, without Etta, she considered her grandmother to be her closest confidante. Bella valued Sophie as a window onto the lives and concerns of young women.

"About this pill," she asked one evening, "what does it actually do?"

An embarrassed Sophie tried to answer as rationally as possible, "It just stops me having babies."

"Don't you want to have babies? Not ever?"

"Yes, but when it's right for me, Gran. Gran..." her voice cajoled and Bella recognised that Sophie was about to ask for a favour.

"Yes?" Bella mimicked her tone.

"I have an interview coming up and nothing to wear. Any ideas?"

Sophie was now living with Chris, who she had met at a badminton class at the local sports centre. She had originally joined in an attempt to break the claustrophobic hold of working, living and socialising with Maggie. When Chris became her boyfriend, and they decided to live together, telling Maggie had been difficult. Telling Bella would be even more so. Chris was a cameraman and had organised a job interview for her at the television station that employed him.

Bella thought that Sophie's contemporary dress style, featuring long flowing shirt dresses, which she wore with her loose hair draped around the collar, was individual and right for her age. But both knew that it was not appropriate for an interview.

"What kind of job?"

"Nothing special, just clerical again but it is at a television station so one step up from filing blueprints."

"Oh, Sophie, you are such an intelligent girl, why didn't you go to university when you had the chance? I would have loved that opportunity but it was not available to us as Jews or women."

"I know, Gran, but hardly any girls went to university from my year, we were just encouraged to type, faster and faster. Anyway, I just wanted to get out there and have some life."

"Do you think university and studying is not life?"

"Of course I don't, but it would have been a rare choice and only for the most academic. I just wanted independence."

"What's the job?"

"It's not glamorous, just typing in the payroll department, but it might lead to something."

"What do you want to wear?" Bella was fiddling with her sketch pad.

"Anything but a grey suit."

"What's wrong with a grey suit?" asked Bella, knowing exactly what was wrong with a grey suit.

"It's what every one wears for job interviews."

Bella showed Sophie the quick sketch she had made of a slim black skirt, black jumper and crimson jacket. She filled in the outline of the legs with black charcoal, indicating black stockings.

"Short skirt – show your legs, you have good legs."

"Mini?"

"Not mini, not for a job interview." Bella indicated the length of the skirt, which was just one inch above the knee. "Courts," she added, drawing an impression of the shape of the shoes. "See, simple, smart and the jacket shows a flourish of personality, better than a grey suit."

"Gran, it's perfect – you are a genius. Where shall I go to buy it?"

Bella looked at Sophie and, shaking her head in amusement, asked, "When did you last buy clothes, Sophie? When do you need it by?"

"Thank you, thank you. If I get this job I'll take you out for a wonderful celebration lunch."

Later, when she called her grandmother, excitedly announcing, "I got the job, I got the job!" she claimed it was the outfit that had secured it for her and indeed it had certainly helped.

# 1972 Bella

Sophie bounded up the stairs of the new Bella Unique headquarters, which were situated in a graceful town house in Mayfair. It was her first visit to the new premises. She was wearing what her mother described as her uniform: a floor-length skirt, large hat, cowboy boots, rows of beaded necklaces and large rings on every finger.

The lift was not working, the building was dark, offices and design studios were empty. They had been struck by one of the electricity cuts, which had been timed to coincide with the three-day working week. These measures were a message to the government from the trade unions. Sophie felt that they were an outrageous insult to her grandmother, who had given so many people jobs throughout her life. But Bella tackled the three-day week and the electricity strikes the same way she had the general strike of 1926, by ignoring them. Transport was disrupted but Danny, her chauffer, had driven her to work as always. There was no possibility that he would go on strike.

Sophie slowed down to admire the sketches of Bella's designs, which Joshua had hung up the stairwell, some black and white and some colour but all in matching frames. The mounts were all a slightly darker shade than the walls, and the sketches were all dated. The first was a rough charcoal from 1905. It had torn edges and had obviously been folded at some time but, mounted and framed, it looked impressive. The most recent was a fully rendered outline of a trouser suit from this year's collection. Despite her many moves of both home and work premises, Bella never threw anything away, so her stairwell displayed an invaluable history of twentieth century dress design.

Her personal office took up most of the executive suite on the top floor. Here, the carpet changed from pale brown to pale gold and this part of the building was known to all as the 'golden mile'. It was reached by a private lift, so in order to visit her, people alighted on the fifth floor and took a separate lift to the sixth. This still had the restored Edwardian gate doors, which clattered as they shut, so that Bella could hear when someone was approaching. The day they moved in, Bella had marched defiantly up the stairs without resting for breath, ignoring anxious protests from Joshua. It was her way of showing her disapproval that he had hired the architect and interior designer responsible for many of Broom's cinemas for her premises, without involving her. Joshua claimed that it was unnecessary for her to waste her time and talents on a mere building when she had collections to design and that this was one of the projects he could take over to ease her workload.

"You can't do it all," said Joshua, "that's why I am here."

"We've had this conversation," answered Bella dismissively, "we must maintain what made the company 'unique', and that is my involvement in everything."

"But this is just a building, Gran...Bella." Joshua frequently found himself sliding into calling her 'Gran' when they had what he described to Sophie as 'a minor disagreement'.

It was noted, but not commented on, that her journey up the stairs was taking a little bit longer and that once up there, she only came down when she had finished her working day.

"This is gorgeous, Gran," exclaimed Sophie as she walked into the office. Bella looked tiny behind her smoky glass desk, which rested on chrome curved legs. She stood up to greet her grandchild, hitting the glass edge as she did. Sophie leant over to kiss her.

"I hate glass," grumbled Bella, hugging her granddaughter, "every time you touch it, it has to be cleaned and these corners are lethal. Do be careful."

"But it is lovely, Gran." Sophie knew that Joshua was finding it frustrating working for Bella but she thought that he at least might have allowed her to choose the décor and furniture for her own office. That would have reassured her that she still maintained control.

The glass table was empty except for a selection of different coloured spectacles and three telephones, all with buttons and lights.

"I can't work any of them," said Bella.

"Just pick up the one that lights up," laughed Sophie. She could understand her grandmother's discomfort at the formality of the space. Bella had never been a neat worker and this new environment was too pristine for her. The only personal object was a portrait of her first great-grandchild, Godfrey, which stood on a shelf behind her desk.

"Oh God, it's God!" a cynical Simon had commented, on being told the name chosen for his first grandchild.

"I'll show you around," said Bella, leading Sophie into the second room on the 'golden mile', which had been designed for Lilly. From her hospital bed she had been allowed to choose its colour scheme from sketches and fabric swatches Bella brought in, spreading them across the bed.

Lilly died before seeing it and Bella rarely went into the room now. It was pale pink and featured a glass cocktail cabinet as its centrepiece. A dark red velvet-covered chaise longue was placed against one wall, a delicate walnut desk against another. The curtains were silk, with wide pale cream stripes against a pink background. It was a room that Joshua wanted to designate for another purpose, but he knew that the loss of Lilly was still too recent to propose it.

"She would have loved it." Sophie put her arms around Bella, knowing how much she missed Lilly.

"She never saw it."

"I know, Gran, but she saw the drawings, chose it herself and knew that you were thinking of her."

After a series of small warning strokes, Lilly had died from a massive one.

"End of an era," Joshua had commented.

"Several eras," Simon added.

Sophie knew that Joshua had found working closely with Lilly almost as difficult as working with Bella. She'd still treated him like a little boy and had a tendency to pick fluff off his collar and tell him to sit up straight in front of the staff. He had been summoning up the courage to suggest to Bella that Lilly did not need to attend board meetings, when she was taken ill.

For a moment, Sophie imagined Lilly's vast frame settling comfortably into the chaise longue in the pink boudoir, enjoying the final fruits of her lifetime of friendship and support for Bella. It had been a long time since Lilly had made any professional contribution to the business, but her presence had provided the personal solidarity that sustained Bella during the toughest times. Despite her fading health, Lilly, picked up by Danny, would still have come to work whenever Bella did.

"You could use this room, Sophie." Bella's voice interrupted the silence.

"What on earth for?" Sophie regretted the astonishment in her voice but meant the question.

Bella led Sophie quickly out and into a small bathroom, complete with shower, bidet, and marble washstand. There was a selection of soaps, perfumes, hand lotions and a glass bowl full of potpourri. Pale coloured towels hung neatly on a rail next to the basin.

Bella pointed at the bidet. "What on earth am I supposed to do with this? What a waste of money."

She then took Sophie into a small kitchenette.

"Useful, isn't it, Gran, since you are so far up? At least you can make a cup of coffee when you want one."

They moved back into Bella's office and sat on the deep white leather sofa.

"Hmm, luxury," said Sophie, sinking backwards.

Bella perched on the edge as if she didn't belong. "I hate this air-conditioning. I am not allowed to open the windows," She paused for a moment. "I mean it, Sophie. I could offer you a job here, I need you.

"What for, what could I do here?"

"Keep me in touch, let me know what is going on."

"Joshua tells me he reports to you daily."

"Joshua is not interested in clothes."

"But he is interested in business and good at it."

"He keeps talking about makeup and perfume. Alright, we'll change the pink."

"What could I do for you? Anyway, I have been promoted." Sophie was sure she did not have Bella's attention yet.

"Joshua only tells me what he wants to tell me," said Bella, reaching towards a box of cigarettes on the glass coffee table in front of them. She picked up a jade table lighter.

"I need to stay in touch. That is what you could do for me."

"Spy?"

"Not spy, just keep me informed. Joshua is too busy, or claims he is anyway, and I don't know what is going on." Bella paused to light her cigarette. "I arrive in the morning, I go upstairs, someone brings me lunch on a tray, everyone is scared to come in."

"But Gran, your stamp is on everything across this business. It always has been. Joshua is just trying to make life a bit easier for you. That is what he is here for."

"Joshua is not respected."

"Why not?"

"Because he has never got his hands dirty. He started at the top because he is my grandson."

"But he works so hard, even Daddy said that."

"He needs to work twice as hard to gain the respect of both the staff and the outside world. He doesn't understand that."

"Gran, the whole idea is that someone you trust takes over the daily running, so that you don't have to. Then you can concentrate

284

on designing and looking after your favourite clients, the part you love. Look, the whole country is doing a three-day week and you are still working seven days."

"I am not comfortable. I feel as if I have been booted upstairs and out of the way. You could make all the difference."

"I'd have the same problem, Gran, it doesn't make sense. You don't need me, this is just growing pains." Sophie touched her grandmother's hand and tried to look into her eyes, but Bella was looking away.

"I don't feel Joshua is working for the business but for himself."

"I know that is not so. He is working for your legacy and he wants to help you keep B.U. at the forefront of the industry."

"B.U? B.U!" Sophie could tell from Bella's face and the tone of her voice that she had made a mistake. Joshua did call the organisation B.U. but was wise enough never to do so in front of Bella.

"It's just corporate speak, Gran. It separates the parent company from the boutiques, collections and mail order. It is the way business people speak these days."

"It means that he doesn't understand the culture." Bella glanced at her watch. "Lunch will be served soon. He told me the other day that what women choose to wear is about how they want to portray their sex life, not their social status or the occasion they are dressing for."

Sophie remained silent, aware that Bella was staring intently into her face.

"I ordered for you." Bella's voice was deflated. "It's just a little picnic, smoked salmon and salad, I hope that's alright."

"Lovely, thank you, but only if we can talk about something else. I have news. I have been promoted, that's what I came to tell you."

"Ah…" Bella's sigh was a mixture of disappointment and pride. "I am pleased, Sophie, really I am. You'll need some new clothes,

285

I think, a couple of new outfits, or are you going to go on looking like a hippie?" She hugged her granddaughter and for a moment held her tightly. "Now…tell me all about this new job."

# 1975 Sophie

"Come on, Gran, I want to know." Sophie was insistent. "Tell me about your childhood and then coming to England."

They were sitting on a bench in Kensington Gardens, between vivid rows of spring flowers. It had rained recently and the air was fresh and sweet. Only the low hum of traffic and the occasional sound of a car horn disturbed the peace. To the left they could see the Albert Memorial imposing its presence over the park, which was now filling with Sunday people.

Only with Sophie did Bella occasionally allow her age to show. She trusted this grandchild completely and the bond between them was growing stronger all the time. Bella admired Sophie's energy and imagination and still hoped that one day she would play a significant role in the future of her company.

"That's not what I want to talk about, Sophie. I don't want to remember the past."

"But if you don't, it will be forgotten." Sophie held Bella's hand and shook it slightly. "You want to talk about the future and I want to talk about the past. How will we manage a conversation?" she laughed.

"So forget it. Let's walk – go on, walk ahead, I want to see how that skirt moves. Thank goodness at least one of my granddaughters wears my clothes."

Sophie swung ahead, her stilettos crunching on the gravel path, her short skirt, slightly flared at the hem, swirling in rhythm with her steps. She wiggled her hips slightly and looked back fondly as Bella noted every detail.

"Stop working for a moment," Sophie said gaily over her shoulders.

"It is a pleasure to see that skirt worn so well, so that is not work. Anyway, I still have to persuade you to join me," said Bella, half in jest.

"Gran, not that again, please," Sophie returned to slip her hand through Bella's.

"I have to do something, Jenna is retiring. She was personally trained by Lilly, you know, and she is a very successful head of sales, very valuable."

"Oh dear, how old is Jenna?"

"Sixty this year. She was never happy working around Joshua, but she waited till sixty. With Jenna gone, I need someone I really trust by my side."

"Oh Gran, or should it be Bella, since I think this is a job offer? I work in television."

"But Sophie, so many people could work in television. There is only one Bella Unique and if you don't join me, it will die with me."

"It won't. Joshua will keep it alive and shouldn't this be his problem?"

"Joshua is out of control. He wants me to design towels now." Bella's voice conveyed that this was an outrageous idea.

"You have other grandchildren."

"Not really. Brynah is busy with her family and, anyway, look at the way she dresses. All that religious covering up, she might as well walk around in a tent."

"Then Rachel?"

"Rachel couldn't."

"Or wouldn't? She's been in a dead-end job for years. I am sure a change would do her good. Why don't you offer her a job?"

"Can you imagine Rachel in that role? She'd be useless. You know that."

"Oh Gran, how can you?"

Bella ignored her and continued. "Anyway, she hates change. She won't even allow me to re-cover the armchair in her bedroom." Bella shook her head in irritation. "And besides, even her father hasn't offered her a job. You would think with a business as large as his, he would have found something for her. Anyway, she is not interested in clothes."

"But nor am I," argued Sophie.

"Of course you are, look at the way you dress. Rachel has no style."

"Oh Gran, that is so rude."

"Not really, just true."

They reached the Albert Memorial, slowly walked up the marble steps and looked at the Commonwealth carvings on each pillar. Bella had moved into a block of flats in Kensington to be near Simon's home in Holland Park. At eighty-eight, she had finally admitted that the Hampstead house was too big. Rachel had moved with her and was comfortably ensconced in a large room with an en-suite bathroom, her routine barely disturbed.

"Little Bella Bromavitch, who would have thought it?" said Bella aloud, leaning against the railings and gazing at the unfamiliar Kensington view. "Shall we have tea, Sophie?"

"Not if you are going to go on nagging me."

"Tell me Sophie, what is so special about working in television?"

"I like it, Gran. In fact I love it and it seems to love me."

"What do you love about it?" asked Bella, curious.

"It's the future, Gran. I want to tell the world what is going on."

"Like your Aunt Etta? She told the world and died doing it."

"Oh Gran, I know, but she went to Israel, which you were proud of at the time, even if you didn't want her to stay there. There was a war. I am not going to war as I am not in the news department. I just make perfectly safe films about local London people. I promise you."

They left the park, crossed the road and turned down Queens Gate. Sophie regretted that the conversation had turned to Etta, noticing the sadness in her grandmother's eyes and feeling the familiar compassion for her. Bella occasionally referred to Etta and Sam and Sophie knew that she would grieve for them all her life; but Bernard was never mentioned. Bella had never come to terms with his suicide.

Bella took the keys out, opened the front door, ignored the lift and briskly walked up three flights of stairs, with Sophie panting her way up behind her. The flat was golden with sunshine glowing softly through the windows. Sophie led Bella to the pale grey sofa covered in silk scatter cushions in various shades of pink.

"Put your feet up and I'll make tea. Then I want you to tell me about Poland."

Bella plonked herself down and threw a cushion onto the Marquette coffee table. She pulled off her shoes. Her feet, complete with corns, bunions and in-grown toenails, the results of a lifetime standing on her feet, were perched on the cushion.

In the kitchen, Sophie made Bella's tea as she knew she liked it, boiling water with a teabag dropped in and almost instantly removed. The tea hardly changed the colour of the water. 'Water with a touch,' Sophie called it. For herself she plopped the same tea bag into a mug and stirred well until the liquid became strong and dark. She added a splash of milk and an exactly measured half teaspoon of sugar. 'Workman's tea,' Bella called it. She placed a few chocolate Olivers onto a plate and put both on a tray. Her grandmother would protest about the biscuits; she would nibble one and then cast it aside.

"Please," Sophie begged.

"Look, Sophie, I've never dwelt on the past. My success has been built on always looking forward. I've never said 'when I was young' or 'in my day.' It's advice for you to listen to. Anyway, why do you want to talk about my childhood?"

"I have an opportunity to produce my own series. It's my idea and it is being considered."

"Ah, an ulterior motive."

"Yes, if you like, but it is inspired by you."

"What does that mean?" Bella sounded suspicious.

"It's called 'Women at Work in London', and it is a series of film portraits about hugely successful women and their achievements. But I am choosing women who have overcome impossible odds. For heaven's sake, I have a perfect example in my own family." Sophie took a small tape recorder out of her large shoulder bag, and inserted a tape. She plugged a microphone into the socket and placed it close to Bella.

"Why didn't you say?" said Bella, showing interest for the first time.

"Because it might not happen and you have no time for failure." Sophie knew that Bella would always respond to news of her career.

"No, for women there is no place for failure." Bella was adamant.

"You see, Gran, you are a feminist!" Sophie pointed to Bella's damaged feet in their sheer nylon stockings. "Oh," she said, caressing them, "do these hurt?"

"A lifetime on my feet, Sophie, it's a small price to pay. At least you have stopped throwing flour and getting arrested."

"But what I want hasn't changed, just the way I am going about getting it."

"I haven't changed my opinion either. You may become chairman, woman, or whatever of the Board, but you will still have to peel the potatoes. You will just double the burden."

"So be it. We have no choice." Sophie walked restlessly around the room.

"I suppose not." Bella noticed her nervousness. "But why do you want to know about Poland? What has that got to do with it?"

"Because being an immigrant with no education and no parents were your insurmountable odds."

"An immigrant? A common story. I'll start from England."

"Can't you remember Poland?"

"I am old enough to have memories of memories," Bella laughed.

"Your life is an inspiration but I need to understand the early years. What happened to your family, do you know? When I was a child I thought you had other family in Poland. Why did I think that? What happened to them?"

Bella stood up and started to clear the tea-cups. "That was a long time ago. Do we have to do my whole life today?"

"Of course not, we'll start and I'll leave the tape recorder with you. But I am going to nag you to use it."

Bella picked up the microphone and held it awkwardly.

"Show me how to work this," she said.

# 1977 Bella

Bella stood upright throughout her entire ninetieth birthday celebration, refusing to use the chair that had been placed strategically for her. Simon was determined to give her a fitting tribute and 'putting on a show' was not a challenge to him. He had the teams, the venues, and the template to create such an event at the push of a button.

Word of mouth had informed the tourists that something special was about to happen in Leicester Square. It was rumoured it might be a royal premiere or at least an opening to be attended by famous stars, as the pavements of the square were cordoned off and guarded by police.

Simon stood magisterially just outside the foyer of his flagship cinema with Lady Penelope by his side. Her streaked blonde hair was swept up into a Gibson girl style, which emphasised her long neck and provided a fitting frame for her long diamond earrings. Her shoulders were covered with a mink stole and her pale cream gown flared beneath it. She held her hands together in defence against having to shake any hands.

Gold rope cordons protected a pathway for the red carpet, which led from the parking spaces for cars with their VIP passengers to the entrance of Broom's Premiere Screen. Security guards were placed discreetly along the outer edges of the carpet. Spotlights, positioned on the opposite side of the square, flooded the front of the building. Its awning was decorated with multi-coloured neon lights, which changed colour as they ran around the façade.

A concierge, his face glowing from the chill wind, wearing a dark blue suit with epaulettes and a peaked cap with a braid surround, stood in wait for the first cars. Men in similar uniforms were stopping the vehicles, checking invitations and directing the invited guests into the secure area. The cars, delayed by this procedure, backed up around the square and into the side streets. Lines of hopeful photographers stood in wait, their cameras held in readiness.

Simon, always at ease wearing a dinner jacket and waiting to greet people, watched the familiarity of the traffic chaos with satisfaction. As the owner of the country's most successful cinema chain, it was a well-practised routine for him, though the guests this time were not the usual film and celebrity community. Instead of famous actors, there were fashion writers, magazine editors, name photographers, models, competitive designers and retailers. There were bankers, property tycoons and business entrepreneurs, representatives of many rich, significant Jewish families who had, as Bella had, made a considerable contribution to British life since their arrival in the early years of the century. Simon had invited a smattering of his film industry contacts – producers, directors and distributors – some of whom had flown in from abroad for the festivities, and a few minor starlets who were always available when the paparazzi were present. Simon had not managed to persuade the stars of the film currently playing to put in an appearance, which he had hoped would gain some extra publicity. As for Lady Penelope, she had ensured the establishment was represented by an elite collection of titled aristocrats.

The entire staff of Bella Unique, from the packers to the managers, had been invited to honour Bella. Simon, or at least Simon's private secretary, had organised the invitations so that their arrival was staggered. Junior staff members were placed in the first cars and, giggling and screeching with delight, jumped out in front of the cinema, amazed at the glittering lights. They had all been given the afternoon off to prepare. The women had been lent Bella

Unique clothes and the men had been given a suit hire allowance. Middle management arrived next, showing a little more dignity, but enthralled at the starry beginning of their big night out in the West End. Those who had travelled by train from outside London had been accommodated at various hotels, the standard of rooms appropriate to their position.

Finally, Bella's most senior colleagues, wearing the best of her collection, wafted in. Simon greeted them all as if they were royalty, and for the one moment when they shook his hand, they felt they were. Lady Penelope nodded regally to each person, relaxed in the knowledge that although his ex-wives had been given seats, they were separated from each other and her.

The onlookers were shouting eagerly but were disappointed as car after car arrived without a well-known face in sight. Expectantly, they pushed against the cordons, assuming these were just the early arrivals and the 'real' celebrities would arrive at any moment. The parade continued until everyone except immediate family were inside and seated.

Bella's rented Daimler drew up and Joshua jumped out to help her alight. A spot light followed her out of the car, hovered as she kissed Simon and his wife, then tracked her as she entered the building, accompanied by Joshua and Simon. Her simple, long, black silk skirt and black top, covered with a matching sequinned jacket, contrasted drastically with the bright colours and flamboyant dresses of the guests. Her understated, elegant style was almost a criticism of the flamboyance of everyone else.

"That's class," someone in the foyer remarked. "Who is she?"

Recognising no one worthy of chasing for an autograph, the disappointed crowd groaned, grumbled and dispersed.

The family followed closely behind in two tight clusters. First, three great-grandchildren marched forward in a line, all wide-eyed but tight-lipped as if they had been threatened with some dreadful punishment if they so much as wriggled or whispered. Brynah's two children held David, Joshua's two-year-old, tightly by each hand. Joshua's new baby Percy had been left at home, the only missing member of the family. Then Brynah, already a matronly figure who looked older than her thirty-two years, swooped forward, holding tightly onto Lionel. Sophie, smiling with pride, searched the auditorium for Chris, who had been invited but, as they were not married, not placed with the 'real' family. She wore a simple, chocolate-brown, closely-fitted floor-length dress and had slung a wide-braided red belt low around her slender hips. A matching red ribbon was plaited through her long wavy hair. Rachel, her dull brown hair tightly permed close to her head, her lips tight with disapproval and shoulders bowed, walked self-consciously beside her. Bella had attempted to persuade Rachel that a simple tailored single-coloured gown would be most appropriate, but she had rejected all Bella's suggestions and bought herself a dress from a department store. She had had no reason to dress formally for many years, and seemed to have poured a lifetime of frustrated femininity into her choice of outfit for this one occasion. It was deep pink chiffon with a feather ruff around her neck and a full and flowing multi-layered skirt. Silver high heels completed the outfit and caused her to stagger rather than walk in the procession.

As the family group entered the auditorium, the entire audience stood up, a live orchestra burst into a jazz rendition of 'We'll meet again' and a thousand lightbulbs projected a flickering '90' onto the giant screen. Strobe lights flashed intermittently into the auditorium.

Bella had been told that the family were planning a celebration of some sort but she had not been warned of the scale or the style. She was reluctant to mark this milestone, particularly as her closest friend, two husbands and three of her children were no longer alive and she felt that to celebrate without them was not appropriate. But both Simon and Joshua had been insistent. Sophie said it was up to her, it could be a grand 'do' if she allowed it to be or a quiet family dinner if she preferred.

"Ninety," she had answered, "what's to celebrate?"

Brynah and Lionel had a keen sense of family history and, although they disapproved of ostentation, felt that their children might gain from recognising their heritage in a tangible way. The children were over-excited at the fancy cars, coloured lights and their place in the centre of the event.

Bella stood still, gazing at the display and the hundreds of people standing in her honour. She felt totally disassociated from it but knew that she could not let her family down. Slowly and steadily she progressed down the central aisle towards the stage. Somewhere, as if from far away, she was aware that an audience of two thousand were applauding.

Supported by Simon and Joshua, she walked up the stairs onto the narrow stage in front of the big screen. Her head was held high, her back, as always, straight. Simon guided her towards a tall winged armchair at the side of the stage and signalled her to sit. She glanced at it then, standing firmly in front of it, turned to face the audience. Despite the spotlights dazzling her eyes, she could just make out blocks of people but was unable to recognise any faces. Simon walked to the podium and introduced the evening. Tripping through the decades, he set her life in context and described her main achievements. Each received a round of applause. The screen displayed designs, posters and advertisements, some of them borrowed from the wall of her headquarters.

Unable to see, Bella fixed a benign smile on her face. Homage was paid to her influence, longevity and inspiration by several fashion experts, the Managing Director of a major department store and the Dean of a university that had recently granted her an honorary degree. One by one they traipsed to the podium and paid their brief respects. Sophie listened from her seat in the front row between Hester and Joshua.

Leaning over and covering her mouth with her hand, Hester whispered into Sophie's ear, "This is awful, just awful, like a living funeral."

Sophie's eyes did not leave her grandmother's face. "She is miserable. I know we shouldn't have done this."

"You tried to stop it, don't feel bad. She is coping."

"Coping, because she can cope with anything, but she is not enjoying herself."

"Shhh!" came a warning from the row behind.

"Oh…here it comes," whispered Sophie.

The choice of pictures for the film montage of Bella's life had caused such animosity amongst the family that even Simon, though committed to the project, was tempted to abandon it. Rachel, the obvious choice since she lived with Bella, had been assigned the task of clandestinely searching through her cupboards and drawers in search of images that could be used to create a visual story of Bella's journey. But Rachel did not have the character of a detective and kept finding excuses not to do her allotted task.

"It feels so sneaky," she protested.

"You're not doing any harm. It's for a wonderful occasion," an irritated Brynah kept repeating.

"I can't do it," Rachel whined. "Peeking into her private drawers, it's just not right. Anyway, how do you know if she has any photographs hidden away?"

"She may not, but you never know."

"Dad has all the family photographs. This is stupid."

While Bella was away on a short spa break in the country, they had all gathered at Simon's to select the photographs that had been found. Simon described a camera that could film every still image and connect them together like a moving film.

"It can even move on them," he said. "For instance, see this photograph of me and Bernard, it can show us together and then move closely into our eyes."

"You can't show pictures of Bernard, what about poor Jenna?" said Brynah.

"What about poor Gran? Dad, we can't do this," added Sophie.

For once Joshua agreed with his father. "We are going to be in a cinema. We have to put something on the screen."

"Well, we can't do family photos, at least not of the early years. All these pictures show Etta, Bernard and Sam. We can't show them yet we can't just miss them out as if they never existed. We have to do something else." Sophie was adamant. "What do you think, Joshua?"

"Well, it is a tribute to her as a person, not just her working life. We should be balanced. She is a mother and a grandmother."

"And a great-grandmother," added Brynah.

"It would be strange to just show great-grandchildren or grandchildren and not the family that started it all," said Joshua.

Sophie held out a photograph of a young Bella with Etta, the twins and Nat, who was holding a grinning baby Sam. "Look, happy children, dead adults. Can you imagine how she would feel if she saw this magnified on your giant screen, Dad? It's inhuman." Sophie stood up and headed towards the coat stand. "If you do this, I won't have any part of it, and I won't be there." She picked up her coat and started to put it on.

"Oh, for heaven's sake calm down." Simon used the conciliatory tone he always saved for his favourite daughter. "How could we explain your absence? Sit down, come on."

Sophie put her coat back on the stand and sat beside her father. She looked into his eyes. He winked and smiled.

"This can't be right," Rachel whined. "We shouldn't be arguing. It is supposed to be a happy occasion."

"It's just family stuff," dismissed Brynah.

"I have an idea," said Sophie suddenly.

"What's that?" Joshua trusted Sophie's ideas and knew that her closeness to her grandmother would mean that whatever she came up with would be to Bella's liking.

"Just take the photographs off the wall of the staircase at the headquarters and turn them into a moving image show. Then have a narrator add the personal milestones of those years. It's a great story and shows how clothes reflect the century. They are pretty and with music and words, it would make a focal point for the evening."

"No family photographs?"

"No family photographs, it's a public occasion."

With the audience on their feet, applauding and cheering, the family were lead out of a back exit and into two waiting cars.

"Just like a funeral," repeated Hester as she slid into the back of a car that also carried Rachel, Sophie, Brynah and Lionel.

"Not the clothes," corrected Sophie.

"No, not the clothes," agreed Rachel, looking down at her own fluffy feathered collar which looked more ragged than it had when she had dressed for the evening.

The young children had been whisked off by nannies and taken to their respective homes. Each had been given a gift as compensation for not taking part in the rest of the evening. Bella sat with Simon, Joshua and Lady Penelope, gazing out of the window as the car slowly drove around various West End streets, delaying her arrival until the allotted time.

The rest of the guests wandered slowly out of the cinema. One hundred selected people, bearing the coveted special invitation to dinner, were herded by ushers into two waiting double-decker buses. In convoy, they were transported out of Leicester Square, round St Martin's lane, back across Covent Garden, along Long Acre, down the beginning of Shaftesbury Avenue around Piccadilly and towards the Café Royal, where another red carpet had been laid out for them.

Inside the foyer, a small choir was singing a medley of twentieth century popular songs, each representing a decade. As Bella entered, flanked by Joshua and Simon, the choir burst into 'For she's a jolly good fellow'. Bella shook off the helping arms of her son and grandson, walked towards the singers and gave a nod of thanks. She entered the ballroom to cheers and whistles and was shown to her place by the head waiter.

Long tables in a U-formation were laid with silver and crystal, each place surrounded by several wine glasses of differing sizes. The rolled napkins were held together by rings bearing the word 'Bella'. Name places, clearly hand-written and handmade in the form of a bow-tie, stood above each place. The menu, printed in silver leaf on white card, was also headed by the word 'Bella'. White arum lilies, tied in upright bunches, had been placed in glass vases on each table. Ushers, checking table plans, helped the guests find their allotted seats. Wine waiters scurried around filling glasses with water and uncorking wine for later.

Bella sat in the centre of the top table, her closest family members spread either side of her. When everyone was seated, a photographer perched on top of a step ladder at the far end of the room and shouted, "Everyone please look at me and smile." His flashbulb momentarily blinded everyone as they looked up at him. He clattered down the ladder, changed some lenses on his camera and started to make his way from table to table.

Bella read the menu. The five courses, selected by Joshua, were her favourites and each dish was accompanied by the appropriate wine. After the first course of tiny gefilte fish balls laid on fresh parsley and decorated by dark red horseradish, champagne was poured into each glass. Simon stood and clinked a fork against his glass.

"Oh God, how much more? Now it's a wedding and it's the father of the bride speech," groaned Hester. Sophie poked her in the ribs. Lady Penelope saw this exchange and threw a warning glance at Simon. He waited for the room to fall silent, aware that the evening was late, the event had overrun and people were hungry. More importantly, everything had already been said.

"To Bella!" he announced and there was the sound of chairs being pushed back and the rustle of clothes as the company stood. Bella smiled and watched as people toasted her.

'Lilly would have loved this,' she thought, watching her guests sit down to eat the elegant meal and drink the fine wines.

# 1980s

# 1982 Sophie

The family were concerned about the strained relationship between Bella and Joshua. Sophie and Brynah rarely found common ground for discussion but, in their totally different ways, both feared the alienation might never be repaired. Even Simon agreed that the family was disintegrating and wanted to preserve at least a semblance of harmony while Bella lived.

Joshua's well-deserved promotion to Chief Executive had escalated the friction between them. She treated him like an enemy alien who was trying to destroy her treasured business. He was incensed that she ignored that he was her grandson who had dedicated his working life to B.U., guiding it into new and profitable directions, despite her objections.

Because of her longevity, energy and charisma, they had not prepared for a time when she might not be there at all, although retirement from the business had been actively encouraged by everyone in the five years since her ninetieth birthday.

Bella was now Chairman of the complex group of companies that comprised B.U. and interpreted the role to mean staying involved. The position had been awarded by the Board of Directors in the hope that she would loosen her grip, at least slightly, but Bella would not let go. There were still strands of the business that she appeared to control, although they were way beyond her comprehension. She was, however, more than a figurehead and still a signatory to most major transactions. Perplexed by the savage marketing conditions of the eighties, she was still able, and prone, to oppose Joshua's decisions. Her arguments over issues such as their advertising campaigns, a strategy she could not understand the need for, made his life difficult and his position uncomfortable. He had considered resigning on a fairly regular basis but always changed his mind, as the emotional tie to the business was overwhelming.

Bella insisted on being driven in regularly to see or be seen by her staff. This was a monthly event scheduled to coincide with board meetings and was greeted with dread by those who could not remember her in her prime. When she arrived, Joshua tried to distract her by showing her the latest designs, for he understood that her heart was always more in the clothes than the business. With a coloured pen in her hand and a sketch book in front of her, she relaxed and became rejuvenated. She sliced millimetres off shoulder pads, altered the shape of skirts and changed colours. She enjoyed being shown into the newly installed computer room to watch as the design of an outfit gradually came to life on screen. She became as animated as a little child and had not lost her ability to add that little bit extra to a garment that turned it from the good into the exceptional. Her eye for what worked, and what didn't, remained undiminished. She still read the fashion press and her eye for detail was impeccable.

"A belt," she would suggest. Then she would watch with excitement as the belt appeared when the designer punched a few keys and drew the belt with a stylus onto a glass frame. Thrilled by the magic of this new grown-up toy, Bella would irritate the designers by changing features, lapels, buttons, pockets and then removing them all again.

She tired easily and the visits were short but after she left, the staff always felt unsettled. Just occasionally, when Joshua caught someone being disrespectful behind her back, he became savagely protective. After one of her disturbing visits, one of the talented young designers faced an irate Joshua across his desk.

"When you are ninety-five, still walking, still involved and still committed enough to drag yourself out of your comfortable home and show up to work, then you can laugh," he exploded.

Brynah's life was devoted to her children and charitable activities associated with her synagogue. She continued to try to unite the family on Friday nights, always hosting a lavish Sabbath gathering for Lionel's brother, two sisters, their spouses and children but longing for her own family to come. Joshua having married 'out', his two older children always seemed to have football practice or dancing classes when she felt they should have been attending the only family gathering that still happened. Hester found reasons to decline almost before the invitation had been presented.

Bella was always invited but she was too old now to go out at night and Rachel wouldn't leave her. She now devoted herself totally to being Bella's companion, for which she received little or no gratitude. She rarely left her grandmother's side and had perpetrated a smooth role-reversal from child to parent, with Bella mischievously trying to escape her mistrustful gaze. Rachel's resentment of Brynah's marriage and family life had not lessened and she rejected all approaches to involve her, claiming that caring for Bella left her no time for herself. She had become less and less confident around other people, even family, and although Brynah's children were well-behaved, Rachel was still intimidated by them. Her face showed all the signs of her frustrated and incomplete life. She looked older than her years and paid little attention to her appearance, a fact that gave Bella fertile grounds for constant criticism.

Brynah always invited her father to the gatherings but he was too busy doing deals. He usually accepted, then called at the last moment to give his apologies. Lady Penelope enjoyed the financial and social benefits of being married to Simon Broom of B.E.E. and trusted that her husband, with his canny business sense, had defended his empire from the downturn in cinema's fortunes. The media were currently publishing worrying reports on the future of cinemas and potential loss of local film houses. The threat came from the spread of home videos, but Simon surprised even Lady Penelope with his foresight when he announced his purchase and development of a High Street chain of video rental shops.

"If the public want to see their movies at home on the sofa with a bottle of wine, that's where I'll show them," he had said, dismissive of her moment of insecurity. "I assure you," he added, "that we'll still be able to turn left on an aeroplane."

Nevertheless, Lady Penelope knew that with two ex-wives to support, their extravagant lifestyle was dependent on continued success. Retiring, which would normally be possible to contemplate at his age of sixty-eight, was not in Simon's plan. He talked business all the time, for the most part totally incomprehensibly to anyone else. Deals, counter-deals, mergers, acquisitions, hostile bids were of no interest unless you were in the centre of them. Penelope accepted that they led separate personal and social lives but the partnership, if not the relationship, worked for both of them. His ambition now was to receive a title in his own right, which he expected in the next New Year's Honours list. It would be acknowledged publicly as a reward for his services to entertainment but, in reality, it would be a recognition of his massive donations to the current government. Privately, although he would not admit it to anyone, Simon hoped that Bella would live long enough to see his visit to the Palace. He knew they had grown apart since his second divorce but somewhere, the little boy inside him still needed his mother's approval.

Like Joshua, Sophie had married 'out' and both Brynah and Rachel were in awe of Sophie and Chris's relationship. Brynah was used to Lionel leaving at the same time every morning and returning home at the same time each night, and could not understand Chris and Sophie's lifestyle. Sophie, busy building her career as a documentary film-maker, travelled extensively and her hours were unsociable. Chris was a cameraman and often away for weeks at a time but when they were together, they always seemed to be devoted and united.

Sophie knew that she did not contact either her father, who did not seem to notice, or Bella, who did, frequently enough. Her marriage to Chris had been spontaneous and she had announced it to the family after the event. Her father's only comment at her speedily arranged trip to the local registry office had been, "Thanks for saving me a lot of money." He then asked if she was pregnant.

She wasn't and it was hard to explain to anyone not in the same business that, as they both travelled a great deal on location, planning and scheduling a big wedding would have been impossible. A large gathering of people she hardly knew was not what she wanted anyway, but she was aware that Bella was disappointed and felt guilty about that. Her ambition had meant certain sacrifices and her family was the biggest one. She also occasionally felt guilty that she had introduced the idea of recording Bella's life story but had dropped it once the project had been cancelled. She was not good at following through ideas unless they were going to culminate in a completed film. Her desk drawers were full of scribbled and abandoned concepts.

She was saddened that Joshua had also refused a family gathering for his fortieth birthday, opting instead for a small dinner with Hester and the children. But she welcomed the opportunity of Godfrey's barmitzvah, recognising it as probably the last occasion for the family to gather with Bella as the figurehead. Bella, although frequently confusing the names of her great-grandchildren, threw herself into the preparations with great excitement and all the energy she could gather, once more taking charge of all the clothes worn by the women in the family. Nobody inhibited her this time and even Rachel and Lady Penelope wore Bella-designed outfits.

"My God, it's God's barmitzvah!" growled Simon, predictably, when informed of the event.

# 1987 Bella

Sophie perched precariously on the edge of the high bed, which was surrounded by safety rails. The smell of urine combined with aerosol was distinct. Bella lay still, except for her hands, which scratched at the candlewick blanket covering her. Sophie wanted to touch her, stroke her face, but felt that any contact might bruise her fragile frame. She cautiously touched her grandmother's hand. Bella opened her eyes and recognised her at once.

"I thought you had forgotten me." The voice was weak. The slight Eastern European inflection that she had never lost, despite eighty-four years in England and lots of effort, had not altered. The familiarity of her voice was strange when connected to the frail, changed body.

"Gran, I was here yesterday."

"Were you?" Bella tried to sit up but could not.

Sophie felt an almost physical pain. She so much wanted Bella back as she had known her all her life, her treasured grandmother who, despite disagreements and sometimes criticism, had always been her main support and best friend. Her grandmother, for whom she had wanted to be a success, would now never know that she was. She looked at Bella's emaciated neck and shoulders peeking through the pale yellow nightdress, which was covered with a lacy bed jacket. Her hair, throughout her life so fashionable, carefully coloured and well-groomed, was now thin, grey and straggly. If she could see it, she would have hated it. Her skin was still almost without wrinkles, but now translucent and drawn tightly across her cheekbones.

Sophie remembered Etta telling her that Bella had been a better grandmother than a mother, and Sophie knew it to be true. She also knew that, despite Bella's relentless attempts to entice her into her organisation, and disappointment when she failed, she was proud of her individual achievements.

Now she wanted to shake her and say, "Gran, come back, it's me, your Sophie, talk to me. I still need you." She said instead, "Gran, I brought you some fashion magazines."

There was no immediate answer and then: "Can you take me to the loo?"

Sophie waited until the moment passed. Bella could no longer get up to go to the toilet and Sophie did not want to remind her of that.

Now she had a question. "Gran, do you remember your sister Rosie?" Sophie's voice was urgent. She knew this was her last opportunity to find the answers she wanted. She brought out the faded photograph she had taken from Bella's bedroom the last time she had gone to check the flat. It had been empty since Bella had 'been away', the way they described her move into residential care. The family were taking turns to visit, to turn on lights, run water, flush the loo, check the post and remove the mounds of junk mail that blocked the front door.

On her last visit, Sophie had scrubbed the kitchen cabinets, removed rotting food from the fridge, released the doors on the bedroom wardrobes to let air in, and pulled open a few drawers. She felt guilty, intrusive and that Bella was watching her. She didn't look carefully at anything. She knew the time for clearing out would come and probably soon, but for now they were all just keeping Bella's home alive.

She found the photo in the top drawer of the dressing table. It was tucked behind old powder compacts, broken mirrors, squashed lipsticks, safety pins, broken eyebrow pencils and a half-empty bottle of perfume. It was covered in dust, the surface cracked with a tear in the centre where it looked as if it might have been intentionally ripped. Through the pale, discoloured image Sophie could make out two young women wearing long skirts and shawls. The taller one was holding a baby heavily wrapped in blankets. She looked as if she had been crying. The shorter one carried a large material sack on her arm, and she was laughing. Sophie recognised Bella's unmistakeable features, even though she was very young. Breathing deeply, she turned it over. In ink, now faded, was written '*Rosie, Bella and Sara, from your loving mother and sister. 1903.*'

"What happened to Rosie?" Sophie repeated, gently stroking her grandmother's forehead.

Bella lay silently. Then suddenly her eyes opened wide.

"Rosie, where is Rosie? Where is Jacob?"

"It's alright, Gran," said Sophie, who couldn't bear to disturb her grandmother's tranquillity. But Bella was alert again.

"My brain, it's out in the street. Where is my brain? Can you take me to the loo?"

"Yes, Gran, don't talk now."

"Tell Rosie the baby is crying again."

Sophie kissed her paper-thin skin and gently whispered directly into her ear. "I have to go now, Gran, I'll see you tomorrow." Gently she kissed her forehead.

"I want to die with red hair!" said Bella, her voice for a moment gaining strength. She lay back on her pillows as Sophie walked to the door, not looking back.

Sophie visited more frequently than anyone else. She regretted now that she had allowed her busy life to prevent her seeing Bella regularly and asking about her history. With the photograph as evidence that Bella had left a family, lost a family, or maybe even somewhere still had a family, the questions she had playfully contemplated as a child were suddenly compelling. She was moved that people remarked how like her grandmother she was and treasured that connection. As she sat beside her bed, watching her weaken, she agonised over the wasted opportunity to understand her own roots. Bella had experienced the momentous historical events that had changed their world throughout the twentieth century. Now it was too late, Sophie was desperate to ask about her experiences. As a documentary film-maker as well as a granddaughter, she was exasperated at her own neglect. She sat by Bella's side, knowing that her expectation was futile but somehow hoping that Bella would return and just tell her story.

Simon visited occasionally, dragging along his resentful wife. He argued that Bella didn't know who he was anyway, so there was no point. Her other regular visitor was Joshua, who made light of the fact that she usually thought he was Sam but was really disturbed by it.

In her lucid moments, Bella loved to talk about the past, although her memory was tangled and confused. She asked about her husbands and seemed to delight in the misconception that she had been married three times.

Raising her shaky, spindly fingers, she would ask her visitor, "Who was first?"

"Oscar." One finger was indicated.

"And next?" she queried.

"Nat." Another finger poked into the air.

"And then?"

"Danny." And nobody would say that Danny wasn't ever a husband. Holding up three fingers, her eyes twinkling, Bella would laugh and sometimes add in admiration, "Three husbands." Then she would ask whoever was visiting, "What happened to them?"

"Divorced, beheaded, died," Simon had muttered once under his breath.

"Again," she said, like a child not wanting the game to finish.

October 16th 1987 was a night like no other. Wind and rain lashed the south east of England. Trees crashed to the ground, tearing away roofs and cars. Scaffolding collapsed, windows were shattered and cars overturned. Plant pots, wood, drainpipes were lifted and

313

smashed to the ground. Debris flew through the air, damaging buildings, cars and people.

In the pandemonium and tumultuous noise, no one heard Bella Bromavitch cry out. She died as she had never lived, alone, while those charged with her care looked out of the window in bewilderment at England's first ever recorded hurricane.


Bushey, the North London cemetery where generations of Jews great, good and indifferent end their journey, was full to capacity. The jungle drums that create a Jewish funeral had played hard and loud. It is a phenomenon of Jewish life that in the prescribed twenty-four hours, except on the Sabbath or High Holidays, or with special dispensation if the next of kin live in Australia or Fiji, even those spread far and wide arrive in time to honour the dead. The rituals include catching up on how the years have treated their relatives.

In the women's section, as always, there was muttering in the background to be heard over the Rabbi's incantations.

"Poor Gertie, hasn't been the same since she lost her husband."

"Naomi's done very well for herself."

"Tragedy."

"He married out."

"Well, what do you expect?"

"Couldn't she have worn a hat?"

Sophie held her father's hand tightly as they entered the funeral chapel. They parted at the entrance and he joined the men on the left and she slowly walked towards the women on the right. Most mourners were standing, though a few elderly people took advantage of the wooden benches on each side. Although her breath was short and her legs felt weak, Sophie knew that sitting at her age would be inappropriate and somehow disrespectful to Bella. She greeted Brynah, who was red-eyed and just starting to show her unplanned late pregnancy, with a cool kiss, then moved towards Rachel for the traditional air kiss. She and Hester hugged, holding onto each other for a moment. She nodded to a few familiar faces and to those she didn't recognise. Most women wore black, with the occasional flash of a coloured scarf or the collar of a blouse showing. They shuffled and murmured and Sophie overheard someone she didn't want to know whisper, "So Bella Bromavitch ended up in North London after all."

She looked towards the men and saw that Simon and Joshua had placed themselves in the front of the group and were staring into their prayer books. Whether they saw them or not, Sophie couldn't tell. Joshua looked uncomfortable in his prayer shawl and Sophie wondered if he had worn one since his barmitzvah. Brynah's husband, Lionel, stood next to them and Sophie could hear his voice above the low hum of others, reciting prayers in Hebrew. Godfrey, a serious, bespectacled eighteen-year-old, and his fifteen-year-old brother Isaac were absorbed in their prayer books. Joshua's twelve-year-old son David stood a step behind them and concentrated on his, although he didn't read Hebrew and his mind was somewhere else. His ten-year-old brother Percy, a name that Bella had never approved, was wedged between his father and grandfather, it seemed, to keep his restless body still. He held a prayer book out in front of him but his eyes were wandering round the scene. He winked across the room at his sister Elspeth, a bubbly eight-year-old with curly blonde hair, who was gripping her mother's hand. Hester leant down to whisper closely into her ear and for a moment she stopped fidgeting.

Sophie was determined not to cry but, not trusting herself, had packed her pockets with tissues, which she now manipulated gently in an effort to stay calm. Observing the surreal scene, she wished she was anywhere else and in any other time. Turning to glance towards the Rabbi, her eyes caught sight of the tiny coffin, which she had so wanted to avoid. Her breath stuck in her throat and her body went rigid. It looked so lonely and defenceless and so little to do with Bella. It was pale oak, a decision that had not been arrived at easily, but somehow in death the family had wanted her

315

to be as elegant as she had been all her life. Sophie stared piercingly at it, trying to imagine Bella's body tucked up inside a box, anything to make this moment less real. She couldn't picture her, Bella, that most vital, vigorous, driving force, now silenced. She tried to remember the sound of her voice, but she could not hear it.

She fingered the photograph in her pocket, which she had wrapped in tissue as a protection, not wanting to add to the damage of years. The image was sharp in her mind and she concentrated on the impression of the young woman in that photograph, as she observed the assembled people in the prayer hall. How had Bella arrived from that scene to this, a funeral of more than two hundred people to mark her passing?

The Rabbi had started the formal service and was directing the congregation to pages as he read them in his monotonous voice. There was a swell of synchronised reciting, louder from the men but with a few confident female voices breaking through. He then stopped and took out some notes and spoke in awe of the dynamic life force, the ambition, the great beauty and the mother, grandmother and great-grandmother. Sophie resented this tribute from someone who had never met or known Bella. She knew that Simon and Joshua had spent time briefing the Rabbi yesterday afternoon, so the detail was probably correct, but it seemed offensive that her grandmother's achievements should be listed so dispassionately by this stranger with the smug smile. He even attempted a little joke.

"No one dared cross her..." is all Sophie heard before she closed her eyes, blocked her ears and mind.

"How dare he?" she thought irrationally.

Now Hester was shaking her arm. The service was over and the congregation was moving towards the back door. Sophie, in a daze, had not noticed the coffin being removed.

"Sophie, come on. Put these on, it's muddy outside." Hester held out some plastic shoe covers. Sophie had seen them once before, in a palace in St Petersburgh. There they had seemed appropriate, as their job was to protect a highly polished parquet floor from the scuffs of tourists' shoes. The congregation of mourners trudged into the muddy cemetery, their shoes covered incongruously with what looked like plastic bags. The children, released from their forced separation of boys on one side, girls on the other, bounced back together and skipped out of the airless funeral hall into the cemetery grounds. The plastic shoe covers made impromptu skateboards and they whooped down the path towards the graveyard, sliding with delight along the muddy gravel as if it were snow. Called back into line by their parents, they still kicked at the ground as the group progressed down the numbered angular paths between the immaculately aligned gravestones.

The cemetery stretched far out of sight. Each grave had its precise space on the grid; the whole area was like a miniature suburban town, so inappropriate for the sophisticated, individual Bella.

She will hate it here, thought Sophie irrationally, so uniform, so formal, so parallel.

A small minibus arrived to pick up the older members of the congregation but the others wandered slowly down the long lines, reading the stones as they passed. They greeted each recognisable name as if it were a jolly reunion or social occasion. It was a large cemetery and about fifteen minutes passed until they reached a newly dug grave. Sophie noticed with relief that Bella would be at the end of a row; she would have been uncomfortable had she been placed in the middle, surrounded by others. She also noticed that Lilly's grave was only two rows away.

"Look," she whispered to Joshua, "now they can natter away into eternity." Joshua hugged her in response and she was grateful. She wondered if it was possible to move graves. She had a fleeting thought that Bella and Lilly should be next to each other forever. Looking at Lilly's headstone, she remembered the discussions they'd had deciding on its wording and Bella's distress at the loss of her friend. She showed her emotions more readily after Lilly's death than she had at the loss of Etta, Bernard or even Sam. Possibly the pain of those three bereavements was too great to even acknowledge and Bella responded in the only way she knew how, by working harder and longer. Sophie tried to remember how long ago it was.

The final ritual of burying the dead began with more prayers from the Rabbi, who stood beside the newly dug hole. The men gathered close, the women halted a little further back. Sophie fingered the photograph in the pocket of her black raincoat and wondered at what moment she would throw it into the grave. Now, before the coffin was lowered, or later so that it lay on top? The finality of the coffin being let down to the low rumble of prayers, punctuated by the occasional sob, shocked her. She knew Bella was dead, Bella was being buried, but she wanted to jump in and rescue her, drag her out, deny the reality. She watched as the men gathered around, and one by one, took the shovel from the Rabbi's hands, drew small clumps of earth from the heap created when the grave was dug, and emptied them onto the top of the oak lid. The sounds of the first clods hitting were hard, then gradually softened as the covering of soil built up. David and Percy manoeuvred themselves into line and took their turns. Their throwing was more enthusiastic than the adults.

Joshua retrieved the spade and handed it out towards the women, his look enquiring if anyone would like to participate. Elspeth tucked her face further into her mother's coat. Sophie watched Brynah and Rachel as they helped to bury their grandmother. She edged closer, holding the picture, then carefully turned it over.

'*Rosie, Bella and Sara, from your loving mother and sister. 1903,*' she read again.

She imagined it sitting concealed inside that pile of earth, lost forever, disintegrating and nowhere near Bella. She shoved it back into her pocket, grabbed the shovel and dug.

The family argued as much over the clearing of Bella's home as they had over the selection of pictures for her ninetieth. After much deliberation, interrupted by various disagreements, Sophie and Joshua were selected to take on the task. Brynah's pregnancy precluded her from all responsibilities outside her home. Rachel had been sitting in an armchair sobbing since the end of the Shiva, and Simon's offer had consisted of sending in 'his people', an idea that was rejected by everyone.

"You have to be savage, everything has got to go. We'll take care of the bequests and chuck out everything else," said Simon. Lady Penelope agreed but Sophie and Joshua wanted to clear Bella's home carefully. The bequests were mainly treasured pieces of jewellery. Each had been carefully labelled with the beneficiary's name hand-written. Simon's ex-wives had not been forgotten. Judith received a pair of Victorian carved jade earrings, which Bella had never worn. Even 'poor' Stella, so-called because their marriage had not lasted a year although because of it she was not poor at all, was left a sapphire and diamond ring. Bella's ruby ring was to be given to Jenna, by agreement.

"That's the only thing we have agreed upon," commented Joshua over drinks with Sophie in the cocktail bar of the Royal Garden Hotel.

"And the drawing pads and paints."

"Ah yes, to God."

"Oh poor boy, don't do that." Sophie had always felt sorry for Brynah's first child Godfrey. Now, at eighteen, he was buried under A-Level pressure and had been rebelling against the orthodoxy of his parents for a number of years. He was showing signs of inheriting his grandmother's artistic talent and wanted to go to art school, a dream that Brynah treated as if he had chosen to become a common criminal. Godfrey had cherished his great-grandmother and felt her loss both as a person and as a supporter of his creative ambitions. Everyone agreed that all her equipment should go to him and his younger brother, Isaac, would be compensated by a generous cheque from Simon.

"OK, so how are we going to do this? I am dreading it," said Sophie, stirring her vodka and tonic.

"Quickly. It's awful but everyone has to do it when they lose a parent."

"Joshua, she is not our parent. Honestly, Dad should be taking care of it. He is so insensitive."

"It's us, or our father and 'his people'. Do you want 'his people' going through Bella's underwear?"

"No," protested Sophie, appalled.

"Well, here we go again. Brynah is pregnant and bovine again, that gives her a perfect excuse, and Rachel is incapable."

"Nothing changes, does it?" Sophie gathered her thoughts. "OK, I'll do all the personal stuff, like clothes and dressing table and that stuff. But can I take Chris?"

"Sure, if he can bear it."

"I expect he'll want to help me. I wish I could get out of it."

"You can – 'his people'," repeated Joshua.

"Don't. I'll start this weekend.

Sophie turned the security lock on the apartment's heavy door, hearing the familiar double click as it opened. She smelt stale air and something rotten as if rubbish had been left out in the hall too long. She hesitated, then turned to Chris for support.

"I'll go in first," he said, responding to the appeal in her expression.

He pushed hard against a barrier of junk mail, bills and get-well cards, then bent and scooped all of it up.

"I'll sort this," he said, turning to coax her in.

Sophie stood still at the open door. "This is horrible."

"I know, but your grandmother would have wanted you to do it. Whatever we find, she would have wanted you to find it first. Come on."

She let him lead her into the living room. He drew the curtains and opened all the windows.

"Sit," he said, "get used to being here."

"Without her?"

"Yes, without her."

Sophie avoided looking at Bella's chair with the little footstool in front of it and sat on the sofa. She leant against the little scatter cushions, which were decorative but had never made it comfortable. Chris pulled some large black bin liners out of a carrier bag, set one on the floor and started to go through the post. He read, chucked, read and chucked.

"Junk, junk," he said in disgust, "it's only when something like this happens that you realise how many forests we are ruining, for no reason."

Sophie sat silently looking around the room, which was still neat but now dusty. One sofa, two armchairs, marble lamps all dating from the 1950s, when Bella had started to make enough money to buy new furniture. It was daringly contemporary then, now it was just dated.

There were pictures on the walls, all original and exquisitely displayed with space surrounding them. The only clutter was on the mantelpiece, which held numerous invitations to events Bella had been too sick to attend, a framed photograph of the family group from her ninetieth party, several pictures of the children and one of her outside Buckingham Palace after collecting her OBE, with Rachel standing awkwardly beside her. Sophie remembered asking why Rachel had been chosen for this and the answer had been "Because she hasn't anything else."

"What do you think we should do with the furniture?" she asked now.

"It's all saleable except perhaps what is in the bedroom."

"Selling seems so disrespectful."

"Disrespectful to what?" asked Chris as he sat next to her, holding her hand.

"Her life."

"It's furniture, a bunch of objects, nothing to do with her life, her achievements, her legacy, her family. Some people only leave furniture when they die." Chris continued to sort the post. Sophie sat silently watching him, then murmured, "That dreadful smell is coming from the kitchen."

"Yes, why don't you go and see what it is?"

Slowly, Sophie stood up and made her way to the kitchen. It was tidy and clean. A few washed dishes stood draining in the sink. But the smell from the fridge was strong and vile. She reached into her handbag and took out the yellow rubber gloves she had brought for the task. She opened the fridge door and stood back as the smell hit her. It was empty but far at the back was a lump of something. It appeared to be moving.

"Oh my God, Chris, look," she cried.

She felt Chris move her quickly out of the way and watched him reach into the fridge. Grimacing, he brought out a decayed piece of meat, crawling with maggots.

Sophie stumbled out into the living room. She plonked herself on the sofa. She tried not to remember the last time she had been here or to feel guilty that she had not been here more often. She could hear Bella's voice in her head, strong as it used to be, not as it was the last time she'd seen her.

"Sophie, Sophie…" Chris was holding out a glass of water. "She was ninety-nine, for Christ's sake. It was a good life and a long life. The smell from the kitchen was a rotten piece of chicken full of maggots. Whoever cleaned out the fridge just missed it. That's all. I've dealt with that. Now, go into the bedroom and start on the clothes. Come on. I don't want to be here all night. Remember, she would have wanted you to be first in."

Sophie was grateful for Chris's reliable practicality. He was a no-nonsense man. He pushed three black bin liners towards her.

"Three?" Sophie queried.

"One to keep, one to chuck, one to go to the charity shop. Go!" he said, pushing her towards the bedroom.

Bella's bedroom, with its double bed, en-suite bathroom and walk-in wardrobe large enough to double as a dressing room, was eerie in the glow from the street light outside. Sophie pushed back the curtains, opened the windows and turned on every light she could find. The sheets had not been changed since Bella's removal to hospital and she shuddered, noticing the indention in the pillows. An old Sunday supplement magazine fashion section still lay across the bedspread and a crystal glass half-full of water remained where it had been for so many weeks.

"Are you alright? Can I help?" Chris shouted from the kitchen, where she could hear him rubbing and scrubbing.

"I am fine," she lied.

The only place of complete privacy in Bella's life was her bedroom. Even her executive office, regularly invaded by assistants and secretaries, had not been a sanctuary for many years; but her bedroom was sacrosanct.

"Remember, she would have wanted you to be first in," she heard Chris yell with his uncanny ability to read her mind.

In the bright overhead light, Sophie ruthlessly pulled the bedclothes off and shoved them into one bin liner. Somehow, with the bed stripped, the room felt less personal. She opened the top drawer of one of the matching bedside tables. She ran her fingers through old pills, hair-pins, bits of old postcards. Finding nothing of interest, she picked everything up and threw it into the bin liner she had designated as the one for stuff to chuck. Then she attacked the other side and, finding the same melee of miscellaneous bits and pieces, threw it impatiently away. Bella's dressing table, where she had previously found the photograph, yielded no more treasures, just broken lipsticks, dried up mascara, two hairbrushes and more pills. A tortoiseshell hair comb was tucked at the back, along with a train ticket to Brighton. Sophie threw them all into the black bag. She removed a J-cloth from the packet, wet it under the bathroom tap and wiped the drawers clean.

"How you doing?"

"Fine, and you?"

"Still sifting the junk, bags of it."

"Anything worth keeping?"

"Bills, they need to go to the solicitors. Nothing much else."

Sophie went into Bella's dressing room. Her clothes were hanging in immaculate rows, mostly in plastic covers, on racks, her shoes neatly lined up underneath. On shelves on the walls were hats and in each hat was a pair of gloves. Her enormous collection of scarves hung separately on a rail intended for men's ties.

"Hats and gloves," said Sophie with surprise. "I never saw her wearing either except at weddings and funerals."

"Perfectly dressed lady," said Chris. "Time for tea?"

"Tea would be good, but there is nothing here…well, nothing safe to drink anyway," said Sophie, looking at the clothes.

"Clever me," said Chris, entering the dressing room with a hot mug of tea. "I'm a good man to have in an emergency. I brought everything." He looked at the rails of clothes. "Hmm, that's a valuable collection. Bella Bromavitch's wardrobe. Sotheby's would like to get their hands on that for a special sale."

"I can't sell her clothes. That would be awful."

"More awful than giving them away or throwing them away?"

Sophie sat on the floor with her mug of tea, staring up at Bella's dresses.

"Maybe a museum, a fashion museum…I don't know. I'll have to discuss this with Joshua and Dad. It's a huge collection, so odd. She wore such simple classic clothes."

Chris joined her on the floor and placed his arm around her shoulders.

"Strange place for tea," said Sophie, leaning her head against Chris' chest, "sitting beneath Bella's skirts."

"I bet you sat beneath her skirts a lot when you were little."

"I can't remember, she was always so busy."

"Right. We can't sit here all day. Shall we have a go at the shoes and hat-boxes or have you had enough for one day? You could wriggle underneath and hand them out to me. OK? It's a bit of a dusty mess down there."

Sophie crawled beneath the rails of dresses, coats and skirts, her fingers tripping lightly over the hems. Some were familiar and she could associate them with particular events. She touched the hem of the black silk skirt Bella had worn to her ninetieth birthday celebration, the pale yellow suit she had worn the momentous day she had been invited to a Buckingham Palace tea party. She had worn it once and never again. There were many outfits Sophie had not seen before, all carefully stored and protected.

"It's just like her warehouse, organised."

She smelt mothballs and traces of perfume. She gradually pulled out shoe-boxes and hat-boxes. "It's dark. I can't see what I am doing. I bet all these shoes and boxes have been here since she moved in."

She coughed from the dust as she progressed across the floor and reached the back wall of the dressing room. At the very end, tucked in a corner and slightly separated from the rest, she found a round leather hat-box. It had a rusty zip and a faded handwritten label in the centre. There was a small padlock which had a key attached to it. Sophie dragged it out with her as she slithered back out into the light.

"Oh, that wasn't fun. Look at this, it looks very old."

Chris came in. "What's that?" he asked.

Sophie was dusting off the leather hat-box. "I don't know, it was separated from the rest. I feel as if we are intruding into something very personal here."

"Maybe we are, but that is what we are here for. It isn't locked. Why don't you open it?"

Sophie hesitated, then ran the zip around the lid. The box was lined with dark green velvet. A pale purple hat sat inside, its delicate upright feathers covered with crumbling tissue paper. It was supported by a tall tin and more tissue paper. Sophie carefully lifted the hat out of the box.

"Oh my goodness," said Chris, "how beautiful."

"Isn't it? I would like to keep this. It's like a piece of art. It is so strange that she placed it in an old tin and not a hat stand. I can't remember her ever wearing it."

"For old tin, think antique tin," said Chris, picking it up. He opened the lid and fell silent.

"I could keep it on my dressing table on a stand, it would look lovely there."

"Sophie, look." Chris handed her a long, buff-coloured envelope. It was marked 'OSCAR' in Bella's familiar handwriting. Sophie watched as he shook the contents onto the carpet. Wrapped in a white handkerchief decorated with a hand-embroidered 'O' was a strip of shoe leather, a fob watch, and a small piece of charcoal. A little package of green felt fell onto the floor. Sophie carefully unwrapped it, then quickly dropped it.

"Oh my God, oh my God, they're my grandfather's false teeth!" she wept, staring at the dentures sitting incongruously on the gold carpet, framed with green felt.

"Go and sit down," Chris commanded, pushing her gently towards an armchair. Sophie continued to sob as Chris picked up the dentures and other objects and carefully replaced them within the envelope. He continued to delve into the tin.

"Sophie." Chris's voice was sharp. "I've found some letters."

He held out a bundle of letters. They had all been opened and were tied together with brown string. Sophie quietly looked at the bundle Chris held out to her.

"They are very old and from Poland, look." Chris pointed out the stamps and the date marks.

"Oh my God, oh my God." Sophie hugged her knees and stared at the letters.

Chris held one out to her. "Do you want to read it?"

Sophie stayed still for a moment, then picked up the letter. She read it silently.

"It's from Rosie," she whispered, "the sister in the photograph." She folded the letter carefully back into the envelope and carefully fanned the other envelopes. "Same handwriting, they all are. Why did she never mention her? Why did she never tell me? Let's take these home, they're precious."

"And the hat?"

"Put it back. It was just her way of hiding her past." Sophie placed the hat carefully back into the leather box.

Chris picked up the tin and peered inside again. "Look, there is a cassette as well."

With unsteady hands, Sophie picked up the cassette and read the label she had written twelve years earlier. The blue ink was now faded to pale green, the paper brittle.

"'London Women Working – Bella Bromavitch, background'," she read, then, followed it with a sequence of dates written by Bella on the label. "Oh, she did it, she recorded the cassette and never told me," Sophie added quietly, her voice unsteady. In despair, Sophie remembered how resistant Bella had been to the idea of telling her memoirs to a microphone. Chris watched her while she put all the letters and the tape back into the tin alongside the buff-coloured envelope and tucked it all into a carrier bag to take home.

"Let's go home now," she said.

# 1990s

# 1990 Sophie

Sophie called her son Bellamy. She was thirty-nine when he was born and remembered Bella telling her that Etta had always just achieved something at "twenty-nine, thirty-nine, just in time," she had said. In her bedroom, she had a framed photograph of Etta and Bella together on a seafront. On the back was written 'Brighton 1964'. They were laughing and Etta, who towered over her mother, had her arm around Bella's shoulders. Sophie had taken it when she had cleared out Bella's flat and now spoke to the picture in moments of extreme stress or indecision. It helped to imagine how they would answer.

Most of the time she was glad Bellamy was not a girl, whom she might have been tempted to call Bella. This would carry too heavy a responsibility for any child. There were, however, dilemmas raised by the birth of a male child in an Anglicised Jewish family, however liberal and modern. Neither she nor Chris practised any form of religion. They exchanged Christmas presents and Easter eggs for fun and found excuses not to join Brynah and Lionel for the family Passover. They agreed that everyone had a right to their beliefs but were deeply opposed to all forms of ritual. Officially, she knew that in the Jewish tradition, children took their mother's religion and had been tempted, on occasion, to write 'committed atheist' on forms that asked.

After Bellamy's birth, the subject of circumcision was raised by Lionel. Sophie was easily able to dismiss the interference as none of his business. She was less able to do so when her father brought up the subject.

Simon had not retired and, determined to work as long as his mother, continued to control his empire from an armchair at home, a golf club in Surrey or by the new mobile telephonic devices from his holiday home in St. Lucia. As her father was no longer an observant Jew, Sophie was surprised at how much Bellamy's circumcision meant to him.

Chris had a straightforward view, seeing it as a medical procedure, so it was not a discussion she could have with him. She acknowledged that there were still compelling reasons to circumcise in the developing world, the same reasons Jews had experienced four thousand years before but she could not relate to them now.

Her predicament made her rethink her Jewishness, a subject she had avoided since Etta's death had made unquestioning Zionism impossible. Etta's paperwork had been given to Sophie, as the result of a personal letter attached to her will. The letter said:

*'Sophie dearest, please follow your own dreams. You have talent, originality and energy. But you need to focus on what is important to you, not me and not beloved Bella. I am leaving you all my paperwork, in case anyone ever wants to know my opinion on the current situation.'*

It was a heavy legacy. It had been many years since Etta's death when Sophie had read these notes. Most had been scrawled in pencil and some were illegible. Sophie remembered that Etta had suggested that the results of Israel's Sinai invasion in 1967 and the subsequent occupation of Palestinian territory would reverberate for generations. At the time she had read them, it was through a wall of grief and the comments seemed little to do with her. Now with Bellamy and unexpected pressure from her father, she felt all aspects of being Jewish were under scrutiny. The dilemma was complicated by her recollection of Etta's remarks.

As a working mother with a travelling husband, there was little time to think of anything other than fulfilling the responsibilities of both those roles. Since the birth of Bellamy, any time not spent mothering or working was wasted time, so struggling with the moral issues surrounding circumcision and being Jewish was not a priority.

Nevertheless, she wanted to please her father and if it mattered to him, it mattered to her so she made the necessary arrangements.

Investigating the history of her family's past, was also not a priority. She had not read any more of the letters found after Bella's death but had wrapped them carefully, protected them with foil and placed them with the sealed cassette at the top of her wardrobe, along with other forgotten memorabilia that held no further value. But she could not bring herself to throw them away. Sometimes she felt curious about the contents of the letters and the cassette but mostly she was just busy coping day by day.

She had told Simon and the rest of the family of their existence but none of them had shown any interest.

"Throw them away," Simon had suggested. "We have to close the door on the past."

She and her father rarely saw each other any more and she missed him. Lady Penelope had created a barrier of social exclusion around him as they climbed further and further up the ranks of English society, and neither his children nor grandchildren were encouraged to remain close. As a patron of many charities, non-executive director of several large companies, Chairman of B.E.E., and now Lord Broom, Simon was quite isolated from his family. However, he did all the appropriate things a dutiful patriarch should, and considered himself a good father and grandfather. All the grandchildren had trust funds, he donated large sums to Brynah's synagogue appeals and to Joshua he gave unsolicited and unwelcome advice on the structure of B.U. Rachel had inherited the flat she had shared with Bella and moved to a small portered apartment block with the proceeds of its sale. She gave up her job and lived comfortably off an allowance from her father, watching television and doing crosswords and inventing excuses not to visit either of her sisters or their children.

Simon considered Sophie to be independent of him, but always noticed her name when it appeared on a television programme and usually remembered to call her. He frequently had a critical comment to make so she dreaded the calls.

"Why are you always so critical?" she once complained.

"I am not," he protested, "I am making an intelligent comment."

Sophie resented that Lady Penelope had resolutely tried to obliterate any signs of Simon's background. Brynah went so far as to call her anti-Semitic but then, to Brynah, all the world outside her conclave of observant North London Jews was anti-Semitic.

Sophie felt that if Simon was not interested in his mother's background, there was no way she should be, but she still had no intention of throwing the letters away. Whenever she had reason to take something out of the top of the cupboard and saw the package, she had a moment of temptation but knew that opening them would require a great degree of self-control and an investment of time and emotion she could not afford.

Joshua was busy with the expansion of B.U., but he and Sophie spoke frequently on the telephone. He was the only one of the grandchildren who still liked to talk about Bella, as her heritage was still central to his daily working life. Nevertheless, the conversation was usually about his three children. Two teenage boys were demanding and required a lot of attention and chauffeuring. Elspeth, strong-willed and bright at eleven and approaching a school change, showed every sign of developing into a defiant and rebellious teenager. She was at odds with her parents about every issue, restriction and house rule.

"It's like living with a baby Bella," Joshua told Sophie after one particularly brutal argument about her right to wear makeup.

"I can imagine what Bella would have said," commented Sophie.

"What's that?"

"At your age…" And they both laughed.

So Joshua and Hester were also busy with the immediate and had no time for reliving history. Maybe Simon was right. The past was the past. Bella's achievements were her legacy.

Then, unexpectedly, Simon died. It was his first and last heart attack.

"Oh bugger," said Lady Penelope, "another three years and he would have had free membership of his golf club."

The death of a member of the House of Lords, a famous entrepreneur, a multi-millionaire benefactor, is a public affair. It was announced on the news on all channels, illustrated with a picture of a young Simon, complete with dark moustache and slicked back hair. The funeral was broadcast, photographs of the grandchildren and famous mourners were pictured arriving at the cemetery. Simon's two ex-wives were featured, almost identical in their simulated sorrow. The future of B.E.E. was deliberated in the business papers and his impact on the entertainment industry discussed at length on television. Representatives of the various charities he supported were interviewed and spoke of the loss of a great humanitarian. Obituaries appeared across the National press and the family background was regurgitated once more.

The shock to his immediate family was deflected by the frenetic pace of events and they found little opportunity to grieve privately. Lady Penelope cleared their London home quickly and left for St. Lucia immediately after the funeral. Boxes of personal belongings arrived unannounced at B.U.'s offices addressed to Joshua and this was her only recognition that her husband had left a family of children and grandchildren.

During the eight months between Simon's funeral and memorial service, Sophie tried to absorb the loss of her father. She shed no tears and there was a vacuum where she had expected grief. When she looked at photographs of them all as children, she was usually holding his hand or sitting on his knee and it was for this younger father and her younger self that she felt sadness. She tried not to compare the way she felt now with the anguish she had experienced after Bella's death. Only Joshua shared and understood the mix of regret and emptiness.

It was her need to reconnect with her fractured family for both herself and her son that eventually drove her back to the letters from Poland.

# 1991 Sophie

Sophie took each letter out of its envelope, keeping them carefully in date order and piling them one by one in front of Joshua. He lazed on her sofa, shoes off, his feet resting on a cushion on the coffee table in front of him. The room still smelt of the takeaway pizzas they had consumed earlier. She had invited him over to share them with her, choosing an evening when Chris was filming late, so they could experience this together. She knew that Joshua was the only member of her family who would give the occasion the respect it deserved and they had agreed not to involve Brynah or Rachel.

She read the first letter, handed it to Joshua and picked up the second. She read that, then the next, handing them, one by one, to Joshua. Sipping glasses of red wine, they read together without comment. Sophie wanted the silence broken but could find no words. Joshua showed no emotion, just occasionally sighed or grunted. Once he shrugged and Sophie felt irritated, trying not to see him out of the corner of her eye.

"What's a bund?" she asked at one point.

"The Bund, a trade union," he answered without looking up. She reached the letter dated 1939, which had been forwarded by the Red Cross in 1946 and held it for a while, not wanting to face the inevitable end of the story. Then Bellamy cried in his sleep and broke the mood.

"It's like reading a novel," said Joshua, after she returned from settling her son back to sleep. His voice was loud in the quiet of the living room.

"It's not a novel, it's real, it's about Gran…well, about her sister." Sophie knew her voice was strident and her reaction was out of proportion.

"Calm down, Sophie, for heaven's sake. What is the matter with you? Have another glass of wine."

"I don't want another glass of wine." Sophie started to sob, loud, long sobs. She curled into Joshua's arms and slowly relaxed.

"Don't you think you are overreacting? This was all a long time ago. It's history. And Bella has been dead for three years."

Sophie pulled herself away from her brother and poured a glass of wine. "I know," she sniffed, "it's just so sad. Imagine this family she lost."

Joshua stood up and started to put his shoes on. "Seems to me she chose to lose them. Look, these letters are begging her to make contact. She didn't want to know."

"Oh, that's just you and Bella, and the way you felt about her. I bet you would have more sympathy if you hadn't had such a hard time working for her. The worst thing you ever did was join B.U." Sophie hated the shrill sound of her own voice. She rarely argued with Joshua but couldn't stop herself.

"Now you are being ridiculous." Joshua left the living room and Sophie heard him walk towards the coat stand.

"I know…please don't go. I don't know why this has got me so worked up. I know it's daft," she wailed.

Joshua returned to the room. "She was not the one who lost. Bella had a large family over here, a successful life in anyone's view. Anyway, it looks as if she ignored the letters on purpose. They are begging for news." Joshua removed his shoes again and plonked himself back on the sofa.

"You sound so hard, Joshua."

"Not hard, just baffled. Why did she cut herself off from her family and never tell anyone? I spent nearly every day of my adult life with Bella and suddenly she has become this new mysterious person with a past."

"Don't you think it's tragic?"

"I don't think she is the one who is tragic. Listen." Joshua skimmed through the letters, reading excerpts aloud. "Nineteen-o-nine, Jacob was in prison; 1915, Rosie is begging for news of her daughter; 1916, she's working as a cleaner in a factory. They are poor and always under threat. What was Bella doing in 1916? She had a growing business, food on the table and three children. Nineteen-twenty-six, they have no money and again she is begging for news of her daughter and help. Bella completely ignored them, abandoned them."

"I know, I know, stop, please," Sophie wept.

"In 1930, they're cold and hungry and persecuted. Just think what Bella's life was like here in the 1930s. The whole Jewish world was trying to get their families out of Europe then, but what was Bella doing? Becoming a saint of success and popularity."

"I know." Sophie's voice had receded into the back of her throat.

"She made no attempt to answer them. In 1937 Rosie is desperate to leave and still no word, no help from her family here," Joshua went on relentlessly. "They were living in one room, while our family was living in a mansion in Hampstead Garden Suburb…"

"Not a mansion," Sophie snivelled.

Joshua ignored her protest, "…and then they stop. Here, read the last letter." He held it out for her.

For a moment Sophie didn't speak. Quietly she placed the letter back in the envelope, put it at the bottom of the pile and put them all back in the package. Joshua waited.

"Don't you think we ought to find out what happened to Rosie and Jacob?"

Joshua pointed to the last letter. "A Jewish family in 1939 in Poland? We can guess what happened to them, this letter was forwarded by the Red Cross. You can call them if you want, they will have records. Maybe by then she was just too ashamed, who knows, but what is the point of trying to uncover it now? Don't start crying again, for heaven's sake."

"But Rosie's child was here. We have to find her or at least what happened to her. Do you think Dad knew about this?"

"I can't believe she would have told him, or that if she had he wouldn't have said or done something. It would be too big a shadow on the family background of the revered philanthropist."

"We might have other family." Sophie was managing to hold her tears back.

"We might but you don't know that. Anyway, you are not even that close to the ones you know you have."

As Sophie watched Joshua prepare to leave, she knew that on this mission, she was on her own.

Sophie removed her makeup with cotton wool steeped in baby oil. In the bathroom mirror she saw Bella's face, not her own. She scrubbed vigorously with a special soap full of unrecognisable properties and bits of grit that she had picked up at Gatwick in Duty Free on her last trip. It scratched her skin and she remembered the simple beauty routine Bella had practised all her life.

She lay in a lukewarm bath, bubbling with lavender essence. There was a glass of wine beside her. The complicated sound system that Chris had installed, with speakers hanging from the ceiling, safe from the spray of the shower, played a gentle Chopin étude. Bella had introduced her to Chopin, saying it reminded her of the excruciating days of the twins' struggle during their piano lessons, before they all gave up and realised the boys had many talents, but playing the piano was not one of them.

Her body was soft and perfumed from the bath as she sat at her dressing table. She covered her face with an expensive night cream, then put a different cream on her neck and yet another on her legs and arms. Bella's face stared back at her. She visualised the disapproval her grandmother would have shown at the amount of money she had just lathered onto her skin.

"Does the cream know the difference between your neck and your legs?" she would have asked. Sophie could hear her voice as if she were by her side.

Wrapped up in two fluffy bath towels, with a smaller one covering her wet hair, Sophie lay on the dark brown leather sofa. She settled into the large cushions and turned on the cassette player. Bella's voice was shockingly familiar, clear with an occasional quaver, the erratic phrasing revealing its Polish origins, tempered by the east end of London, Hampstead via Dalston and Crouch End, and the adopted inflections of Kensington.

*"I was born in a village in Poland. So were my parents and my grandparents and I can still describe the village. I can see it right now in front of my eyes. It was divided into two parts. One part was the landowners who had acres and acres of land. They had orchards and grew vegetables. We used to call them Lords and Ladies just as we do here. The village had two churches, a Russian church with a Russian priest and a Polish church with a Polish priest. All the children were educated by priests. Jewish children didn't have an education as their parents were worried that they would be converted. Sometimes it happened. The priests would give them things they couldn't have at home, so they became Christian.*

*When my parents died, I don't want to talk about how, Jacob sent for me to help my sister Rosie with her baby, as she was weak after the birth. I had no one else, so they became my family, Jacob, Rosie and the baby…"*

When Chris returned home at 1am, Sophie was asleep on the sofa. The cassette had finished, the player was still on. He pulled her gently onto her feet and manoeuvred her towards their bedroom. Bewildered, she pointed towards the cassette player.

"Come on, Sophie, it's finished."

In the morning Sophie told Chris about the contents of the letters and the tape recording. She also explained how disappointed she was with Joshua's lack of interest.

"Well, why are you so obsessed with this, since obviously nobody else cares?" he asked, spreading butter on his toast.

Sophie poured coffee into two mugs. "It's just the idea that there might be someone around with Bella's DNA," she answered thoughtfully.

"But there are plenty of you with Bella's DNA. Look at the way your sister Brynah is multiplying. We could go on multiplying, if it is DNA you are after." Chris left his breakfast and walked round to her side of the table. He slid his hand beneath her robe.

"I can't explain," said Sophie, withdrawing from his touch. "You had to have known her. Stop, we both have to go to work."

# 1994 Sophie

A glance through the Yellow Pages suggested a world where many people were looking for someone or something, maybe to divorce, maybe to sue, maybe even to award with an inheritance and maybe just to reunite with a lost relative. Certainly the market in private detectives was thriving.

The headlines announced:

*'No find, no fee!'*

*'Utmost confidentiality!'*

*'Your records kept under lock and key!'*

*'Extensive and full knowledge of the law!'*

*'A team of dedicated professionals!'*

Sophie felt guilty just reading the proclaimers, as if she had inadvertently thrown herself into a suspect and criminal world. She pointed them out to her assistant, Melissa, who seemed excited at these unfamiliar and exotic possibilities.

"It's another world," gasped Sophie.

"It's another planet," Melissa was leaning over her shoulder, surveying the pages and pages of options listed under 'Private Investigators'.

"I wonder if I ought to look for a Jewish one. It's a common Jewish story, looking for your ancestors. Everyone is interested in who their grandparents were and where they came from. The private detectives are making a bundle."

"But you know all that. Everyone knew about Bella." Melissa walked back to her desk and turned her computer on.

"We thought we did, but apparently not." Sophie put her pencil into the electric sharpener and, as always, was comforted by the

343

buzz it made and the sharp points it produced. "Come on, Melissa, we have to get this budget done."

As a successful documentary film producer, Sophie had a wealth of systems available to help her research any subject. She also had teams of researchers at her disposal, but she felt this particular quest was too personal to delegate to anyone. Melissa had suggested hiring a private detective. Seeking her boss's long-lost family seemed a perfect opportunity to enhance her own job prospects, although Sophie, having taken her advice, soon became very discreet about the progress.

"Look…" Melissa's voice was staring at the screen "…we can get all this stuff for free."

"What stuff?" Sophie interrupted the budget she had started to calculate.

"Spy equipment. Look, let's send for it. It says we can send for samples of covert equipment."

"Don't be ridiculous, what on earth would we do with it?"

"Listening devices, bugging devices, receivers, car trackers. All very James Bond. Oh come on, Sophie, just for fun."

"Crazy, isn't it? All I had to do was ask," Sophie mused "and now look at what we have to go through."

"But she obviously had something to hide, otherwise she would have told you."

"I can't think what my grandmother would have said about me hiring a private detective."

"Why are you anyway? Is there an inheritance or something?" Melissa looked embarrassed at her own question. "Sorry, I didn't mean to pry."

Melissa did not believe Sophie's reasons for taking this step. She knew, and many in the small world of television production knew, that Chris had left Sophie. Sophie, now alone with Bellamy, had put on a very brave face, but Melissa thought it was too co-incidental that she was suddenly determined to hire a private detective and didn't believe the grandmother story. Sophie did not tell her that she only felt free to do it now that Chris had left. He had been totally opposed to Sophie's need to find out if she had family somewhere and accused her of being obsessive. It was a drive she had not been able to articulate, even while they were still friends. Not acting had not saved her marriage, but at least it had given them one less issue to argue about whilst they were still together.

"No, it's alright. It is just that Bella was so special and my family is so fragmented."

Melissa was writing down a list of names from the internet. "Golly, so is mine and am I glad. I can't stand any of them. Here," she said, handing Sophie the list with a flourish. "That should get you started. But do let me know if you want me to make any calls for you."

Sophie was running her pencil through the list. "I would love to find out that I suddenly have a whole raft of cousins, or aunts and uncles. I knew that there was this possibility since I was a child."

"Why didn't you ask her?"

"I sort of did, but not loudly enough, I was too busy being young and trendy."

Sophie was producing a television series about the challenges facing ethnic minorities finding homes to rent. She travelled all over the country filming and struggled with child care during her absence, so it took her a while to find time to sieve through Melissa's list.

Although Joshua had also accused her of being obsessive, between her absorbing job and looking after Bellamy, Sophie often forgot what she had started. In the back of her mind was the need to pursue the conviction that somewhere she had another family, as it had been with her since childhood. The practicalities of seeking them, however, kept getting pushed to the bottom of her priority list.

As well as work and mothering, there were responsibilities to be shared with her siblings towards the care and attention of her mother and two stepmothers. All were now elderly and, although rich, all three were demanding, lonely and difficult. Sophie wished she could bunch them altogether in one home with a team of nurses, but they didn't speak to each other. Even while all other elements of their lives were subject to forgetfulness, they each remembered they loathed each other. She visited her mother twice a week and each stepmother once a month. That added up to a lot of time.

It took her another year before she proceeded.

# 1995 Sophie

Private detective work is not as profitable as I assumed, thought Sophie as she sat on the wine-coloured, cracked-leather sofa. Wooden storage shelves, perilously uneven and full of buff-covered files, lined three walls. Folders, boxes and piles of letters crowded the top of a long table. Sophie was comforted to see a computer at one end of it. There was a damp patch in one corner of the ceiling and wood poking through the linoleum floor.

Her career as a film-maker had thrown her into many unfamiliar environments, from building sites to factories to Formula One race tracks. Sophie was used to approaching them with confidence. Now, however, she felt nervous and out of place in the silence of this shambolic basement office. It didn't help that she alone in the family had felt the need to go on this quest. She had chosen Mr William Appleton, private investigator, on instinct after a series of telephone calls to the list of names she and Melissa had compiled together. He had sounded positive when she briefly described what she was looking for, but was the only one who did not suggest it would be easy. He also insisted on a meeting before she awarded him the contract. That impressed her.

Mr Appleton appeared, carrying yet more papers. His hand, outstretched to meet hers, was half-covered by a jacket sleeve too long for his arm. His glasses hovered down his nose, his eyes regarded her over them. His face was thin, his body bent. He sat at the large table and summoned her to sit next to him. He smelt of stale tobacco.

"Whatever happened to the paperless office?" she laughed anxiously.

"Hmm, not in the world of the private investigator. Too much of our information is old and given to us on paper. Isn't that what you have in your briefcase?" He pointed to the briefcase beside her. His voice was high-pitched and scratchy.

"Yes, letters," said Sophie, suddenly resenting his supercilious tone and wanting to leave immediately.

"But," he said, pointing proudly to his computer, "we have the best of both worlds." He waved his hand over the table. "It's not as chaotic as it looks but if it makes you nervous, I'll open a file." Mr Appleton picked up an empty buff folder. Sophie, irrationally, wondered what he would do if she said it did not make her nervous. In black pen he wrote *Sophie Mitchell* in capital letters across the front. He then added a forward slash.

"And?" he looked at her expectantly.

"And? Sorry…what?"

"Who are we looking for?"

"I don't know." Sophie rarely felt foolish and was annoyed that this man was making her feel so. She opened her briefcase and brought out the photograph and letters. "I don't have copies," she added, placing them cautiously on the untidy table with the photograph on top. She tentatively added the cassette.

Mr Appleton stared but did not make a move to touch them. "Let's start with why, then," he said brusquely.

"Why?"

"Yes, is it the person or the descendants of the person in the photograph you want to find?"

"Yes." Sophie barely recognised her own voice.

"Why? It helps if I know why. It is usually money. Is there money you wish to claim?"

"No, no money." Her voice showed her shock.

"To give?"

"Oh my goodness, no, at least…no, I don't think so. I never thought of that."

Mr Appleton's expression softened. "Right dear, tell me what you are looking for."

Sophie was surprised at how clearly she could describe as much as she knew about the history of her family. Her tone softened when she described Bella. Mr Appleton listened attentively, making notes as she spoke, and her voice resumed its normal confidence. "I know it's a tall order," she finished.

Mr Appleton stood up and wandered thoughtfully around the table. "You know," he said, "I never promise anything, but Jews are good record-keepers."

"Gosh, not my grandmother, she never wrote anything down about her early life, all we have are…"

"A photograph, letters, a cassette," he finished. "Richness, Mrs Mitchell, I assure you. There is a lot to work on. What looks like a closed door to you holds many possibilities for me."

Sophie recognised the assured tone she had first heard on the telephone. She had to make a decision. Despite the paucity of his office, Mr Appleton's fee was high.

"How would you start?" she asked, assuming her television interviewer's voice.

Mr Appleton picked up the photograph and held it gingerly by one corner. "With two questions. The first is, who do you think this baby is?" He turned the photograph over and read the back. "Sara. Do you think she is your aunt?"

This was the question Sophie had not dared ask herself. Was this baby Bella's first child? She picked up a pencil and doodled on a piece of paper in front of her. Mr Appleton waited. She stood and walked towards the wall, staring unseeingly at a certificate announcing his qualifications. She ran her eyes down it, not registering its content.

"No," she said finally, her back still towards him, "Bella would never abandon a child. I think she is my grandmother's sister's child, for some reason brought up by my grandmother in England. I suppose that is what I need to find out about, and whether she is still alive."

Mr Appleton made a note as she returned to her seat. "So, next question: did your father ever mention her?"

"I asked him once. He was a very busy man."

"And what did he say?" Mr Appleton's voice was gentle.

"He said that he remembered a nanny or a maid called Sara. When he was young, she looked after him and his brother, his late brother. He thought she was given the sack after his father's death. He said there was lots of whispering and no one was allowed to mention her name again. He said his baby brother, Sam, the one who died in the war, cried for her a lot and his mother got very cross. I think it was very painful for him to remember because of the loss of his brothers and then his sister."

Mr Appleton closed his notebook and placed his pen in a pot full of others in the centre of the table. "My dear Mrs Mitchell, my philosophy is that whatever families choose not to talk about is written down somewhere. I suggest you think about it and telephone me if you want me to proceed." His tone suggested the consultation was over and it was business or not, from now on. "Let me reassure you that there are many good sources. Firstly, your grandmother arrived with many others at the beginning of the century. Every vessel was met and every arrival noted. There will be ledgers for me to scour. How correct the information is depends on how much truth the immigrant told, but if she came into this country, she will be there, recorded in some form. If she arrived with a child, that will be written down, even if the name is assumed or indeed changed. There will be birth certificates, marriage certificates and, sadly, death certificates. Medical records, school records – she must have gone to school. Later the internet will come and aid us, but for now there will be information in the Public Records office, the telephone directory, the tax office, the census – we just have to know how to access and interpret them. My dear, that is what I do."

Sophie watched him walk towards the door and hold it open. She was offended by his patronising attitude and knew she was being dismissed.

"You sound very hopeful."

"These letters…" He finally touched the letters as if they contained pure gold. "They will be my guide."

"But the last one was 1939."

"Nineteen thirty-nine, a Jewish family in Poland…my dear, I know that is unlikely to be happy news but it means your relatives are traceable. I am afraid bad news for a family is usually good news for a detective. Call me when you have made up your mind."

Sophie and Melissa were sitting in an editing suite in central London, viewing some material that had been recorded the previous day. Typically, as a working single parent with elderly relatives to care for, Sophie's concentration was fragmented. She was trying to give her full attention to the film being shown to her, but was also thinking of Bellamy's latest school report and pondering on ways to make the care of three old women easier. So the telephone call was a surprise and almost an intrusion.

"It's Sherlock Holmes," declared Melissa as she handed Sophie the telephone.

She asked the editor to pause the flickering images as she took the call. Sliding off her stool and stretching the telephone lead, she pulled it so that she was half out of the door and had a degree of privacy. As she listened, she watched Melissa straining to hear her conversation. William Appleton sounded confident as he made an appointment for her to visit his office.

William Appleton had earned his high fee and proved, undeniably, that he was able to access and interpret old records. The report he gleefully handed to Sophie was comprehensive. He obviously had literary aspirations, as the facts were embellished with personal comment and detail. Sophie thought he might have invented them, but he claimed not.

"Luckily," he said, "the subject did not change her name until she married and luckily, prostitutes live longer than we expect them to."

"Prostitute?"

"Oh my dear, no, your relative worked amongst them and is famous for the care she gave them. The story of how she came to work amongst…um…the ladies is still told today and the legend of her good deeds lives on."

Sophie hoped his report was clearer than his excited speech. "But how…?"

"Luckily, she died during the war. I mean, luckily for us…tragically for her, of course," he said, flustered at his own insensitivity. Noticing Sophie's anguished face, he added, "You are right, she was not your grandmother's child but her niece and there are descendents – alive. I'll make some tea."

"No tea, thank you."

Anxiously, she flicked through the file, which had a case number, dates and a list of names and addresses. There were copious typewritten notes about sources he had consulted, the time spent on each one meticulously logged and the corresponding travel expenses entered alongside. There were transcripts of interviews, dates, places and times carefully annotated, as well as relevance to the investigation. Mr Appleton had been liberal with his use of coloured felt-tipped pens and next to each transcript was either a flamboyant red cross or a green tick. In contrast to the formality of the reference and code numbers, the pink and yellow lines and symbols linking details gave the report a vibrant appearance. There was a report of an interview with a Madame Rita, an address in Dean Street, and in brackets he had written '*ex prostitute, now 86, no longer working!!!!!!!!!!!!!*' The exclamation marks were orange.

"Can I take this now?" Sophie was shaking and thought she would be able to absorb the information better in her own home.

"My dear," he started, as Sophie vowed one day to tell him not to call her 'my dear', "it is yours." Sophie thanked him for his service, asked for the invoice to be sent to her and escaped as graciously as she could.

*

As Sophie pieced together the formal documentary evidence and Mr Appleton's gratuitous editorial comments, the story of Sara emerged. Sophie recognised that there were fictional embellishments, particularly at the beginning, as much of it had been spread through gossip and rumour.

Sara, had apparently arrived in Soho in 1925, by taxi. The driver had stopped to offer her a lift when he had seen her running down the street by herself in dense fog, crying. He left her to cry for a while in the back of his cab, then asked where she would like to go. She did not reply for a while, and he named several possibilities. She had no idea of a destination but just happened to nod, or he thought he saw her nod, when he mentioned, without seriously meaning it, Soho.

Soho in the 1920s was used to welcoming lost souls, particularly female lost souls, without asking any questions. Sara found a warmth and acceptance she had never experienced as the 'Cinderella' of the Bromavitch family.

To begin with she lodged with prostitutes, using the skills she had gained looking after Bella's children to nurture these grown-up children. They adored her and she earned her rent and food by doing their laundry and healing their wounded hearts. They gave her the nickname 'Sara Saviour'. This was the legend that Madame Rita remembered and had recounted to a new generation.

Sara used the experience of slaving for Bella to find herself a job in a vegetable shop. She continued to lodge with the prostitutes and this life suited her, until she met Leonard one Saturday morning in one of the many little synagogues that served the Soho community of Jews.

Sara's regular attendance at synagogue was more to do with the need for companionship and comfort than God, and that had become even more important in the thirties when the anti-Semitism that had spread across Europe tickled the edges of London's geographically spread Jewish communities.

Sara and Leonard were married in 1938 and moved to Wanstead. Sara secretly loved the idea that Bella would have hated their move back to the East End but she didn't discuss this with Leonard. In those days, it was accepted that many Jewish people had backgrounds so painful that, even within a happy marriage, they were not discussed. They opened a general store, resided above the shop and lived comfortably and quietly. Their daughter Nancy was born in 1940, just at the beginning of the mayhem and violence that afflicted London for five long years.

Sara and Leonard lost their lives in one of the first vicious bombing raids to hit the East End. One-year-old Nancy was fostered and later adopted by a teacher and his family, who lived in a small cottage in Cookham in Berkshire. They also adopted a boy called John, two years younger than her. No one talked about her birth parents and she had no reason to be curious about her identity. This arrangement was so common in the turbulence of the Second World War that it was not considered strange that she asked no further questions. Nancy was happy with her adoptive family. She had a mother, a father and a brother and that is all she knew. They went to Church, played cricket and ate scones with jam.

She could not possibly have known that the little boutique in Marlow where she bought her wedding dress was owned by her Great Aunt and that the famous Bella Unique label, which Nancy had left on her wedding dress to impress her friends, was her Great Aunt's own label. She didn't know that, when she was sixteen and discussing an article about the hanging of Ruth Ellis as part of her general knowledge course at school, the article had been written by her second cousin, Etta. She didn't know that, when she went to the cinema in her twenties, it was owned by another second cousin, Simon. She didn't know when she heard, but paid no attention to, the television announcement of the sudden and unexpected death of the famous Lord Broom, that he was family. If she had, she might have watched with more interest.

Nancy Porter, née Carey, the adopted daughter of Cynthia and Henry Carey, wife of Richard Porter, mother of Hilary, Andrew and Mark, knew nothing of this until a television producer called Sophie Mitchell wrote to her. She opened the letter just as she returned home from the baptism of her first grandchild in the Church of the Good Shepherd in Maidenhead.

# 1995 Nancy

The blue holdall that Sophie used to identify herself contained the history of the family Nancy had not known about. Birth certificates, wedding photographs, obituaries, Mr Appleton's report as well as a family tree that covered five generations, all labelled and explained, were inside. Rosie's letters, now safely copied, were also included. She swung the bag high so that it could be seen as she walked across the pedestrian bridge to the booking hall, their designated meeting place.

Sophie could see that Nancy's body was taut with anticipation as she, an unknown woman who had arrived from nowhere to claim a place in her heart, shyly placed her arms around her. Nancy, alarmed, withdrew slightly; the immediate intimacy embarrassed her. Sophie looked into her face, seeking some family resemblance, and, eerily, Bella's eyes looked back at her.

Nancy drove silently towards her little cottage in a village just outside Haslemere. Inside, after the pleasantries of offering tea or coffee were complete, Nancy invited Sophie to the window. She had set two chairs close together beneath an old standard lamp, and a card table was placed strategically between them.

Nancy described how astonished she had been to receive Sophie's letter, and how she'd felt when she discovered her relationship with the famous Broom/Bromavitch dynasty. She joked that going to a Broom's cinema would never be the same again.

The morning was intense as Sophie talked Nancy through the story of how she, thanks to Mr Appleton, had traced her.

"This explains so much," said Nancy. "Despite my life, my husband, the children and now a grandchild, I have always felt incomplete. I don't remember my birth mother and my adoptive mother told me so little. I didn't even realise I was Jewish. There is always something missing when you are adopted but I never felt the need to search for it. Then at the doctor's once, for one of the children, I was asked to fill out a form about inherited diseases and I had no idea."

"What did you do?"

"I just scrawled 'adopted' against all the unknown questions. But I felt so inadequate."

Nancy looked sad but Sophie was eager to understand more. "Wouldn't your mother tell you?" she asked.

"She always told us we were adopted and they had chosen us specially. We had no reason to question beyond that. John and I were happy and the war had created many orphans. I don't know how much she knew anyway. In those days the process was so different, secretive even, and there was no law saying that you had the right to the information."

"She just needed to ignore it, I suppose." Aware of the slight tension between them, Sophie inwardly berated herself for taking so long to make this journey.

"Yes, I can imagine if you have adopted a child it would be hard to accept that they wanted to find their birth parents. It would take a huge degree of generosity and there was always the possibility that the search would not reveal a comfortable story with a happy ending, particularly for war babies." Nancy shrugged. "Shall we eat?"

Sophie welcomed a lunch break and a chance to chat about ordinary things – the weather, train strikes, the cost of food, inconsequential but a relief from the emotion. Champagne was poured, a sure sign of the importance of the occasion, to accompany the lunch of baked salmon, peas, carrots and boiled potatoes. They ate in the kitchen.

"I hope you don't mind but you are family," said Nancy apologetically, "although I can't quite believe it."

After a flurry of clearing up and piling dishes into the dishwasher, they returned to their window retreat. It was getting dark and Nancy turned lights on, moving the standard lamp around until it was directly over the small card table.

Sophie brought the blue holdall to the table. She opened it up with small flourish, as if revealing the inside of a magic box, and pulled out the report from William Appleton and the family tree, which she had drawn in pencil on four A3 sheets of paper. It had been much scribbled on and corrected and looked like a giant geometric spider's web. The names Jacob and Rosie were underlined in red; some names were ticked in green.

"A green tick means alive," she said.

A bewildered Nancy watched as Sophie pointed a pencil at Jacob and Rosie, then indicated a straight line down through Sara and continued the line through the chart directly to Nancy. She heard Nancy gasp as she spread all her relatives before her.

December 14th 2000

# Press release

## FASHION HOUSE CHANGES OWNERSHIP

The financial conglomerate run by the German industrialist Klaus von Wullf has bought the international fashion empire Bella Unique. The business includes a chain of boutiques in London, New York and Paris and the mail order catalogue 'Bella by Post'.

Joshua Broom, the current Chief Executive, will be retained as Fashion Director. The firm was founded in 1910 by his grandmother, the designer Bella Bromavitch.

Future expansion plans include scarves, men's shirts and ties, a makeup range, 'Bella Perfume' and an exclusive collection of bathroom accessories. A move into Germany for the 'Bella' chain is planned for 2003.

Note: For immediate circulation